SHADOW SOUL

THE FOURTH EMPIRE
BOOK 4

KAT ROSS

SHADOW SOUL

First Edition

Map by the author.
Cover by Atraluna.
Chapter images by Rawpixel.

ISBN-13: 978-1-957358-18-5 (Ebook)
ISBN-13: 978-1-957358-19-2 (Paperback)

For Spike

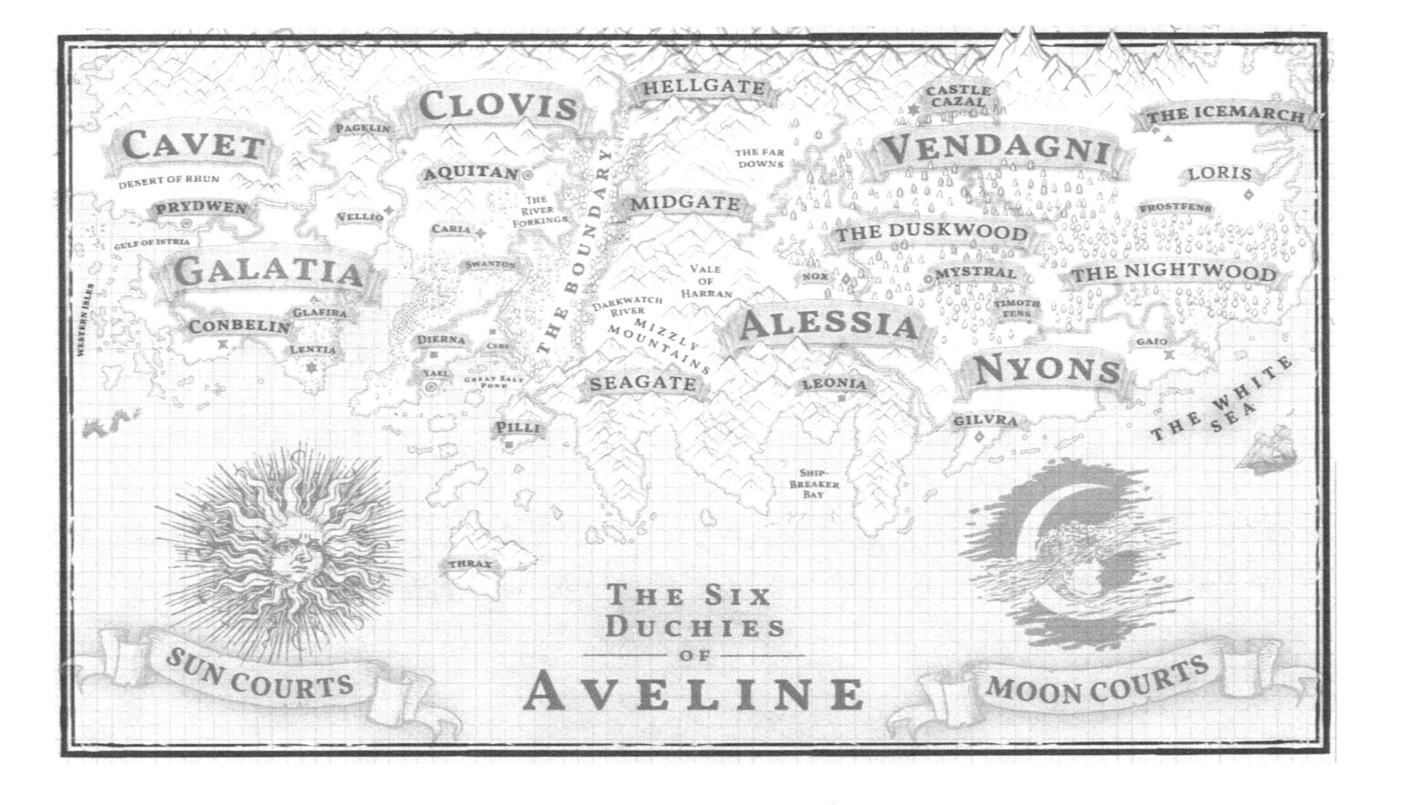
THE SIX DUCHIES OF AVELINE
CAVET
DESERT OF RHUN
PRYDWEN
GULF OF ISTRIA
GALATIA
WESTERN ISLES
GLAFIRA
CONBELIN
LENTIA
PAGELIN
VELLIO
CLOVIS
AQUITAN
CARIA
THE RIVER FORKINGS
SWANTON
DIERNA
CERE
YAEL
GREAT SALT POND
PILLI
THRAX
THE BOUNDARY
HELLGATE
MIDGATE
THE FAR DOWNS
VALE OF HARRAN
DARKWATCH RIVER
MIZZLY MOUNTAINS
SEAGATE
ALESSIA
NOX
LEONIA
SHIP-BREAKER BAY
CASTLE CAZAL
VENDAGNI
THE DUSKWOOD
MYSTRAL
TIMOTH FENS
NYONS
GILVRA
THE ICEMARCH
LORIS
FROSTFENS
THE NIGHTWOOD
GAIO
THE WHITE SEA
SUN COURTS
MOON COURTS

One

Lo crouched at the foot of the slender stone bridge, her cloak blending with the darkness. Across the chasm, Castle Cazal stood against the stars, a sharp silhouette clinging to a rocky spire. The keep's obsidian walls reflected no light, lending it an aura of gloom.

The last time she had visited, a single window glowed high in the central tower, but even that feeble light was now gone. Where was Nathan Ouvrard? And more importantly, where was Nabu-bal-idinna and the damned necromancer he'd run off with?

Kaethe, the goddess of death, believed they might come here since it was Jaskin Cazal's ancestral seat. It was Lo's only lead.

"I suppose they could be inside, sitting there in the dark like weirdos," she muttered. "Gods, please make this easy for me."

She rose, wincing as her kneecap banged into one of the bridge supports. Her divided soul attracted misfortunes large and small like bloodflies to carrion. She took extra care crossing the bridge. Tentacled monsters dwelt in the mist below; the way her luck was running, if she slipped, she'd probably fall straight into an open maw.

Toward the far side, her footfalls changed from stone to wood. The drawbridge. Happily, it was lowered, permitting access to the keep. She shrugged off the concealing cloak, stuffed it into her pack, and strode to the stone lintel carved with leering gargoyles. Lo banged a fist against the door, the hollow thuds muffled by the fog.

After a long wait, the door creaked open, revealing Nathan's mortifex servant, Vigo. His giant frame filled the doorway, white hair gleaming in the moonlight. Pale irises with pinpricks of flame regarded Lo with icy disdain.

"The master is away," Vigo said, his deep, gravelly voice devoid of recognition even though they'd just seen each other a few weeks before. "Come back later."

Heavy rings with rubies and sapphires glittered as he started to shut the door.

Lo jammed her boot into the gap. "I watched Nathan walk through a gate from Kaethe's domain less than a fortnight ago. He was headed here."

"His Grace did stop home briefly," Vigo conceded. "Then he left again by carriage."

"Left for where?" Lo asked, tamping down her impatience.

Vigo eyed her haughtily. "I'm not at liberty to say. Now remove yourself before I do it for you."

Lo craned her neck, trying to peer past his broad shoulders into the darkened foyer. "Is anyone else home?"

The question seemed to befuddle the mortifex. "Such as?"

"Like, say, Jaskin Cazal?"

Vigo stared at her. "The master informed me that Jaskin escaped his black mirror. However, I have not seen him."

Lo chewed her lip, considering. There was no way she'd

leave without searching the keep herself. Vigo had served the necromancers of Vendagni for a thousand years. He would say whatever Jaskin told him to.

But she'd prefer not to fight him head on. Mortifexes were dangerous to say the least. It was time to find out if her ability to lie had returned, now that she'd left the land of the dead.

"That's a shame," she said, holding his burning gaze. "However, Nathan left an important relic for me in his workshop." The falsehood rolled smoothly off her tongue, buoying her mood considerably. "I must retrieve it posthaste."

Vigo crossed his arms. "I know of no such relic, and he would have left express instructions if that were the case. You mistake me for a fool. Be gone before I toss you into the chasm."

He heaved his shoulder against the door, but Lo wedged herself into the gap. "I'm here at Kaethe's bidding," she snapped. "Let me pass or I'll open a portal and send you to the depths of the lower planes."

Vigo threw his head back and laughed, a harsh bark. "Piss off," he declared.

"As you wish," she replied a bit breathlessly, still caught in the crack of the doorjamb.

Lo reached for her shadow magic and ripped open a churning vortex at Vigo's feet. The mortifex roared as he sank into the maelstrom — but then the black wind of the portal sputtered and died.

Shit! In a rage at losing her consort, Kaethe had locked the doors to her realm. That included portals.

Lo looked down and bit back a startled laugh. Vigo was trapped in the stone floor up to his chest like a sheep in a mire. He struggled and cursed, but the half-formed portal held him fast. Lo forced the door wide and stepped inside, keeping away from his flailing arms. She scooped up the candelabra that Vigo had left on a side table, venturing into the drafty hall.

"Nabu!" she called out, her voice echoing off the black walls. "Kaethe's not angry with you, she just wants you to come home. She misses you terribly!"

More lies. Kaethe was in a towering fury. But only silence answered her. Well, besides Vigo's bellows.

With a sigh, she hurried for the stairs and began to search the keep floor by floor. She found nothing animate, not even Nathan's ash servants. Just room after empty room, the furniture covered in black sheets. Eventually, she reached Nathan's workshop. Sinister tools littered the worktables — saws and blades and hooked implements whose purposes she didn't care to guess at. Row upon row of glass jars lined the shelves, filled with viscous fluids and floating specimens. The stench of decay mingled with acrid chemical odors.

Using a spark of elemental fire, she lit the melted stubs of black candles affixed to the tables. Floor-to-ceiling bookshelves created a labyrinthine maze along one side, packed with grimoires and moldering scrolls. Lo paced the room, peering into the shadowed recesses, but found no sign of the two fugitives.

The real problem was that Nabu-bal-idinna was not, in fact, a mortal man who had stumbled over Kaethe's tower and fallen in love with her, as everyone believed. Far-fetched as it seemed, he was really the sun god Bel, whom Kaethe had bewitched. As long as Bel remained in her tower, he would not remember his true nature. But now that he had run off with Jaskin Cazal, his memories would return.

And Kaethe claimed that Bel was not a very nice god at all.

Lo's desperate gaze fell on a long row of ornate mirrors dominating the far wall. Wraith-like figures stirred within the smoky depths, the spirits of Nathan's ancestors. Their pale faces shrank back when she approached.

Lo rapped sharply on the first mirror. "All right, pay attention," she said, "I have some questions, and you'd best answer truthfully unless you want the Vigo treatment."

One by one, generations of necromancers drifted into view, filling the mirrors with their ghostly reflections. They wore antiquated garments from centuries past, eyes gleaming with malevolence... and a touch of fear. They remembered the woman who had banished two of their kin to the netherworld.

"When was the last time you saw Jaskin Cazal?" Lo demanded, moving down the line of mirrors. "Speak!"

A gaunt specter in a high-collared doublet with a devilish pointy beard bowed his head. "Not since you took his own mirror away, mistress," he whispered. "This I swear."

The others quickly echoed his claim. Lo swore under her breath. Another dead end. Her eyes roved the workroom, searching for any clue she might have missed.

"If Jaskin were on the run," she said, turning back to the mirrors with a hard stare, "where do you suppose he'd go? Think carefully now."

The spirits muttered amongst themselves, a susurrus of dry whispers.

"The ruins of Vhaskali?"

"No, no, the hidden ossuaries beneath Llum!"

"Fool, those were swallowed by the quakes long ago! The Whispering Barrows, more like."

Lo listened with growing impatience as they bickered, tossing out names that meant nothing to her.

"Belladonna has your answer, Shadow Soul." The voice, feminine yet harsh as a rasp on bone, cut through the others. Lo quickly found its source — a mirror second from the end.

There hung the specter of a dark-eyed young woman. She was missing her left ear. Belladonna. Nathan's cousin, Lo recalled. The specter lifted a finger, pointing deeper into the room. "Jaskin's journal. Third bookcase, behind the jar of toenail clippings." Her mouth twitched. "Jaskin always was a meticulous record-keeper. If he has a secret hideaway, it will be there."

Lo strode into the maze of towering shelves, following Belladonna's directions as she scanned the titles. *The Shadowbinder's Compendium. Ars Notoria. Nine Hundred Types of Ash and Their Uses. The Body Snatcher's Ossuary.* Others were scientific tomes on plants and animals, horticulture and biology. Jaskin Cazal had harnessed the power of the Grand Menotte to bring life to the darklands.

"The next shelf," Belladonna called. "On the bottom."

Lo crouched down and saw a thick volume. She slid it out and opened the brittle pages. They were filled with spidery handwriting. She began to read, lips moving silently as she deciphered the old-fashioned script.

"Through the blessed Darkness I have found enlightenment. By weaving together the Elemental Magicks — that of Earth, Air, Water, and Fire — I have coaxed the Night Blooms to unfurl their petals beneath the triple moons. In my glass garden, these delicate flowers take sustenance from naught but starlight and shadow. A miracle of elemental power, made possible by the undead mortifexes I have bound to the Grand Menotte!

"Next I shall turn my attention to the trees and mosses, those stolid ancients who remember when the Sundering first fell. If I can but persuade them to embrace the Eternal Night, then the eastern forests shall rise anew. And what a dark Eden it shall be! Insects that sing only to the constellations, birds who navigate by the ghostly lines of force, the small scurrying mammals who know no fear of light.

"But I must make haste. The voices, ever present, grow louder by the hour. Madness claws at the edges of my mind, and I fear that time grows short. I am determined to see this work completed ere my faculties abandon me completely."

Lo sat back on her heels, considering. Jaskin's words painted a picture of a man on the precipice of sanity, but there was no denying that his experiment had worked. The forest she had just traveled through was a testament to that. It had not seen the sun in a thousand years, yet trees, plants and animals thrived within its moonlit haunts.

Across the White Sea, in the land of her birth, daēvas had done much the same. Bending the forces of nature to adapt to a world sundered between night and day.

This made her think of her parents, and how Kaethe, in her fury at losing Bel, had hurled Nazafareen and Darius back to Nocturne. Two days. That was all the time Lo had spent with them before they were ripped away once more.

But dwelling on the past would not help. She had to find Jaskin and Bel. Only then would her debt to Kaethe be paid. Only then could she find Cas and bring him home with her, to marvel at the Acropolis of Delphi and the storied Rock of Ariamazes. She missed his quick wit, the way he could always startle a laugh from her, even in the darkest moments. She prayed to any god who would listen that he and Felippa had found their father and brother in Prydwen.

Lo forced herself to focus on the present. Castle Cazal was a dead end. If Jaskin had planned to return here, he'd have arrived already. No, she needed another way to find him. If the journal failed, Nathan was her last hope. He knew his ancestor's twisted mind far better than she did. And perhaps some of Nathan's necromantic spells still worked. She shut the journal and stood up.

Across the room, one of the candles sputtered out. Then another. And another. One by one, as if snuffed by an unseen hand.

Two

In two heartbeats, the last candle guttered out, plunging Nathan's workshop into blackness. Lo groped for a stub of candle and conjured a weak flame.

"Is someone there?" she called out. "Vigo? If so, I apologize!"

The wick wavered, making the shadows writhe. She couldn't see much beyond its tight circle of light.

"It's the Devouring Darkness," a spirit whispered.

"What's that?" Lo hissed back. She set the candle down and threw the magic cloak over her shoulders, willing it to conceal her.

Then she spotted movement. A black substance like tar oozing across the floor. It made no sound. Just an impenetrable void swallowing everything in its path. Lo edged backwards, eyes fixed on the thing. The spirits whispered excitedly.

"It will suck the marrow from your bones!" one cried.

"Turn your flesh to jelly!"

"And your heart to stone!"

She feinted left, but the Devouring Darkness was, regretfully, not stupid. It pooled before the door, blocking escape.

"That cloak won't hide you," a spirit tittered. "It sees all, hears all."

Lo snatched up Jaskin's journal and shoved it into her pack. "How do I beat it? Someone better tell me right now."

"The Devouring Darkness is ancient, older than time," Belladonna said gravely. "It makes Kaethe look like a dewy-eyed maid. Some fool's experiment centuries ago let it leak through from another plane."

The spirits erupted into an argument over whose fault that was, a hubbub of accusing voices.

"Shut up," Lo snapped. She needed to think. Her gaze darted around the workshop, searching for another way out.

"What does it want?" she hissed, backing away as the Darkness oozed closer. Inky tendrils reached out and she yanked her foot from its grasp, half-climbing a bookcase that immediately began to tilt under her weight.

"To absorb all heat and light," Belladonna replied. "It senses the life within you."

Lo's skin prickled as the temperature dropped, her breath misting. "Then order it to go away!"

A spirit laughed. "It only obeys the master of the keep."

"But Nathan's not here," Lo said, leaping over the thing and slipping into the next aisle of books.

"Then it must have been sent by Vigo," Belladonna replied.

She couldn't let it end like this. She slung her pack over one shoulder. Then she grabbed a heavy grimoire from the shelf and hurled it across the room. It hit the far wall and fell with the pages splayed wide. Lo reached within herself, tapping into the elemental power of the Nexus. Flames burst from the ancient vellum.

The spirits howled. "That volume is priceless!" "Irreplaceable!" "*What have you done?*"

In the flickering firelight, Belladonna caught Lo's eye and gave her a tiny smile.

The Devouring Darkness surged towards the flames, drawn to their warmth and energy. Lo seized her chance, darting past the distracted entity and wrenching open the door. She flew down the twisting stone steps, her footsteps echoing off the obsidian walls. The spirits' whispers chased her, but she knew the way now.

Lo burst through the front door, pulse thudding. Mist swirled around her, curling like ghostly fingers. She squinted, expecting to see Vigo, but the courtyard was empty.

He must still be searching inside.

She raced across the flagstones, boots slipping in the damp. The chasm yawned before her. She stopped at the edge, breath catching in her throat. "Bloody hells," she panted, furious.

The drawbridge was raised, cutting off her escape.

A deep, resonant voice cut through the fog. "Leaving so soon?"

Lo spun around. Vigo strode out of the mist, white hair fluttering behind him. Satisfaction glinted in his eyes. "What are you really doing here?" he demanded.

Lo grasped for a suitable lie. "I told you, I'm looking for a talisman—"

"Enough!" Vigo snarled, closing the distance between them in two long strides. "I grow weary of your deception." He grabbed her arm, cold fingers digging into her flesh. "Perhaps a trip down the chute into the Blood Labyrinth will loosen your tongue."

She couldn't fight him, not with her Shadow powers weakened. "Wait!" she cried. "I'll tell you the truth."

Vigo's grip loosened slightly. "Speak, then."

Lo took a shuddering breath. The urge to lie was so very strong, but she doubted Vigo would offer another chance. "Kaethe sent me to find Jaskin and her consort, Nabu-bal-Idinna. They ran off together."

She related how Nathan's distant ancestor, Jaskin Cazal, had abandoned them and vanished through a portal. Vigo must have already heard the story from Nathan for he nodded without surprise. But his eyes did widen when she explained that Kaethe's hounds had tracked Jaskin to the Lady's tower, only for him to escape with Nabu's help.

The only detail she omitted was Nabu's true identity. Kaethe had sworn her to secrecy.

"That is the truth," she said, shoulders sagging. "Kaethe was so angry, she sealed the doors to her realm until I bring Nabu back to her."

Vigo studied her, his gaze piercing. "Why didn't you tell me this in the first place?" he asked more calmly.

How could she make him understand that just as she couldn't lie beyond the Veil, now that she was back among the living, the truth felt foreign on her tongue?

"I should have," she admitted. "I'm sorry."

Vigo regarded her for a long moment, his expression unreadable. Then he released her arm and stepped back.

"Come inside," he said, gesturing towards the keep. "We can discuss this further over supper."

Lo had no burning desire to dine with Nathan's mortifex, but Vigo might know something useful. And with the draw-bridge raised, she had little choice.

"I'd be delighted," she said with a smile, the lie coming easily.

As they entered the keep, a flicker of movement in a corner of the ceiling caught her eye. The Devouring Darkness lurked in the shadows. It had no eyes, yet Lo could feel its hungry regard.

Vigo waved a hand. “Return to the labyrinth,” he commanded.

The Darkness undulated in silent protest. Then, slowly, it retreated, slithering down the wall and disappearing into the stone floor.

“I insist on cooking for you,” Vigo said, leading her towards the cavernous dining hall. “It’s the least I can do after our misunderstanding.”

“That’s very kind of you.” Lo paused. “I don’t suppose there’s something other than tentacles?”

Vigo looked disappointed. “I shall examine the larder.”

He bowed and withdrew. The dining hall was just as she remembered it from her first meeting with Nathan. A snowy cloth covered the long table, the silverware glinting in the light of blue flames dancing in an enormous hearth.

Vigo pulled out a chair and she sat down. He disappeared into the kitchen, leaving her alone with her thoughts. Minutes ticked by, each one an eternity as Lo imagined her quarry getting further away. Finally, Vigo returned carrying a silver tray. He whipped the cover off with a flourish and set a plate in front of her.

“I’m afraid we only had the tentacles,” he said.

Lo tried to sound nonchalant, though she cringed inwardly. “Oh, that’s fine. I’ve eaten them before.”

The mortifex sat across from her as she speared a rubbery mass with her knife and raised it to her lips. She chewed slowly and thoroughly, which was the only way to eat gully squid, as Cas called them. Vigo’s flaming eyes bored into her, studying her every reaction.

“It’s ... very nice,” she said huskily, washing down the lump with a generous swallow of wine.

He smiled. "I am glad you like it."

The silence stretched, broken only by the clink of silverware and the sound of her own labored chewing. At last, he leaned forward, white hair gleaming in the candlelight. "So," he said, his voice a deep rumble, "do you know who has the Grand Menotte?"

Lo coughed, eyes watering. Vigo leapt up to pour more wine. She downed half a glass, rinsing the salty taste away.

"A fair question," she replied, "but I have no idea."

"I can sense its power. It brought great sorrow and grief to my master's family."

Lo snuck the last tentacle into her napkin and pushed her plate away. "Kaethe promised to destroy it if I brought her consort back. Jaskin persuaded him to run away."

"If you do find Jaskin Cazal," Vigo said, his eyes meeting hers, "I hope that Kaethe will keep him locked up forever."

Lo hoped for a worse punishment than that. "I must tell Nathan what's happened," she said.

Vigo nodded. "My master took the coach to Mystral to see the Courtenays."

"Is there another coach?" she asked with a flicker of hope.

"I'm afraid not."

It was a three-day trek on foot to Mystral, but she had no choice. She bid Vigo farewell and set out along the road leading south. It followed a river, its merry song a welcome companion. Lo paused at the bank, filling her waterskin with the clear, frigid water. It glimmered like silver in the moonlight, a stark contrast to the dark woods ahead.

As she entered the forest, a stealthy sound caught her attention, the snap of a twig somewhere behind. Lo stopped, head cocked. Could Vigo be following? But no, he would never leave the keep unguarded. And why pursue her when he already knew her destination?

Lo dropped her pack on the forest floor. She knelt beside it, unslinging her crossbow with what she hoped looked like practiced ease. Then she wedged her foot in the cock stirrup and used both hands to draw the string back until it settled into the notch with a click. She chose a silver-tipped quarrel, its wicked point gleaming in the dim light. With a fluid motion, she loaded the bolt into the crossbow, the weapon now ready to fire.

Rising to her feet, Lo scanned the forest for a suitable target. A sturdy oak about thirty paces away caught her eye. She raised the crossbow, aligning the sights. Her finger rested lightly on the trigger, a moment of stillness before the release. Then the bolt thrummed through the air, a whisper of death, before embedding itself deep into the bark.

Lo strode towards the tree, kicking her feet loudly through the leaf mulch. “Smooth mechanism!” she said with satisfaction, examining the quarrel’s placement.

A firm tug and it slid out of the trunk, leaving a small hole in its wake. Lo used a bit of earth magic to heal the sap wound, then turned the quarrel over in her hand, inspecting the silver tip for any damage.

Satisfied, she slung the crossbow and pack across her back and set out down the road once more. The quarrel remained in her hand, a silent warning to whoever — or whatever — might be lurking in the shadows.

Three

Cas hunched in his saddle, stiff fingers gripping the reins as a bitter wind swirled around him. The horse plodded through drifts that rose to its fetlocks, head down against the stinging sleet. Felippa pressed against his back, shivering.

"Still alive back there?" Cas turned his head slightly to be heard over the wind.

"Aye," his sister replied, her voice muffled. "My cloak helps. Even if it did belong to a dead person."

She'd taken it from the lair of the mortifexes in the Cold Sea, an adventure that already seemed two lifetimes ago. Cas squinted ahead but could barely make out Gui on his black charger or the hunched shapes of Teo and Da on their own mounts. The road east from Prydwen was a white ribbon between pine boughs heavy with snow, blue shadows pooling beneath.

Cas had hoped to take the straightest route to the Cavetti border, but they heard at an inn that a mob had burned the ferry. So they'd been forced to turn north and hope the next one was still running.

They'd be lucky to make a few more leagues before stopping to camp. Cas's stomach growled at the thought, and not just for rest. A hot meal and a spot by a fire seemed as distant as their chances of reaching the Boundary.

So far they'd managed to avoid the worst of the chaos. Oh, there'd been signs enough — desperate refugees struggling along the frozen road; hard-eyed sell-swords riding atop coaches; men with red rags tied around their arms whose gazes lingered on the horses. Once, a messenger in livery had galloped past, bringing word of the troubles to the border margraves, no doubt.

Cas touched the stout hickory staff tied to his saddle. He'd get his family to safety without spilling blood if he could, but he wasn't letting anyone take the horses. Other than their mounts, they had little of value and looked as ragged as everyone else. Which was probably why they'd been left alone.

The wind sliced through the pines. Cas urged his horse on into the teeth of the storm. One step. Then another. Each bringing them closer to warmth, to shelter, to crossing the border into Galatia and leaving this frozen purgatory behind — or so he told himself.

As the leagues fell away behind them, the traffic on the road thinned. Soon they rode alone through a stark landscape, silent except for the crunch of hooves on snow and Da's rattling cough. Felippa had given him her talisman of healing, but it did no good. That cough was worsening by the hour.

"There's a town a few leagues on," Gui said, as if reading his thoughts. "With luck, we'll find a room."

"Aye," Teo said. "And if not, I'll throw someone out of theirs."

Cas snorted. "That'll go over well."

His brother gave a tired smile. "You have a better idea? I'm all ears."

Before Cas could reply, two figures materialized out of the swirling snow ahead. A man and woman of middle years, bent against the wind. They drew up short at the sight of riders, expressions wary.

Cas raised a hand in greeting, and the man bobbed his graying head. He had sharp brown eyes and was still handsome despite the gauntness of his face. "Good day to you. Harsh weather for travel, eh?"

"That it is," Cas agreed. His gaze flicked over their few belongings. More refugees. "Where are you headed?"

"Caria," the woman said, brightening somewhat. She was plumper than her husband, with light auburn hair and cheeks ruddy from the cold. "We have family there."

The man peered at Felippa. "Why, you look just like our granddaughter Martine. She has flaxen hair, too. I used to tell her she must have been left on the doorstep by wood sprites on account her parents are both redheads like my Sarra."

The man's wife shook her head with fond exasperation. Felippa managed a polite reply, though her teeth were chattering. The man rummaged in his sack and held out a hunk of hard bread. "You look half-starved, child."

"I couldn't," Felippa said, "but you're very kind to offer."

It was plain the couple had little enough for themselves. Cas dug into his purse and held out a silver ferry, one of the few he had left. "A gift for luck. We aren't so bad off."

The woman hesitated. It was clear she had pride. "We weren't so bad off, either," she admitted with some bitterness, "until we were robbed of every copper by a greedy innkeeper. His ruffians threw us out the next morning and told us we were lucky they didn't slit our throats."

"Which inn?" Cas asked.

"The Blue Bear."

The odd name rang a bell. They'd almost stopped there two days ago, but Cas had misliked the shifty look of the men gathered in front.

"Please," he said, holding out the silver. "Take it."

The man's eyes glistened as he accepted the coin. "Bel protect you and yours."

"And you," Cas said.

He touched his heels to his mare's sides. They rode on in silence, the couple lost to the swirling snow. A sad story, but not the worst he'd heard. There was no law in the west anymore. Cas wondered if the duchies east of the Boundary would be any better.

Teo cocked his head, twisting in the saddle. "Horses."

Cas heard it a heartbeat later. Drumming hooves, muffled by the snow. A large party of mounted men crested the hill ahead, perhaps two hundred riders. Brigands or soldiers, there was no telling. Cas drew rein, pulse surging. He knew trouble when he saw it. "Off the road. Now!"

Gui shot him a sharp glance. No time to run, not with Da's bad lungs. They'd have to brazen it out and hope for the best.

Cas wheeled his horse around. "I'm going back," he said. "Wait in the trees."

He kicked his mare to a gallop and charged down the road. The couple appeared a minute later, trudging along with their meager belongings. The thunder of hooves grew louder behind him.

"Riders!" he shouted. "Make way, quick!"

Their heads lifted in alarm. The woman stumbled and was steadied by her husband. The riders were nearly upon them, a long double column with pikes and lances. At their head rode a bearded man wearing a rich blue cloak. He paid Cas the same attention he would a mangy dog. One contemptuous glance and then he was past.

The tension eased in Cas's shoulders until he saw a pair of hooded riders approaching — different from the rest. The garments were black as ink. Grinning skull masks gleamed within raised cowls. One deliberately steered his horse towards the couple huddled on the far shoulder. Before Cas could shout a warning, the rider went straight over the man, trampling him.

Cas leapt from the saddle and sprinted to the crumpled form. The man lay on his side, blood staining the snow. The riders had already vanished ahead, but four soldiers from the column reined up.

"Drag that body out of the way, peasant," one ordered.

Cas looked up, a challenge in his eyes. "Why don't you get off your feckin' horse and lend a hand?"

The soldier's face darkened. Gloved fingers touched the pommel of his sword. "Mind your tongue before I cut it out."

"Try it and I'll send you to the ninth hell," Cas snarled.

"Ivo! Jans!" an irate commander shouted from the head of the column. "Get back in line!"

The soldiers hesitated. The one who nearly drew steel spat in Cas's direction. "Count yourself lucky, churl." They wheeled their horses and cantered off.

Cas grasped the man's hand. It was icy cold. Blood bubbled from his lips with each breath. The wife gave a keening wail. Cas watched the departing column, helpless rage knotting his gut. When he looked back, the old man shuddered once and went still.

Cas fished in his pocket for one of the precious iron coins he'd been saving for emergencies. He placed it on the man's tongue and spoke a prayer to Kaethe, asking her to watch over him on his journey to the Cold Sea. The others rode up as he got to his feet. Teo looked like he might be sick. Felippa just stared after the soldiers, her face carved in stone.

"I saw their colors," she said. "A trefoil leaf on a green field. Sir Richart Mortimer. One of Vazsoly's margraves."

Cas noted the name. He turned to the dead man's wife, who sobbed on her knees in the snow. Gui dismounted to help her up. She looked dazed, frozen tears glittering on her cheeks. "What's your name?" Gui asked gently.

"S-sarra," she managed.

"Come with us, Sarra. It's not safe for you here."

Teo and Cas carried the dead man into the woods, where they made a bier of snow. It was the best they could do.

Sir Richart Mortimer. Cas imagined several painful ends for the margrave — though justice felt like another empty promise. Nobles did as they pleased.

He swung into the saddle and leaned toward Gui, who now had Sarra behind him. "We have to get off the road. For good."

Gui frowned, looking west where the soldiers had gone. "Aye, but the Galatian border won't be far—"

"We'll ride cross-country. Find another way."

Gui searched his face. After a moment, he nodded. "As you say."

Cas wondered when he'd become their leader. Gui didn't call him "lad" anymore either. It felt strange.

"We'll cut northeast," Cas said. "Keep to the woods for cover as far as we can."

They pushed the horses as hard as they dared. After a league or so, the snow-laden pines gave way to open, rolling hills. Good country for riding. Cas kept glancing over his shoulder, half-expecting to see men on horseback cresting the horizon behind them.

The weather worsened, the snow thickening. Presently,

they reached a hollow shielded by firs on three sides. Cas called a halt. "We'll camp here. Teo, see to the horses."

His brother had been a stableboy for Duc Marcel, and the horses instinctively trusted him. But Teo had always had an easy way with animals, bringing home orphans and strays when he was a child and nursing them back to health. Now he started clearing a patch of green grass for the horses to graze.

Cas turned to Felippa. "Let's gather some kindling. Dead brush, anything dry."

"What if someone sees the smoke?" she asked nervously.

"Would you rather freeze to death?"

Da gave an awful hacking cough, and Felippa sighed. "No. I suppose we're far enough away."

Cas followed her into the trees, fingers numb inside his gloves. He yanked them off, stuffing them into his belt, and started snapping branches off a deadfall.

"Your hand!" Felippa exclaimed.

She was staring at him in shock. He followed her gaze down to the webbing of his left hand between thumb and forefinger. The blue star tattoo marking him a Quietus was gone.

"It just disappeared," he confessed. "A few days ago."

She propped her hands on hips like Ma used to do. "And you didn't think to tell me about it?"

"I figured you had enough to worry about."

Felippa snorted.

"All right," he said. "I suppose I didn't mention it because I have no idea what it means, but it can't be good."

Her brow creased. "Is Kaethe angry with you?"

Cas met her blue eyes, saw his own fear mirrored there. "Maybe. Gui's mark is gone, too. We don't know why."

Felippa digested this. "Well, if anything like that happens again," she said tartly, "don't keep it to yourself."

"I won't, I promise. And Lip, I am sorry. You deserved to know."

She threw him a scowl, then softened. "You're forgiven." She shook her head with a wry laugh. "I always wanted to see snow. Now I've had my fill of it."

The weather was another mystery. This far west, it should have been blazing hot. They gathered armfuls of kindling in silence and headed back. Cas tried to put the tattoo out of his mind, but he couldn't shake a sense that the worst was yet to come.

Da sat against a tree, a blanket around his thin shoulders, coughing into his fist. Cas looked at his father's haggard face. He was leading them, aye, but to what? Certain death? The Boundary was still a hundred leagues away.

He crouched and started building the fire, feeding the small flame with infinite care. It seemed a fragile thing against the rising twilight. Teo knelt beside the widow Sarra and gave her his own blanket. "There now, missus. I'll make us a nice pot of tea." He guided her to a spot near the growing flames and busied himself filling the kettle with fresh snow. Sarra stared into the flames with hollow eyes, hands limp in her lap.

Cas joined his brother, adding larger sticks. Together, they coaxed the blaze higher. The heat washed over his face, his chapped hands. Snowflakes vanished in the updraft.

Sarra spoke then. "My Roalt made the prettiest shoes for the ladies at Duc Marcel's court. Such delicate slippers of kidskin and brocade. And I sewed hats and gloves to match. Twenty-three years we had our shop on Turnkey Lane..."

Teo pressed a steaming mug into her hand. "He sounds like a fine cobbler. I bet the Cavetti ladies fought duels for a pair of his shoes."

Sarra laughed, then covered her mouth and began to weep. Most boys Teo's age would have been embarrassed, but for all his bluster, he had a soft heart and just sat with her, patting her back.

Cas listened with half an ear, trying to plot out their journey. If they stayed off the roads, they might just have a chance of reaching the Boundary. Tomorrow, they'd push on for the river and hope the ferry was running. Once they were in Clovis, he knew the way well.

Cas glanced up and saw Gui moving between the trees, his stiff knee giving him a rolling gait like a sailor too long at sea. Now he'd taken first watch without being asked.

When Cas looked back, Sarra was curled on her side, her breathing slow. Good. Sleep was sometimes the best medicine for grief.

Cas took off his wet boots and set them near the fire — close enough to dry, not so close they'd go up in flames, which had happened to him once when he was camping with Gui.

"How are you feeling, Da?" he asked.

His father gave a brave nod. "Better, son. I—" He broke off as the cough rattled again, a wet, tearing sound.

Cas felt helpless. He knew which plants to gather for a cough — mallow or horehound — but horehound liked sunny meadows and fallow fields, and right now everything was covered with snow.

That made him think of his mother and her final illness. He still wasn't sure if Justinian had killed her, or the fever.

"I found the mortifex that came to the barn that night," Cas said abruptly. "A friend dispatched him. He's gone forever."

Da pressed a fist to his mouth. Teo's head jerked up. "Good," he said savagely. "I hope it suffered."

Cas might have told his brother that Justinian had already suffered for the last thousand years, bound to the Grand Menotte. That as much as Cas still hated him for what he'd done to Felippa, he'd found a measure of pity for the half-life to which Jaskin Cazal had condemned the man.

But they were all exhausted, and he knew Teo wouldn't understand.

"It did," he said.

Then Da started coughing again and his brother didn't ask any more about it.

One by one, they rolled themselves in blankets. Cas pillowed his head on his saddle, listening to the fire snap and hiss. His heavy eyes followed Gui's stout shape weaving between the trees.

He hoped Lo was safe. He'd give anything to hold her again, to tell her all that had happened and ask what she thought about it. A smile curled his lips. Of course, her advice was usually terrible, but he didn't care. He felt like his own soul was divided and she kept half in her pocket. But how was he supposed to find her now?

Movement in the darkness snagged his eye. He tensed, then relaxed. Just Gui coming around again. But the figure that shuffled into the firelight wasn't Gui. It was the man who'd died on the road. The man whose lips he'd sealed with an iron coin.

"It can't be," Cas whispered, adrenaline jolting through him.

Frozen blood caked the side of the man's head. His eyes shone like a cat's in the firelight.

"Roalt!" Sarra cried, scrambling from her bedroll. Cas leapt up and caught her around the waist. "He's alive!" she sobbed, anguish lending her strength as she fought to escape. "He's alive and we left him behind. Let me go to him!"

Roalt's head snapped toward her. His blue lips moved. "Karam atu. Nergal ish ekki."

Help me. It hurts.

Cas's heart clenched. By all the gods, it shouldn't be possible. The iron on his tongue should have stopped him from rising.

Then Gui appeared from the woods, pulling vials of Kaethe's Tears from his braces. He tossed one to Cas, who unstoppered it with his teeth. Together, they emptied the vials in Roalt's face. The man should have staggered back, skin smoking. Kaethe's Tears were akin to potent lye for the risen. But it had no effect at all.

The horses screamed, rearing against their tethers. Dark silhouettes materialized out of the swirling snow. More dead were coming, and Cas had no idea how to stop them.

Four

The risen man came forward, his eyes vacant black pools. Cas had watched Roalt die hours before — had placed the iron coin on his tongue himself — but here he was, moving with terrible purpose toward the camp.

Cas seized a burning brand from the fire and swung it in a wide arc. Roalt recoiled, raising an arm against the light. A deep, guttural sound escaped his throat.

"Get up!" Cas shouted. "Move!"

Bedrolls rustled. Felippa gasped, then snatched her own burning stick from the fire and waved it about.

"There's another!" she cried, pointing.

Cas risked a glance and saw a second figure, this one a young woman in a dirty, torn blue dress, walking through the trees. Her head lolled at an unnatural angle.

"Teo, ready the horses!" Cas shouted.

His father heaved himself to his feet, coughing in great wracking gasps. The sickness worsened with each night they spent in the open. Teo sprinted toward the panicked mounts, murmuring soothing words.

"Easy now, easy." He caught the reins of the bay mare as she tossed her head. "I know, I know you smell them."

Sarra stood frozen at the sight of her dead husband come back. Gui took her shoulders, turning her to face him. "It's not really him," he said grimly. "You know that." She released a breath and gave a tearful nod.

The thing who had been Roalt circled wide around Cas's fire, seeking a path past the flame. Its movements were less erratic now. More purposeful. Cas backed away, keeping the burning brand between them. The risen's eyes followed the light, but Cas sensed an intelligence gathering behind them — something learning, adapting.

"Hurry!" he shouted to the others.

His boots still sat drying by the fire. Cas needed them if he didn't want to lose his toes to frostbite. Keeping a close eye on Roalt, he managed to reach the boots and awkwardly jam them on his feet, hopping first on one leg, then the other, the torch bobbing. It might have been funny if it fecking wasn't at all.

Gui tossed the last pack onto his horse and turned to help Da into the saddle. The older man's face was gray in the firelight, sweat beading his brow despite the biting cold.

"Felippa, get over here now!" Cas snapped as she jabbed her flaming branch at the dead woman like it was a rapier.

Lip backpedaled, never turning her back on the risen. He'd taught her well.

Teo led the last horse up. "All ready!"

"Mount up," Cas ordered, finally looking away from Roalt to ensure his family obeyed.

Felippa tossed her torch at the feet of the risen woman and scrambled onto the horse behind Cas. As they galloped off, he saw Roalt stepping through the fire, his clothes catching like dry grain.

"Don't look back," he told Felippa, feeling her arms tighten around his waist.

They rode hard across a long stretch of rolling hills. The gray light cast everything in shades of silver shadow. Behind them, the fire dwindled to a speck.

Cas's mind whirled. Risen that could no longer be banished by Kaethe's Tears or cold iron? If the old weapons were useless... well, they were in a heap of trouble.

After an hour of hard riding, their mounts began to show signs of exhaustion. Foam flecked their bits, their breathing labored in the frigid air.

"We can't keep this pace," Gui said, voice low. "They'll founder."

"And we'll freeze," Teo added, his face pinched with cold.

They slowed to a walk, the horses' heads drooping, steam rising from their sweating flanks.

"How far to the Dolcetto River?" Cas asked.

Gui considered, scanning the countryside for familiar landmarks. "Close, I think. But I can't say for certain."

"Will running water even stop them?" Felippa wondered.

"I don't know," Cas admitted. "But the river's our best chance."

"Look," Teo said, pointing to a ridge in the distance.

Cas squinted through the falling snow. Dark shapes moved against the white, a dozen at least, with shambling gaits.

"Feck!" he muttered.

Da hadn't spoken in hours, and Cas looked over to see him slumped forward in the saddle.

"He needs shelter," Teo said. "His breathing's worse."

"I know," Cas replied, a weight pressing down on him like a physical force. "We'll find something. A farm, a woodcutter's hut. Anything."

But all he could see were more snow-covered hills. They plodded onward, the horses stumbling now. With mounting dread, Cas realized the risen on the ridge had spotted them, changing direction to cut them off.

"We can't fight them," Gui said.

Cas nodded wearily. "So we just keep moving."

They emerged from a gap between two low hills, and his hopes died. A milling crowd of risen blocked the path. They were close enough to make out details. A rich velvet doublet on that one, peasant's russet on the next. One woman wore a shop's worth of jewelry, and Cas imagined her putting it all on and fleeing, only to die in some way. He guessed not even the boldest thieves dared to get close enough to take it from her.

"Kaethe preserve us," Sarra murmured.

"I wish she fecking would," Teo replied.

Before Cas could decide whether to risk galloping past or wheel around and try to turn back, a volley of flaming arrows streaked past. The risen staggered, fire blooming. One by one, they toppled into the snow, burning like grotesque candles.

"Mother of Shadows, receive these souls with open arms and guide them to your borders," Cas whispered in a rush, feeling an odd mixture of horror and gratitude.

A dozen men rode up. They wore helmets with horsehair crests and cloaks over dark pleated skirts.

"Hold there!" called one, whose crimson cloak denoted a higher rank, probably captain. "Identify yourselves!"

Cas raised his hands. "Refugees from Prydwen," he said. "Hoping to reach Galatia."

It didn't seem wise to admit they were headed for the Boundary. People could be funny about the mountains between east and west, where the three Greater Gates to Kaethe's domain sat in the high passes. He'd grown up there and loved the peaceful woods, but the Boundary had a fey reputation.

The captain rode up, assessing them with cool gray eyes. His gaze lingered on Gui, in particular.

"The Sons of Bel offer protection to the faithful," the captain said. "Are you faithful?"

"Aye," Cas replied quickly, making a starburst with his fingers. "We stand in Bel's light."

The captain nodded slowly. "The Strategos will want to speak with you."

"Strategos?" Cas asked, unfamiliar with the term.

"Our leader," the captain said curtly. "You'll come with us."

It wasn't a request. Cas exchanged a worried glance with Gui, but they had no choice anyway. Da needed shelter, their supplies were low, and the risen were everywhere.

They followed the priests along a winding track, one of the region's smaller byways. Now that they traveled with armed escort, Cas relaxed enough to take in his surroundings. The eastern part of Cavet was prosperous wine country, with terraced vineyards climbing the hillsides. Fine manor houses stood in the distance, but no smoke rose from their chimneys, and no lights shone in their windows. The area had been abandoned, its people either dead or fled.

"Everything will be better now," Cas whispered to Felippa, who rode behind him. "We'll get Da warm, get some food, rest a bit."

"Hmmm," she grunted, obviously skeptical.

After an hour's ride, they crested a hill and saw the camp spread before them — about three hundred tents arranged in orderly rows with dozens of campfires between. A palisade of sharpened stakes surrounded it, and men in cloaks and pleated kilts patrolled its perimeter. The smell of cooking food drifted upward, making Cas's empty stomach clench painfully.

They were led through the camp's main entrance, past more armed men who eyed them with suspicion. Everywhere, Cas saw preparations for war — weapons being sharpened, armor being mended, men drilling in small groups.

At the center of the camp stood the largest tent, its canvas dyed a fiery yellow. Priests flanked its entrance. The captain conferred with them in low tones, then ducked inside. He emerged a minute later and gestured for them to enter.

Inside, the air was warmed by braziers of hot coals. Maps covered a large table. Standing over it was a tall man with sharp features and piercing eyes. He wore a boiled leather cuirass, and a short-sword hung at his hip, its pommel decorated with a golden filigree sunburst.

"Strategos," the captain announced. "The travelers we encountered near the north road."

The man's cold eyes swept over them. "Refugees from Prydwen, is it?" His voice was raspy, as though he shouted all the time.

"Aye," Cas confirmed. "We travel to Galatia."

"Galatia," he repeated with a harsh laugh. "You'll not find it an improvement. Dark rumors come out of Vellio. The young Damiata is consorting with demons, they say." His fingers touched the red rash at his neck, then fell to his side again. "Tell me, why does a group of Cavetti refugees travel with a servant of Orlaith Redvayne?"

He stared at the phoenix clasp securing Gui's cloak. Cas silently cursed. Stupid not to have thrown that away when they had the chance.

"I no longer serve the Ducissa of Clovis," Gui said evenly. "I left her employ months ago."

"Yet you wear her symbol." The priest's lip curled. "Orlaith

Redvayne is a heretic. I have heard that a giant statue to Kaethe looms over her manor house in Aquitan. It is this demon-worshipping that has brought the plague of risen upon us all."

A fanatical light entered the man's eyes. "The dead rise because Kaethe wills it, and her nuns do nothing to stop this calamity. It is pure knavery!" He slammed a palm down on the table. "You expect me to believe you're not a Redvayne spy?"

It would take more than a puffed-up zealot to ruffle Gui. "Whatever you think of me, my companions are innocent," he said mildly. "I only met them on the road yesterday. They know nothing of my past service."

"Is it true?" the priest asked softly, turning to Cas.

"Aye," Cas replied, hating himself but seeing no point in making matters worse for his family. "We walk in Bel's light, as all decent folk do."

"You do not know this man well?"

"No. He said he'd protect us from brigands if we shared our food. The rest of us are family. That's my Da and Ma." He glanced at the widow Sarra, who nodded despite her fear. "My sister and brother."

The priest frowned, considering. Despite his air of authority, he wasn't very old. Thirty years, maybe. Cas wondered how he'd gained command of the Sons of Bel.

Now he gestured to the guards standing at the tent flap. "Search them."

The men groped their clothing and emptied their pockets. Cas tensed when they examined his hands, for once glad the tattoo that marked him a Quietus was gone.

"There's nothing, Strategos," the soldiers reported.

Still, he glared at them all for a long moment. Then he jerked his long, beardless chin at Gui. "Clap the spy in irons. I will question him thoroughly later."

Gui let them drag him away without a fuss. As he passed,

he gave Cas a small nod. It was meant to reassure, but Cas didn't feel reassured in the least.

"What about the others?" the captain asked.

The Strategos waved a hand. "They're free to go. But their horses and supplies are seized in Bel's name to compensate us for the trouble they've caused."

The captain frowned.

What the feck? Cas tamped down a hot rush of fury, forcing humility into his voice. "Please, my father is very sick. He can't walk far. Can't you at least share some food—"

"We have no room for refugees," the Strategos interrupted in an irritated tone. "Be glad I'm letting you leave at all."

The captain and another soldier escorted them from the tent. Gui was already gone from sight, but their horses were being led to the picket lines. At the edge of the camp, the captain who had found them stopped, looking uncomfortable.

"The road south leads to a village," he said. "Half a day's walk, perhaps. You might find shelter there."

"Half a day," Cas repeated, looking at his father's ashen face. "He won't make it half a day in this cold."

The captain glanced around to ensure they weren't observed. He pulled a cloth-wrapped bundle from his pack and pressed it into Cas's hands.

"Bread and cheese," he muttered. "Not much, but it's all I can spare."

Cas nodded, surprised by the small mercy, though he was still fuming inside.

"Go," the captain urged. "Before the Strategos changes his mind and decides you're all spies."

Cas couldn't be sure, but he got the feeling the man didn't like his leader much. Still, he seemed unwilling to disobey his orders.

With no choice, they left the camp behind, trudging along

the frozen road. "They won't kill him straight away," Felippa said tightly. "That flaming arsehole said he meant to question Gui again. So we're going to get him out before they do kill him."

Cas studied her stony face. Her ordeal among the mortifexes had changed her. She'd always been clever, but now she was even tougher than he was.

"I need to scout it first," he said. "Learn the camp's layout and find where they're keeping him." He paused under a massive spruce tree, with thick spreading branches that offered easy footholds. "In the meantime, you all climb up there until I get back. I've never seen a risen climb a tree."

Cas watched as Teo hauled himself up first, then reached down to pull their father after him. Plump Sarra followed with impressive agility. Felippa went last, pausing on the lowest branch. "Be careful," she whispered. "I don't want to have to rescue you again."

Cas smiled up at her. "See you soon."

The snow began falling faster as he left the road and cut through the trees, retracing his path to the camp. Growing up in the Boundary had taught him woodcraft. A broken twig here, a disturbed patch of snow there — the scouts and sentries weren't bothering to hide their trail. Why would they? They traveled in force, with fire to ward off the dead. But Cas moved alone, and he moved like a ghost.

The tang of woodsmoke reached him first, then the distant murmur of voices. He crouched beneath the snow-heavy boughs of a fir tree. Torchlight glimmered through the whirling snow. He advanced inch by careful inch until the palisade of freshly cut logs appeared. Torches burned at regular intervals, casting uneven shadows across the snow, and men paced the perimeter, dark silhouettes against the orange glow.

Cas circled the camp, counting the guards, noting their

patterns. Four at the main entrance, two at the rear, and six more spread around the walls.

The snow was his ally, muffling his movements and erasing his footprints. Still, getting past those sentries wouldn't be easy. He watched a patrol pass, counting their seconds between groups. Six minutes. That was his window.

So where were they holding Gui? Cas climbed a thick oak tree and studied the camp from above. It was all orderly rows except for a tent near the middle. Lantern light shone through the cracks, while most of the other tents were dark. This one wasn't as big as the command pavilion, yet two guards stood before it, their postures alert.

Shite. It looked hard to get to.

Cas climbed down and worked his way closer, using the trees for cover. The palisade was roughly eight feet tall, the logs sharpened to points at the top. He was weighing his options when a cold hand clamped over his mouth.

Cas slammed his elbow back, connecting with something solid as an oak stump. The grip didn't loosen. He twisted, scrabbling for his knife, then remembered that the fecking priests had taken it.

"*Be still,*" came a hiss in his ear. Cas went rigid. He knew that dry voice. The hand slowly released him and Cas turned, meeting a pair of amused eyes with pinpricks of flame floating in their emerald depths.

"Lucius?" he breathed in disbelief.

The mortifex gave a feral grin. "Fancy meeting you here."

It was too bizarre. Cas had left him in Prydwen weeks before.

"What are you doing out here?" Cas whispered.

"Same as you, I imagine. Skulking about, hatching devious plans." As usual, Lucius looked like he'd just walked out of some noble's audience chamber. Not a copper hair was out of place. He wore his usual midnight blue cloak, although the golden phoenix clasp of House Redvayne had been replaced with a crouching lynx. Black gloves covered his hands.

Cas kept his voice low. "Gui's being held prisoner in there."

They had all served Orlaith, and Lucius knew him well.

"Gui Harcourt?" Lucius's eyes narrowed. "When did this happen?"

"Not an hour past. They caught us on the road and accused him of being Orlaith's spy."

"Us?" Lucius arched a brow. "Who else are you with?"

Cas hesitated. Lucius always played his own game, but he obviously wasn't in league with the priests. "My family," he said. "We're on our way to the Boundary."

"Ah." Lucius studied the palisade. In the gray light, with snow gathering on his hair, he looked human — until you noticed that no chill mist of breath left his lips.

"Will you help me?" Cas asked. "You could walk in there right now and bring him out."

Lucius's lips thinned. "It's not that simple."

"Isn't it?" he replied bluntly. "I've seen you kill. They wouldn't stand a chance. Not a hundred of them armed to the teeth."

"They're priests," Lucius replied sourly. "And I serve Brennos Fearghal, the true Strategos of the Sons of Bel."

Brennos Fearghal. Cas chewed over the name for a moment, his thoughts slow from cold and not enough sleep. "Was he the man who called himself the Red Rogue?"

Lucius nodded.

"Brennos Fearghal is *here*?" Cas pressed. Things were getting even stranger.

"Not far." Lucius gestured eastward. "He's camped on the banks of the Dolcetto. I take it you met Brother Arnulf?"

"The pious peacock?"

Lucius laughed softly. "Yes, that one. Arnulf is a zealot who's appointed himself leader of a splinter faction. He's been hunting the nuns of Kaethe, burning their convents."

Cas shook his head in disgust. "I can't say I'm surprised. But what does that have to do with rescuing Gui?"

Lucius looked annoyed. "Brennos won't permit an attack on his own brothers, no matter how misguided they've become. He still hopes to bring them back to the fold. And I..." He grimaced. "I respect his wishes."

"Since when do you respect anyone's wishes?"

"Since I found myself free of my bondage to the Redvaynes." Lucius's gaze hardened. "Since I discovered what it means to choose my own path."

Cas stared at him. "Are you joking with me, Lucius?"

The mortifex pulled up the sleeve of his doublet. The iron band that once circled it was gone, leaving a strip of alabaster skin. "I am free," he said.

Cas stared in amazement. "I'm glad for you," he said, meaning it. "But how?"

"I'm still not sure. But I suspect we have much to discuss." His gaze tracked the bobbing torches of the sentries. "And this is not the place to do it. Let's collect your family and get you to Bren's camp."

Cas hesitated. "I can't leave Gui."

"And I'm not asking you to abandon the man to his fate," Lucius growled. "Arnulf will be dealt with, you can trust me on that." He gave a grim smile. "Gui will keep for a single night."

Cas glanced back at the camp. His gut screamed at him to act now, but he still had no idea how to get past the guards, and if he was caught it would only make matters worse.

"My family's waiting about half a league back down the road," he said finally. "Up in a tree. Seemed like the safest place."

Lucius nodded. "I've little to fear from the risen," he said wryly, "but they are a nuisance."

Cas snorted. They slipped through the forest together, the snow blanketing the world in silence. Cas glanced over his shoulder once, where the torches of Arnulf's camp flickered like tiny stars fallen to earth. Somewhere among them, Gui waited. Cas vowed to return for him — this time, with an army at his back.

Five

Lo strode through the crowded streets of Mystral, shadow cloak swirling behind her. After three days traveling alone in the Duskwood, it was nice to be around people again, though she steered clear of the loup-garou with their long, dark tresses and alluring eyes who prowled the alleys between shops selling all manner of arcane curiosities.

The manor house of the Courtenays perched on a rise ahead, a living palace of ancient trees whose boughs formed twisted towers and knotted domes. When Lo neared the gates, also woven from golden-leaved trees, a centaur cantered out to greet her, green hair flowing nearly to her waist.

"Delilah Dessarian." The centaur's tone was cool.

"Hello, Astris." Lo inclined her head. "I seek an audience with Ladies Chaos and Caul."

Astris tossed her head. "They are expecting you. Come, mortal, do not keep Their Graces waiting." The centaur trotted ahead through an arch of vines. Lo followed her swishing tail, ducking as bats fluttered overhead and owls swooped past on silent wings.

The air hung heavy and damp, thick with the scent of earth and night-blooming flowers. Mushrooms sprouted from mossy roots snaking along the walls. Despite the dimness, Lo navigated the overgrown passages deftly, pupils widening to catch what shreds of light filtered down.

At last they reached a high rampart, the breeze carrying the perfume of the night gardens. Sable flowers unfurled beneath the moonlight, drinking in its glow. Lo traced a finger along the petal of a black rose. All this beauty, born from the suffering wrought by the Grand Menotte.

Chaos and Caul rose from a bench at her approach. Chaos, the warmer of the two, came forward on her silver canes. "We hear you bested Magnus the Merciless," she said with a smile. "Freeing your parents and the Reaper's sister, as well."

"Felippa," Lo clarified. "Yes, she is safe with Castelio. But I'm afraid I bring bad news on that front. Hello, Nathan."

He was leaning against the parapet, arms and ankles crossed. The scruffy traveler she had spent weeks with in the Cold Sea was gone. Nathan's dark hair was swept back, his attire impeccable. "If it has anything to do with the dead rising in numbers never before seen, and refusing to obey our commands, we are eager to hear it."

All three of them were necromancers, but they were not evil as Lo had first believed. Just... a bit weird.

"Funny you should mention that." Lo drew a deep breath. "The Grand Menotte wasn't destroyed after all. Someone is wearing it and commands the mortifexes, but not even Kaethe knows who."

"It must be Jaskin," Nathan growled.

"I know, he's the first person I'd suspect," Lo agreed. "But he's the only one we can rule out."

She quickly related how the old necromancer had been caught by Kaethe's hounds and dragged before the goddess. "He was thoroughly searched and he didn't have it. When she asked who did, he babbled some nonsense. Kaethe locked him up and intended to question him once his wits returned."

"Don't tell me he managed to escape," Nathan said flatly.

Lo nodded. "With the help of Kaethe's consort, Nabu-ba-idinna. They've run off together." She felt proud of herself for sticking mostly to the truth. What they could *never* know was Nabu's true identity.

"I'm hunting them both and thought you might have some idea where Jaskin has gone." She gave a regretful smile. "You should probably do something about the Grand Menotte, too. Whoever has it is going mad as we speak."

Caul muttered a vile oath. "We knew something was wrong. The Veil is no longer open to our sight."

"Oh yeah," Lo said, "that's the other problem. Jaskin stole a talisman that locks the gates to the land of the dead." Now that part *was* a lie, but it might convince them to help her find him.

Chaos sucked a breath through her teeth. "I have never heard of such a thing."

"Kaethe kept it secret for obvious reasons," Lo said. "It's called the Orb of Carnage. Fashioned by an entity named Bonoth the Maggot."

Nathan cast her a suspicious look. "And what reason could Jaskin have for locking the doors to the afterlife?"

Lo shrugged. "Who can fathom the motives of a lunatic?"

Chaos began to pace, her gown trailing through the black clover. "It's been obvious something was amiss. I can no longer speak to the dead behind the Veil or call forth spirits." She glanced at Lo, her gaze piercing. "Some of my charms have lost their power as well, though others still function. It is… haphazard."

"Yet the dead on *this* side of the Veil are more numerous," Caul added. "Travelers have been vanishing in the Nightwood at an alarming rate, even for that perilous forest."

Nathan pushed off the rampart. "We must call a gathering," he said, "of all the lords and ladies of the Moon Courts. The centaurs, the loup-garou, everyone. To discuss these strange happenings and prepare our defenses."

Chaos nodded at Astris, who stood waiting. "Send messengers at once. We will convene under the light of the full moons three days hence."

Lo listened with half an ear as they laid their plans. She wished them luck, but finding Bel was her only priority. "You know Jaskin better than anyone," she said to Nathan. "Where do you think he would go?"

"I had planned to hunt him down myself, actually. I only stopped here first to, ah…" His eyes flicked to Chaos. "Pay a visit to my neighbors. But I will go with you. Together we'll find Jaskin and this orb."

Lo's heart sank. She couldn't let Nathan accompany her. Nabu's true identity had to remain secret. If it came out, who knew what Kaethe might do in her fury?

"No," Lo said firmly. "You're needed here. And I cannot wait three days for this council to be over."

He frowned. "You intend to hunt Jaskin alone? You know how dangerous he is."

"I can handle him," she bluffed. "But anything you can tell me about him would be invaluable." She hesitated. "He's on his last life, isn't he?"

Something flickered in Nathan's dark eyes. "So he claimed."

"Then he'll be affected by the Quickening."

"As will you," Nathan reminded her.

Lo turned to Chaos and Caul. "Kaethe said the Quickening is a power beyond hers. Something that affects all Shadow Souls nearing their final death. You are both scholars of dark magic. Tell me, is it deliberate or just random bad luck?"

The Courtenay twins exchanged a silent look. Finally, Chaos spoke, her voice grave. "There are ancient powers in this world. Ones that make Kaethe seem a dewy-eyed maid."

Great. "Kaethe mentioned 'other chthonic deities'. Is that who she meant?"

Chaos nodded. "The Lady of Shadows has three sisters."

"Nona, Decima and Morta," Caul said. "The ones who bind the world."

Lo felt a chill. "Kaethe said my very existence was an affront to them. That they want me dead."

"Yet they have not succeeded," Nathan said with a smile.

He meant to be kind, but a bitter laugh escaped her. "Haven't they? I've died eight times, including the lightning strike that I mistook for sending the mortifexes to the far shore!"

She could still feel the searing heat, the blinding flash. What a fool she had been to think it was a victory. "Justinian and the others vanished," she explained, "but only because some fool put on the Grand Menotte and summoned them."

"Eight lives," Caul murmured. "So you have one left."

Lo thought of Bel, his memories returning with each passing hour. Of the Grand Menotte and its undead army.

"Yes, so I can't waste it. If I find Jaskin and the orb, I can reopen the gates."

The wind whispered through the ramparts, carrying the scent of moon-flowers and the distant hum of Mystral.

"This orb," Nathan said. "Who created it again?"

"Ah, Argoth the Maggot."

"I thought you said Bonoth the Maggot."

Lo stared back at him, unblinking. Fuck you, Nathan. "No, I said Arnoth."

Nathan opened his mouth, clearly about to argue, when she was saved by the Courtenays' mortifex, Mace. He strode up one of the pathways. "My ladies, a riot has broken out in the city."

"A riot?" Chaos echoed. "What was the cause?"

"No one knows, but it's spreading fast."

"Misfortune and trouble," Nathan said with a tight smile. "Why does that sound so *very* familiar?"

"Could be the Quickening," Lo agreed. "If Jaskin is the cause, we can't let him slip away."

Caul nodded. "Mace, ready a coach. We shall see for ourselves what's happening."

He hurried to obey, and Lo felt a surge of excitement. It *couldn't* be this easy, could it?

Six

Jaskin Cazal crouched behind an empty ale barrel, peering around the staves. The street beyond crackled with thumps and screams and breaking glass. The brawl was spreading like wind-driven wildfire.

Nabu-bal-idinna squatted next to Jaskin in the dingy alley. He clutched his purple robes, whimpering like a kicked puppy. "It was a mistake to come here." The alchemist's timid brown eyes darted about. "I want to return to Kaethe's tower." When no reply came, his plaintive voice climbed an octave. "You promised I could go home whenever I wanted to!"

"Quiet your nattering," Jaskin hissed, "or the angry wenches will hear." He scanned the alley again, mapping out potential escape routes.

Nabu moaned, rocking back and forth. "'My Lady will punish me grievously for this." He cast Jaskin a reproachful look. "I should never have listened to you."

Jaskin bit back a sharp retort. Nabu had been an amusing companion at first, with his slack-jawed wonder at the world beyond Kaethe's tower. But now the man's constant whining grated like a dull saw on bone.

How long had he been Kaethe's pet, locked away in that gilded cage? Jaskin had asked him questions, but Nabu's sense of time was addled, like everything else in his great soggy mushroom of a brain. He spoke of epochs and eons, months and centuries, all jumbled together.

Jaskin tensed as a shadow drifted past the mouth of the alley. Just a stray spirit. But the smoke was growing thicker and they couldn't hide there much longer. He seized his sniveling companion by the shoulders.

"We shall run," Jaskin whispered, "swift as deer. Follow and stay close."

With luck, the alchemist would trip over his robes and fall on his face. Then he'd be rid of him.

Nabu nodded resentfully. Drawing a deep breath, Jaskin unfolded his spidery limbs and dashed into the smoke-filled night, Nabu stumbling in his wake. As they dodged a knife fight between two blue-haired centaurs, Jaskin tried to grasp how they had landed in this predicament.

Upon escaping Kaethe's tower, he'd been tempted to return to Castle Cazal. But the Lady of Shadows would be hunting him, and his ancestral home was the first place she would look. Feeling rather cunning, Jaskin had instead brought them to Mystral. It would be a simple matter, he thought, to disappear into the throngs.

The evening had begun pleasantly enough. They found a raucous tavern packed with revelers of every stripe. Jaskin ordered a bottle of wormwood cordial, hoping it might loosen Nabu's tongue about Kaethe's secrets. The alchemist had coughed at the first sip, tears leaking from his eyes. But as the night wore on and his cup was refilled, the priggish pout had loosened. Soon he was matching Jaskin drink for drink, his voice rising in boisterous toasts.

As the liquor flowed, Jaskin's gaze wandered to a table of loups garou, their tawny eyes flashing beneath silken hoods of deep crimson. He leaned in, murmuring a bawdy jest that set them howling with laughter. Even Nabu, emboldened by drink, offered the ladies some slurred but earnest compliments.

To Jaskin's displeasure, the wolf women were charmed by the guileless alchemist. They crowded around him, tweaking his beard and cooing endearments. Nabu basked in the attention, grinning foolishly.

Soon, the busty lycanthropes began squabbling over who would claim him. Hackles lifted. Teeth bared. Steel glimmered in the candlelight. When the dispute erupted into a full-fledged melee, Jaskin had dragged Nabu through a back exit. He'd hoped to vanish again, but the chaos had already spilled into the street like an overturned flagon. Fists and hooves flew, along with bottles and plates and anything that came to hand.

"What madness has gripped this city?" Nabu panted, as he ducked beneath a flying pail of what looked and smelled like human waste.

"'Tis the Quickening," Jaskin muttered. He could feel it, a current of malice lapping at his heels, a hot breath of misfortune dancing along his skin. The tinkle of breaking glass drew Jaskin's gaze to the shop across the way. A mob had hurled something through the front windows and were storming inside, emerging with armfuls of looted goods. Two streets off, the city watch advanced to quell the uprising.

"We must flee," he hissed, seizing Nabu's elbow, "lest we be clapped in irons or worse."

"But Kaethe—"

"Will flay both our hides if we're caught!" Jaskin snapped.

"Now move, you great goose, before I leave you for the wolf women!"

Nabu blanched and scurried after him, stumbling over the hem of his ridiculous purple robe but never quite falling. Jaskin set his jaw and plunged ahead, praying to whatever minor gods might still favor him that they would escape this wretched night unscathed. Sweat beaded his brow as he led Nabu deeper into the alleyways. The stench of refuse clung to the walls. Overhead, the three moons leered down like the eyes of a beast.

"Where... where are we going?" Nabu panted, his face ashen.

"Far from this accursed city," Jaskin replied.

He paused at the mouth of another nameless alley. The street beyond was deserted. But how long until the madness found them again? He sought his Shadow magic. The air rippled as a portal struggled to take shape. But his power was faint. The gateway flickered once, twice, then guttered out like a spent candle.

"No," Jaskin whispered. He tried again, pouring all his will into the spell.

"What's happening?" Nabu asked. "Why isn't it working?"

"I know not," Jaskin snapped, raking a hand through his crest of raven hair. "But 'tis a small setback only—"

A flaming bottle arced over the rooftops and shattered at their feet. Nabu yelped and leapt back, patting at his smoldering hem.

"All is well," Jaskin said quickly, stamping out the flames. "We just need to—"

The clatter of wheels froze the words in his throat. He turned, slowly. A black coach with a stooping Nightjar painted on the door stood at the end of the alley. It was drawn by skeletal steeds that pawed the ground, striking blue sparks. Jaskin groaned. Chaos and Caul Courtenay.

Then the door swung open. Jaskin's irritating heir Nathan Ouvrard emerged, along with a woman with cold blue eyes and ragged black hair. Jaskin remembered her well. Delilah was another Shadow Soul, but she was no ally. She was Kaethe's creature through and through.

For a moment, hunter and prey stared at each other. Then her lips curved in a satisfied smile. "Hey, shithead!" she shouted, barreling down the alley.

Jaskin seized Nabu's arm and dragged him into a run. They pelted in the opposite direction, Nabu gibbering some nonsense that Jaskin ignored. He risked a glance over his shoulder. The hunter was gaining, and Nathan was close behind her.

Ahead, the alley split into three wider lanes. Jaskin veered right, careened around a corner, skidded through some vile puddle, caught himself and kept running. The warren of back streets seemed endless. They dodged through makeshift markets, leapt past carts and shoved through startled crowds. At every turn, Jaskin hoped Nabu would flag. But the man kept pace, panting and wheezing yet never falling more than a step behind.

As they slunk beneath a shadowed portico, Jaskin risked another look back. Their pursuers had vanished! And ahead... He squinted. It was the same pox-ridden tavern where the whole kerfuffle had started. He'd gone in a huge circle.

Jaskin slowed to a walk, fighting to steady his breathing. Beside him, Nabu bent double, wheezing like a broken bellows. "We lost them?" the alchemist asked between gasps.

"For now." The street was quiet. The city watch must have forcibly dispersed the rioters. Jaskin caught sight of the Courtenays' black coach, which was drawn up in front of the tavern. A smile spread across his face. "Come," he said. "I have an idea."

They crept towards the coach. The bone horses stamped

and snorted, rolling their fiery eyes. Jaskin raised a finger to his lips, gesturing for Nabu to stay back. He approached the lead horse, murmuring a snatch of Tongues under his breath. The creature allowed Jaskin to stroke its muzzle, skeletal head dipping in submission. Grinning, Jaskin was about to clamber into the driver's seat when Nathan appeared.

"You're not going anywhere," he said with icy anger. "The game is over, uncle."

"I am not your uncle," Jaskin retorted. "But *you* are a pious scoundrel. Stand aside, you half-witted lemming."

"I'm a scoundrel?" Nathan exclaimed. "*You* stole the Orb of Carnage!"

Jaskin frowned. "What in all the devils are you talking about?"

A flash of purple caught his eye. Nabu was creeping up behind Nathan, a broken chair leg in one hand. The alchemist's moon face glowed in the darkness. Before Jaskin could blink, his makeshift club came crashing down on Nathan's head. The heir of Vendagni crumpled to the ground. Nabu stood over him, mouth agape as though he scarcely believed what he'd just done.

Jaskin leaped into the driver's seat. "Bravo, my friend! I knew you had some fire in you!"

In fact, he'd known nothing of the sort, but now Jaskin felt a renewed fondness for his accomplice. Nabu scrambled up to the bench. Jaskin gathered the reins just as the Courtenays emerged from the tavern. One was tall and one was small, but their faces wore identical expressions of fury.

Jaskin paused to sweep a mocking bow. Then he flicked the reins and the bone steeds surged forward, ironshod wheels clattering on the skulls that served as cobblestones. Nabu yelped as he was thrown back against the seat.

Jaskin gave a monkey-like hoot, drunk on their daring

escape. But his mirth died as a familiar figure stepped into the road directly ahead. Delilah, her crossbow leveled at Jaskin's forehead. He flung himself sideways. The quarrel buzzed past his ear and lodged in the coach's canopy.

They sped past, leaving her to fling a stream of curses that were swallowed by the creaking wheels. Jaskin guided the horses to the eastern road. The lights of Mystral faded behind as they galloped towards the Duskwood. Beside him, Nabu still gripped the seat, knuckles white. A smear of blood stained the front of his robe.

"I haven't had that much fun in ages," he blurted. Then he started to laugh. It grew louder until tears streamed down his face.

"You sound like a madlark," Jaskin admonished, but he found himself laughing too.

Let Kaethe put a bounty on him. Let the Quickening try to claim his final soul. He would outrun them all, one step ahead, as he always had.

SEVEN

Fresh snow squeaked under Cas's boots as he hiked through the forest, breath steaming in the frigid air. Lucius strode along next to him. Behind, Teo murmured soft encouragements to a listless Sarra. Felippa and Da brought up the rear, their faces wan with exhaustion.

"What news from Galatia?" Cas asked in a low voice.

Lucius glanced at him sidelong. "Enrigo Redvayne is dead. Poisoned by his own mother."

Cas frowned. Orlaith was a cruel and selfish woman, but that seemed excessive even for her. "Why?"

"It was an accident. She intended the wine for the Damiata Beatriu and Vazsoly Marcel on their wedding day. Enrigo drank it by mistake." Lucius's mouth twisted. "It broke her mind. She was raving when I left her in Vellio."

Cas felt sorry for the young Redvayne heir. Enrigo had seemed better than either of his parents.

"How long were you in Vellio?" he asked.

Lucius was silent for a long moment, his green eyes scanning the snow-laden trees. "Before I was freed, I was passed around like a trinket at the bazaar," he said wryly. "First Orlaith gave me to Enrigo. The poor boy barely had me a day before the Damiata talked him into handing me over to her instead."

Cas halted in his tracks. "You were bound to Beatriu do Santillan?" He couldn't keep the incredulity from his voice.

"For a brief time." Lucius touched the ruby-eyed lynx clasp at his throat. "The girl is more cunning than she appears." His shoulders shrugged with a sigh, though it made no mist in the frigid air. "In any event, it matters little. Our bond broke at the wedding. Rather violently, I might add."

Cas thought of the dark rumors he'd heard on the road. "What happened?"

"Morgen Nadezhda." Lucius grimaced. "Apparently she's Vazsoly's half-sister by the old Duc Andrzej. Her mother was the man's necromancer and he abused her badly. The Marcels are all brutes. Vazsoly got the death he deserved."

"Good for her," Cas said.

"Then a man came claiming to be Jaskin Cazal. He and Morgen nearly tore Kaethe's temple apart fighting each other over the Grand Menotte. I think one of them summoned the mortifexes bound to it."

Cas shook his head. "No, you're wrong. Delilah used her power to free them. She sent them onward to the far shore."

"I wish it were so, but I watched it happen. The temple has a nine-pointed star carved into the floor. Vazsoly's blood poured into the grooves, racing to complete the conjuring." Lucius went still, his gaze distant. "A darkness gathered at the center. I cannot describe it, but I *know*." He glanced at the sky. "And this freakish weather. How else do you explain it?"

Cas had never seen Lucius show fear, not even when they stood shoulder to shoulder staring down Kaethe's monstrous hounds. But now his face held a haunted quality. The sight unsettled Cas more than he cared to admit.

"You lost something, too." Lucius glanced pointedly at Cas's hand.

Cas flexed his fingers. He still felt oddly naked without the tattoo. "Aye, Kaethe's mark vanished as we rode out from Prydwen." He frowned. "I'm guessing you already know that the usual weapons no longer work against the dead."

Lucius gave a brusque nod. "You must tell Brennos everything you know— He cut off, ears pricking at some distant sound. "Get down!"

Cas barely had time to register the hissed command before Lucius yanked him behind the broad trunk of an ancient oak. The others scrambled to follow, pressing themselves flat against the rough bark. Cas strained to hear past the frantic thudding of his own heart. Then faint voices reached him. A patrol.

Two of Arnulf's priests emerged from the trees. They passed a flask between them, steps weaving across the frozen earth. Would Lucius kill if his hand was forced? Cas wasn't sure how deep his loyalty to Brennos ran. And the mortifex had a habit of vanishing when trouble appeared.

The moment he thought this, Cas felt a twinge of shame. Da wouldn't be here if not for Lucius, who'd saved him from a flaming pyre in Prydwen. Perhaps he really was a changed man.

The seconds stretched as the patrol came closer. Cas hoped they wouldn't notice the telltale footprints in the snow. But they seemed too preoccupied with the flask to care.

Relief coursed through him as the voices faded, but it was short-lived. He was weak with hunger. When had they last eaten? Before Roalt appeared. Roalt the Risen. Cas bit his lip against a bark of grim laughter.

The party pressed onwards, meeting no more patrols. At last, a whiff of woodsmoke reached his nose. The red glow of fires lit the trees.

The camp was a sad affair, reminiscent of the makeshift

settlements they'd passed on the road. Hollow-faced men huddled around sputtering cook fires. Their numbers were half of Arnulf's camp, and only a dozen horses stood along a picket line.

Cas's spirits sank as he surveyed Brennos's army. These men didn't look like they could stand up to a stiff breeze, let alone a legion of fanatical warriors.

"I know it looks bad," Lucius admitted. "The blizzard caught them unprepared. Blankets threadbare, food stores low. And with Arnulf threatening to burn any town that aids us..."

Cas swore under his breath. "What about Brennos?"

"He took a nasty cut in a skirmish with Arnulf's soldiers." Lucius's jaw tensed. "But he's recovering. Come."

He led them through the camp. Two Sons of Bel guarded a tent larger than the others. They stepped aside, allowing Lucius and the others to enter. The tent was as cold as the outside air, lit by three lanterns. A cot and camp table took up most of the space, along with a few trunks.

Brennos struggled to sit, blankets falling away to reveal bandaged ribs. It was the first time that Cas saw the face of the man who'd called himself the Red Rogue. He was young, no more than thirty or so, with coal-black hair and olive skin. He had the sort of classical good looks that would draw every gaze, either with desire or envy, despite the pitted scars on his cheeks. "My scout has returned," he said, eyes kindling as they found Lucius.

"With friends." Lucius moved to Brennos's side, hands gentle as he helped him upright.

Brennos's gaze settled on Felippa with a start of recognition. "The young scribe from Prydwen!"

Felippa looked pleased that he remembered her. She gave a little curtsy and Brennos laughed, but it had kindness in it. "No need for that. Tell me how you have come here."

She drew a breath. “We’re just trying to reach the Boundary. But Arnulf took one of our party prisoner.”

“And stole our horses, too.” Teo put in. He rubbed his arm and glared at Felippa. “Don’t pinch.”

“The horses don’t matter as much as Gui,” she whispered, loud enough for all to hear.

“Did I say they did? Don’t put words in my mouth.”

Cas stepped forward as Brennos watched the pair bicker with evident amusement.

“I’ve been inside the camp,” he said. “Arnulf has at least four hundred men, well-armed and provisioned. Close to the same number of horses, too.”

He described the defenses he’d observed, the patrols and sentries, with Lucius confirming his account and adding a detail here and there. Brennos’s face grew stonier with every word. When Cas finished, he shook his head.

“We can’t kill them all,” he said. “They’ve been led astray, but they’re still my brothers. We must win them over to our side with reason and logic.”

Cas wondered how he planned to do that from a sickbed.

“We must give them something to believe in.” Brennos struggled to sit up straighter, wincing. “Something worth fighting for. If we can just make them see that the nuns of Kaethe are not to blame—”

“There’s no time,” Lucius cut in. “Prydwen is under siege. The margraves have brought in mercenaries, and they’re gathering at the gates as we speak. If we don’t act soon, the city will fall.”

Cas thought of the troops they’d passed on the road, banners snapping in the wind. “Sir Mortimer has joined them,” he said. “We saw him riding west with hundreds of men.”

Brennos looked bleak. “Mortimer was the last holdout. If

he's thrown his lot in with the others..." He shook his head. "Then you are right. We're out of time."

Lucius turned to Cas. "Our spies say that Mortimer's been on the fence, unwilling to commit himself and join forces with the other margraves, but they must have persuaded him to their cause. He controls the Westmarch, commanding over a thousand men. If he's joined the fray, Prydwen will soon fall."

Before Cas could reply, the tent flap opened and a young messenger entered, cheeks pink from running. "Strategos," he gasped. "The usurper has agreed to meet with you."

Brennos didn't seem surprised. "The god wills it," he said. "I told you, Lucius, I will win them over without bloodshed. Now, we must talk. Please see that our guests are cared for."

It was a clear dismissal. Lucius handed them over to a gangly priest named Brother Serl. Then he dragged a camp chair over to Brennos's cot, their heads bent together in quiet conversation.

Cas realized how little there was to spare when Serl ordered two priests to grab their things and squeeze into a tent with their brethren. "Who the hells are they?" one demanded, shooting Cas a dirty look. "Esteemed guests of the Strategos," Serl replied with a dirty look of his own. "Now move it!"

The men did, with grunts of displeasure. Serl passed out blankets and hot broth, then ducked back out into the cold. Cas sipped the thin soup, barely tasting it. His mind churned with worry.

"Do you think he can do it?" Felippa asked. "Win Arnulf over?"

Cas stared into the flames. "I hope so." But in his heart, he doubted it. Men like Arnulf didn't yield power easily.

Felippa pulled her knees up to her chest. "If he can't, what will happen to Gui?"

"Don't think like that." Cas forced more conviction into

his voice than he felt. "Bren was the Red Rogue. He led a revolution, didn't he? And they won. If anyone can outmaneuver Arnulf, it's him. Plus he's got Lucius on his side."

The words sounded hollow, but Felippa nodded. She cupped the tin cup of broth, her gaze distant. Behind her, Teo, Da and Sarra were laying out their blankets, Da coughing miserably all the while. Cas's eyes strayed to the tent flap. Outside, the snow was still falling.

Prydwen was running out of time. And so were they.

Eight

Early the next day, Lucius rode alongside his general, a dozen of the most loyal men behind them. Brennos sat tall despite the half-healed wounds, his face set in grim lines. It only softened when the clouds parted and the sun streamed down, making the hilts of their swords glint.

"Bel's light shines upon us," he remarked. "A good omen."

Lucius made a noncommittal noise and raised the hood of his heavy cloak. Iron might have lost its potency, but sunlight still burned.

Bren caught his eye. "I want to name you my First Flame."

The title would make him second in command. Lucius blinked. "I'm honored, but I cannot accept. I'm no priest."

"You could always convert," Bren said.

A dry laugh escaped Lucius's lips. "I doubt your men would take kindly to that. One such as I, leading them in matters of faith?"

"Why not? Bel crafted the daēvas in his image, blessed you with power over fire itself. Who better to serve as First Flame?"

Lucius sighed. "I may wield fire, but I do not worship your

god. Surely there are brothers among your ranks far more qualified."

Bren looked annoyed at the refusal. He nodded curtly. "I will give it more thought."

Which meant, Lucius knew, that Bren wished to speak no more of it — until he argued his case again. The Strategos had a talent for redirecting conversations that displeased him. Lucius did not press the matter further. Let Bren name a true believer as First Flame, one the Sons of Bel would obey without question.

They pressed on through the silent forest. A bitter wind knifed through the trees, though Lucius barely felt it. From the corner of his eye, he studied Bren's profile. The firm chin, the bold nose. It belonged to an ancient hero of legend, yet for all his noble bearing, Lucius feared his notions of honor would be his undoing.

Lucius urged his mount closer, lowering his voice. "You should take Arnulf captive. There will be no better chance."

Bren turned to him, brows knitted. "At a parley? That is treacherous and ignoble."

Lucius snorted. "Your opponent is more treacherous and ignoble. He robs travelers, sows chaos in the land, and refuses to aid a city in need." Lucius's tone sharpened. "Need I remind you the margraves have vowed to punish this rebellion? To make an example of Prydwen? We both know what that means. Men put to the sword, women defiled, children—"

"Enough," Brennos cut him off gruffly. "I am aware."

But Lucius would not relent. "Arnulf is a fanatic, a mockery of a true priest. He does not deserve to claim Bel's mantle."

Bren's lips pressed into a line. "That may be so, but I cannot believe all in his camp are the same. If I sink to his level, why should they follow me?"

"Your virtue will not save the city, Brennos."

"Yet without it," Bren retorted, "I have nothing."

An old argument, one they had engaged in countless times. Lucius tamped down his frustration. What was the point in learning hard lessons when, despite your wise counsel, others insisted on repeating them?

The trees began to thin and the chosen field opened before them, a blanket of white broken only by the dark smudge of Arnulf's pavilion. Lucius reined in his horse as unwanted memories flooded back. "I died in a place much like this," he muttered. "Also for the sake of honor."

Bren cast him an exasperated look. "I will not die here, Lucius."

"I know you won't," Lucius agreed tightly. "Because I won't allow it."

The memory of their disastrous parley with Duc Marcel at Bel Mara was still fresh, but unless Arnulf had a necromancer hidden among his men, Lucius could reduce them all to ash with a single thought. Bren seemed to read his mind. "Promise you'll keep your power leashed."

Lucius met his gaze. "I will. Unless they attack first."

Bren considered a moment, then nodded. "Agreed."

They urged their mounts forward, closing the distance to the pavilion. Arnulf waited with a dozen priests, the same number Brennos had brought. First Flame Odhrán stood at his shoulder, a tall man with a shaved head and pale eyes. Lucius scanned the terrain but saw no hidden traps, no lurking archers. Perhaps Arnulf truly meant to parley.

Or perhaps he was just a good liar.

They dismounted before the tent. Bren betrayed no hint of the pain Lucius knew his wound caused him. He greeted Arnulf politely, but without his false title. "Brother."

Arnulf stared at them both, a smirk playing about his thin

lips. He reminded Lucius of Farrumohr, the king's counselor from his mortal days. A man who always seemed privy to some jape only he was in on. Lucius had never trusted him either.

Bren began without preamble. "I propose we should set our differences aside for now. Join forces and ride together to break the siege of Prydwen. The city is in dire need."

Arnulf's smirk deepened. "And after? Perhaps we'll settle the question of who is the rightful Strategos of the Sons of Bel over a game of dice?"

"If you wish," Brennos replied. "But the people cannot wait for us to resolve our dispute. Thousands of lives hang in the balance."

"Prydwen," Arnulf said dismissively, "is a cesspool of thieves and whores." He stared directly at Bren as he spoke the last word, giving it a slight emphasis, and Lucius fought the desire to immolate him on the spot. "I am more concerned with the heretical nuns at the nearby convent." His eyes flashed. "They will be cleansed in Bel's purifying flame for their sins."

Bren looked weary. "And what sins are those?"

"Their mistress Kaethe has wronged Bel. I dreamt of it. She imprisoned him in her black tower. It is Kaethe's doing that the sun sits frozen in the sky. Her doing that the dead walk the land." Arnulf's smirk died. "Here is my counteroffer. You will deliver your men to me, their true Strategos, and go back to your whoring ways."

Bren's jaw tightened. "The Sons of Bel are not chattel to be bartered. They follow me of their own free will."

"Free will?" Arnulf scoffed. "What need have they of free will when Bel's will is clear? I am his chosen leader, his right hand on this earth. It's not too late for you, whore. Renounce your prideful ways and submit to me. Bel may yet show you mercy."

Bren's knuckles whitened on his sword hilt, but his voice stayed even. "I'll not renounce anything, least of all my pride as a free man. The only one here guilty of pride is you. It blinds you to the suffering of innocents."

"Innocents?" Arnulf made a disgusted noise. "The wretches in Prydwen are sinners all, no better than those wanton nuns. They've turned from Bel's light and must be scoured clean."

"Listen to yourself. You are as bad as the old Duc." Bren's horse stamped restlessly, sensing his agitation. "I won't let you condemn a city to death for your twisted crusade."

Arnulf's face mottled purple. Spittle flew from his lips as he stabbed a finger. "You dare lecture me? I walked the righteous path while you were on your back getting fucked by half the court. If you're too craven to stand for the light, then get out of my way!"

Bren merely smiled. "I notice you're not so eager to ride toward a true battle. Is it cowardice that keeps you from facing Marcel's margraves in the field? Ah, well. Don't feel ashamed, brother. It *is* easier to slaughter unarmed, elderly nuns than fight hardened soldiers of the Westmarch."

Arnulf looked like he might suffer a stroke. Lucius watched a wormy blue vein throb at his temple. He was sorely tempted to help the process along.

"Cowardice? I fear no mortal army! Bel's fire flows in my veins." Arnulf's gauntleted hands clenched to fists. "I hope the margraves burn Prydwen to ash and piss on the cinders!"

Speaking of pissing on cinders... Lucius caught Bren's eye and cocked a pleading brow. To his vast disappointment, Bren gave a minute shake of his head.

"If you won't join me in defending Prydwen," Brennos said, still striving for reason, "at least release your prisoner, Gui

Harcourt. He's no spy, just another traveler you snatched from the road."

Arnulf's mad fervor receded, replaced by an equally unsettling calm. "The Quietus? I think not. He is a servant of Kaethe, that much is certain." The zealot's eyes gleamed. "Consider him an incentive to stay out of my way, Brennos. If you interfere with Bel's divine justice, I'll send the old man straight to that demon Kaethe."

Without another word, Arnulf wheeled his horse and galloped off, his guards following. Lucius watched him go. "You should have let me deal with him. It was a mistake to let him leave."

Bren sighed. "Killing Arnulf would only make him a martyr and turn his followers against us. He may be mad, but he still wields influence."

"A fanatic is always dangerous, but more so when he commands loyalty through lies and fear." He glanced at Bren, noting the stubborn set of his jaw. "You won't sway Arnulf's followers. Their minds are too poisoned."

"Most of those men are not evil, only misled," Bren insisted as he guided his horse back towards their camp. "They have not committed any great wrongs yet. It is a small number who have been wreaking havoc. If I can stop Arnulf before his madness drives them to it, they may see the truth."

"And if they don't? Will you absolve them of the outrages they commit at Arnulf's behest, simply because he ordered it?"

Bren's shoulders tensed. "Of course not. But I must try to reach them first. Arnulf's death alone will not end this. Another fanatic would just take his place."

Another would take his place... Lucius frowned. He sensed an unseen hand at work, goading Arnulf, stoking the fires of his obsession. But whose?

Bren rode on, his brow furrowed in thought. Lucius had

seen that look before, usually preceding some idealistic but risky scheme.

Snow began to fall again, muffling the world in silence. Lucius knew too well the mayhem one charismatic zealot could unleash. *I failed my legion once by not acting soon enough. I will not fail these men the same way.*

By the time they reached the camp, Bren slouched in his saddle, face pale. "I have much to think on," he said tightly as he dismounted. "I know that you wish to pester me further, Lucius, but I ask that you leave me to my own counsel tonight. See that the men are fed."

Lucius watched him trudge to his tent, one arm pressed against his side. The wound still pained him, though Bren would never admit it. Stubborn man. Yet wasn't that one of the things Lucius admired about him?

Shaking his head, he went looking for Castelio. Lucius found him huddled over his father in their tent. "How is he?" Lucius asked.

Castelio glanced up, his eyes hooded. "The fever worsens. He needs a proper healer." He wet a cloth in the basin and laid it across his father's brow, then studied Lucius's face for a long moment. "So the parley failed."

Lucius nodded. "Arnulf will not see reason. But don't lose hope. We'll find another way to free Gui Harcourt."

"Aye. We must." Cas's jaw tightened. "What now?"

Indeed. What now? "Brennos is forming another plan. He's aware that time is short."

"I hope you're right," Castelio muttered.

"He's the doing the best he can," Lucius said defensively. "He's in a difficult position."

"I know. But it's hard for me to pity those men. They could come to our side if they didn't like the prick they're following. Which makes them pricks, too."

It was an argument Lucius had used himself. "I'll have extra blankets sent," he said, glancing at the ashen father. "Call me if you need anything else."

Outside, restless energy crackled through the camp. Men paced and muttered, resentful of what new hardships the morrow might bring. They needed purpose. Direction. Lucius gathered the youngest and strongest, and ordered them to assemble in the practice field. Appraising the motley bunch, he barked the first orders that came to mind. "You there! Tighten that strap. And you, raise that shield."

They scrambled to obey. He drilled them relentlessly for hours, correcting stances and demonstrating strikes, channeling his frustration into bellowing at the men. "Keep your guard up!" Lucius smashed his practice blade against a shield. "You think Arnulf's thugs will go easy? They mean to slaughter you!"

By the time he released them, they stood taller, moved with a bit more confidence. Lucius stalked back to Bren's tent. He'd been told to keep away, but he was more in the mood to give orders than obey them. The guards shifted uneasily as he approached, not meeting his eyes. He shouldered past them into the tent. Bren's armor hung on the stand, his sword propped beside the cot. Which sat empty.

No. Surely he wouldn't be so foolish...

Lucius whirled on the guards, his voice low and tight. "Where is the Strategos?"

The men exchanged a glance. One gathered his courage. "He... he ordered us to keep silent, Lord Bittencourt. But he rode off an hour ago."

In a blink, Lucius slammed him against the tentpole. "You idiot," he hissed. "He's gone to his death. Next time, you fetch me right away. Understand?"

"Y-yes, lord," the guard choked out.

Lucius stepped back, and the man crumpled, gasping. In a blur of preternatural speed, he raced across the camp and vaulted onto his horse. Lucius galloped bareback, icy wind stinging his face, his thoughts outpacing the stallion's drumming hoofbeats. At the valley's rim, he reined to a halt. Arnulf's tents were pitched below, but only two hundred or so priests were visible, fewer than had been camped here yesterday.

When a sentry stepped out to challenge him, Lucius slid from his horse and gripped the man by the throat, lifting him off his feet.

"Where is Arnulf?" he demanded. "Where has he taken his forces?"

The sentry clawed at his iron grip, eyes bulging. Lucius's fingers tightened, lips curling back from his teeth. Darkness gathered at the edges of his vision, red thirst rising in his throat.

The man would answer, one way or another.

Nine

Sister Judith inspected a pea vine, its pods shriveled and white with frost. "All gone," she murmured. "Every last leaf."

The carrots, lettuce, squash and tomatoes were dead too. Beside her, Sister Valeria drew her woolen shawl tighter. "What will we eat? When the stores run out?"

Judith straightened, joints popping. At her age, winter settled deep in the bones. She surveyed the convent with its weathered timbers and thatch roof, more like a ramshackle farmhouse. Yet the convent near the Galatian border had stood for centuries. Surely it would withstand one untimely snowfall.

"I've seen worse," she said, keeping her tone light. "Twenty summers ago, we had a terrible drought. The wells went sour, and the creek dried up, and we had to haul water from the Dolcetto a league away, bucket by bucket."

Valeria bit her lip her head. "I'm too young to remember."

"Well, we buried three sisters that year," Judith said. "They returned to the Mother's embrace, but that's nothing to be afraid of. Kaethe welcomes her children home in her own time. And the rest of us survived. Just as we'll survive this." She glanced at the flat gray sky. No hint of a thaw, but the Mother's will moved in mysterious ways. They would muddle through, as they always had.

"Sister." Valeria tugged at her sleeve. "Look."

Judith followed her gaze. A mass of armed men marched up the road in tight formation, sunlight glinting off mail and helmets. The convent perched exposed atop its hill, the whitewashed walls offering no protection. It was in the far east of Cavet, much closer to the Galatian border than the Cavetti capital of Prydwen. In fact, most of the nuns were from villages in Galatia, which had always worshipped Kaethe.

"The Lady preserve us," Valeria breathed. The crests of horsehair marked them as Sons of Bel, a sight rarely seen. Judith counted at least threescore, maybe more. "Fetch Mother Mencia," she said, more calmly than she felt. "Quickly now."

Valeria hitched up her white skirts and ran for the convent. Judith squared her shoulders as the priests reined up in the courtyard. Their leader was a tall man, hair cropped short beneath his helm, a face lean and angular. "Good day, Sister," he said with a smile. His gaze flicked over the neat garden plots, the sturdy outbuildings. "A pretty spot. How many dwell within these walls?"

Judith hid her unease. There was something wrong about him, though she couldn't put her finger on it. "We are but two dozen, devoted to Kaethe's service," she said.

"I suppose you have lived here all your life?"

"I have known no other home," Judith admitted. Nor wished to. "I fear we can offer scant hospitality in these times, but what we have is yours. Will you take refreshment?" Meager as their stores were, the custom was clear, though how she would feed a hundred men, Judith had no idea.

The man's smile faded. "I do not wish to share your table. Tell your sisters to attend me. Assemble them here."

"For what purpose?" Judith asked. "We are occupied with our work."

"Your work," he echoed slowly. "Raising the dead, you mean?"

She nearly laughed at the foolishness of the charge but thought better of it. "They rise on their own," she said dryly. "That has been the way of things for a very long time, though I allow it has been worse of late. As you must know, we anoint the bodies to prevent them from coming back."

That thin, mocking smile hovered at the edges of his lips. "Of course. Let me be clear. I carry a message. No harm will befall those who heed my words."

Despite his courteous tone, Judith's apprehension grew. She reminded herself that the last raids by the priests were distant memory. "May I ask your name?" she said.

"Brother Arnulf."

Behind her, shuffling footsteps heralded the approach of Mother Mencia at the head of a small contingent. The abbess moved stiffly, her aged back bent, but her eyes were sharp beneath her wimple. "I am Mother Mencia. What matter brings you to our door, Brother?" Her voice, though aged, held authority.

"I come on Bel's behalf to demand justice," Brother Arnulf said.

The abbess frowned. "Justice? I do not take your meaning—"

"You will." Arnulf jerked his chin. About a third of the priests dismounted. Judith's heart seized, her cheeks flaming, as one of them ripped away Mother Mencia's chain of office, silver with a nine-pointed star, and stomped it into the dirt. Judith tried to run to the abbess, but an arm closed around her neck. She struggled against the bruising hold. Wetness pricked her eyes. Kaethe, let this cup pass from us.

Priests swarmed into the convent, dragging out those who had not come willingly. Most of the men stayed out of it, but they did nothing to stop the others. The air grew thick with smoke. Flames licked at the whitewashed walls.

The priests dragged them all to a stand of sweet chestnuts. The trees had been ancient even before the convent was built. In late summer, Judith would gather the nuts by the basket-load and grind them for flour. They made a delicious pastry crust.

Now, the priests busied themselves throwing ropes over the lower limbs. Judith's sisters, most of them elderly, huddled together among the great roots. Sister Amelia was crying, poor thing, but the rest were dry-eyed like Judith. It will not be an easy end, she thought, holding her courage tight. Not the death I imagined, snug in my bed with my dear sisters gathered round. But the pain will pass. And one day, Kaethe will judge them, too.

"You will carry a message to your mistress," Arnulf announced loudly, trotting over. A sick light shone in his eyes. "Bel's Sons demand his return, and we shall not rest until he is restored to his throne of glory. Your deaths are her doing, not mine." He turned to the priests. "Hang them all. But do it one at a time, so the rest may watch. The abbess first."

Mother Mencia lifted her bruised face. It was not Arnulf she spoke to but the nuns. "Kaethe welcomes her daughters home. We go to her in peace and joy."

Judith's knees buckled as the noose fell around Mother Mencia's neck. Ungentle hands jerked her upright. Valeria wept softly. "Be strong," Judith whispered. "Show these butchers what we are made of." She pushed aside her horror and began to speak the catechism. After a moment, others joined her, voices carrying across the windswept hill. "Bless us, Kaethe. Guide us through the thickets of night. Let our feet not lose the path."

"Hold your filthy tongues," Arnulf snarled, a flush creeping up his pale skin.

Judith paid him no mind. "And at the last hour, when your cold hand beckons, lend us courage to cross the stormless sea." She watched flames lick at the leaden sky. "Bless us, Kaethe—" There was a blur at the corner of her vision. Pain bloomed, a dizzying blow that knocked her flat.

"I told you to be quiet." Arnulf's indistinct form rose above her. His horse stood inches away and she thought he might trample her, but then steel rasped from a scabbard. "Since you will not comply of your own accord, I am forced to take your tongue."

Suddenly, Arnulf turned away, distracted. From the east came drumming hoofbeats. Valeria crouched next to Judith and helped her to sit. A lone rider crested the road. Judith's hopes sank when she saw he was a priest, too. Even if he was coming to their aid, what could one man do against so many?

Arnulf's face twisted. "Are you here to pray with the sisters?" he said to the rider. "If you love the goddess of death so dearly, you are welcome to join them!"

The priest dismounted. Judith had tended many injuries in her seventy years and saw right away that he was concealing pain. He moved stiffly, carefully. "It is you I will pray for, since you have lost your way." His voice held a dangerous edge. When his gaze swept across the other priests, they avoided his eye. "Release these women at once."

Arnulf threw back his head and laughed. "You are not in command here. We are doing Bel's work. But I have had enough of your meddling. Shall I hang you? Or do you prefer cold steel?"

The man regarded him without fear. His face was comely but scarred by fire. Judith felt a slight chill. Just as she had known that Arnulf was rancid inside, there was something different about this one, too. The phrase *God-touched* sprang unbidden to her mind.

"You cannot kill me," he said. "Bel will not allow it."

Mutters rippled through the legion. Some laughed. Others shifted uneasily. Arnulf's eyes glittered with a fevered light. "Let us test this fascinating theory." He turned to his ranks. "Kitt! You are my finest archer. Shoot the blasphemer dead."

A heavyset man with a shaved head stepped forward, nocking an arrow to bowstring. He was twenty paces from his target. Judith knew little of archery, but at that distance he could not miss. Kitt drew back his muscled arm, sighting down the shaft. The priest simply stood there, gazing back with unshakeable faith. *He is mad, too,* she thought.

Then something strange happened. First, the heavy banks of clouds rolled away. Dazzling light bathed the snowy fields. The priests shielded their eyes, staring upward. Judith squinted, a thrill of superstitious terror electrifying her gut.

The sun, which had sat at the same meridian since Aveline was founded a thousand years ago, a hand's width east of its zenith, was now moving across the vault of the sky.

LUCIUS CRESTED the last hill and galloped down the back side. The smudge of smoke on the horizon had led him true. To his left was the convent of Kaethe, its upper story alight with flames. To his right, the nuns. They stood beneath a magnificent old tree, surrounded by about a dozen of Arnulf's men. And between the two...

Brennos faced an archer, their shadows pooling on the snow. Lucius raised his hood against a sudden hot prickle of sun. Then he watched in astonishment as the shadows stretched long and black, the quality of the light shifting. Colors sang along the horizon. Red and orange. Kaethe's tits! With effort, he recalled the word for this bizarre phenomenon. *Setting.* The sun was setting.

Brennos laughed, a sound of pure delight.

The archer's longbow had fallen to his side. He stood with his head tilted back, one arm shading his brow. The priests sank to their knees. "A miracle!" someone cried. "The god lives again!"

Only Arnulf seemed unmoved. He drew his sword and kicked his mount to a gallop. Brennos was too entranced by the heavenly spectacle to notice.

Which is why you need me, you heroic fool, Lucius thought. He formed a bludgeon of air and knocked Arnulf from the saddle. The priest flew backwards and slammed into the ground with a stunned groan.

That done, Lucius drew the fire devouring the convent into himself. He was so angry, the heat boiling inside him absorbed it with barely a ripple. Lucius rode over to the sun god's heir apparent. Their eyes met. Bren's held defiance and a touch of guilt. "You may chastise me later, Lucius," he said quietly.

Oh, you can count on it. For now, with the legion watching, Lucius pressed a fist to his heart. "Strategos." His gaze fell on Arnulf. "What of the usurper?"

"Take him prisoner."

Lucius pushed through the shaken men at the chestnut tree. He unwound one of the ropes they'd brought for the nuns and used it to bind Arnulf, tight enough to elicit more groans. Brennos approached the sisters, every gaze following him. "Are any among you hurt?" he asked. "Were you... abused in any other way?"

The eldest spoke. "No," she said tartly. "Though we stood at the Mother's doorstep."

Relief showed in the softening of his shoulders. "I am deeply sorry for these men's actions." His voice was grave. "They bring shame upon us all. How would you see them punished?"

A few of the priests muttered at this. Brennos turned around. The force of his gaze commanded instant silence. In the low sun, his white scars stood out lividly against his tanned skin. "If I did not need you," he snapped, "I would strip you all naked and flog you until you bled."

Lucius watched, gauging their reactions. A few still knelt in the snow, but most had risen, uncertainty and caution warring across their faces.

"Mother...?" Brennos ventured.

"Mencia," the abbess answered. She studied him for a long moment. "Bel's hand intervened today. If he sent you here, I trust your judgment."

Something unspoken passed between them. "Help me," he said quietly. "Which ones?"

Her gnarled hand pointed. Those it landed upon licked their lips, resentful and afraid. All stood near the hanging tree.

"First Flame!" Brennos shouted without taking his gaze from the unfortunate chosen. Lucius sighed inwardly. He could not refuse the title now. Not in front of them all. "Disarm these men," Brennos said. "Escort them to the next village. They are expelled from the brotherhood."

Lucius searched his face. Found the answer he sought. It was the right one. He brought a fist to his heart. "You heard the Strategos," he said, striding towards the sullen group. "Throw your weapons down."

They looked about to balk until they saw the flames in his eyes. Swords and shields were discarded with alacrity.

"The rest of you will beg forgiveness from Mother Mencia," Brennos said loudly. "If you refuse, you may join the outcasts. Step forward now if you believe it is god's work to murder innocent women."

Most of the men hung their heads, shamefaced. But eleven came forward, hatred in their eyes. It was fewer than Lucius expected. The usurper had had months to spread his poison.

"Tricks," spat a weasel-faced priest. He glared at Lucius. "The demon deceived you with his dark magic! Stand with us!"

When none of the rest seemed eager to join their cause, he and the other ten stomped over to the group that Mother Mencia had picked out. Altogether, they numbered nineteen.

"Get out of my sight," Brennos told them. "The rest of you, form a line."

As the men shuffled forward, Lucius gathered six who looked reasonably intelligent. They were alarmed, fearing some special punishment awaited. "First Flame," one stammered, "we meant no harm, by Bel's light. Arnulf said he meant to scare them, that's all." "We would've stopped it," another claimed, "before it went too far."

Lucius stared at them until they shut up. "You are fortunate," he said, "that the Strategos is a merciful man." They made starbursts with their fingers and praised Bel. "However," he added, "I am not. Guard his back until I return. And watch Arnulf." He did not issue a threat. Let them imagine what it might be.

They bobbed their heads and formed a ring around their former leader, who had shit himself judging by the smell. One eye was half-open, the other closed. A head injury? Lucius hoped so.

He mounted and escorted the nineteen excommunicates

up the road and over the hill. Once they were beyond shouting distance to the convent, he reined up. "You will travel through the forest from here," he said. "Bel bless you."

Maybe it was his feral smile that tipped them off. Lucius watched them run across a field of barley stubble, his nostrils flaring at the rank stench of fear. A head start was only fair. When the last one vanished into the tree line, he dismounted, led his horse to a pleasant spot with shade and a creek, and stripped to the skin. He left his clothes folded on a log and padded into the cool, dim woods.

It was not so long before he returned. The sun still sat just above the trees. Lucius rinsed off in the icy creek. He laid a palm against his chest, savoring the steady thump of his heart. The warmth of his skin and fullness of his belly. What a curious thing it was to be dead one moment and alive the next. Perhaps not fully alive, but close enough as made no difference.

There'd been too many to guard. Too many to feed. Let them go and they might have returned to the convent out of spite. Instead, he'd left a gift for the foxes and crows. Ah, the cycle of life!

When he returned to the convent, the last of the penitents were begging Mother Mencia's clemency while Bren looked on with crossed arms and a satisfied expression. They exchanged a brief look. Lucius nodded. *It is done.* Brennos looked grim, but he nodded once in turn. He is learning, Lucius thought, when to give quarter and when to make a quick end of those who would harm you.

A flash of metal caught his eye. Lucius wandered over to where Arnulf's sword lay abandoned on the ground. He crouched down to examine it. The blade was Cavetti steel, keen and perfectly balanced. But it was the pommel that stood out — a starburst wrought in gleaming gold filigree, with three large garnets. No simple priest could afford such a weapon.

Maybe it was stolen. Or maybe someone wealthy was backing Arnulf's crusade. But to what end? The persecution of a few nuns hardly seemed worth such expense.

Lucius rose, sword in hand. He was glad the usurper hadn't broken his neck in the fall. It would be interesting to see what he had to say on the matter.

Ten

The coach sped along the uneven road, bouncing the two fugitives — one wearing purple robes covered with astrological symbols, the other in an old-fashioned black frock coat sporting frothy lace at the cuffs — with each rut.

Jaskin Cazal frowned at the unfamiliar landscape. Fields stretched away to a dark line of forest, the three moons casting it all in a silvery light. "I do not recall ever taking this byway," he remarked.

He rubbed his forehead, trying to coax out some memory, but none surfaced. "Perhaps we are not headed north after all," he mused aloud. On the bench across from him, Nabu-bal-idinna sat with his bearded face half in shadow, dark eyes gleaming.

Jaskin slouched against the velvet upholstery. "My sense of direction used to be splendid, but I spent too many centuries trapped in that accursed mirror. Unchanging, while the world spun on without me." He glanced at Nabu. "Perhaps you are the same, eh? Neither of us has ventured out into the world for so long that we no longer recognize it." He sighed.

"A lonely feeling, to be so old," Jaskin continued pensively, his gaze drifting back to the darkness beyond the window. "But 'twould be worse if I were truly alone." He managed a faint smile. "I am glad for your company, alchemist. Even if neither of us knows where we're going."

He looked again at Nabu, expecting a response, but the man stared straight ahead. Jaskin leaned forward, searching for any flicker of recognition, but the alchemist sat rigid as a wax mannequin. A prickle of unease crept up Jaskin's spine. He reached out and poked Nabu's shoulder. No reaction. He poked again, harder.

Nabu's head snapped up, eyes blazing. His face contorted into a rictus. "Why do you hound me?" he snarled, his voice deep and resonant, nothing like the mild demeanor of Kaethe's consort.

Jaskin recoiled. For a moment, he thought he glimpsed something ancient and powerful lurking behind Nabu's eyes. "I... Forgive me," Jaskin stammered, thrown off balance. "I meant no offense."

As quickly as it had come, the rage drained from Nabu's face. He blinked once, owlishly. "Why, I must have drifted off," he said.

Jaskin frowned. "Do you often slumber with your eyes open?"

Nabu did not reply for a long moment. "I dreamt of two men," he said at last. "Brothers. One good, one evil. They were locked in battle." He shook his head as if to dislodge the vision. "Never mind. Where are we?"

Jaskin shifted, still rattled by the abrupt outburst. "That's the difficulty," he admitted. "I am not sure. Do you perchance know which direction we travel?" He eyed the arcane symbols on Nabu's robe. "You are a learned man. Can't you navigate by the stars?"

"I... I can't remember," Nabu stammered. "Are we lost?"

Jaskin suppressed a sigh. The fool really was useless. He had planned to abandon him at the first chance, but Jaskin was beginning to realize that he didn't wish to be alone. He'd been alone for centuries, with only his own maddened thoughts for company.

"Of course we are not lost," Jaskin lied, forcing a smile. "And the worst is behind us now. There are many wonders yet to see—"

He cut off as the coach hit a very deep hole that knocked their heads against the silk-lined roof. Jaskin swore, grabbing for a handhold. The coach ground to a halt, listing to one side. Nabu clutched at Jaskin's sleeve, eyes wide. "What's happening?" he squealed.

Jaskin pried the man's fingers from his arm. "Mayhap a wheel has broken," he said, trying to keep his tone light. "I shall go and check—"

Before he could finish, a thunderous crack split the air. The coach gave a shuddering lurch, throwing Jaskin against the door. He scrabbled for the handle. Cold, murky water gushed into the coach as he wrenched the door open. They were stuck in a mire, the boggy ground sucking at the wheels. Jaskin leaped out, boots squelching in the muck. He turned back to offer a hand to Nabu, but his coat snagged on a spur of shattered wheel.

Then the whole contraption started sinking fast. Black water rushed in, dragging Jaskin down. He thrashed, lungs burning, but his coat was caught fast. Panic clawed at his chest. Not like this. Not his final life, drowned in some gods-forsaken swamp!

A hand seized his collar, hauling him up. Jaskin broke the

surface, coughing and sputtering. The two men paddled to a hummock of matted reeds. Jaskin hauled himself up, limbs quaking. He twisted around in time to see the roof of the coach vanish beneath the surface, along with the bone steeds.

Beside him, a mud-covered Nabu hugged his knees to his chest, rocking back and forth. "I wish I were in my nice toasty kitchen," he moaned. "I never should have left the tower. I'm not meant for adventures."

Jaskin forced himself to take a deep breath. The Quickening dogged his steps, the curse of a Shadow Soul nearing his final death. It would have claimed him if Nabu hadn't intervened. Jaskin shuddered. When he crossed the Veil for the last time, Kaethe would not give him a warm reception, not after he stole away her paramour. He *had* to persuade the cowardly alchemist to continue.

"There now, my friend," Jaskin said. "You have the heart of a lion, leaping in to save me like that. Why, you're a hero!"

Nabu eyed him doubtfully. "I am?"

Jaskin clapped him on the shoulder. "Indeed. And a hero doesn't turn back at the first spot of bother, now does he?"

Nabu wavered. Jaskin pressed his advantage. "Just think of the tales you'll have to tell. Why, you'll be the talk of every tavern from here to the Boundary. Nabu the Valiant, they'll call you."

"Nabu the Valiant," the alchemist repeated slowly, a tentative smile touching his lips. "I rather like the sound of that."

Jaskin grinned, though it felt more like a grimace. "Then let us onward, my valiant friend." He made to rise but paused as a flurry of bubbles disturbed the murky surface. Nabu's new courage evaporated. "W-what's that? You don't suppose anything lives in this dreadful mire, do you?"

More bubbles streamed up, larger this time. "It's not a mire, it's a fen," Jaskin replied testily. His mind dredged up long-forgotten knowledge. They had indeed gone south rather than north, as he'd intended. "I know where we are now. These are the Timoth Fens—"

Nabu gave a girlish shriek as the bone steeds erupted from the depths. Hooves churning, blue witchfire blazing in their eye sockets, the skeletal horses dragged the sunken coach up from the bottom of the bog. Mud and weeds streamed from the spokes.

"Our coach!" Nabu exclaimed.

Jaskin shot to his feet. "Quick, we must try to swim back—"

Before he could finish, the bone steeds wheeled around and went thundering back up the road toward Mystral, the coach bouncing wildly on three wheels behind them. In an instant, they vanished into the night.

Nabu gaped. "They left without us!"

"Stupid creatures," Jaskin muttered acidly.

The alchemist pulled a slimy reed from his beard. "I suppose we ought to go after them."

Jaskin shook his head. "They will head straight to the Courtenays. A simple spell would reveal our location." This was likely untrue, but he had no intention of returning to Mystral. "Our only choice is to press on. We must traverse the fens to the other side."

Nabu blanched. "But you promised to take me back to Kaethe's tower whenever I chose!"

Jaskin gave him a regretful look. "I would be delighted to," he said, "but I cannot open a portal. My sorcery fails me."

He expected an emotional outburst, but Nabu simply stared at him. The cold glitter of his eyes made Jaskin uneasy. A tense silence stretched, broken only by the chittering insects of the fen. Jaskin opened his mouth to offer another false apology, but before he could speak the words, a hiss drifted from the darkness.

Jaskin raised a finger to his lips. Nabu stiffened as he too heard it. "What's out there?" he whispered.

"I mislike the sound of it," Jaskin murmured. "And I do not intend to stay and make introductions." He scanned the fen, searching for a path. There, a ragged line of hummocks, half-drowned in mist. It would have to do.

He turned a hard eye on Nabu. "I leave the choice to you, my brave friend. Stay here and wait for whatever lurks in the dark... or come with me."

With that, Jaskin leaped for the first hummock. He overbalanced and nearly pitched headlong into the muck, boots scrambling for purchase. He tottered on the brink for a moment, then steadied himself. Nabu still hesitated behind him, wringing his soft hands.

The slithering hiss came again, much closer now. The alchemist cast a frightened glance over his shoulder. With a choked cry, he sprang after Jaskin. His leap fell short. For a terrible moment, Nabu-bal-idinna floundered in the muck, arms windmilling as he slowly sank. Jaskin lunged and seized a fistful of his robe, hauling him to safety.

"My thanks," Nabu gasped, but Jaskin was already moving, bounding to the next precarious island.

As they plunged deeper into the fen, the Quickening's curse made itself felt. Vines snagged at Jaskin's ankles, sending him sprawling. Twice he fell in the water and had to drag himself out. A chorus of chirps and croaks surrounded them. Jaskin glanced behind and saw Nabu doggedly following. His robe was splattered with mud and he looked as wretched as a drowned muskrat.

Jaskin felt a pang of sympathy. He knew what it was to be

lost and afraid. When he'd first been trapped in the mirror— No. He shook off the memories. They helped nothing.

Jaskin stumbled to a halt, frowning. These trees, festooned with hanging moss... hadn't they passed them before? By all the eldritch gods, they were going in circles.

But he couldn't let Nabu see his fear. Mustering his most confident tone, Jaskin called back, "Not much further now!"

Nabu made no reply. He merely fixed Jaskin with a glare of pure loathing.

They stumbled onward, trekking for hours. Jaskin was so weary that it took him several minutes to realize that he no longer heard the splash of Nabu's footsteps. He turned in alarm, fearing they'd been separated, and saw with a start that Nabu was right behind him.

I thought you were lost! he exclaimed.

Or tried to. His lips formed the words, but no sound emerged. In fact, the entire fen had gone still as a tomb. Then the truth struck him.

Nabu watched with a worried expression as Jaskin danced a little jig. He had built this place himself, centuries ago, a secret route in and out of the treacherous fens. The Silent Valley.

Jaskin turned to Nabu, jabbing a finger toward the ravine ahead of them. The alchemist cocked his head. Jaskin mimed walking with two fingers, then pointed again more emphatically. Understanding dawned and Nabu nodded.

An unnatural hush enveloped them as they forged on. The ground firmed, but their footsteps made no sound. It was as if the whole world had been wrapped in wool.

Jaskin had created this place to escape the voices that plagued him. Of course, they were inside his head so it had done little good. But now, with centuries to mellow the worst of his madness, Jaskin found it calming.

The downside was that anything might creep up on them

unawares. He signed to Nabu that they must keep a sharp eye on their surroundings.

When the end of the valley came into view, Jaskin allowed himself a breath of relief. They had made it. Safety was within reach.

That's when the vines struck.

One moment Nabu was walking beside him. The next he was gone, yanked off the path in a thrashing green tangle. Jaskin whirled in time to see his companion vanish into the undergrowth, mouth wide in a soundless scream.

Then the vines came for him. They lashed around his legs, his chest, his throat, lifting him off his feet. Jaskin struggled, but their grip was unbreakable. Through the haze, he saw Nabu thrashing weakly a few feet away, already half-cocooned. A tendril snaked around the alchemist's arm, thorns like fangs sinking deep into the flesh.

No blood came. Instead, what welled up from the wound appeared to be molten gold. It shone with a blinding radiance, searing Jaskin's eyes. He squeezed them shut against the glare.

The coils around him convulsed. Their grip slackened, then released. Jaskin tumbled to the ground. When he cracked his eyes open, he saw the predatory vines slithering back into the shadows, their leaves smoking and blackened. Nabu stood on the path, staring at the golden ichor dripping down his arm. He seemed more perplexed than alarmed.

Questions whirled through Jaskin's mind. What exactly *was* Nabu-bal-idinna? A daēva? A demon? Something else entirely? But he held his tongue. The last thing he needed was Nabu growing suspicious of him in turn. So he hauled himself upright, making a show of brushing off his coat.

"Well, that was bracing!" His voice emerged as a croak. He cleared his throat and tried again. "A good thing you, er... drove them off. Shall we continue?"

Nabu blinked at him, then down at his arm. The golden flow had already stopped, leaving only a few smears of drying luminance. "I... Yes. Yes, let us go on."

Jaskin limped along at the briskest pace he could muster, eager to leave the Silent Valley behind. As they passed beneath the last of the overhanging trees, sound came rushing back like a held breath released. Birdsong, wind in the leaves, small animals scurrying through the undergrowth.

Jaskin barely noticed. His mind was preoccupied with his mysterious companion. He took an absent-minded step and felt a sudden sting in his calf. Wincing, he bent to pluck a small white thorn from his flesh. The skin around the puncture mark was already reddening, itching fiercely.

Devil's snare. One of his own creations, a mildly poisonous plant he'd bred centuries ago during a fallow period between schemes. The damn things had gone feral, spreading beyond his ability to control, yet another unwanted legacy.

Ah, well. Devil's snare was more nuisance than lethal. He'd have a welt the size of a duck egg. But Nabu, it seemed, was immune. The vines had recoiled from his luminous blood, and he showed no ill effects from their thorns. *Who are you really, my friend?* Jaskin wondered as they entered the western fringe of the Nightwood. And what other secrets do you hide?

They trudged onward, weaving between ancient oaks and elms. Jaskin felt safer here, but the throbbing pain in his leg was getting worse. He called a halt when they reached a moonlit clearing, dropping heavily onto a log. Nabu sat beside him, dark eyes watchful. "How do you fare?"

"Never better," Jaskin gritted out, rolling up his pant leg. The flesh around the puncture was an angry red, hot to the touch and swollen. He prodded it gingerly. "I fear the Devil's snare has evolved."

"In what way?" Nabu peered at the wound.

"Grown more potent." Jaskin shook his head ruefully. "My own fault. Without a master's hand to tend them, they have grown dangerous."

"Can't you heal yourself with magic?"

Jaskin snorted at the man's innocence. "Necromancy is the opposite of healing. No, we must make for Loris. It lies in the far northwest. A city of herbalists and thaumaturges."

Nabu looked doubtful. "You don't look well. Perhaps you should try again and see if you can open a portal directly to this place?"

Jaskin knew it was futile, but he closed his eyes and sought the black whirlwind. At first it seemed he could touch it... but the power slipped through his fingers like smoke.

"It's no use," he sighed. "We'll have to walk."

"How far is it?"

"A few days." Jaskin levered himself upright, ignoring the dizziness that washed over him. "But there's a gate in Loris, one that leads back to Kaethe's domain. With luck, you can return to your mistress once we arrive."

Nabu patted his hand and gave a weak smile. "Do not worry, I will carry you there if I must."

Jaskin felt an unfamiliar weight upon his chest. Could it be... guilt?

"I am sorry," he said quietly. "I only wanted to enjoy my last life to the fullest. To see my creations one last time. But I was selfish, dragging you along."

Nabu's eyes widened slightly at this admission, but he remained silent.

"I was trapped in a magical prison for a very long time," Jaskin explained. "With no company save my idiot heir, Nathan Ouvrard." He shuddered, remembering the endless days, each the same, and Nathan's tiresome prattle. "Even the refuge of sleep was taken from me."

Nabu's expression softened. He laid a hand on Jaskin's shoulder. "We all do things we regret when we're afraid."

"Thank you," he said gruffly. "I appreciate your understanding. And your companionship."

Jaskin shivered, the chill of the night seeping into his bones.

"You're cold!" Nabu exclaimed. "I'll gather some wood for a fire." He rose, brushing the dried mud from his robes. "Wait here."

Jaskin watched Nabu disappear into the trees. Then he closed his eyes, trying to ignore the throbbing pain in his leg. A short while later, Nabu returned, arms laden with branches and twigs. He stacked them in a triangular pile, then reached into a pocket and produced a handful of black walnuts.

"I found these as well," he said, setting them aside. "They'll make a nice snack once roasted."

Jaskin eyed the kindling. "That's all well and good, but we don't have a dry flint. How do you propose we start the fire?"

Nabu's face went weirdly blank, just as it had in the coach. He stood motionless, gaze unfocused.

"One of his thrice-damned trances," Jaskin muttered, reaching for a walnut. "And how am I supposed to crack this open—"

Without warning, the heap of twigs erupted into a roaring inferno. Flames licked at the black sky. Jaskin reared back, one coat sleeve alight. He rolled on the ground to extinguish it, the stench of burnt fabric in his nose.

"I… I don't know what happened," Nabu stammered, wringing his hands. "I'm sorry, I didn't mean to—"

"How did you do that?" Jaskin demanded, his voice harsh. He struggled to his feet, wincing as pain shot through his injured leg. "What manner of sorcery do you wield?"

Nabu shook his head in denial. "I just… I wished for fire

and it came!" He swallowed hard. "Some alchemy I have forgotten, perhaps?"

The explanation was weak, and even Nabu knew it. Jaskin narrowed his gaze, studying the man in the flickering red light. The timid, gentle scholar he traveled with was being replaced by something far more powerful and enigmatic. And Jaskin didn't like it one bit.

A wave of dizziness washed over him. He sat heavily on the log, vision blurring.

"Here, friend, the fire has died down and left us some fine embers," Nabu said, too cheerfully. "Perfect for roasting chestnuts!"

Jaskin nodded, a chill walking across his skin. Three more days. Could he make it? Well, he would have to. They could not reach Loris fast enough.

Eleven

Lo slumped against the plush seat, the hypnotic rocking of the coach lulling her into a half-doze. Her mind drifted back to her argument with Lady Caul, who had wanted her to bring an escort of armed centaurs into the Nightwood.

"I must follow Jaskin Cazal alone," Lo had insisted. "It's too dangerous. I won't risk the lives of companions."

Caul propped a hand on her hip, bone bracelets rattling. "And what about your own safety?"

Lo shrugged. "Jaskin is caught by the Quickening too. His misfortune will be my good luck."

She knew this theory was nonsensical and expected Nathan to object, but he was too preoccupied with the Grand Menotte. In the end, she'd coaxed them into giving her another coach. Jaskin had last been sighted careening south along this road, and she hoped to overtake him—

Her eyes flew open as the bone steeds screamed, an unearthly sound. Lo stuck her head out the window. Another coach was hurtling out of the gloom, straight at them. She ducked back inside as it flew past, but the road was too narrow to accommodate both and it sideswiped her own coach with a crunch of splintering wood.

The world tilted as her coach overturned. Leaves and branches slapped at the windows. Inside, Lo was flung about like a ragdoll. The coach rolled once, twice, then came to a halt against a massive tree trunk.

She lay still for a moment, breathing hard. Hot warmth trickled into her eye from a cut on her forehead. Gritting her teeth, she reached up and wrenched open the door, which was now directly above her. Ignoring the dull ache in her ribs, she pulled herself up and out, tumbling onto the loamy ground.

The other coach sat askew in the middle of the road, traces of mist curling around the wheels. Like her own, it was painted with the stooping Nightjar of Nyons.

Jaskin's stolen coach.

Motherfucker! Lo headed for the coach at a limping run. She yanked the door open, ready to punch Jaskin in his weasel face, grab Bel, and make a dash for it. A waft of fetid air gusted out, reeking of swamp water. The interior was dark and empty. Sodden clumps of reeds clung to the upholstery.

Lo rocked back on her heels, chewing her lower lip in fury. She turned to the bone steeds and approached with her palms up. *Where have your passengers gone?* she asked in Tongues, the language of the dead.

The steeds stood there, silent and inscrutable. She sighed. Okay, so they didn't talk.

Limping back to her own fallen coach, Lo assessed the damage. The axle had snapped clean through, rendering it useless. She unfastened the traces of her own horses first, then the others. "You've done your duty," she said glumly. "Go on home."

With grateful whickers, the four bone steeds cantered off down the road to Mystral.

Lo ducked back into her coach, rummaging until she found her pack. She slung it over one shoulder, then retrieved her crossbow and quiver. Examining the weapon, she was relieved to find it undamaged.

Then she checked the hidden pocket sewn inside her cloak. She drew out a small wax-paper packet. Kaethe's knockout tea. God's bane would render Bel senseless and erase his memories long enough for her to return him to the Lady's custody.

Stowing the precious packet, she started down the road in the direction the coach had come from. Before long, it disappeared into a vast swamp. Lo paused at the edge. Wheel ruts from the other coach led straight into the fetid water.

No footprints besides her own led out of the swamp. They must have continued through it. Or ... they were at the bottom.

Nabu is immortal, she reminded herself. *He cannot drown. Jaskin, however, is a man. And if he did die, I feel not a shred of pity for him.*

A pale gleam caught her eye. Something glinted on a distant hummock. Unslinging her pack, Lo held it high above her head. With a resigned sigh, she waded into the black swamp.

Swirling patterns disturbed the surface, hinting at deep, treacherous pools. Glowing fungi sprouted from half-rotted logs. The air hung heavy and still, thick with decay. Lo's foot slid on a submerged root. She caught herself, pack teetering. Hissing a curse, she sought the glint she'd spotted from the road.

There. Wedged between gnarled roots, something white shone in the dimness. Lo snatched it up before the swamp could claim it. A fancy antique button, carved from bone. Jaskin's, certainly.

So he'd made it this far. She turned the button over in her fingers, then studied the swamp. A string of small islands made a path, each within leaping distance of the next. Someone nimble could traverse it without getting mired.

She leapt for the first tussock. Frogs croaked in annoyance and plopped into the swamp. Regaining her balance, she gauged the distance to the next bit of solid ground. As she jumped from island to island, the prickle between her shoulder blades returned. She'd felt it on and off since she left Kaethe's domain and entered the mountains north of Castle Cazal.

Unseen eyes upon her back.

Lo's hand drifted to the crossbow slung at her hip. It wasn't just nerves; of that, she was certain. Though this gods-forsaken place was enough to fray anyone's wits, with its eerie will-o-wisps bobbing above the water and faint ripples, like something gliding just beneath the surface.

Lo spied a large gray boulder jutting from the swamp ahead, the first truly solid ground she'd seen. Her legs ached from leaping between narrow tussocks and gnarled roots. Just a moment's rest, she promised herself, reaching for her waterskin.

As her foot touched it, the boulder heaved upward. Mud sloughed from a mottled shell sprouting stalks with little black eyes. A crab, she realized. One with foreclaws that could snap her in two.

She leapt back as a pincer swiped inches from her face. Until it moved, the thing's carapace blended seamlessly with the swamp.

Lo snatched the crossbow from her shoulder, nocking a bolt with clumsy hands. The first shot went wide, splashing into the water. She reloaded, forcing herself to breathe. This time, her aim was true. The quarrel sank into the neck juncture.

The monster convulsed. It keeled over with a splash. Lo allowed herself a grim smile, which faded as mandibles clicked behind her. She spun to see another crab skittering from the water, and another. Two became six. All converging on her tiny island.

"Nine hells." It took thirty seconds to draw the string back, hook it, and position a new bolt. She couldn't reload fast enough, not with half a dozen of the things speeding towards her.

She set her jaw and raised the crossbow, determined to go down fighting. If this was to be her final life, ended by a pack of hungry crabs, she'd make them earn their supper.

As she loosed another bolt, a cloaked figure leapt into the fray. It was a sturdily built young woman with flaxen hair. In one hand she gripped a cudgel, in the other a long, flashing dagger. The girl swung the club in vicious arcs, expertly flipping the crabs onto their backs. Then she darted in, stabbing her blade into the soft junctures where carapace met abdomen.

Lo cranked the crossbow and sent a few more bolts zipping true. Between the two of them, the crabs decided they didn't like the odds so much after all. Clacking in dismay, the survivors fled, vanishing into the swamp. Lo lowered her weapon and turned to the girl, chest heaving. "I owe you my life. What's your name?"

"Dravka," the girl replied. She looked barely out of her teens, but her blue eyes held a hard glint.

Lo was about to ask what she was doing there when a tall woman with short-cropped hair stepped out of the shadows. She wore a gown of forest greens and smoky blues that blended into the shadows. Her eyes were as dark and cold as a midwinter morning.

Morgen Nadezhda.

Like Lo, Morgen was a Shadow Soul. The last time they met, she'd stolen the Grand Menotte and vanished through a portal.

What the hells?

Lo aimed the crossbow, ready to unleash a bolt through the woman's heart if she so much as coughed. "You're the one who's been following me. Why?"

Morgen stared back, unafraid. "We hunt the same man."

"No clue what you're talking about," Lo replied.

Impatience flickered across Morgen's austere features. "Jaskin Cazal, of course. I assume you are chasing him for the same reason. To retrieve the Grand Menotte."

Well now, *that* was interesting. Morgen didn't have it anymore. Even better, she believed Jaskin *did.*

Lo calculated the odds of making it through the swamp on her own. Even if she hadn't been cursed with bad luck, they weren't good. But with Morgen and Dravka, she might stand a chance. Still, best not to look too eager.

"Why should I trust you?" Lo demanded. "You've been dogging my trail since Castle Cazal."

Morgen frowned. "We stayed well back. How did you...? Ah, yes, you have the ears of a daēva." She waved a hand. "I meant you no harm. I hoped you might lead me to Jaskin. And when you *did* need aid, we showed ourselves."

"*Dravka* showed herself," Lo clarified. She turned to the younger woman. "For which I am grateful."

Dravka gave a brusque nod. The two were a study in contrasts. Where Morgen was lean as a willow reed, Dravka had broad shoulders and strong legs. Her hair was white-blond and raggedly shorn, her eyes a pale blue. She wore tunic and breeches over muddy boots. An apprentice?

Morgen gazed past Lo's shoulder into the swamp. "The

crabs will return soon, in greater numbers. Shall we travel together? The choice is yours."

Lo slung the crossbow over her shoulder, keeping a wary eye on Duc Marcel's former consort. "Lead on."

Morgen strode off, her long legs devouring the ground. Dravka followed, with Lo deliberately taking the rear. She kept her crossbow at hand, ready to whip it out at the first sign of treachery — though Morgen could have attacked long before if that was her aim.

For long minutes, they slogged through the muck in silence broken only by the eerie music of the mire's denizens. Lo scanned the water for telltale ripples or moss-covered humps. She noticed Dravka doing the same.

At last, the ground began to firm. Wisps of fog drifted between the gnarled trees, curling around them like skeletal fingers. Morgen called a halt at a dry patch. "We should be beyond their hunting grounds now," she said.

Lo hoped she was right. Her stomach felt hollow as a drum. Morgen unslung her pack and pulled out some nuts and berries. Dravka munched on a hunk of pungent cheese. After a moment's hesitation, Lo took out an apple plucked from the Courtenays' night orchard. It was deep violet like an eggplant, but the fruit tasted sweet and crisp when she bit into it.

"So," Lo said, through a mouthful, "when we find Jaskin, what do you plan to do with the Grand Menotte? Name yourself empress of the known world?"

A humorless smile twisted Morgen's full lips. "I am no fool. The talisman is poison. I intend to throw it into the deepest part of the sea."

Lo tossed the apple core into the woods. "Sure you will."

"You doubt me?" Morgen shook her head. "Well, I care not what you think." She stared into the darkness, her eyes unfocused. "Let us hope he hasn't put it on yet. Perhaps some small spark of sanity stays his hand. But it's only a matter of time before temptation overwhelms him. No one should possess that much power."

"We agree on that," Lo said. "How did you find me anyway?"

"I had been watching Castle Cazal, thinking Jaskin might return to his ancestral seat. Imagine my surprise when I spotted you doing the same." Morgen took a swig from her waterskin. "When you left, I decided to follow. The gamble paid off when you led us to Mystral — and Jaskin."

"But he escaped us both," Lo said ruefully.

A muscle ticked in Morgen's jaw. "When the civil guard arrived to break up the riots, we were nearly arrested."

"It was a fucking fiasco," Dravka muttered.

Yes, Lo thought, that described the ridiculous chase Jaskin had led her on. One that ended with him stealing the Courtenays' coach and poor Nathan nursing a lump on his head.

It occurred to her that she and Jaskin might not be the only ones in the grip of the Quickening. If Morgen was, too... What would happen when the three of them were in close proximity?

She looked up and realized Morgen was staring at her.

"Jaskin travels with Kaethe's consort," Morgen said. "Nabu-bal-idinna. Do you know why?"

Lo met her flinty gaze. Damnit, how had the woman recognized him? Then she recalled what Kaethe said. Morgen had spent time in the goddess's tower as a child.

"I've no idea," Lo said. "And I don't care. I just want to stop him from using the Grand Menotte."

Morgen gazed at her for a long moment, then gave a curt nod.

"The thing must be destroyed," Dravka said decisively. "My

brother had it in his possession, but he lacked the spell to open the iron box. If he had put it on…" She shuddered.

Brother? Lo studied the girl more closely. Her sky-blue eyes and silver hair. "You're a Marcel!" she exclaimed in surprise.

Dravka nodded. She gazed at Morgen with obvious admiration. "And we are half-sisters."

The plot thickened. Lo reached into her pack and pulled out a leather-bound book. "I might have a way out of this mire. Jaskin's journal. I took it from Castle Cazal. He speaks of a Silent Valley." She offered it to Morgen. "See for yourself."

Morgen arched a black brow. She opened the book to the black ribbon marking the relevant page and scanned the faded script. After a long moment, she looked up. "I've heard rumors of the valley. This journal could prove useful. Well done."

The praise was reluctant, but Lo grinned. "Why, thank you."

"May I see it?" Dravka asked.

Morgen passed her the journal and Dravka began flipping through the pages. The apple had hardly put a dent in Lo's hunger. She dug through her pack again and found a heel of black bread studded with raisins. It was hard but still delicious.

"Fuck *me*," Dravka muttered, scanning Jaskin's spidery handwriting.

"What is it?" Morgen asked.

Dravka cleared her throat and read aloud in a gruff voice. "Within the deepest reaches of the Nightwood dwell the creatures known as night-ghasts. Once, they were men, necromancers who traded their souls for the span of centuries. Alas, the wretched fools knew not the true cost. As the decades passed, their mortal flesh twisted into grotesque forms, until they could no longer abide their own hideousness. They fled into the shadows of the wood, condemned to a waking nightmare, hungering eternally for the flesh of the living.'"

"Nice," Lo said, eyeing the last crumbs with regret. "Do you think those crabs were night-ghasts?"

Dravka turned the page, reading for a minute more. "Could have been. He never specifies what they looked like."

"Other than grotesque and hideous," Morgen added drily, "which describes many of Jaskin's creations."

Dravka ran her finger down the page. "Actually, he didn't like them either. Listen: 'I confess, I would not have crafted such unpleasant things myself. They proved a vexing problem, harrying the trade caravans bound for Loris. I dispatched armed parties into the wood to hunt them down, but half the centaurs never returned. In the end, I abandoned the effort. Perhaps, in time, the dreadful creatures will die out on their own. One can only hope.'"

She snapped the book shut and handed it back to Lo. "Sounds like nasty pieces of work."

Lo tucked the journal safely into her pack. Morgen stood, brushing dry leaves from her skirts. "It's been a thousand years since he wrote those words. If these night-ghasts ever existed, they're probably long gone."

"And if not, we'll run in the opposite direction." Lo shouldered her pack, the crossbow a reassuring weight at her hip. "For now, we need to find that Silent Valley."

Morgen nodded. "Agreed. Jaskin has enough of a head start already. We must make haste to catch his trail."

Lo fell into step behind the necromancer, Dravka bringing up the rear this time. She was glad for the company, but she couldn't afford to trust them. How she wished Cas were with her. He'd have her laughing instead of keeping one hand on a weapon. *Ah, Sleepy-Eyes. Where are you now? Safe with your family, I hope.*

Was he waiting in Prydwen, wondering why she hadn't come back for him? The thought was a dagger to the heart.

Lo's jaw tightened. She just wanted to finish the job and get out of here. How far could one old lunatic and a muddle-headed god run?

And when the time came, she'd do whatever it took to capture Bel and bring him home to Kaethe. Even if it meant betraying her newfound allies.

Twelve

Cas stood on a grassy knoll, the wind tugging his collar as he studied the camp below. The newly unified army of Brennos and Arnulf swarmed like ants along the riverbank, sorting themselves into regiments under Lucius's terse commands.

"I overheard talk at the cookfires," Cas said. "They don't trust him because of who he is. *What* he is."

"But they'll obey out of fear, if nothing else," Gui said dryly. "And the worst of Arnulf's men are gone. Those who volunteered to raid the convents and carried out the killing. The rest seem relieved to have Brennos leading them."

He was right on that score. More than a few cheers had erupted at the news of the change in command. Watching them now, hope kindled. There was a fresh vigor in the camp, a sense of purpose that had been absent before. Still, many were hardly more than Teo's age. How would they fare against Sir Mortimer's battle-hardened troops? The knights of the Westmarch were no green recruits.

Well, at least he had Gui back. Cas had found him tied up

in one of the tents, hungry and bruised but whole. Gui's weathered face had split into a grin when Cas cut his bonds and told him of Arnulf's capture.

Now Gui shifted his weight with a wince, leaning heavily on his good leg. "I've been feeling useless of late," he confessed. "I'm no good as a soldier. The infection from that ghoul bite just never healed right." He held up his unmarked hand. "And Kaethe's taken back her blessing, so I'm no good against the risen either."

Cas opened his mouth to protest, but Gui waved a hand. "No, I've made my peace with it. But I think I've hit upon a way I can still be of use." He nodded to the men below. "Most of them hardly know one end of a sword from the other. But I served in Robert Redvayne's army before I became a Quietus to his widow. I could help them stay alive when they face the Cavetti margraves."

Cas smiled. "You'd be a brilliant teacher."

"Happy to do it." Gui looked grave. "But I'm just as willing to keep heading east if that's the way you decide. I'll not abandon you again."

Cas's throat tightened. He'd been so angry after his mother died. Angry that Gui had left and not returned for years. But the past was buried now. "I'm not sure what I mean to do next," he admitted. "But I'm grateful for your counsel."

Gui just gripped his shoulder. For a minute they stood together atop the rise, watching the fledgling army take shape below. At last, Cas drew in a breath. "I'd better talk this over with Felippa. She kept our family together all those years I spent on the road. She deserves a say." He smiled wryly. "And if she doesn't get one, I'll suffer for it."

Gui laughed. "That you would. I'll go see about our mounts. They'll be ready, whatever you both decide." With a parting clap on the back, he limped away down the hill.

Cas watched him go, heavy with the weight of the choice before him. He made his way through the bustling camp to his family's tent. Felippa greeted him at the flap, exhaustion making her seem older than her thirteen years. "I was just about to look for you."

Cas's heart nearly stopped. "Is Da…?"

"His fever's broken," she said with a smile. "He even took a bit of broth. The worst has passed."

Relief crashed through Cas like a wave. He looked past Felippa to where his father lay sleeping, color already returning to his wasted face. The widow Sarra sat beside him, pressing a cloth to his brow. She glanced up and gave Cas an encouraging nod.

Felippa took his hands. Her blue eyes searched his face, seeing too much as always. "Something's troubling you," she said quietly. "Something besides Da.."

He drew her outside, glancing around to make sure they had privacy. "Brennos will march on Prydwen to break the siege. We could travel with his army."

"But what about crossing the Boundary?"

"Here's the thing. I spoke to Brennos. He promised that if he wins, he'll find us a ship bound for Alessia."

"*If* he gets there in time," Felippa said. "But the city might have already fallen."

"Aye." Cas scrubbed a hand over his face. "Feck, I don't know what to do. Trying to reach the Boundary on our own… It'll be mad dangerous. But if we go back to Prydwen, we might all wind up dead."

She was quiet, worrying at her lower lip. Finally, she lifted her chin. "I think we should go with Brennos."

He wasn't surprised. "Tell me why."

"Because I believe in him." Her face glowed with conviction. "You were sleeping, but I saw it! He made the sun move in the sky!"

Cas shifted uneasily, glancing at the fiery orange ball hanging low on the horizon. The so-called miracle that everyone was talking about. "It's changed position, I'll give you that." He shook his head. "But it doesn't mean Bel has blessed Brennos. Maybe whatever magic caused the Sundering is getting weak. Or it's connected to this sudden plague of risen."

Felippa gave him an exasperated look. "You doubt everything, Cas. You need to have more faith."

Something hot and bitter surged up. "I used to have faith. I believed in Orlaith Redvayne. I believed I was carrying out Kaethe's will. And what did it get me? A good friend dead and a warrant on my head for her murder. It was all for nothing, Lip. All of it!"

She frowned, opening her mouth to argue, but his anger drained away as quickly as it had come. "Never mind." He thought of the packs of risen roaming the countryside, and the living — far worse, in his opinion — who were robbing defenseless travelers like Sarra of all they owned. "You're right. Going back to Prydwen with Brennos is the safest course. As feckin' insane as that sounds."

She threw her arms around his neck. "We'll get through this," she whispered in his ear. "Together, like we always have."

Cas managed a faint smile. "Aye. Together." He turned to survey the camp once more. "I do hope Lo is waiting there," he admitted. "We promised to meet in the city. Remember?"

Felippa's face brightened. "Of course I remember. Oh, I hope we find her!"

That cold knot of worry tightened again. "I keep wondering if her meeting with Kaethe went well." He trailed off, not wanting to voice the dark possibilities lurking in his mind.

"You shouldn't fret so much," Felippa chided. "You two are destined to be together. You'll meet again. I know it in my bones."

Cas pulled her into a fierce hug. "What would I do without your bottomless well of optimism, eh?" He dropped a kiss on the top of her fair head. "I'm a fortunate man to have such a wise sister."

She giggled and swatted at him as he released her. "And don't you forget it."

Cas looked around. "Where's Teo?"

"Brennos made him a messenger. He's been racing around delivering orders." Felippa's blue eyes shone with mirth. "You should've seen his chest puff out. I think he's still in awe at meeting the Red Rogue."

Cas smiled fondly. "Aye, well, you let Sarra and Da know the plan. I'll go track down our young messenger and fill him in."

Felippa nodded. "I'll get our things together. There's not much to pack, but we should be ready to leave as soon as they give the order."

With a squeeze of her hand, Cas strode off into the camp. A hive of activity buzzed around him, men striking tents, saddling horses, sharpening weapons. He scanned faces as he passed, searching for his brother's red-gold hair. Teo had found his place here; he'd be glad to know they were staying. And he'd lived in Prydwen for almost half of his sixteen years. He must have friends there, people he worried about.

With a pang of guilt, Cas realized how little he knew of his brother's life. They had been separated for so long, each walking their own path. He resolved to remedy that on the journey back to the city. It was past time they got reacquainted.

But as he wove through the camp, he saw no sign of Teo. Cas made his way to the perimeter, where a line of stakes had been driven into the ground, torches lashed atop them to ward off the risen. Sentries stood with watchful eyes, bows ready to fire flaming arrows at the first sign of trouble.

"Any of you seen my brother?" Cas called as he approached. "Teo? He's been running messages."

One of the men jerked his chin toward the road. "He passed through not a quarter hour ago. Carried orders for the forward scouts."

Cas eyed the gloomy forest beyond the stakes. He knew the scouts were essential, but he didn't like the thought of his little brother out there alone beyond the safety of the palisade.

Well, Teo was nearly a grown man. Cas couldn't protect him forever. He had to find his own way in this world, make his own choices. Cas nodded his thanks to the sentries and squeezed through the line of stakes.

The road was a rutted, half-frozen track wending through snow-clad pines. His boots broke a thin crust as he walked, breath pluming in the frigid air. The wan sun vanished behind a bank of clouds, and the temperature plummeted. Fresh flurries came whirling down.

He wondered how far the forward post was when a sound pricked his ears. Cas cocked his head, listening. It came again, faint but unmistakable. Muffled sobs, somewhere off the path. Cas knew his own brother's voice and felt sure it wasn't Teo. Habit sent his hand reaching for the braces under his coat, though they were empty of vials. And even if he had Kaethe's Tears, it wouldn't do any good.

It sounded like a child. One of the refugees, wandered away from their parents? He stepped off the road and headed deeper into the woods. Branches snatched at his coat and slouching banks of snow slid from the trees to land with muffled thumps. The weeping grew louder.

Finally, he spotted a hollow. A silhouette crouched in the

shadows. Cas approached cautiously. "Hello?" he called. "I won't harm you."

The figure lifted its head. A young man, hardly more than a boy. His face was gaunt, his eyes large and dark. No plume of breath issued from his mouth.

Cas studied the risen boy. It was hard to tell how he'd died. Starvation perhaps, or some wasting illness. He looked more pathetic than frightening.

You must not linger here, Cas urged in Tongues. *Go to the Mother's embrace.*

The young replied in a rasping whisper, his throat working. *I am caught between worlds. There is no passage through. The gates are closed. Help me!*

A thrill of dread coursed through him. Cas had suspected as much, but to hear it from the lips of the dead... He was about to reply when a sound made him turn. Three Sons of Bel were coming from the road, two with arrows nocked, a third gripping a torch to light the oil-soaked rags. Cas stepped quickly into their path, placing himself between the soldiers and the risen boy. "Don't shoot!"

The men scowled. "Are you daft? Get out of the way!" one snapped.

"He's no threat," Cas retorted. "He's as confused as we are!"

The soldiers glanced at each other. Cas heard twigs snapping as the boy staggered off into the woods behind him.

The two priests lowered their bows. "Not a threat? They can kill with a touch, don't you know?"

"Aye, I'm aware. He's gone now, and I don't need saving." Cas shouldered past them, knowing his anger was unfair and not caring. How many more risen were out there, lost and terrified? He nearly cursed the Lady of Shadows for her cruelty but thought better of it.

When he reached the road, Cas was glad to see his brother run up, red-faced and out of breath. Teo cut a glance at the irate soldiers stomping out of the woods. "Everything all right?"

"Fine," Cas bit out. "Let's get back to camp."

Felippa waited at the palisade. She looked relieved to see them both. "The army's about to march! Da's riding in a wagon with Sarra. I've made him comfortable."

She led him and Teo to one of the mule-drawn baggage carts. Da lay swaddled in blankets, eyes closed. He still wheezed a bit, but his face had lost its feverish flush. Cas tucked the blankets more securely around his shoulders.

As he straightened, he noticed the gaunt man in the next wagon, hands and feet trussed, armed guards watching him. Arnulf met Cas's gaze and smiled. His eyes glittered with dark amusement. Either the fanatic had lost his mind or he knew something they didn't.

A worrying prospect, but it was too late to turn back now.

Cas scoured the ranks until he spotted Lucius's tall, lean frame astride a charger beside Brennos and Gui at the head of the column. He pushed through and related his encounter with the dead boy in the woods.

"He told me the gates to Kaethe's realm were closed," Cas warned. "It's going to get worse. A lot worse."

Brennos took the news without expression. He was not a man easily rattled. "For now, fire slows them down." He held up a hand. "You may not like it, but we have little choice in the matter." He turned to Lucius. "First Flame, give the order."

Lucius wheeled his horse around to face the army. "Second Flame, attend!" he bellowed at a man with a mournful face and keen gray eyes. "Forward march to Prydwen!"

Down the line, the call was taken up by the Third Flame. "Ready torches! Fall in line!"

A red pennant went up, whipping in the breeze. Cas joined Felippa and Teo in the rear, both looking excited at the tumult. A rattle came of spears against bucklers, and the Sons of Bel marched forth beneath a leaden sky. Would they find a city besieged? Or one already put to the sword? Cas fumbled for Felippa's hand, lacing their fingers together as he used to do in the hayloft as children. *Faith.*

How he wished he had more of it.

Thirteen

Orlaith sipped her bitter black tea and carefully set the porcelain teacup on its saucer. It slid an inch to the left... then halted. Her sharp gaze cut to Margrave Widmunt Dufay, who knelt on all fours, a silver tray balanced precariously on his back. Sweat beaded his brow.

He shot her a pleading look. Stupid man. What was Orlaith supposed to do about it?

She ignored him, turning to Beatriu. The eleven-year-old empress nestled in an embroidered armchair of green and gold, her ringlets perfectly arranged against her white gown. She selected a sugar-dusted pastry from the tiered platter atop Dufay's back.

He let out a tiny whimper as the tray wobbled again, a bead of moisture trickling from hairline to ruddy jowls.

The tradition of *biscochos*, or afternoon biscuits, was popular among the Galatian nobility, and Beatriu took it very seriously. On the eastward march to Caria, a town in Orlaith's duchy of Clovis, her army had halted every day at four o'clock so the little empress could have her tea and cakes.

Beatriu bit into the cake, chewing slowly. Dufay's baker stood nearby, hands twisting in her apron. After an agonizing moment, Beatriu swallowed.

"A bit dry," she pronounced.

The baker blanched. "My deepest apologies, Your Highness," the woman stammered, bobbing a curtsey. "Shall I take them away and bring something else?"

Beatriu regarded the platter, her left eye twitching almost imperceptibly. Orlaith tensed. That twitch never boded well.

"I want marchpane," Beatriu said.

"M-marchpane?" The baker's voice quavered. "I fear I do not have any almonds, Your Highness."

Beatriu's pale gaze slid to the trembling woman. "But I want marchpane."

She did not raise her voice, but the baker flinched. She curtsied again, lower this time. "I shall find some straight away, Your Highness."

"You may leave the tray," Beatriu instructed. She was already reaching for another cake. Dufay made a strangled sound as the tray listed dangerously to one side.

It was his own fault. They had arrived at Dufay's manor the night before. Orlaith had informed him of the situation. The child commanded an army of mortifexes. She was now the Empress of Aveline, Kaethe's divine representative on earth, and they must cater to her every whim, no matter how capricious or impossible it might be.

But Dufay, being a fat old fool, had drunk too much wine at supper and got Beatriu's father's name wrong. This made her quite cross. She had decided he would serve as a table, and if he failed in this task, he would meet a far worse fate.

"More tea, Your Majesty?" Orlaith inquired in honeyed tones.

Beatriu shook her head. Sugar smeared her rosebud lips, but Orlaith would not dare to offer a napkin.

The dark-haired mortifex captain called Janus moved aside to let the baker scurry out. When Orlaith glanced up, she found him studying her, amusement in his burning gaze. She looked away, unsettled. If not for the flames in his eyes, he could pass for a living man.

Orlaith had expected the rivers between Galatia and Clovis to delay the undead army's advance, but the winged mounts had simply carried their riders across, far above the rushing waters. Beatriu's mortal army took longer, but they too had arrived, tents sprawling across the snowy fields beyond Caria's walls like a second town.

From here, they would march to Aquitan, then cross the Boundary and crush the Moon Courts. Orlaith dreamt of it every night as she curled at the foot of Beatriu's bed. Chaos and Caul, begging for mercy that would never come. Nathan Ouvrard strung up while he was slowly flayed alive—

A knock jolted her from this pleasant daydream. The door opened to admit a young woman, snowmelt dripping from her curly hair. Janus conferred with her for a moment.

"A Quietus to see you, Your Highness," he said. "Adith Finch."

Orlaith stood, surprised. She'd always liked Adith. The woman had steady nerves. She must already know of Beatriu's ascension and Orlaith's allegiance, but if she was troubled by this turn of events, she hid it well.

Adith knelt before Beatriu, head bowed. "Your Majesty. I bring news from the south."

Beatriu popped another cake into her mouth. "Rise and report," she mumbled.

Adith stood. "I rode from Dierna, Your Majesty, meaning to continue on to Aquitan, but then I was informed of the, ah..." Her brown eyes flicked to Orlaith. "New political situation," she finished. "The dead are rising in numbers I've never seen before. The iron lines have failed, every last one. Those who can are fleeing." She met Beatriu's pale gaze. "I fear it's the same everywhere, Your Majesty."

Beatriu continued to chew, but Orlaith saw that telltale twitch of her left eye. The strain of wearing the Grand Menotte was finally beginning to show.

"Kaethe is angry," Beatriu said. "I must go to her shrine and pray for guidance." She turned to Orlaith. "You will accompany me."

The child rose, and Dufay sagged with relief, then stiffened as the tray nearly toppled over. Orlaith stood as well, fighting exhaustion. Sleep had been elusive these past nights. Beatriu demanded stories and songs until the small hours of morning. Even then, the girl tossed and turned, the thick iron cuff glinting on her slender arm in the candlelight.

"Of course, Your Majesty," Orlaith murmured.

Beatriu swept from the room, Orlaith a pace behind. Janus and three other mortifex knights fell into step beside them, their faces impassive.

The streets of Caria were deserted, the few people about making themselves scarce at the first sight of Beatriu and her entourage. Orlaith looked around at the sagging roofs and crumbling walls. Refuse littered the narrow alleys, and gray laundry fluttered between boarded-up windows. How tawdry the town had become!

Had it always been this way? Orlaith flinched from the thought. No, it couldn't be her fault. She had always acted with her people's best interests at heart. Everything, every sacrifice, every compromise, had been for them.

At last they reached the shrine, a rundown building next to a fountain. The usual faceless statue of Kaethe loomed over the murky water, her blank hood seeming to watch their approach. As they drew near, the door to the convent opened. A single nun emerged, her white robe threadbare.

She eyed Beatriu warily. "Your Majesty. What brings you to our humble shrine?"

Beatriu looked around. "Where are the other nuns?"

"I am the only one left," the sister replied.

Beatriu frowned. "Why is this?"

"Four sisters died tending to the unhallowed dead. The rest fled to the main convent in Aquitan. I chose to remain, to guard the holy relics."

Her face held serene acceptance. Orlaith envied her. But Beatriu was obviously displeased. "Leave us. I must commune with Kaethe alone."

The nun nodded and withdrew into the convent. Beatriu gestured sharply to her guards. "Wait here."

She hitched up her skirts and waded into the fountain. Then she sank to her knees before the statue and bowed her head.

Orlaith feared Beautriu would beckon her into the icy water, but she did not. So she stood on the sidelines, waiting. That was her life now. Waiting to start marching. Waiting to stop marching and make camp. Waiting to discover what Beatriu wanted for breakfast, which tale or song she wished to hear. Waiting to learn if today would be the day her luck ran out. Largely, the days consisted of tedium interrupted by bouts of terror if she misspoke or fumbled a silver button on the child's shoe.

Orlaith admired Adith Finch's composure. She was made of sterner stuff than that sniveling worm Dufay. This in turn made Orlaith think of Castelio zah Nerides. Where was he? Was he still alive? It seemed ridiculous now to worry about what he might have known about her plot against the Courtenays. With Enrigo dead, none of it mattered anymore.

Castelio had been like a son. She suddenly yearned to tell him his betrayal was forgiven, that she held no more anger. She wished she could mend the rift between them, but it was likely too late now.

A faint splash dragged Orlaith back to the present. She had no idea how long she had been standing there, but her toes were numb. Beatriu was wading out of the fountain, shivering. She looked uncertain, for once like the little girl she was.

"Kaethe would not answer," Beatriu admitted. "We must make haste to the great shrine in Aquitan. That is where the Lady of Shadows' spirit dwells. I will pray again there." She fixed Orlaith with a hard stare. "You will kneel to me in front of the court and proclaim that Clovis is now a province under my dominion."

Orlaith inclined her head. "As you command, Your Majesty."

Janus conjured a hot wind to dry the child's clothes and they returned to the manor. When they entered Dufay's extravagantly furnished sitting room, Beatriu's marchpane was waiting on his bony back.

"I sent my master's fastest rider to the next town to fetch the almond flour," the baker said anxiously. "I hope it is to Her Majesty's liking."

She had even put nine tiny white stars on each cookie in imitation of the empress's sigil.

Beatriu eyed the marchpane with a surly expression. "I don't want it anymore."

Orlaith snapped her fingers and the baker whisked it away. She chose her next words carefully. "Your Majesty, may I suggest that we send my former steward Albion ahead to Aquitan? He can ensure you are granted a worthy reception when we arrive."

Beatriu considered, then nodded. "I want the shrine prepared for my arrival, with all the proper rites."

"Albion is capable and efficient," Orlaith assured her. "He has served House Redvayne his entire life. Now he will serve Your Majesty with the same devotion."

Albion had been found cowering behind sacks of onions in the Alcazar's root cellar after Beatriu's disastrous wedding to the now-dead Vaszoly Marcel. He'd been one of the few survivors.

Orlaith rose and sent for the steward. His long crimson surcoat was fraying, his hose sagging at the knees, but he still wore the phoenix ring of House Redvayne on his pinky finger. She gave him instructions, then leaned close to whisper in his ear. "Observe the nobles upon your arrival in Aquitan. Note those who seem the most reluctant to embrace Her Majesty's rule. Report back to me discreetly what you learn."

Albion gave the barest nod of acknowledgment. "My lady."

Orlaith studied the elderly steward as they stepped into the courtyard. He had more hair sprouting from his ears than on his scalp. Yet even now, with the world crumbling around them, he would not abandon her. She felt a pang of something like affection. With Lucius gone, he was the closest thing she had to a confidant.

"Have a safe journey," she said. "I will be but a few days behind you."

A mortifex took Albion by the arm, its eyes flaring like banked coals. The steward looked as though he might faint as he was bundled onto an abbadax and buckled into a harness. The reptilian creature screeched and tore furrows in the frozen earth with its claws.

"Remember your orders," Orlaith called after Albion as the

mortifex mounted behind him. "We shall follow in due course."

The abbadax unfurled its leathery wings and launched skyward, bearing Albion away to an uncertain reception in Aquitan. Orlaith watched until they dwindled to a speck against the clouds. Her fingers drifted to the iron cuff encircling her wrist. Once it had held Lucius, bound him to her will. Now it was a constant reminder of her own precarious position.

When she turned back to the manor, Beatriu was watching her through the window. Those pale eyes were *always* watching.

"Your Majesty," Orlaith said, dipping into a curtsey as she entered the sitting room. "Now that Albion speeds ahead to prepare Aquitan for your glorious arrival, perhaps it is time we informed the rest of your new empire of the blessed change in rulership."

She held her breath as Beatriu weighed the proposal. It was so hard to predict what would anger her these days.

"We agree," Beatriu said at last, causing Orlaith to heave an inward sigh of relief. "The Moon Courts must know of my ascension." She touched the iron cuff around her arm, twice the size of the one Orlaith wore.

"Allow me to draft the imperial decrees in your name, Majesty," she offered. "I can dispatch envoys within the hour to deliver them."

Beatriu's gaze had wandered to Dufay, still on his hands and knees. "We are *most* displeased with you!" she snapped. "The state of Kaethe's shrine was unacceptable."

Dufay quaked, sweating like a pig despite the chill in the room. "A thousand apologies, Your Highness! I beg forgiveness. I shall have it restored at once, on my honor!"

"We care nothing for your *honor*," Beatriu growled. "You

will serve as a writing desk while my lady-in-waiting pens our decrees. If so much as a drop of ink is spilled, we shall be *most* vexed."

"Yes, Your Highness," Dufay said in a resigned tone.

Orlaith eyed his bowed back and knobby spine. "I fear my penmanship will suffer," she remarked dryly.

Janus smirked. "If I may, Your Grace, a writing board could be fetched."

"An excellent proposal," Orlaith agreed. Soon enough, a smooth plank of wood was produced and laid across the margrave's back. Dufay grunted but dared not protest.

Orlaith took up quill and parchment and began to write in an elegant, flowing hand, savoring each line. The Courtenays, the Ouvrards, all the nobles who had schemed against House Redvayne — soon they would read her words and tremble.

With every stroke of the quill, the cold knot in her chest loosened. For so long she had dreamed of vengeance, and now it was close enough to taste, paid for with the blood of her husband and son.

Let the cowards bluster and rage, Orlaith thought as she sanded the finished letters. Let them muster their armies and make their defiant stands. In the end, they would fall before the power of the undead, and House Redvayne would be gloriously avenged.

Orlaith smiled. The game was not over. It had only just begun.

Fourteen

Jaskin Cazal gritted his teeth against the pain that shot through his leg with each step. He dared not look upon the festering wound, though he could feel the devil's snare poison burning in his veins.

The three moons illuminated a vast moorland broken by six spires of colored glass that thrust up from the ground like the fangs of some ancient leviathan. A discordant hum filled the air, rising and falling with the wind.

Jaskin's eyes were drawn upward to the tips of the spires, where shimmering visions swirled — glimpses of alien lands and fantastical realms. He saw palaces of liquid smoke perched on purple mountainsides, strange ships with crimson sails speeding across silver seas, and countless more wonders that made his head spin.

Nabu-bal-idinna halted. His scholarly face seemed to shift in the moonlight, hardening into something else, at once severe and unknowable.

It is the fever, Jaskin thought. *Making the mundane seem monstrous.*

"What are they?" Nabu asked. His voice was changed, too. Deeper and resonant with power.

"I named them the Obsidian Spires," Jaskin replied, his own words sounding thin and reedy. A cackle of mad laughter threatened to bubble up, but he forced it down.

"You created them?"

"No. I discovered them when I first came to the darklands many centuries ago. Some elder race must have built them long before my people arrived. Though I know not what befell those ancients."

They watched the visions in silence, the colors and shapes morphing from one fantastical scene to the next. An underwater city with whales swimming between honeycombed buildings as tall as cliffs. A blasted wasteland where two suns hung above half-buried ruins. A jungle where huge dragonflies darted between vivid blue trees.

"Are they real?" Nabu turned to him. "Or merely an illusion?"

Jaskin hesitated. He had no certain answer despite his long study of the spires. "I believe they are real. Windows into other worlds, mayhap."

"Have you tried to pass through?"

Jaskin's expression was part wistful smile, part grimace. He'd spent countless hours staring up at those tantalizing visions, his mind awhirl with possibilities. Later, when he was trapped in the mirror, he often daydreamed about the wonders he'd glimpsed.

"I must have attempted every spell and ritual known to necromancy," he confessed, "but if there is a door to reach those other realms, I never found it. In the end, I had to concede defeat. And now..." He gestured at his wounded leg." I fear my exploring days are behind me."

Nabu regarded him thoughtfully. "Did you ever feel you were meant to be someone else? To walk a different path?"

The question caught Jaskin off guard. He barked a rueful laugh. "Many a time, my friend. Many a time." He shook his head, mirth fading. "I have enjoyed nine lives, you know. And wasted most of them on selfish pursuits."

He gazed at the Obsidian Spires. "Yet for all my failings, I do believe I used the Grand Menotte to achieve some good. To bring life to barren lands. Create beauty where once there was only desolation. That is my legacy. Not gold or glory, but..." He spread his arms wide. "*This.* And it will outlive me. Outlive us all, I daresay."

To his surprise, Jaskin felt a tear slide down his weathered cheek. He brushed it away. The poison must be addling his wits, making him maudlin.

"This is my last life," he said quietly. "I must reach Loris. If the healers cannot aid me, then I shall face Kaethe's judgment."

At the mention of the goddess, Nabu went still. His gentle face became a cold mask. "The Lady of Shadows," he muttered, lip curling. "She speaks with a forked tongue."

Jaskin was taken aback. "I thought you loved her."

Nabu stared at him, unblinking. There was something in that empty gaze that sent a clawed animal skittering down Jaskin's spine. Then pinpricks of light began to glimmer at the center of his pupils, like distant stars. Or the eyes of a wolf. They grew larger, brighter, twin pools of molten gold. Jaskin lurched back, transfixed, as Nabu opened his mouth.

It yawned impossibly wide, a cavernous door swinging open to reveal a roaring furnace within. Heat seared Jaskin's face. He flung up an arm, staggering away from the scorching wind that howled from his companion's throat.

The air shimmered, distorted by waves of blistering heat. Nabu's purple robes flapped in the gale. And in the heart of that fiery maelstrom, his form changed, growing taller, broader…

Jaskin's knees gave way. He collapsed to the ground, gaping in disbelief at the towering figure wreathed in flames above him. A being of light, both beautiful and terrible to behold.

LO STEPPED CAUTIOUSLY into the small clearing ringed by ancient pines. A circle of blackened stones surrounded the remnants of a fire. Scattered chestnuts, their shells cracked and charred, littered the ground nearby.

Morgen knelt and sifted a handful of ash through her fingers. "Still warm. Someone camped here not long ago, and it looks like they left in a hurry." Her ice-chip eyes narrowed. "I think we have found Jaskin's trail."

Lo nodded distractedly, her gaze fixed on a pine tree. The trunk looked scorched, the lower branches also blackened by fire. It had to be Bel. The god was waking. *Shit!*

"I hope so," she said, keeping her voice calm. "Jaskin can't be far ahead now. We should keep going."

Morgen nodded, but Dravka spoke up. "We've been walking for hours. If we don't rest, we'll be useless when we do catch up to him."

Lo desperately wanted to press on, but the girl was right. "Let's stop here, then," she said. "But only for an hour or two."

Dravka busied herself building up the fire. Lo sat on a log and took out Jaskin's journal. She thumbed through the pages, poring over his cramped script and meticulous sketches of flora and fauna.

Morgen squatted across from her, palms out to the growing flames. "What are you looking for?"

Lo traced her finger along a lovingly detailed rendering of

an orchid. "Answers, I suppose. To who Jaskin Cazal truly is. The things he did with the power of the mortifexes... Much of it seems admirable. Restoring life in a land abandoned to eternal darkness."

Morgen's lips thinned. "Whatever he accomplished with that cursed power, the cost was too high."

"I'll concede that the man is a villainous canker," Dravka said. "But I am impressed with his creations. I cannot honestly call them all evil."

Morgen cut her a look. "The ends never justify the means."

Lo arched a brow. "Oh, really? I seem to recall you stealing the Grand Menotte from me."

"Only so you wouldn't give it to Nathan Ouvrard."

"Well," Lo retorted, snapping the journal shut, "you managed to lose it, and now..." She was about to say, "We've no clue who has it," but remembered her own lie in the nick of time. "...It's in the possession of a madman!" she finished, injecting the statement with the appropriate note of outrage.

Morgen scowled. "Which is why I intend to take it back."

Lo tucked the journal away. Perhaps she could share a crumb of truth. "There's something else you should know about Jaskin Cazal." She paused, savoring the moment. "He's a Shadow Soul."

Morgen looked up, shock on her face. "What?"

Lo leaned forward. "Why do think he's still around after all these years?"

"I thought... a necromantic spell..."

"No. He has nine lives, just like us. But he's on his last one."

They regarded each other for a long moment.

"How many do *you* have left?" Morgen asked.

Lo scoffed. "Why should I tell you?"

"I'll tell you mine," she offered with a grim smile. "One for one."

Lo gazed into the flames. Part of her was intrigued by the game. Other than Jaskin, this woman was the only other person in the world who knew what it was like to die and come back.

"All right," she said. "But you first."

Dravka sat cross-legged, watching them both with fascination.

"I came into this world with the umbilical cord around my neck," Morgen said. "Dead in the womb before I was even born."

Her eyes challenged, *Top that.*

Lo tossed another twig into the flames. "I crashed my wind ship. Twice."

"I fell into a well and drowned."

"I drowned once, too," Lo said. "Not my favorite death, I'll tell you that."

The memory of her descent into Khaf-hor's trench was still fresh. He was one of the five gods of the Cold Sea, the ocean that lay between Kaethe's border and the afterlife. Unlike her other deaths, that one had been deliberate. She'd wrapped chains around her waist and jumped from the rail of the *Wind-Witch*. It was the only way to reach the giant eel's realm six hundred fathoms deep.

Lo had struck a bargain for the location of her parents, who were being held by Magnus the Merciless. She'd promised to come back when Khaf-hor summoned her — another contract with a shady deity that had yet to be fulfilled.

But she wasn't about to tell Morgen all of that. "Your turn," she said.

"A fever got me when I was five."

Lo scoffed. "Run-of-the-mill."

Morgen frowned. "Once I mistook death cap mushrooms for edible straw mushrooms. That was easily the worst one. The violent sickness lasted for three days."

Lo winced. "I'm sorry."

"Then I started to feel better. I believed I was through the worst of it. Now I know that stage is called the 'false recovery.' On the fourth day, my skin turned yellow. The seizures began. I was dead by evening."

Lo felt a pang of sympathy. "I was struck by lightning a couple of times." She pulled up her sleeves and showed Morgen the branching scars running along her arms. "It hurt, but it was quick."

"I was thrown out a window," Morgen said. "Painful, but also quick."

"I was touched by a lich."

Morgen leaned forward, the firelight playing across her face. She was a stunningly beautiful woman, even if her personality didn't exactly match the outside. "What was it like?"

"Cold. I don't remember much else. Your turn."

"I broke my neck coming through the portal from Kaethe's house. You witnessed that one."

Lo nodded. "I did feel bad, though you'd just tried to rob me. Oh, I've got one more. Breaking a blood pact with a necromancer."

"Which one?"

"Nathan Ouvrard. In fairness, he tried to find a loophole in our contract. There wasn't one."

"That's eight deaths," Morgen said. "You're on your last life."

"And you're on your seventh."

"Eighth," Morgen corrected. "I was stabbed in the heart by Vazsoly Marcel."

"Son of a bitch!" Lo said.

Morgen's smile was chilling. "Imagine his surprise when I came back."

"She turned the prick inside out at his own wedding," Dravka said, her voice tinged with awe. "In front of the Damiata Beatriu's whole court."

Lo was impressed. "Literally *inside-out*?" Not a pretty image, but if anyone deserved such an end it was Duc Marcel.

Morgen nodded. "That's when Jaskin Cazal showed up and tried to take the box with the Grand Menotte. It was chaos. I fled with Dravka and her sister Jaelle before we were all killed."

So that's why she believed Jaskin had it.

"You've burned through seven lives already," Lo said. "Don't you think it's peculiar how often we've both died considering neither of us is past thirty?"

Morgen shrugged, but the question clearly unsettled her. Lo leaned in. "Have you heard of the Quickening?"

"Of course. My mother warned me about it."

"Is there any way to stop it?"

"No." Morgen's reply was flat. "It is the Fates, tugging at the warp and weft of our lives."

"Kaethe's older sisters," Lo said. "Nona, Decima, and Morta."

Surprise colored Morgen's face. "You know their names."

"The Ducissas of Nyons told me. But that's all they knew."

Morgen drew her cloak tighter around her shoulders. "Nona measures the thread and decides how long you will live. Decima weaves the main events of your life. And Morta..." She made a snipping motion with her fingers. "Cuts your thread when the time comes."

Lo frowned. The idea that the Fates controlled her destiny sat like a stone in her gut. If it were true, she might as well give up right now.

As if reading her thoughts, Morgen gave a sour nod. "I do not like it either," she said. "But I see no point in dwelling upon it. If they wish to torment us, we are at their mercy."

On cue, the sky opened up, cold rain pattering on the pine boughs overhead. Lo took the first watch, but she could not shake her dark thoughts. After a stretch, Morgen roused herself and took over, feeding twigs to the sputtering fire as Lo wrapped herself up in her cloak.

She jerked awake sometime later, thoroughly damp. Dravka lay a few feet away, snoring like a hibernating bear. Morgen was nowhere to be seen. Lo scanned the trees and caught a flash of movement, a figure stalking slowly through the undergrowth. What was she up to?

Suspicion rising, Lo swirled her cloak around her, raising the hood to conceal her face. She crept after Morgen, placing each foot with care. Ahead, the woman drifted like a ghost between the trees. She paused now and then, peering into the shadows as if searching for something. Once, she glanced back, her gaze sweeping directly over Lo. But the cloak did its work, blending with the dappled grays and greens of the forest.

Lo drew closer, near enough to reach out and touch the other woman's shoulder. She held her breath, pulse loud in her ears. Perhaps she should simply reveal herself and ask—

Morgen stopped abruptly. At the same instant, Lo's toe caught on a root. She stumbled, slamming into Morgen's back. The necromancer let out a grunt of surprise. They staggered forward... And the ground disappeared beneath their feet.

Lo had a brief glimpse of Morgen's startled face before they plunged into darkness.

She came to with a groan, muddy water soaking her clothes. Lo pushed herself up on one elbow. The movement sent a bolt of agony lancing through her skull. Gingerly, she touched her brow. Her fingers came away sticky with blood.

A figure crouched a few feet away, little more than a silhouette in the gloom. "You're awake." Morgen's voice was dry as ever, but Lo detected a hint of relief. The woman moved to her side, fingers probing at Lo's skull. Lo flinched away.

"Be still," Morgen ordered. "You took a nasty knock on the head."

Lo ignored her and struggled into a sitting position. Her back rested against one of the fallen branches that had crashed down with them, forming a partial roof over the pit.

"What is this place?" She squinted through the drizzle. Muddy walls loomed on all sides, too deep and regular to be a sinkhole. "Some kind of trap?"

Morgen looked irritated. "It appears so. I found scat nearby when I was keeping watch. From a large predator, judging by the size and clumps of fur."

Predator? Lo wrapped her arms around herself, shivering. "Animals d-don't dig p-pits and conceal them with b-branches," she stammered, the words fuzzy on her tongue.

Morgen's black eyes glittered. "No, they do not. I hope we're gone before we find out what did."

Lo touched her head, then immediately regretted it as pain lanced through her skull. She watched Morgen move to the pit wall and use protruding roots for handholds. She made it halfway up before a root snapped and she tumbled back down in a shower of curses, landing hard on her backside.

A laugh burst out before Lo could stop it. Morgen shot her a glare.

"I'm sorry," Lo said. "It's just... You look like someone hit you in the face with a mud pie."

Morgen flicked a handful of muck at her. “There, now we match.”

Lo scowled. “Can’t you use magic to turn one of these branches into a ladder?”

Morgen held up a sodden pouch. “My spell dust is ruined. What about your elemental power?”

Lo closed her eyes and sought the quiet space of the Nexus, but her aching head made it hard to focus. A faint sound in the forest above snapped her eyes open. Morgen heard it too. They both tensed as a shadow fell across the opening above.

“Bel’s bleeding boils,” a voice called down, “I’ve been looking for you two for hours!”

Lo and Morgen shared a look of relief. “Help us get out of here!” Lo called hoarsely.

Dravka peered over the edge, silver-blonde hair plastered to her forehead. “I do have a bit of rope, but it’s not nearly long enough. Hold on.” She vanished for a few minutes, then returned and ordered them to make way. With a grunt, Dravka rolled a mossy log into the pit. Morgen angled it against one side, testing its stability with a shake. It held. She began to creep up, arms spread for balance.

Lo watched, silently cheering her on. The log shifted under Morgen’s weight, but she kept climbing, inch by inch. Dravka stretched out her arm.

“Almost there!” she said encouragingly.

Morgen reached up, but the log fell short and a foot of empty air separated their hands. She lifted up to her toes. Lo held her breath. A bit closer now... Then Morgen wavered, teetered. The log rolled out from under her and she plummeted back down, landing in an ungraceful heap.

She lay still for a moment, chest heaving. Then she pushed herself up, expression thunderous. This time, Lo wisely kept her mouth shut.

"I have another idea," Dravka called. "I'll cut down some saplings and tie them together. There's enough rope for that. Then I'll lower the whole thing down."

Lo nodded. It was a solid plan. As her footsteps retreated, Lo turned to Morgen. Rain cut rivulets down her mud-streaked face.

"I'm sorry," she said. "This is my fault. I thought..." She hesitated. "I thought you were up to something and followed."

Morgen regarded her for a long moment, eyes unreadable. "I don't blame you. We hardly know each other."

Memories surfaced of how she used to bully Morgen when they were children at Kaethe's house. Chasing her through the halls with her hands hooked into claws, pretending to be a ravenous monster. The woman had forgotten — or didn't realize Lo was her tormenter.

Now was probably not the time to bring it up.

They sat on the log. "How did you end up with Dravka Marcel?" Lo asked, trying to distract herself from her pounding head.

"I rescued her and her younger sister, Jaelle. Vazsoly had exiled them to the convent of Kaethe outside Prydwen. After the city fell to the Red Rogue and his rebels, Vaszoly fled. A mob came looking for him at the convent. He wasn't there, but they were content to string up his sisters," she said dryly.

"I happened to be there looking for him myself," Morgen continued. "I didn't plan to take the girls with me, but Dravka had spirit. I decided not to leave them to such a grisly fate."

"So where's the other one?" Lo asked.

"I left Jaelle at my cottage in the Western Isles. She will be safe there until we return."

Lo tried to picture Morgen spiriting away two frightened girls. It seemed at odds with the cold, ruthless woman she'd come to know. But then, people were rarely simple.

They lapsed into silence, waiting for Dravka's return. Rain dripped from the branches above. In the soggiest corner of the pit, two frogs conducted a croaking argument, or perhaps a courtship. As the minutes passed, Lo felt a little better. Less dizzy, at least. She hoped she'd be strong enough to climb out.

When the leaves rustled, they both rose to their feet. Morgen strode to the edge of the pit, head tilted back. "I am more than ready to escape this place," she muttered. "We've lost too much time as it is."

Lo cocked her head, listening. Something was off. Instead of Dravka's steady tread, she heard a strange hissing.

She gestured urgently at Morgen, who hurried over. Without a word, Lo swept her cloak around them both, tucking them into its shadowy folds. They huddled together, motionless. The hissing drew closer to the pit's edge. Then a pause, a held breath, and two heavy splashes.

Lo couldn't see a thing, but her other senses sharpened. She heard the intruders moving about the pit. "Where is it hiding?" one rasped. "Nothing escapes the trap. Never has."

"Must be here," came the guttural response. "Keep looking."

Lo raised her head slightly, peering through a crack in her hood. The darkness and rain obscured her view, but she could just make out two bizarre shapes prowling the pit.

"It be *here*," one insisted. "Smell it, I do!"

They came closer. Morgen stiffened beside her, coiled like a spring. The snuffling grew louder, until it was right on top of them. Something brushed against the cloak.

In a flash, Morgen stood. The cloak fell back and Lo blinked in a sudden burst of light. It emanated from the creatures' mouths, a cold, eldritch glow. They recoiled as Morgen chanted a spell in Tongues, the words harsh and jagged. She held out a hand, fingers moving as though coaxing something forth. But before she could finish the incantation, one moved with blinding speed. Black threads shot from its mouth as long, jointed legs spun her round and round, like a spider wrapping a fly.

Lo was reaching for her boot knife when something gripped her ankle. She was hoisted into the air. The beat of wings filled her ears, and the pit lurched away. The creatures bounded through the forest in great, bone-jarring leaps. Lo dangled upside down, fingers scrabbling for her knife. They brushed the hilt…

The creature stopped and made a clacking sound. Sticky threads erupted from its mouth, trapping her arms tight against her body. Then it resumed its relentless forward motion, disappearing into the dark heart of the forest.

FIFTEEN

Lo lay curled on one side, arms bound, the stench of decay filling her nose. Beside her, Morgen was similarly trussed in black threads. Bones littered the ground, ivory in the firelight.

Their captors had brought them to a clearing in the forest. A huge cauldron hung suspended over the flames, along with several wicked-looking hooks. Five tall, gangly creatures capered in the orange glow.

Ridged fungal growths on their skin matched the dark grays and greens of the forest. Like the swamp crabs, whose shells were camouflaged to resemble mossy rocks, they were perfectly adapted to their environment. Small, hairless heads bobbed atop long, oddly-jointed arms.

"Build fire up big," one rasped. "Game look tasty."

Lo's mind raced, seeking any way out, but the sticky threads pinning her arms and feet allowed little movement.

"I tried to rip out their souls," Morgen whispered, dark eyes flashing. "They have none."

"No souls?" Lo whispered back. "Are they dead?"

Morgen shook her head. "The dead have no appetite for meat, or food of any kind. Even mortifexes only consume blood. No, I fear we have met the night-ghasts Jaskin spoke of in his journal."

Lo's head had cleared enough to remember the entry:

Once, they were men, necromancers who traded their souls for the span of centuries. Alas, the wretched fools knew not the true cost. As the decades passed, their mortal flesh twisted into grotesque forms, until they could no longer abide their own hideousness. They fled into the shadows of the wood, condemned to a waking nightmare, hungering eternally for the flesh of the living.

Well, that sounded about right.

Now the night-ghasts were arguing over how to cook the "game."

"Roast on hook taste best," one hissed, its crystal teeth clacking with anticipation. "Skin crackle and crisp. More juicy."

"No, soup best!" another countered, skittering over to prod Lo with a disturbingly human finger. "Boil long time, make game soft and tender."

Lo eyed the hooks and cauldron, suppressing a shudder. The ghast leaned close, its small eyes glittering with a twisted intelligence.

Gods, she was thirsty. "Listen," she croaked. "If you let us go, I can promise you all a reward. Big reward!"

The night-ghasts paused their debate, swiveling hairless skulls to peer at her. For a moment, Lo dared to hope. Then they broke into rasping laughter.

"No want gold," one chortled. "Want game. Celebrate bitter-moon. Fire-moon. Long time no catch fat game."

"Fear make game sweeter," added the one hovering above her, prodding Lo again. "Wait little bit, get even more tasty."

"Need more sticks for fire," another ghast declared. It sniffed the air, nostril slits flaring. Two of them bounded into the darkness, propelled by their strange hopping gait.

Her last life, filling the bellies of night-ghasts. It was a bad joke.

"At least Dravka got away," Lo said softly.

Morgen's expression was grim. "The girl is no coward. I fear she'll do something stupid."

"Like try to rescue us?" Lo's gaze was drawn to the cookpot again. Clouds of steam rose from the simmering water inside. A very small part of her hoped Dravka would run and not look back, but the rest desperately wanted the girl to show up with her cudgel and long knife.

A thought struck her. The knife! If it hadn't fallen out during the trip from the pit to the clearing, it might still be in her boot sheath. She whispered her plan to Morgen, who gave a cool nod. The woman's unshakeable calm was reassuring.

Slowly, carefully, Morgen shifted position, drawing up her own legs to help conceal Lo's efforts. The ghasts had settled on soup and were arguing over the seasoning for the broth, but they still glanced over often, watching their captives with sharp eyes.

After much wiggling and picking at the threads with her ragged fingernails, Lo brushed the hilt of the knife. She began to work it free, hardly daring to breathe. The ghasts ladled broth into a bowl made from a human skull, tasting it and smacking their lipless mouths.

"More salt root. More bitter bark," cried one, stirring the broth with a yellowed thighbone.

Another tasted the mixture and made a clacking sound that somehow conveyed picky displeasure. "Need pinch of sweet-moss."

"Too much sweet-moss make game stringy," countered a third.

"Pinch, I say!" the first huffed.

They took turns dipping bones into the broth and licking them clean, adjusting the seasoning with each taste. They were meticulous about their cooking, for all their monstrous nature.

Lo's fingers tugged gently at the hilt of her knife. With agonizing slowness, she eased it from its sheath. The blade wasn't large—barely the length of her palm—but its edge was well-honed.

"Got it," she murmured to Morgen, as they edged back-to-back. "Now hold still—"

She was interrupted by a triumphant cry from the tallest ghast. "Broth perfect! Ready for game!"

Three of the creatures bounded toward them, stunted wings fluttering in excitement. Lo frantically sawed at the thick threads binding Morgen's wrists, keeping the knife concealed between their bodies. The bonds were tough, giving way a strand at a time.

"Hurry," Morgen breathed, her serene facade finally cracking.

The night-ghasts were five bounds away. Sweat slicked Lo's palms. The ropes had an oily residue, making the knife handle slippery in her grasp. One more strand, then two—

A commotion from the trees drew everyone's attention. One of the ghasts that had gone for wood hopped into the clearing, pointing a long, knobby finger at the branches of a pine whose boughs extended over the cookpot.

"Found third one!"

It launched itself aloft, wings flapping furiously. There was an angry curse as the ghast dragged a struggling figure down from the crook of a massive limb. Dravka's silver-blonde hair gleamed in the firelight as she kicked and swore, fighting like a cornered wildcat.

"Get off, you wart-ridden codpiece!" she snarled, landing a solid kick to the ghast's jointed leg.

The creature barely flinched, dragging her across the clearing to the fire. The other ghasts chittered with excitement.

"Three game now! Rich gravy!"

"More meat for fire-moon feast!"

While their captors were distracted, Lo sawed frantically at the last thread binding Morgen's wrists. She could feel it parting when a ghast grabbed her by the hair. Two others lifted a cursing Morgen as if she weighed nothing. They were dragged toward the bubbling pot.

"Game go in now!" announced the tallest ghast, stirring the broth one final time. "Simmer slow, 'til meat fall off bones..."

It stopped mid-sentence. The ghast blinked its small eyes in confusion, then staggered sideways. Around the fire, three others began showing similar signs of distress—wings drooping, movements sluggish.

"What happen?" one slurred thickly. "Where..." The creature trailed off.

One by one, the ghasts collapsed, their limbs twitching before they went still. Only the tallest remained upright, though it, too, wobbled unsteadily. Its eyes fixed on Dravka with sudden fury.

"What game do?" it shrieked, its voice rising to a bone-chilling pitch. "What game put in broth?" Its mouth gaped wide and something emerged from deep in its throat. A pale appendage, unfurling like a nightmarish flower.

Lo used the knife to slice her left hand free. She dashed forward, snatching a burning brand from the fire. The ghast's strange throat-flower pushed past its teeth, black threads shooting from its center.

Whipping her arm back, Lo threw the flaming branch directly into the creature's open mouth. The threads caught instantly, flames racing along their length back down into the ghast's throat. It screamed—a sound like a mace scraping plate armor—as the fire spread to the fungal growths covering its body.

"Dravka!" Lo called, tossing her knife toward the girl.

Dravka caught the blade deftly and set to work on Morgen's remaining bonds. Lo spotted her crossbow at the edge of the clearing, where the night-ghasts had dumped their packs. She sprinted toward it and snatched up the weapon, loading a silver quarrel with practiced speed.

Behind her, the burning ghast rolled on the ground, extinguishing most of the flames. It rose to its feet, charred and smoking, its eyes fixed on Dravka and Morgen with murderous rage. Its hind legs bunched, preparing to leap.

Lo raised the crossbow, drew a slow, even breath, and fired. The silver quarrel whistled through the air and struck the ghast directly in the eye. The creature howled, a sound that made Lo's teeth ache. It staggered backward, clawing at the bolt embedded in its skull, then retreated into the darkness beyond the firelight.

"Let's go!" Lo shouted, slinging the crossbow over her shoulder and grabbing her pack. "Before it comes back!"

Dravka finished cutting Morgen free, and the three women threw their packs on with frantic haste. The ghasts were already beginning to stir. Morgen strode to the fire and kicked one of the burning logs. It rolled to the creatures and set them alight.

"This way!" She pointed toward a gap in the trees. They plunged into the darkness, leaving the burning ghasts and bubbling pot behind. Lo threw a glance over her shoulder, catching a final glimpse of the clearing—the bones, the hooks, the flailing soulless. Then the forest swallowed them, and they ran as if the shadows themselves had grown teeth and claws.

Lo took the rear, crashing through dense underbrush. One hand gripped her crossbow, the other caught whipping branches that tried to smack her face. The hissing voices of the night-ghasts rose and fell, sometimes distant, then suddenly close enough to smell their fetid stench. There were more of them now—many more.

"Faster," Morgen hissed, a second before her foot caught on something and she flew face-first into the dirt. Lo tripped over her back, the crossbow flying into a tangle of ferns. Cursing the Quickening, she scrambled to her knees, hands groping through the darkness.

"Leave it," Dravka snarled, yanking her up by the arm. "They're gaining!"

Lo abandoned the search and ran, ignoring the sting of scratches and ache in her lungs. They scrambled up a long hill, then down into a gully where water soaked their boots. The swift current tugged at Lo's knees, nearly toppling her again.

"This way," Morgen commanded, veering along the stream. Her cool demeanor was back, as if being hunted by creatures from nightmare was merely an inconvenience. Lo envied the woman's composure. Her own heart hammered against her ribs like an animal trying to escape a cage.

"Have we lost them?" Dravka gasped.

No one answered. Who the hells knew? They were moving blind through unfamiliar territory. Lo chanced a glance over her shoulder and got her answer. Shapes moved in the darkness behind them—tall, emaciated figures with too-long limbs that bent at unnatural angles. Their eyes gleamed like droplets of oil catching firelight.

They abandoned the stream, clambering up another steep embankment. Lo's fingers dug into the soft earth as she hauled herself up. A rock came loose in her hand, and she slid back with a muffled cry. Morgen reached down, dragging her upward.

They crested the hill and plunged down the other side, weaving between ancient trees whose massive trunks might have offered hiding places if the night-ghasts weren't able to scent their prey. Lo's legs were aflame, her shirt soaked with sweat.

Then, between one labored breath and the next, the world went quiet, as if they'd fallen into a pool of deep, still water.

"The Silent Valley," Morgen mouthed.

The ravine before them was narrow, its walls rising steeply on either side. Gnarled trees clung to the slopes. Lo glanced again over her shoulder, unsettled by the oppressive hush. This time, the ghasts appeared to be gone — though it failed to reassure her.

The valley floor was strewn with rocks that threatened to turn an ankle with every step. Her boots slipped twice on patches of moss, and she had to catch herself against the rough wall. The stone felt unnaturally cold.

After what felt like hours but was likely only minutes, the canyon began to widen. The walls grew less steep, and trees thinned out. Morgen and Dravka quickened their pace, and Lo followed, still watching their backtrail.

They emerged onto a gently sloping hillside. The silence receded like a tide, sound returning in a flood that made her ears pop. A fresh breeze stirred tall grasses. Insects chirped. Their own harsh breathing rasped in the still air. There was still no sign of pursuit.

Without discussion, they collapsed on the ground. Lo lay on her back, staring up at the stars, waiting for her racing heart to slow. Her pack dug into her spine, but she couldn't summon the energy to take it off.

After several minutes, Dravka fumbled with her water skin and took a long drink. She passed it to Morgen, who accepted with a nod.

"Here," Morgen said, offering it to Lo.

Lo pushed herself to sitting and took the skin. The water was warm and tasted of leather, but she'd never had anything more refreshing. She drank deeply, then poured a small amount onto her sleeve, using the damp fabric to scrub at the sticky black residue coating her wrists—remnants of the thread-like tendrils the night-ghasts had used to bind her. It reeked of rot and old blood.

"Disgusting," she muttered.

"Be grateful," Morgen said. "If Dravka hadn't risked herself, we'd be stew by now."

"Soup," Lo corrected. "And about that..." She turned to Dravka, a dark suspicion rising. "I *am* grateful. But how did you manage to poison them?"

"Not poison." The girl's sweaty face broke into a grin. "I dropped a packet of sleeping potion into their nasty fucking pot."

Lo's heart sank. *Shit! Double shit!*

"Sleeping potion?" Morgen repeated, staring hard at Lo.

"Lady Caul gave it to me," she said casually. "For Jaskin. She wants him captured alive."

The lie came easily, as always. Neither Morgen nor Dravka knew about Bel, or that Lo's true mission was to find the amnesiac sun god. She planned to keep it that way.

Dravka stretched her long legs. "It took a few minutes to kick in. I was just starting to worry when those paunchy toads dropped like stones."

Lo wanted to scream and throw something, but she smiled instead. Hard to be mad under the circumstances, even if it complicated fucking *everything*.

"How did you know it was a sleeping potion?" she asked. The packet had been unlabeled, and she'd certainly never mentioned it.

"I didn't at first," Dravka replied. "I was going through our packs looking for weapons, and I accidentally spilled a little." She rubbed her nose ruefully. "Just the scent knocked me out cold. Lucky the ghasts didn't find me before I woke up."

She pulled out a strip of dried fruit and bit off a chunk. "Once I did, I followed your trail. When I saw that massive cookpot..." She shrugged. "It seemed worth a try."

"But how did you drop it in?" Lo asked.

"Well, I couldn't get anywhere near the pot. The gray pricks were standing around it, tasting their maggoty broth." A hint of pride crept into Dravka's voice. "So I climbed a tree and dropped it from a branch hanging *over* the pot."

Lo was impressed despite herself. The girl was resourceful.

"I kept the packet." Dravka pulled a crumpled wad of wax paper from her pocket. "If you want it back."

"Is there any left?" Lo asked hopefully.

Dravka shook her head. "I used it all, just to be safe."

"Let me see that," Morgen said, holding out her hand.

Triple shit. She probably knows what it is. And she isn't stupid.

Dravka passed it over. Morgen unfolded the paper packet, holding it at arm's length. She inhaled. Even from several paces away, Lo caught a whiff of mint, with an underlying bitterness.

"God's bane," Morgen said without hesitation. "A rare herb."

"Like, how rare?" Lo asked casually.

"Rare as hen's teeth." Her eyes narrowed, studying Lo with the look of someone who suspects deceit but lacks proof.

"I'll need more," Lo said. "Jaskin could be wearing the

Grand Menotte by now. If he is, we'll need to drug him." Another lie, but close enough to the truth to be convincing.

After a long moment, Morgen nodded grudgingly and tucked the paper in a pocket. "There's only one place we might find god's bane," she said. "The Night Bazaar of Loris. It's where all the rare herbs and potions of the darklands are traded."

"Loris," Lo repeated, committing the name to memory. "How far is it?"

"A few days' north." Morgen rose, brushing grass from her skirts. "The sooner we start walking, the sooner we arrive."

Lo groaned. She wanted to lie down and not move for a good while. But they were still near the ghasts' territory, and her mission had just been dealt a serious blow. Bel was somewhere in the vast Nightwood, but even if she found him, she had no way to bring him back without the god's bane.

They gathered their belongings, shouldering packs that seemed to have grown heavier during their brief rest. Lo felt the absence of her crossbow keenly. She'd have to acquire another weapon in Loris.

The forest fell behind them, the land opening up to gentle hills covered in black grass. It swayed like the surface of a whispering sea, beautiful in the starlight. As they set off across the strange prairie, Lo couldn't shake the feeling that their escape had been too fortuitous. Finding the entrance to the Silent Valley while running blindly, panicked and lost, stretched coincidence. Someone—or something—wanted her to take this path.

She sighed. Wicked schemes or not, there was no choice but to press on to Loris.

Sixteen

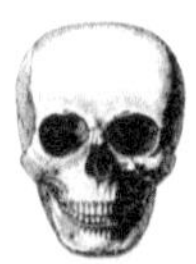

Wid Thorel squinted through the smoke hazing the plain below, his eyes gritty with exhaustion. To the west, a blood-red sun hung a hand's breadth above the horizon. Siege towers loomed like sentinels in the fiery twilight.

"We can't hold much longer," his son Den said beside him. "Not without more Bel's fire."

"I know it." Wid rubbed his sore shoulder, aching from days spent plying his bow. "But we haven't any left."

His youngest son Colm leaned on a merlon, face aged a decade in a fortnight. "They'll put us all to the sword when they break through."

"If," Wid said. "If they break through."

Den shook his head, despairing. "It's only a matter of time. The walls are crumbling, our supplies gone. The dead rise faster than we can burn them. And now these thrice-damned spirits..."

As if summoned, a spectre drifted past, no more than a shimmer in the air. Wid tensed, but it kept moving. They'd learned to avoid the phantoms after the first defenders brushed too close and fell senseless to the ground, lost in the spirit's anguish and bewilderment.

At first it had seemed they would prevail when they rained Bel's fire down upon the margraves' ships and soldiers. The viscous substance burned even through water, clinging and consuming. The screams of the dying haunted Wid still. But then the bodies stirred and rose, more than he had ever seen.

"Should've known better than to use the fire of an angry god," Colm muttered. "No good can come of that."

"It was all we had," Wid said. His limbs felt heavy as lead. He just hoped to die before Colm and Den.

"We hold until the end," he told his sons. "Take as many of the bastards with us as we can. For Prydwen."

"For Prydwen," they echoed. A vow and a dirge in the dying light.

Through the spyglass, Wid studied the distant tree line where the margraves' forces gathered, poised like a wolf about to leap for the throat. Their numbers had swelled with the arrival of the soldiers of the Westmarch, men who had spent years beating back the heathen raiders from across the sea.

"They planned this," Wid said bitterly. "Baited us into using up the fire, knowing we'd have naught left to face a true assault."

Den spat over the parapet. "Mortimer's a cunning bastard, I'll give him that."

A mournful horn shattered the taut silence, rising from the margraves' camp. Wid raised the glass again, searching for the banner with Mortimer's silver trefoil leaf fluttering in the smoky air. He found it at the center of the lines, and his breath caught as he spied six robed and hooded figures flanking the lord, skull masks leering beneath crimson cowls. They carried staffs of twisted black wood, and an aura of dread emanated from them even at this distance.

"What fresh devilry is this?" Wid muttered.

The horn sounded again, strident and commanding, and the assembled forces began to advance. Mortimer's cavalry took up positions at the rear, while scores of pikemen and archers marched forward in tight formations. Wid knew in his bones that this was no mere harassing foray. This was the final assault, the bloody crescendo they had dreaded for a fortnight.

"Make ready!" he shouted to the weary defenders ranged along the wall. Bows creaked as they nocked their last arrows. Catapults were winched back and pikes bristled over the guard towers flanking the city gates.

Wid sent a final plea to any god who might still be listening. *Let my arrows fly true. Let my arms stay strong until the end. And if I am to fall, let me take a hundred of these whoresons with me into the dark.*

He drew a deep steadying breath, sighting down the shaft of his arrow as the margraves' force surged forward.

Lucius hunched under his heavy cloak, the merciless sun sapping his strength. He rode in silence, ignoring the taunts of the man chained in the wagon beside him.

"You're an abomination," Arnulf spat. "A desperate, accursed thing. We must pray against you as against all enemies of our salvation, indeed, as we pray against the demon Kaethe herself!"

Lucius didn't rise to the bait. He had heard such words a thousand times before. They'd long since lost their sting. And yet... His hand tightened on the reins as a wave of thirst crashed over him. It would be so easy to drag Arnulf from the cart, to tear open his throat and drink deep...

He wrestled the impulse down. There would be killing enough before the day was done.

Brennos called a halt as the scouts returned, their horses lathered. "Mortimer's army is massing for the attack," one reported grimly. "At least three times our number."

Brennos digested that, his fingers lightly tracing the pock-marked scars on his face, as he often did when thoughtful or anxious. He turned to Lucius. "Can your power even those odds?"

"Perhaps. But I'll need to be close. More than half a league and I'll barely singe their banners." Lucius glanced at Arnulf, lowering his voice. "We could be riding into a trap."

Brennos followed his gaze. "You think he knows something?"

"Perhaps. I beg leave to question him. Privately."

Understanding passed between them. The Brennos of old would have balked, but that man was gone, forged into something sterner. He gave a curt nod. "Do it."

At his signal, two burly priests seized Arnulf and hauled him from the cart. They dragged him into the woods, Lucius following like a shadow. When they were deep in the trees, out of sight of the road, the priests threw him to the ground and left.

Arnulf lay bound on his side, trying for defiance, but Lucius could smell the fear seeping from his pores. "You think you can break me, creature?" His lip curled in a sneer. "Nothing suits you save for hypocrisy, flattery, and lies. But you will face the chains of Bel's divine judgment, bound in hell like all the devils!"

Lucius said nothing. He merely stared until Arnulf began to squirm.

"What do you want from me?" the priest asked hoarsely.

Lucius raised his hand and flames blossomed in his palm, white-hot and hungry. The memory of Justinian rose, unbidden. Justinian, who had held a similar flame to Brennos's face, demanding the location of the Grand Menotte.

Lucius firmed his resolve. This was different. Justinian's cruelty had been petty, selfish. What Lucius did, he did for the greater good. To save lives, not destroy them.

Or so he told himself, even as dark satisfaction unfurled in his chest at Arnulf's flinch. In truth, he yearned to see the zealot brought low. To make him suffer.

"I'll take your confession, *brother*," Lucius said softly. "In full."

Arnulf barked a laugh. "I have nothing to confess to you, abomination." He spat, narrowly missing Lucius's boot.

In a blur of speed, Lucius seized Arnulf's arm and wrenched the sleeve of his stinking goat-hair shirt up to his elbow. The flame flared as he pressed it to the exposed flesh. Arnulf screamed.

"Sir Mortimer!" he gasped. "He freed me from Blackwater Jail after Duc Marcel arrested me for heresy."

"And?"

Arnulf screamed again. "Mortimer paid me... Paid me to gather the priests, to raise an army!"

Well, that was quick.

"To what end?" Lucius demanded, relenting.

Arnulf panted, his brow coated with sweat. "At first, to overthrow Marcel. But the rebels beat him to it. So Mortimer...he commanded me to sow chaos instead. Harass the bitches of Kaethe. Raze villages. Then... then he would play the savior. Restore order." Arnulf slumped.

"What else?" Lucius hissed.

Arnulf lifted his face, a deeper fear in his eyes. "He hired necromancers from the north."

Lucius gave a low growl. They would be the linchpin, the most dangerous foes on the field.

"That's all I know," Arnulf said hoarsely. "Go on, kill me."

"Not yet." Lucius whistled and the priests returned. They seized Arnulf and hauled him back toward the wagon.

Lucius found Brennos and Gui beside the supply cart. He relayed Arnulf's intelligence, glossing over the way he extracted it.

"Necromancers," Brennos said in disgust. "No matter. If the defenders see our banners, they'll rally. We'll hit Mortimer from behind."

"And be cut down like wheat by his archers," Lucius cut in. "That open plain is a killing field. Your troops are still green. They'll never reach the gates."

Brennos touched the pits on his face, gaze distant. Frustration etched lines around his mouth. "Then what do you propose?"

Lucius's smile was a death's-head grin.

Sir Richart Mortimer reined up before the six northmen, their faces concealed behind leering skull masks. He had to crane his neck to meet their eyes; even dismounted, the necromancers towered head and shoulders above him. Mortimer tossed a pouch at their feet. It struck the earth with a hefty clink.

"Half the gold now. Half after the city falls."

The tallest northman stooped to collect the purse. His voice was muffled behind an ivory rictus. "And the slaves?"

"Take your pick," Mortimer said. "Once the defenders are broken, you may keep as many as you can herd."

It was all proceeding to plan. Mortimer had not risen to control the Westmarch by leaving the game to chance. Every contingency was accounted for, every possibility weighed and prepared for. It was how he had kept order on the frontier for thirty years. How he had weathered the whims of Vaszoly Marcel's brief, impetuous reign.

The Marcel dynasty's end had been a long time coming. Andrzej, for all his cunning, had been too deep in the Brotherhood's pocket. The priests set the duchy policy, and Andrzej danced to their tune. Then Vaszoly — the boy had no instinct for rule. No tact or skill at mollifying his subjects. Vicious, entitled, utterly lacking his father's political acumen.

In truth, Vaszoly's cruelty had done Mortimer a favor, stoking the fires of uprising. The rebels had cast down the Marcels with scarcely a nudge from Mortimer's agents. Now a new noble house would rise to fill the void.

Mortimer could already picture his own trefoil standard snapping from Prydwen's ramparts. Let the peasants play at governing themselves for a few more hours. By nightfall, they would kneel. The ones he spared, at least.

A scuffle broke out at the edge of the camp. Mortimer turned to see his men-at-arms hauling a pair of children between them. A boy and girl, ragged and filthy, their bare feet dragging furrows in the mud.

The men shoved them to their knees. The girl, who could not have been more than eight, glared up at Mortimer with defiant eyes. The boy twisted in the soldier's grip, trying to run.

One of the necromancers nodded approval. "As we discussed, milord, the working requires an offering. Innocents taken at the cusp of battle. The death magic has been...unreliable of late. This sacrifice will lend us the power."

Mortimer's mouth tightened. He thought of his granddaughter Melisant, who had just passed her eighth name day. For a moment, his resolve wavered.

No. This was necessary. The duchy had to be secured swiftly, and Mortimer refused to spend months starving out Prydwen. Not with chaos brewing in the south and rumors flying from Galatia. He needed to seize the capital and establish his rule. Then, and only then, could he determine what was happening beyond his borders.

"I leave the details in your hands," Mortimer said curtly. He swung up into the saddle of his courser. "But be quick about it. I want those walls breached within the hour."

As he turned his mount toward the knoll where his co-conspirators waited, he heard the rasp of blades being unsheathed. He did not look back. Some things, a man was better off not witnessing.

The last of Cavet's margraves stood their horses in a loose half-circle, watching Prydwen with avid eyes. They would squabble over the spoils later, Mortimer knew, but for now they deferred to him. His forces, his siege engines, his necromancers. The city would fall at his word.

And fall it would. The defenders had used up their tricks, expended their store of Bel's fire. Mortimer's army outnumbered them five to one. The great trebuchets were already trundling into position, their cranks and wheels creaking like the bones of giants.

No, the city would not hold long once the assault began in earnest. But Mortimer would leave nothing to chance. The ringleaders, those who had whipped the populace to rebellion —for them, he would devise special punishments.

Their wives, their brats, their doddering fathers, all would face the noose while the rebel lords watched. Then it would be their own turns, and Mortimer would make certain those deaths were not clean ones. Fear, he had learned, was the great lubricant of obedience. A few public examples, and the people of Prydwen would fall meekly into line.

All the pieces were in place now. All that remained was let the game play out.

Mortimer's skin tingled as the necromancers began their blood rites. The sky bruised to black, clouds boiling across the sun. Lightning forked earthward in jagged bolts. Wind lashed his cloak as the darkness grew thicker. It pooled around the base of the hill, tendrils snaking toward Prydwen's walls. His horse trembled, stamping uneasily. He mastered it with a sharp tug of the reins.

Giselher and the other skull-masked mages rode to him through the eldritch gloom. Mortimer watched their approach warily. Like rabid dogs, northmen could turn on the hand that fed them.

"It is done," Giselher rasped, his voice muffled behind the grinning rictus of bone. "The Nameless are summoned."

Mortimer swallowed bile, suddenly unsure if he had chosen rightly. He heard the margraves whispering behind him. Even they, hard men all, felt the weight of it.

"And when it's finished?" Mortimer asked. His mouth had gone dry as chalk. "When the city is ours? You will call them back?"

Giselher's face was hidden, but Mortimer heard the mocking laughter lacing his words. "For more gold and slaves... yes."

Seventeen

The legion of the Sons of Bel galloped along the eastern road, Brennos and Lucius at the vanguard. When they reached the outskirts of Prydwen, Lucius veered away from the main column to clear out Mortimer's rear scouts.

He melted into the trees, listening for the sounds of men. Soon enough, he caught the snap of a twig. In a flash, his blade slit the patrol's throats before they could utter a sound. Two others soon joined them.

The rest of the legion followed through the woods, breaking formation to ride in ragged lines while Lucius cleared the path ahead and ensured they would arrive unannounced.

At last they reached the plain's edge. The sky swirled an inky black. Six monstrous forms shambled toward the city walls, horned heads swaying, branch-like growths writhing on their backs. They towered as high as the ramparts, shadow made flesh.

"Bel have mercy," Brennos said softly.

Lucius scanned a distant hilltop, studying the pennants snapping in the wind. Mortimer's trefoil leaf, and others he cared nothing for. Then his gaze locked on six scarlet-robed figures. The necromancers. He itched to stop their foul hearts, but at this distance, he couldn't be certain of killing them. It might only alert them to the danger. Lucius cursed under his breath. He needed to get closer.

Lucius signaled to Bren, and they set their plan in motion. A Son of Bel rode forth carrying a white banner. He crossed the open ground and was met by one of Mortimer's men. They exchanged words and Bren's messenger rode back, cheeks flushed with excitement.

"He's carrying word that we're Arnulf's force, come to join the siege," the young priest said.

"Now we must hope Sir Mortimer believes the ruse," Brennos murmured.

Lucius turned to Arnulf, his gaze pitiless. "You will pretend to be the Strategos until we get close to Mortimer. If you're convincing, you'll live to see another day." He leaned in, his voice dropping to a whisper. "But if you betray us, I will burn your manhood off, followed by your ears and nose. And that's just the beginning. I know how to keep a man alive for a very long time."

Arnulf swallowed hard, his throat bobbing. "I understand."

They untied his hands so he could mount. His face was ashen, but he managed to keep his back straight in the saddle. Brennos flanked him, pretending to be his First Flame.

The rider from Mortimer's camp returned, his lip curling as he looked them over. "His Grace wants Arnulf. Which one of you is he?"

Arnulf lifted his chin, the old arrogance resurfacing. "I am the Strategos."

The knight looked unimpressed, his gaze flicking over Arnulf's dirty cloak and scraggly beard. "Come on, then."

Arnulf spurred his horse forward. Lucius and Bren followed close behind.

"Hold!" the knight snapped. "Who are they?"

"My First and Second Flames," Arnulf replied.

Lucius kept his eyes downcast. He felt the knight appraising them both, but after a long moment, the man seemed to decide that three priests of Bel posed no threat. With a grunt, he wheeled his horse around and trotted towards the distant command post.

Lucius tried to envision how this gambit would play out. Everything hinged on getting close to the necromancers — and on Arnulf not betraying them. One misstep and the game would be over.

As they drew nearer to the wall, a scene of devastation unfolded. The shadow creatures, their forms as inky as the darkening sky, tore at the gates with thick arms. The hinges shrieked as the monsters ripped them loose, along with chunks of the watchtowers, sending men tumbling to their deaths.

Lucius wrenched his gaze away. He focused instead on the command post ahead, where Sir Richart Mortimer stood scowling, his blue cloak snapping in the wind.

"You weren't supposed to come here," Mortimer shouted as they drew near, irritation sharpening his words. "That was not your task. I gave you explicit orders!"

In the pause that followed, Lucius drew on the well of fire within himself. "Answer him," he hissed.

"I thought you might need our shields, Your Grace," Arnulf called back.

Mortimer's icy eyes narrowed. "I don't pay you to think," he growled. "Now, take your fucking priests—"

"High Dead!" The warning cut the air. One of the necromancers stared straight at Lucius, skull-mask gleaming.

Before Lucius could react, Brennos drew his blade and charged. A necromancer flung a fistful of glittering dust, chanting in Tongues. Lucius locked his gaze on the man and stopped his heart with a thought. Blood dripped from beneath the mask as the northman crumpled.

Lucius wheeled to face the rest as Mortimer's knights thundered towards him. The margraves shouted, trying to control their rearing mounts. With a snarl, Lucius unleashed a blistering wall of flame. Through the smoke, he glimpsed a figure galloping away. Arnulf, seizing his chance to flee in the chaos. Lucius muttered a curse, but there was no time to give chase. Four of the northmen were dead or dying, yet one still stood.

He targeted the last necromancer. The man screamed as his blood began to boil, skin blackening and peeling away. As the corpse hit the ground, the towering shadow-creatures at the walls shuddered and collapsed, sending tremors through the earth.

They'd gotten very, very lucky, Lucius realized.The necromancers had bound the creatures to their own souls. Now the giants were unraveling.

Lucius raised his blade. "To me!" he bellowed.

At the signal, the legion rode forth from the trees. Lucius had taught them the *barritus*, an ancient war cry from his own time that began as a low murmuring and slowly rose to an ear-splitting roar. Mortimer's cavalry milled for a moment, confused at the attack from the rear, then wheeled to face them.

Lucius grabbed a screaming margrave and quickly drained him. Fresh blood surged through his veins. Sunlight pierced the smoke, but Lucius barely felt its sting. "For Prydwen!" he cried.

"For Prydwen! For Bel!" The legion took up the chant as they clashed against Mortimer's forces.

Brennos and the margrave of the Westmarch traded blows, their swords a whirl of deadly steel. Brennos fought like a mongoose, darting in with bared teeth, turning aside Mortimer's heavy strikes with a flick of his wrist. But the older man had experience on his side, and his blade slipped past Brennos's guard, scoring a line of crimson. Brennos stumbled and Mortimer pressed his advantage, hammering hard.

It was agony, watching the man he loved nearly lose his head, again and again. Lucius longed to intervene but knew Bren would not thank him for it.

Finish the bastard, Lucius silently urged. *You're quicker. Smarter.*

As if hearing his thoughts, Brennos rallied. He parried a vicious cut and lunged inside Mortimer's guard. Their blades locked, faces inches apart as they strained against each other. Then Brennos managed to twist free. His sword found the gap between shoulder and breastplate, angling deep. Mortimer looked astonished. Then he sank to his knees and toppled over.

Brennos yanked his blade free. "The Lord of the Westmarch is slain!" He held Mortimer's shield high.

The margraves' soldiers reeled back as Prydwen's surviving defenders streamed out through the shattered gates to trap them between the two forces.

"First Flame, to me!" Brennos shouted. Lucius galloped over and they threw themselves into the fray, fighting shoulder to shoulder. Men screamed and fell. Blood and mud churned beneath trampling feet. The sun beat down, the heat thick and oppressive. He glimpsed Castelio, staff spinning, alongside Gui and a knot of priests.

At last, Mortimer's battered army broke and fled. The rest threw down their arms in surrender. As the defenders raised a ragged cheer, Lucius scanned the field, his elation fading. The cost had been high. Around him, priests moved among the fallen, dispatching the dying and searching for their own wounded.

Castelio jogged over. "I can't find Lip. She was supposed to stay with the supply wagons, but they said she left." The words tumbled out in a rush, thickening his Boundary accent.

Lucius dismounted. "She can't have gone far. I'll help you search."

Cas swallowed hard and nodded. They split up, picking their way across the battlefield.

Carrion birds were already gathering. Lucius walked among the carnage, a leaden weight in his gut. Felippa was a clever girl, but so very small. If she'd been caught up in the fighting...

Then a flash of fair hair caught his eye. He hurried over to find her kneeling beside one of the margraves' conscripts. This was no hardened soldier of the Westmarch. The boy looked about fifteen and he was mortally wounded, Lucius could see that right away. Felippa pressed something into the dying boy's hand and curled his fingers around it. Bowing her head, she shut her eyes as if in prayer.

Lucius hesitated. Then he called her name. Felippa's head snapped up. Her face was streaked with mud, her braid coming unraveled.

"I keep trying but it won't work," she said angrily. "Why won't it work?"

Lucius knelt beside her. "What won't work?"

She gently opened the boy's fingers, revealing a silver disk in his palm. It was engraved with a sun on one side and a moon on the other. "It's supposed to be a talisman of healing," she said. "It saved me from some poison berries. And it saved Cas once, too, when he had an arrow in his lung."

Lucius stared at the talisman. "The bridge at Nox," he said softly. "I was there. How did you come by this?"

"Delilah gave it to me. She said she didn't need it anymore."

"Ah." Lucius picked it up, turning it over in his fingers. "I do know something about talismans. I am... I *was* of the Vatra daēva clan. This work is ours."

Hope kindled in Felippa's blue eyes. "Then you can make it heal him!"

Lucius regretfully shook his head. "Healing is beyond my abilities. My magic only kills."

She bit her lip. "Most of them will die anyway. What harm can it do to try?"

If she had tried to bully or shame him, Lucius would have bristled. But he was free now. Free to make his own choices — and mistakes.

"Very well." He curled his fingers around the talisman, coaxing threads of power into the silver disk. Earth and water. Fire and clean salt wind from the Bay of Istria. The metal warmed against his palm. He laced his fingers with the dying boy's, the talisman pressed between them.

The boy gasped, back arching. For a terrible moment, Lucius thought he'd miscalculated. Used too much power. Then the young soldier blinked in shock, touching the blood-soaked gash in his tunic with trembling fingers.

"Let me see," Felippa said briskly. When she lifted the garment, the skin beneath bore a puckered scar.

Lucius glanced around. No one was paying them any attention. "Go back to your village," he urged. "Now, while you still can."

The boy scooted away, fear and awe on his face. He scrambled to his feet and stumbled toward the trees. After a minute, his gait steadied and he broke into a flat-out run.

Lucius had grown accustomed to his power only serving death and pain. To use it in another way… It cracked something open inside him, like a key turning in a rusty lock.

Felippa grinned as if she'd expected no less. Lucius laughed. Rising to his feet, he held out a hand. "Come. Let us see how many we can save together."

EIGHTEEN

The light from Orlaith's candle flickered across damp stone walls as she hurried through the passageway deep beneath Redvayne manor. Cobwebs tickled her face and dust motes danced in the wavering flame. How many times had she come this way with Lucius, back when he served as her loyal advisor? Before he betrayed her darkest secrets to Enrigo. Filled her son's head with vile lies.

One day I will find you, Lucius. And I will take from you what you have taken from me.

At last, she reached the heavy iron-bound door, its surface pitted with age, and slid the key into the lock. She shouldered it open, the hinges groaning in protest. Orlaith glanced back the way she had come, straining to listen over the frantic thudding of her heart. Was that a footstep in the distance? No, just the scurrying of rats.

Beatriu would still be at her daily prayers to Kaethe. Safe, for a time. But she could not tarry long. Sometimes the girl stayed away all day, sometimes only for a few hours.

Orlaith crossed the empty wine cellar, her slippered feet

silent on the flagstones. She paused before the inner door, fingers tightening on the iron key.

"My love?" Her voice seemed small in the darkness. "It's me."

From within came the familiar clinking of chains. She unlocked the door and eased it open. In the weak candlelight, she could make out the hunched figure shackled to the far wall.

Orlaith approached slowly. Forced herself to smile as she met his dull, clouded eyes. "You look well, dear husband. Handsome as ever."

With effort, and a bit of squinting, she could pretend not to see the gray skin pulled taut over bone. The brittle wisps of hair still clinging to his leathery scalp. In her mind, Robert was whole and hale, with a thick black beard and barrel chest, boisterous laughter and unshakeable confidence. Funny, how little Enrigo took after his father.

Pain lanced through her heart. Her beautiful boy, cut down on the cusp of manhood. Lucius, in his cruelty, had denied her plea to bring Enrigo back, as he had Robert. Although, looking at her husband now… Perhaps it was for the best.

Orlaith's words poured out in a torrent, all the pent-up anguish and rage. She told Robert of the ill-fated journey to Galatia to woo the young Damiata. Beatriu's growing madness, but also her determination to march on the Moon Courts.

"She means to crush our enemies, my love. To grind them into dust beneath her heel." Orlaith paced the cramped cell, just beyond the reach of Robert's chains. "And I shall be at her side when she does. I will see the Courtenays brought low, and that fork-tongued traitor Nathan Ouvrard. They will pay for what they did to us."

Robert's eyes gleamed in the guttering candlelight. Did he understand her words? Without Lucius to translate them into the guttural language of Tongues, she couldn't be certain. But in her heart, she felt he must. Surely he knew she would never rest until she had avenged him.

Orlaith sagged against the wall. Sharing her woes aloud left her feeling scraped raw inside, but lighter too. As if a weight had fallen from her shoulders...

Without warning, Robert lunged forward. Orlaith staggered back with a startled cry. The iron links snapped taut, and he gnashed his black teeth, growling something in the gabbling pidgin of the dead.

"I—I love you too, my darling." Her voice quavered only a little. "I'll return to you soon. I swear it."

She all but fled the room, fumbling with the key in the lock. But as she hurried back through the underground passages, she carefully revised the encounter to a joyful reunion. Robert had reacted to her. He understood. Everything would be all right now.

In her mind's eye, she could already see it. The mortifex army sweeping into Mystral, the Courtenays dragged before her in chains. They would grovel at her feet, begging for mercy that would not come.

In this fantasy, it was Orlaith who wore the Grand Menotte. She pictured Caul and Chaos's faces, the dawning horror as she pronounced their doom. Cleansed in flame, along with all the unnatural creatures of the Moon Courts. A smile, the first in many days, touched her lips at the thought.

She took the cramped stairs upward two at a time, almost giddy with renewed purpose. As she stepped through the nondescript door into the manor proper, Orlaith faltered. One of her nobles, Lady Voisin, was striding down the gallery, yellow hair piled in an elaborate updo strung with pearls. When she saw Orlaith, she halted, eyes flashing.

"You've brought the House of Redvayne to ruin," Voisin

spat. "The heir dead, your mortifex gone. And now I am expected to bend my knee to a child? A *Galatian*, no less? It's outrageous!"

At first, Orlaith had feared that Lady Voisin knew about Robert. But she was the same brainless twit she'd always been. When Orlaith had ruled the duchy, Voisin had sucked up to her, while privately whispering venom behind her back. She'd only found her courage now that she had nothing to lose.

Orlaith didn't bother defending herself. What was there to say?

"You're a disgrace," Lady Voisin continued. "Your scheming has destroyed us all!" Her contemptuous gaze raked Orlaith up and down. "Just look at you. As filthy as a scullery." With a last glare of disgust, she brushed past, silk skirts swishing.

Something snapped. It was like another person seized control of Orlaith's body, propelling her forward. Three swift strides and she caught up to Lady Voisin.

The woman heard her coming. She half turned as the heavy brass candlestick came crashing down on her perfectly coiffed head. There was an audible crack. Voisin dropped like a sack of barley. Orlaith knelt and struck her again and again, until the expensive silk dress was soaked crimson and Voisin's face was a ruin.

Breathing hard, Orlaith rocked back on her haunches. She carefully set the candlestick down and smoothed a lock of hair from her face.

She had never killed anyone with her own hands before. It was easier than she'd expected.

Orlaith looked around, but the gallery was empty. All the servants had fled days ago. Still, if Lady Voisin had been wandering about, there could be others.

Moving swiftly, she seized her under the arms. The woman

was heavier than she looked. A dead weight. Orlaith bit back a giggle. She dragged Voisin through the door to the underground warren. Her limp head bumped each stair on the way down.

At the bottom, Orlaith rolled the body into a dark corner. She would attend to it later. First she needed to clean up the evidence.

In the kitchens, she splashed water on her face, rinsing away the speckles of blood. Then she found a bucket, rags, and a stiff-bristled brush. Lugged it all back to the gallery. As Orlaith attacked the stain, she noticed that she no longer had the soft hands of a lady. Her nails were ragged, her knuckles rough and red from hours submerged in a scalding washtub, scrubbing Beatriu's smallclothes.

I am strong. Stronger than they ever suspected.

The flagstones were nearly clean when rapid footsteps rang behind her. She looked up to see Janus, the stern-faced captain of Beatriu's knights, striding down the hall, his white cloak billowing.

She climbed to her feet, praying he would not look down and notice the bucket brimming with bloody water. It was lucky she still wore mourning black. The bombazine fabric hid the stains.

"Lady Redvayne." Janus halted before her. "Her Majesty requires your presence."

Orlaith's heart leapt to her throat. "Of course." She raised her chin. As Beatriu's lady-in-waiting, she still had noble rank. "I shall come presently."

His eyes, dark and penetrating with tiny flames writhing at the center, nailed her in place. "You shall come *now*."

She swallowed. "Very well." Abandoning the bucket where it sat, she scurried after him, half running to match his long strides.

Janus led her to the audience chamber where she used to hold court and threw open the oaken doors. Beatriu sat upon the Redvayne throne, mortifex knights arrayed around her. The undead soldiers stood unnaturally still, hands resting upon their bonewood swords.

Beatriu had stripped the place of all adornments, every stitch of tapestry. The only light came from the blazing hearth, which cast orange shadows across the child's face. A muscle beneath her left eye fluttered and twitched.

Did she know about Voisin? Orlaith's legs buckled, but she covered it with a deep curtsey, trying to master her racing heart. When she dared to look up, Beatriu beckoned impatiently. "Attend me."

Orlaith hurried forward, climbing the steps of the dais to kneel beside the throne. She clasped her fingers to steady their trembling, the cold iron of the petit menotte biting into her wrist.

"Bring in the sisters," Beatriu commanded.

Janus departed with a bow. Moments later, he escorted five bedraggled nuns into the audience chamber. Beatriu's expression softened. "Tell us what has befallen you, daughters of Kaethe."

One stepped forward, nervously smoothing her robe. "Your Majesty, we walked from Cavet. A man who called himself Brother Arnulf came to the convent in Lindow, along with about twenty Sons of Bel." She paused to compose herself and brush away an angry tear. "They put our convent to the torch. Cut down those who tried to flee." She glanced at the rest, who nodded. "We alone escaped."

"I have heard the same tale from others, Your Majesty," Janus added grimly. "More than one convent has burned."

Beatriu's face darkened like a gathering tempest. She gripped the arms of the throne, fingers whitening. "You have endured much, sisters. Go now to the convent in Aquitan. You will be safe there."

"Kaethe's blessings upon you." The nuns bowed and departed, murmuring prayers.

Orlaith watched them go, unease stirring. Beatriu had spent most of the last week sequestered inside Aquitan's towering statue of Kaethe, beseeching the goddess for an end to the rising dead. It was an unwelcome development.

Beatriu brooded in silence for long minutes, only the twitch of her eye betraying her agitation. Orlaith waited, absently twisting the petite menotte round and round her wrist until the skin was raw.

At last, the empress spoke. "Kaethe's anger is plain. Her will has been made known through the mouths of her daughters. The Sons of Bel have brought this plague upon us." She locked eyes with Janus. "You will fly west and send these killers to face Kaethe's judgment. Leave none alive." Her tiny fist banged the arm of the throne, rage flushing her cheeks. "Not one, do you hear!"

Orlaith bit her tongue until she tasted blood. Her vengeance could not be delayed yet again. Not when it was so close! She forced herself to draw a calming breath. *I must appear obedient. Sensible.*

"Your Majesty," she ventured. "What of the conquest of the Moon Courts? Surely that is our most pressing concern—"

Beatriu cut her off with a sharp gesture. "It must wait. Kaethe demands retribution." A flurry of twitches spasmed her left eye. "I want the priests dead to a man. Only then will the goddess open her gates again."

Nineteen

Felippa stood atop the ramparts of Bel Mara monastery, the salt breeze whipping her flaxen hair. Cas leaned against the parapet beside her, fingers tapping a restless rhythm on the weathered stone. The causeway below snaked across glittering water to the docks of Prydwen, now bustling with activity as ships filled the bay.

"Look at all those cutters," Cas said, shading his eyes. "Must be from the Western Isles, aye? Bringing in goods now the siege is broken."

"About time," Felippa said. "Those people suffered under the Marcels for centuries. They're glad to help the new council, I expect."

Cas grunted agreement. Across the bay, the ringing of hammers carried across the calm water from the Shambles, where stilt homes were rising above the marsh.

"They're rebuilding fast," Felippa observed.

"From what I heard, the council gave the captured soldiers a choice. Rot in Blackwater or swear fealty and work off their debt. With the margraves dead, they didn't have to think too hard."

Satisfaction bloomed in Felippa's chest as she watched the ant-like figures laboring in the distant ruins. Prydwen would rise anew, this time led not just by men drunk on power but wise women too. A more just rule.

"Still no word of Lo?" Felippa asked.

"Nothing. I've asked everywhere." Cas stared out to sea, his jaw tight.

Lo loved her brother, Felippa felt sure of it. If she'd broken her word, something was wrong. But Cas didn't need to hear that. He already knew it.

"We'll find her," Felippa said, "just like we found Da and Teo."

Cas didn't turn, but after a long moment, he covered her hand with his own. "Faith, right?" His lips twisted wryly. "I'm working on it, Lip."

He still forgot sometimes, but she didn't correct him. Somehow the old nickname didn't bother her anymore.

A priest in mail and kilt emerged from the archway. He looked at Felippa. "The Strategos requests your counsel."

She and Cas exchanged a curious glance before following him into the temple. He led them up a cramped spiral staircase, narrow steps worn smooth by centuries of use. Felippa's short legs burned as they climbed ever higher. Finally, they entered a round tower facing south above the city.

Brennos Fearhgal sat at a plain table littered with papers, his handsome features pensive. Lucius lounged in the shadows of a broad windowsill, where doves pecked at seed. He smiled when he saw them and Felippa was struck by how human he looked. How *alive*. A far cry from Orlaith Redvayne's terrifying servant.

"Any sign of Arnulf?" Cas asked.

Lucius's smile faded. "No. I fear he got away."

"We still have much to be glad for," Brennos said. "The main market has reopened. A civil constabulary is dealing with the criminal gangs." He cleared his throat. "But there is still the matter of..."

"The dead," Cas finished.

Brennos nodded. "Most have faded to spirit. They hide in the shadows. Only the canals and bright sunlight keep them from overrunning the city." He leaned forward. "You served as a Quietus. Do you know why Kaethe has turned her face from us?"

Her brother met Bren's imploring gaze. "I've no idea. I wish I did."

Brennos sat back, disappointed. Silence descended, broken only by the cooing from the dovecote in the rafters. "It is our main problem," he said at last. "And it's only getting worse."

Lucius shifted. "With all due respect, you are wrong."

His bluntness didn't appear to faze Brennos, who merely raised an eyebrow as if accustomed to such candor.

"The Grand Menotte," Lucius said gravely. "That is your biggest problem, even if you cannot see it yet."

Brennos exhaled wearily, a hand coming up to massage the scars on his cheeks. "I do not make light of it, but we don't even know who has the cursed thing. If anyone does at all."

Lucius's lips compressed into a line. "I was *there.* I saw the nine-pointed star, the blood racing to complete its pattern. The talisman has been claimed. If you had witnessed it yourself, you would not doubt me."

Brennos lifted a placating hand. "Peace, I never said I doubted you." He frowned, considering. "I could send a rider to Vellio to learn what transpired. We should have word within a fortnight."

Felippa found herself speaking up. "Strategos, there is a

way to know right now." Cas turned to stare at her. She ignored him. "Summon the mortifex Justinian. He must be serving whoever it is. Just ask him."

Cas muttered an oath. Brennos frowned. But Lucius... a glint of satisfaction lit his emerald eyes, as if her suggestion was precisely what he'd hoped for. With a flash of insight, she realized this was why he'd requested her presence in the first place. For some reason, Lucius had wanted this idea to come from her, not him.

She forged ahead. "I've spoken with Justinian. All he wants is to be free, to cross the Cold Sea. But the talisman binds him here. He might even help you defeat his new master, whoever it may be."

Again, Brennos's fingers went to the pitted scars on his face. His gaze turned distant. "The council would never sanction such a thing. Justinian burned the Shambles. He slaughtered countless innocents when he served the Duc. The people despise him nearly as much as they do Marcel."

"Which is why the council needn't know," Lucius argued. "We do it here, quietly. He will be trapped inside the star as surely as an iron cage. If he proves difficult, he can be banished with a word."

"I'll call him myself, if you like," Felippa offered, rather amazed at her own bravado.

This was the creature who had fed on her life force, leaving her body weak and stunted. Who, minutes before that, had probably killed her mother.

Cas tensed. She braced for a vehement objection, but to her complete and utter shock, he gave a slow nod. "My sister is tougher than you can imagine. Let her try."

It was Lucius who protested. "I've known Justinian since he was a living man. We were close then. I'm the one who should question him."

Felippa had the feeling he was wrong, but she'd said her piece. Let the Strategos decide.

Brennos looked deeply unhappy. At last he sighed. "Whatever you claim, I think he is dangerous. But I agree it's the fastest way to learn the truth and put this argument to rest. So I will do it myself." A humorless smile touched his lips. "Surely this will be the first time in history that Kaethe's sigil is drawn in Bel's temple."

Lucius handed him a dagger hilt-first. The blade gleamed in the light slanting through the windows as Brennos drew it across his palm. Without a word, Cas unsheathed his own knife and did the same. Together they knelt and drew a bloody nine-pointed star on the stone floor.

When it was done, Brennos turned to Felippa and Cas. "Conceal yourselves. Do not interfere, no matter what occurs. Understood?"

They nodded and withdrew to the staircase. *We're spying, aye?* Cas mouthed. She nodded nervously. They peered around the curving wall into the tower chamber. Brennos stood just outside the star, Lucius at his side.

"Let me question him alone," Lucius urged. "He will respond better to me."

Brennos gave a short nod. His hand half-rose to touch his scars, but he lowered it with an effort. "I summon you, Justinian!" he snapped.

Sudden darkness fell. Crackling frost crept across the flagstones. Felippa shuddered, tugging her cloak tighter. Beside her, Cas went very still.

Then, a flickering glow slowly illuminated the room. A man stood in the center of the star. He looked nothing like the monster she had last seen at the mortifex citadel in the Cold Sea. HIs hair was dark and thick. The deathly pallor of his skin had warmed to a living hue. He wore a snow-white tabard with

Kaethe's sign embroidered on the breast in scarlet thread, a match to the star that bound him.

"Captain," Lucius said calmly. "It has been some time."

Justinian's head snapped up. His gaze swept the room, taking in the round walls, the ladder to the dovecote. "I know this place," he said. "I came here once before. The monastery of Bel Mara. It was the old archivist's chamber." Justinian turned to Lucius, his expression hardening. "You cannot help me now. It is too late for that."

"I'm sorry for your bondage," Lucius said. "Whom do you serve?"

Justinian gave a harsh laugh. "You speak as if you have authority, but I know better. A mortifex cannot summon another mortifex. Only the living enjoy that power." His eyes narrowed. "So I ask you, Claudius, whom do *you* serve?"

Silence stretched between them, taut as a bowstring. Then a figure detached from the shadows across the room. Brennos stepped forward.

Justinian's lip curled. "The Red Rogue. I see my handiwork remains." He studied the burns marring Brennos's face with a twisted grin.

"Enough," Lucius growled. "Just listen to me. Help us, and I will find a way to release you."

Justinian shook his head, a mocking smile still playing about his mouth. "You have nothing to offer me. But if you let me out…" The grin widened. "Perhaps then we can bargain."

Brennos looked worried, Lucius frustrated.

I knew he was wrong. Felippa tugged free of her brother's restraining hand and stepped out from the staircase. At the sight of her, Justinian's mouth dropped open, astonishment writ across his face. "Little one?" he rasped.

Felippa approached the star, hoping she didn't look as scared as she felt. He was still the thing of her nightmares. "On my honor, they mean you no harm. We only want to know what we're up against."

Justinian stared at her, still wrong-footed. She realized he wore the raiment of Kaethe. A uniform.

"Someone has bonded you," Felippa said. "We'll know who it is soon enough. Won't you just tell us? I swear to let you go."

Blue flames licked the inside of the star. She thought he would refuse again, but he finally gave a brusque nod. "It is no secret. I serve Beatriu Do Santillan, empress of Aveline. She means to bring the Moon Courts under her banner. Even now, messengers ride to the eastern duchies, informing them of her intentions."

Beatriu? The child ruler of Galatia? Felippa covered her shock. "Thank you," she said. "One more thing. This plague of risen dead. Do you know what's causing it?"

Justinian scowled and jerked his chin at Brennos. "His fucking priests have been attacking convents and assaulting the nuns of Kaethe."

"That was *not* my men," Brennos said firmly. "I condemn their actions in the strongest terms. There was a deranged brother called Arnulf. He falsely named himself Strategos. But he is..." A pause. "Gone now."

"I know the name, though it matters not. One dead priest won't satisfy my mistress. The blood of Bel's children will darken this land in a red tide." The nine-pointed star began to bubble as his agitation mounted. "I am a wolf nipping at your heels," Justinian snarled, "and I will not stop until every last one of you is ash in the wind—"

A sudden scream tore from his throat. Sunlight pierced the gloom, falling directly across the mortifex's face, raising blisters on his skin. He threw up an arm, but the cloth of his tunic started to smoke. "Please..." he gasped.

Without thinking, Felippa stepped forward, her hand outstretched. "I banish you, Justinian!"

The star flared once, blindingly bright. When the spots cleared from her vision, he was gone. Only the blackened stone and the lingering reek of burned blood remained.

"Who told you to do that?" Lucius rounded on her, eyes blazing. "I had more questions for him!"

Felippa met his furious gaze. She could still hear Justinian's screams ringing in her ears. "No one deserves to suffer so. Not even him."

"You have no idea what he deserves," Lucius spat. "If Bel sought to punish him, it is no business of ours to intervene."

"Ah," Cas said, "so now you're a true believer, are you?"

Lucius shot him a venomous glare.

Felippa turned her back, cheeks flaming, and sketched a bow in Brennos's direction. "Strategos, I beg your leave."

He nodded, looking troubled. "Of course. Go in peace, both of you."

Cas fell into step beside her as they descended the narrow staircase. She could feel the weight of her brother's gaze but he held his tongue until they reached the foot of the tower.

"Lip..." He touched her shoulder gently. "I hate Justinian, but you did the right thing. Lucius spoke out of turn. I think he's more angry at himself than you."

She managed a wan smile. "Beatriu? She's even younger than me and commanding a mortifex army. *Fecking bleeding shit-hells.*"

Cas rubbed his head. "That sums it up."

LUCIUS PACED THE TOWER CHAMBER, sending the agitated doves fluttering into the rafters.

"Beatriu's forces will meet resistance in the Moon Courts," he said. "That is where you must march."

Brennos shook his head. "I will not leave Prydwen. Not when there is so much yet to be done. The city needs me."

Lucius halted mid-stride. "And after she conquers the east, how long do you think Prydwen will stand against her? A month? A week?"

"They held out against the margraves—"

"This is different!" Frustration sharpened Lucius's voice. He reined in his temper with effort. "You cannot fight this war alone. You will need allies."

"Allies." Brennos's mouth twisted around the word. "You mean necromancers."

"They are not slavers like the northmen," Lucius replied. "And you do not need to approve of their magic. All that matters is that Chaos and Caul Courtenay will fight." He hesitated. "Nathan Ouvrard, I do not trust. The man has no loyalty beyond his own skin. But Duc Scalici and the others—"

"Are still practitioners of the dark arts. I will not stand with them."

"Even if it means saving your precious city?"

"This is not only about Prydwen!" Brennos slammed a palm on the desk, his composure finally shattering. "All my life, I have dreamed of building something better. A place where people are judged by their deeds, not their blood. Where money and titles hold no sway. I fought for that dream, bled for it. I took up the mask of the Red Rogue and I brought the Marcels to their knees.

"And now, when that dream is finally within reach, you want me to abandon it? To turn my back on everything I believe in and march across not one but *two* hostile duchies to ally with dark wizards who worship the Lady of Shadows!"

"I only ask that you listen to reason," Lucius said tightly. "I have walked this road before, and I know where it ends. Your intentions are good, but Beatriu is hungry. Ambitious. She will come west eventually, and when she does, there will be no one left to aid you."

Lucius hardly noticed that the air around him shimmered dangerously, that the temperature in the tower was rising. "If your people were vassals under the Marcels, I can promise you, Beatriu will be far worse. Even now, the Grand Menotte is surely driving her mad, just as it did to Jaskin Cazal. You must think beyond your own borders!"

The papers on the desk erupted into flame. Lucius flinched back, startled, then drew the fire into himself with a sharp gesture. In an instant, his anger seeped away. He stood motionless, watching the wisps of ash drift out the window.

"Apologies, Strategos." His voice sounded cold. Distant. "I am losing control."

Bren drew a deep breath. "Explain."

"The Redvayne menotte... it linked me to the living world. Now that it's gone, my soul is... I don't know. Fading, I think." His gaze fell on the scorched star.

Brennos took a step closer. "You used your power to heal. You saved many lives after the battle."

"Not I." Lucius shook his head. "The talisman did that. I tortured Arnulf and enjoyed it. Far too much." He passed a weary hand over his face. "I am becoming like Justinian. A shell with no heart."

"You will never be like him." Brennos's warm hand fell on his shoulder. "Not in a thousand years."

Their eyes met and held. Brennos leaned in, capturing Lucius's mouth with his own. The kiss was searing. "First Flame," he murmured. "I can feel your heat beating."

"Stolen life," Lucius confessed, as his pulse quickened further.

"From who?"

"One of the margraves."

Brennos grinned. "Then let us savor this gift while it lasts."

CAS FOUND Gui drilling young priests in a dusty yard below the main temple. Sunlight glinted off pikes as the men moved through their paces, boots stamping in unison. They were no longer the hungry, miserable band Cas had first encountered at the camp by the Dolcetto. They were disciplined now, proud. A true fighting force.

Gui caught sight of him and called a halt. He dismissed the men and limped over, snow white hair stark against his brown skin. "You look like you have something on your mind."

"Aye." Cas fell into step beside Gui as they walked through a grove of orange trees. The sweet scent of blossoms hung in the air. "There's a restlessness in me, telling me I don't belong here."

Gui shot him a sidelong look. "And where do you belong?"

"I'm not sure." Cas kicked at a pebble, sending it skittering. The world was crumbling around their ears and he had no notion what to do about it. "Somewhere else. Not Prydwen."

"Have you told your father?"

"I have. He and Teo want to stay, move back into the city. It's their home now." Cas shrugged. "I figure Felippa will do the same."

But he couldn't. There was a woman he loved, and he needed to find her. The yearning was a constant ache in his chest.

"Brennos won't stop you?"

"He said I'm free to go. Though he did ask me to carry some letters to Nyons."

Gui's eyes sharpened. "You know what they contain?"

Cas shook his head. "The Strategos didn't say. Wasn't my place to ask."

"Well, I'm mighty curious, but I'd never ask you to break a confidence."

They reached the edge of the grove. Gui enfolded him in a tight embrace, one broad hand cradling the back of Cas's head like he was a child again. "May you find what you seek. I hope better times lie ahead for us all."

Cas returned the hug fiercely. "Aye. Better times."

They spoke for a while more. Roalt's widow, Sarra, had chosen to remain in Prydwen as well, which Gui seemed pleased about. Then Cas returned to his small sleeping cell, the stone walls bare save for a laurel wreath hanging above the cot. He packed his few belongings — a change of clothes, a whetstone, flint and tinder, some provisions. Last was the staff leaning in the corner. The wood was smooth in his grip, the runes quiet as always. He snorted. It would be good for walking, at least.

"Leaving, are you?"

Cas turned to find Felippa framed in the doorway, hands on her hips and an accusing look on her elfin face. "Aye. I was about to look for you."

She lifted her chin. "No need. I'm coming with you."

"What? No. It's too dangerous. And you're needed here—"

"You need me more." She stepped closer, blue eyes fierce. "I won't let you go alone, Cas."

"I am a grown man," he reminded her gently.

She arched a brow. "One in dire need of my charming company."

He opened his mouth to argue, then shut it. They'd grown close these past weeks, and in truth, he'd be glad to have her along. It was dangerous everywhere. Who's to say she'd be safer in Prydwen? Besides which, perhaps her optimism would keep his demons at bay.

"Fine," he said. "But it'll be close quarters on the ship. And I snore."

Felippa waved a hand. "I've listened to it for years."

Cas patted his coat pocket to make sure the messages were there. "Better go tell Da."

She smirked. "I already did."

A laugh escaped him. "I suppose I shouldn't be surprised. You could probably take on Beatriu's whole army of mortifexes single-handed."

She grinned. Then her smile gentled. "It'll be all right, Cas. We'll find her."

He could only nod, throat thick.

"Where are we going anyway?" she asked.

"Gilvra," he said. "It's a port city in Alessia. From there we head north to Mystral to deliver a letter to the Courtenays."

Her eyes widened. "Mystral? Will I see centaurs?"

Cas absently rubbed the old arrow wound on his chest. "Probably."

Felippa grinned.

"But it'll be a long voyage," he added. "We're stopping at Yael, and maybe some other ports, too."

"I don't mind." Her grin widened. "Ooooh, how about loup garou? I've always wanted to meet one of those..."

THEY CROSSED the causeway on foot, packs slung over their shoulders. The harbor was crowded with ships. Gulls wheeled overhead, raucous cries filling the air. After some searching, they located their vessel, a swift merchant cutter called the

Merry Maid. Brennos had pulled some strings with the captain, a barrel-chested man with a salt-and-pepper beard.

"I was told to expect a single passenger," he said, frowning slightly.

"This is my sister," Cas said. "We can share a berth. I hope it isn't a problem."

His weathered face creased in a smile. "She doesn't look like she eats more than a sparrow. I suppose it won't matter."

Felippa gave a strained smile in return, though Cas knew such offhand comments annoyed her.

"We'll be sailing with the tide," the captain continued. "I'll show you to your cabin."

It was small and dim, with a narrow bunk and a porthole. The only other furnishing was a wooden sea chest. Cas stowed their packs and they went back up on deck for some fresh air. The city walls rose in the distance, a patchwork of scorched stone and new timber. Smoke curled from cookfires in the Shambles. Atop the highest tower of the ducal palace, where the cockatrice of the Marcels once flew, a plain scarlet banner fluttered in the breeze.

"Do you think we'll come back?" Felippa asked. "See Teo and Da again?"

He was about to say, *Of course we will*. But the time for lying was past. "I don't know." Cas draped an arm around her narrow shoulders. "I hope so."

She leaned into him, and together they watched Prydwen dwindle to a smudge on the horizon as the *Merry Maid* carried them towards the long, deep swells of the open ocean.

Twenty

Jaskin's leg burned like a brand as he dragged himself through the narrow, twisting streets of Loris. Snowflakes swirled in the pools of lamplight, as blurry as his vision. He squinted at the signs above the crooked doorways, lettering in the strange angular script of the far east.

A bout of dizziness buckled his knees. He caught himself on his walking stick with a grunt of pain. The devil's snare coursed like black fire through his veins. Without the antidote, he was done for. He judged that he had only a few hours left before it reached his heart.

Jaskin glanced over his shoulder, scanning the shadows. Had that flicker of movement been a trick of the fever? Or was Nabu-bal-idinna following?

Jaskin had abandoned his companion at their last campsite, sneaking away as Nabu tossed in his sleep, rambling about Kaethe and his "fire children." Whatever the man's true nature, he wasn't human. Jaskin's singed coat attested to that. When flames had erupted from Nabu's mouth at the Obsidian Spires, it was the last straw. Let Kaethe's consort fend for himself.

Jaskin grimaced. A shame. If he hadn't been grievously injured, he might have found a way to use Nabu's power. The fool seemed ignorant of it except when he lost his temper. Perhaps Jaskin could still use him, eventually. Once he was healed of this damnable wound.

Gritting his teeth, Jaskin limped on. The crooked little houses hunched close as if whispering secrets. Frost-rimed windows winked like watchful eyes.

A shudder of dread rippled through Jaskin's bony frame as he considered his ninth and final death. He'd be trapped forever in Kaethe's house, just as he had been in the mirror. Anything was better than that fate.

Rallying, he decided that once he procured the antidote and regained his strength, he would resume his hunt for the Grand Menotte. The cuff belonged to him. He had made it, after all. Wearing it again would grant him centuries more of life. Power unimaginable.

A tiny voice in the back of his mind whispered a warning, reminding him what happened the last time he put on the cuff. The madness. His family, nearly all slaughtered by his own hand. Jaskin shook his head, dispelling the memory. This time would be different.

He squinted through the feverish haze, searching for the hothouses of the Night Bazaar. *There.* A massive structure of glass and wood loomed ahead, lit from within by a golden glow. Jaskin stumbled through the entrance.

Inside, the air was humid and heavy with the scent of a thousand herbs and tinctures. Loris was famous for its potions and elixirs, salves and extracts. Every known plant and herb could be found here, fresh-cut or dried in bunches, powdered or boiled to a paste, stirred into thick syrups or distilled in tiny vials.

Moisture beaded the glass walls. Figures browsed the stalls, some human, others not. A hunched creature shuffled past, citrine-yellow eyes gleaming from the depths of its hood. Hairy hands clutched a basket filled with dried purple flowers.

"Eau de troll's warts," rasped a voice like dead leaves. "Guaranteed to soothe the fussiest babe."

Jaskin turned to an old woman, her skin waxy as tallow. She held out a bottle of grayish liquid.

"Nay, I have no need of such," he said impatiently. "'Tis an antidote to devil's snare I seek."

The crone's smile evaporated. "Just sold out." She thrust the bottle beneath her long coat and hurried off.

Jaskin limped on, pausing at each stall to repeat his query. Sweat beaded his brow, the wound in his leg throbbing like a rotten tooth with each step.

"Virgin's kiss? Nay, we don't carry it anymore," said a portly man with a walrus mustache.

A wizened gnome shook his head. "Ran out yesterday, I'm afraid."

Despairing, Jaskin reached the last table. It was the smallest and most pathetic in the bazaar. Half the plants were dried out husks, the other half spotted with mildew. Still, no other option remained. He dragged himself closer, looking for the proprietor.

"I don't suppose you have any virgin's kiss?" he asked.

Jaskin addressed himself to an apple-cheeked child of indeterminate gender, who perched upon a stool. A bit of yarn dangled from their fist, which was being vigorously batted by a black cat.

"No virgin's kiss here, good sir," the waif said regretfully. "But my aunties carry it for certain. They run an apothecary on Weft Street."

Hope sparked. "Weft Street, you say? And the name of this shop?"

The child told him, then turned back to the cat. Jaskin repeated the name under his breath. Gritting his teeth, he stepped out into the chill night, his bad leg dragging in the snow. He tried not to think about how far he had yet to go. One step, then another.

Slush soaked through his boots as he trudged down the street, squinting at the signs. Weft Street, Weft Street... There! A rather gloomy lane, lit by a few guttering streetlamps. He limped toward it, stick tapping on the cobblestones.

Several apothecaries lined the street, herbs and bottles visible through the front windows. Jaskin scanned the signs until he found the one he sought. *Tinctures, Tonics & Yarn — Remedies for All That Ails You!* Relief surged through him. He hurried to the door and grasped the handle.

It didn't budge. Locked. Jaskin sagged against the doorframe, his leg throbbing. He had come so far, only to be thwarted. Then he noticed a brass hand with a bellpull, nearly hidden in the shadows. He seized it and yanked. A faint tinkling sounded from within.

Footsteps approached and the door swung open. Jaskin found himself face to face with a hearty young woman in a spotless apron. She looked him up and down, taking in his haggard appearance.

Remembering his courtly manners, Jaskin attempted a bow and nearly toppled over. The woman reached out a strong hand to steady him.

"I was told by your, ah ... agent at the market that you have virgin's kiss?" Jaskin said, hating how weak and thready his voice sounded.

The young woman smiled, her eyes warm with sympathy. "We do indeed! You poor thing, I'll mix up a poultice right away. Come in, come in."

She stepped back and Jaskin stumbled across the threshold.

Everything would be all right now.

Lo picked at her stew, shoving chunks of potato and carrot around the bowl. The food was fresh, but she had no appetite. Her thoughts churned like a whirlpool, always circling back to the same inescapable fact — she'd lost Jaskin's trail, and with it, any hope of finding Bel.

Across the table, Morgen and Dravka tucked into their meals with gusto. They'd arrived in Loris an hour before. Lo had wanted to go straight to the Night Bazaar, but it was the first town of any size they'd seen in a week and Dravka begged for a hot meal. Not camp food — real food. So here they were, at the Lucky Loon tavern.

"D'you want that?" Dravka wiped her own bowl clean with a hunk of bread and eyed Lo's half-eaten supper.

Lo pushed it forward. "Go ahead."

Dravka pulled it closer and started shoveling stew down her gullet like a newly released prisoner.

"While we're here," Morgen said, "I might as well pick up some spellcraft supplies. I've always wanted to come to Loris. They claim you can find anything here."

"Like what?" Dravka mumbled between mouthfuls.

"Belladonna, useful for calling the dead to the middle realm. Thorn apple, mandrake, and wolfsbane." Morgen sipped her ale. "Glow worms are quite fond of mandrake leaves. That is why in the west we call it devil's lamp."

Their chatter washed over Lo as she contemplated her next move. On the way to Loris, she'd seen a charred patch on the plain half a league wide. Maybe it was just a grass fire. But maybe it was an angry sun god.

"What do you make of this Empress Beatriu?" a man at the next table said in a low voice.

Lo's ears pricked up.

"I heard she's got an army of High Dead," his companion whispered back. "They burn all who oppose her."

A shudder ran through the first man. "Best kneel right quick when she gets here, lest we end up like that poor bastard Lazlo."

There were murmurs of agreement.

Who was Beatriu? And what had happened to Lazlo? Lo didn't have a clue, but they were obviously talking about the Grand Menotte.

Morgen's voice cut through her racing thoughts. "Shall we go to the market?" She looked expectantly at Lo, who plastered on a smile.

"I do need to find more of that god's bane tea," Lo said.

And get out of this town before you hear anything about an empress commanding mortifexes.

They paid for their meal and stepped into the cold. A fresh layer of snow blanketed the cobblestones. As they crossed the public square, a large proclamation nailed to the oak at its center caught her eye. She tried to steer Morgen and Dravka around it, but it was too late.

"What is this?" Morgen strode toward the tree, her dark cloak swirling.

Dread in her gut, Lo followed. The parchment read:

Let It Be Known That This Land and All Others from the Icemarch to the Western Isles are Now Under the Just and Divine Rule of Kaethe's Regent, the Empress Beatriu.

Morgen stared at the words, her face unreadable. Lo sidled up beside her, feigning surprise. "Beatriu... Who is that?"

"The child queen of Galatia." Morgen's voice was flat.

A woman hurried past, her head bowed against the wind.

Morgen stepped into her path. "Pardon me, madam. When was this proclamation posted?"

The woman glanced at the parchment, then leaned in, eyes gleaming with the pleasure of gossip. "Yesterday eve. They say it was brought by a fearsome flying beast with an undead rider."

Morgen's voice was calm. Too calm. "An undead rider. You mean a mortifex?"

The woman nodded, dropping her voice to a stage whisper. "My cousin's dressmaker saw it land with her own eyes. They say the young empress has a hundred of them as her royal guard."

Morgen thanked the woman with a sharp nod. Then she turned around, black eyes flat. "You knew."

"*What?*" Lo feigned outrage. "I had no idea—"

"Don't bother lying. You knew all along that Jaskin Cazal didn't have the Grand Menotte. You used me."

Lo searched for a plausible denial. "You have it all wrong. I truly believed—"

"Enough! I'm done listening to you," Morgen snarled. "You are a bungling magpie, croaking loudly and without meaning."

Dravka glanced between them. "Maybe we should hear her out—"

Morgen spun on her heel and stalked away. With an apologetic shrug, Dravka followed, jogging to catch up with her sister's furious strides. Lo watched them leave, a hollow feeling in her chest. Well, it was inevitable. She operated better alone anyway.

A small voice whispered that it was her own fault, that she should have been honest from the start, but she silenced it. It was too late now.

Lo melted into the crowds, making her way toward the

Night Bazaar. She stopped at every stall, asking for god's bane tea, but the run of ill luck continued and she found no sellers. Frustration mounting, she was about to give up when a scruffy kid at a ramshackle booth piped up.

"Try Tinctures, Tonics & Yarn. It's an apothecary around the corner. I bet they've got some. They have everything."

Lo followed the kid's directions to a narrow, crooked street. A sign creaked in the wind above a nondescript door. She pulled the bell chain and waited, shifting from foot to foot.

The door swung open, revealing a plump, rosy-cheeked woman in a crisp apron. She smiled, her eyes crinkling at the corners. "Welcome, dear. How can I help you?"

A lie was forming on Lo's tongue before she could think. She bit her lip hard and tried again. "I need god's bane leaves. I was told you might carry them."

The woman's smile widened. "Oh yes, we have a dram or two left. Come in, come in." She stepped back, ushering Lo into the shop.

The interior was dim and cramped, the air pungent with dried herbs. Shelves lined the walls, crammed with glass jars and clay pots of every shape and size. Bunches of plants hung from the rafters. Baskets overflowed with skeins of yarn in a riot of hues.

As Lo's eyes adjusted to the gloom, she saw something odd. A plump black cat regarded her lazily from atop a wicker basket. It stretched, kneading white paws. *Peculiar.* The cat looked exactly like the one she'd seen at the market stall.

"Sister!" the rosy-cheeked woman called out. "We have a customer in need of god's bane."

From the back of the shop emerged another woman, tall and whip-thin, with sharp foxlike features. She looked Lo up and down, her gaze lingering on the shadow-cloak.

"God's bane, you say? We keep that in the back. I'll fetch it for you." She disappeared through a half-open door.

Lo fidgeted, uneasy in the musty, close confines of the shop. To distract herself, she watched the cat bat at a stray ball of yarn, its needle-sharp claws snagging in the fibers. A rhythmic sound drifted from beyond the door. She strained to make it out.

Snick, snick, snick.

It sounded like the soft whisk of scissors opening and closing.

The cat. The yarn. The gods-damned Quickening....

A spike of ice stabbed Lo's spine. She leapt for the door, but it vanished just before her fingers touched the handle. The walls warped and shrugged, the street-facing window melting into unyielding stone.

The two sisters appeared and Lo shoved past them, dashing through the half-open doorway at the rear of the shop. In the corner, a shadowy figure hunched over, gleaming scissors flashing in its hands. Lo didn't pause, just ran, plunging into another chamber piled high with overflowing baskets of yarn. Breathing hard, she wrenched open the far door and stumbled through...

Only to find herself back in the main shop. The black cat hissed, tail swishing. The two sisters were waiting for her. Their lips curved, but their eyes were flat.

Lo stared at her adversaries, heart thudding. "Nona," she guessed. The buxom sister inclined her head. Lo's gaze slid to the thin one. "And Decima. I suppose the one with the shears is Morta?"

"Clever girl," Nona said, clapping her strong hands together. "Now we've caught two little mice!"

Two? Lo frowned. She looked down just as a trapdoor sprang open beneath her feet. The fall into darkness was short but brutal, and she landed painfully in a damp, earthen-smelling space.

Faint light leaked through the gaps in the planks above, illuminating stacks of barrels and burlap sacks. A root cellar. And there, against the far wall, a figure sat with his knees drawn up, greasy black hair falling over his face. Eyes glittered in the dark.

Jaskin Cazal.

It took but an instant to cross the cellar. Lo grabbed his singed coat, hauled him upright, and slammed him against the wall. "Where's Nabu-bal-idinna?" she demanded.

He twisted and writhed, but she was stronger. "I don't know!" he cried. "I left him in the forest, by my troth!"

Lo shook him harder. "So he's not here?"

"No!" Jaskin snapped. "I just said I came alone, you witless harpy. Unhand me!"

Lo released him with a disgusted snort. "You're an idiot," she muttered, stalking back to the opposite wall. Jaskin skittered away, putting as much distance between them as the cramped cellar allowed.

"You do know who's caught us?" he ventured in a sour tone.

Lo sat down and tipped her head back. "The Fates."

Jaskin plucked at his ragged garments, weaselly eyes darting. "They're far worse than Kaethe. Vindictive hags, persecuting us when we've done no wrong."

"What do they want?" Lo asked. If she knew their motives, perhaps she could spin this to her advantage.

"I've no notion. I only arrived a few hours ago myself, seeking a cure for devil's snare." He hiked up his trouser leg, revealing a nasty wound, the veins around it black and pulsing. The sickly-sweet stench of infection wafted across the cellar.

"That looks bad," Lo said. "I hope it kills you slowly."

Jaskin lowered the fabric with a wince. "'Twas a little imp at the market who sent me to this thrice-damned place."

Lo glanced sidelong. "The kid with the dead plants?" He nodded. "Great," she said. "We're well and truly fucked now."

Still, she paced the confines of the root cellar, running her hands over the rough earthen walls, searching for any hidden crevice or loose stone.

"I already looked," Jaskin said dourly.

"Good for you," she snapped. "I'm looking again."

After an hour, she had to concede that there was no way out except the trapdoor above. Lo rested her forehead on her arms. Exhaustion pressed in and she drifted into a light doze.

She startled awake sometime later, disoriented in the unchanging gloom. Jaskin still huddled against the opposite wall, ashen and shivering as the poison ravaged his body. Lo stood and shouted up at the trapdoor until her voice cracked, but no one came.

She rounded on Jaskin, fists clenched. "This is all your doing. You made Kaethe so angry she sealed the gates to her realm! And now some brat named Beatriu has the Grand Menotte and is busy taking over the world. Anything to say for yourself?"

Jaskin bridled. "Naught of this is my fault!" he spluttered.

She lunged forward and seized him by his lapels again. "Not your fault? You created the thing! You—"

A faint tinkle sounded from above. Lo froze. The bell on the shop door.

A customer!

Twenty-One

Morgen stood on the apothecary steps, lips pursed in a tight line. The argument replayed in her mind. Dravka's chiding that she'd been too harsh, her own icy retorts. She had stormed out of the inn in a fury, but now doubts crept in.

Perhaps Dravka had a point. Morgen knew she could be unyielding. She had spent so long plotting her revenge against Vazsoly Marcel that she had forgotten how to forgive.

But it ran deeper than that. She had only half a soul. That was the real problem.

Earlier, Morgen had stalked through the Night Bazaar, relief flooding through her when she saw no sign of Lo among the stalls. She made her purchases with clipped words and a hooded gaze, all the while asking after soul-mending potions in hushed tones. The merchants had no answers for her.

Then the child had approached, barefoot and begrimed. "My aunties have what you seek, m'lady," the urchin whispered. "The most potent remedies in Loris!"

Tinctures, Tonics & Yarn. Morgen had little hope they'd be able to aid her, but it was worth trying before she left. The apothecary door swung open with a tinkling of bells, jolting Morgen from her reverie. A fresh-faced young woman greeted her with a smile that seemed too bright for the late hour. "Welcome! Please come inside."

Morgen stepped across the threshold. The shop's smell was a blend of the common — lavender and sage — and the rare — powdered leeches and midnight amber. She handed the apothecary a list of ingredients, then hesitated, weighing her words.

"I have a friend," Morgen began. "Her soul is ... divided. Is there any way to make it whole again?"

The apothecary's eyes widened. "That sounds serious." She patted Morgen's hand with a kindly touch that made Morgen want to recoil. "But don't you worry. I'm certain I can help. Let me just check what I have in the back."

With that, the woman vanished through a doorway at the rear of the shop, one shoe squeaking faintly as she walked. Morgen paced the worn floorboards. Foolish, to let herself hope. What were the chances this unassuming little shop could mend a Shadow Soul?

In the dank root cellar, Lo's head snapped up at the creak of footsteps overhead. Faint voices filtered through gaps in the wooden planks.

"Help!" she shouted, leaping to her feet. "Down here!"

The conversation above continued without a pause. She climbed atop a barrel and pounded against the ceiling, raining dust on their heads. "Help! Please, we're captives!"

Still no response. Jaskin let out a mirthless chuckle. "Those she-devils must have warded the cellar. Sound only travels one way, I'm afraid."

The voices fell quiet, and whoever had arrived started to pace up and down. Lo bit her lip in frustration. Again, she shouted and banged on the ceiling to no avail. Then she heard a squeaky tread approach. "Nona's coming back," she hissed.

A brief scuffle ensued, punctuated by muffled curses. The trapdoor flew open and Morgen dropped into the cellar. She landed like a cat, dusting off her black skirts with sharp, angry movements. When she saw Jaskin, she looked even more enraged.

"*You*," Morgen spat. "I should have known you'd be mixed up in this."

Jaskin stared daggers. "You cost me the Grand Menotte," he snarled. "Where is it?"

"The talisman was mine," Morgen retorted. "I died for it!"

"So did I!" His monkey-like fingers hooked into claws. "Come then, let us duel. I shall make a mincemeat pie of you!"

Morgen laughed in his face. "You don't stand a chance, old man."

"Shut up, both of you," Lo snapped. "Forget the Grand Menotte. We're in a heap of trouble."

Morgen gave her a surly look. "How did you end up here?"

"Same as you. The kid at the Night Bazaar. He said his aunties had god's bane."

"They promised me virgin's kiss," Jaskin muttered. "What did *you* come for?"

"None of your business," Morgen said tartly. She turned back to Lo. "What are they, witches? Organ traffickers?"

"Worse," Lo said.

Abruptly, the trapdoor creaked open and a ladder dropped down. They all winced at the sudden light.

"Come out, come out!" Nona's voice drifted down.

Jaskin gestured to the ladder. "After you," he said mockingly.

Morgen shouldered past him with a scowl. She climbed the ladder, Lo close behind. Jaskin made a production of hauling himself up last, groaning and cursing his injured leg.

Nona and Decima stood waiting above, identical smiles on their faces. Of Morta, there was no sign. Nona clapped her plump hands. "The three little mice are together at last!"

Lo stared at her with loathing. "Go ahead. Just kill us and be done with it."

Jaskin shot her a baleful look. "Speak for thyself, girl."

Nona's laughter tinkled like shards of glass. "Kill you? Why, we don't want to kill you, silly mice!" She reached into the folds of her robe, producing a small vial. "Here, Master Cazal. As promised, your virgin's kiss."

Jaskin accepted the vial gingerly, as if it might bite him. He uncorked it and sniffed, wrinkling his blade of a nose. With a grimace, he tipped the contents down his throat.

"Gah!" He shuddered. "Vile stuff."

"Medicine oft is," Nona said sweetly.

Decima glided forward, cunning eyes studying each of them in turn. She halted first before Morgen, who glowered back, arms crossed.

"Morgen, daughter of Ingharad," Decima said in formal tones, like a judge pronouncing sentence. "Born in the Dominion on the banks of the River Acheron. Your soul is forfeit."

Morgen paled but said nothing. Decima turned next to Jaskin. "Master Cazal. Your parents were necromancers who traveled often through the gate in northern Eddyn, exploring the shadowlands."

"And it was during one of those jaunts to the land of the dead that you were conceived," Nona added with a wink.

He raised a finger to speak but Decima cut him off. "Your soul is forfeit," she pronounced.

Nona turned to Lo. "And you, Delilah Dessarian. Your mother's thread was cut, but Kaethe saw fit to bring her back. You should never have been born at all."

"Your soul is forfeit," Decima intoned.

Lo looked at her grim-faced companions and nodded slowly. "I think we'd all love some clarification. What exactly do you mean when you say *forfeit*?"

Nona chuckled. "It means that you belong to us now. You will be our servants for as long as it pleases us."

"So a few months?" Lo pressed. "A year? Or are we talking eternity?"

Decima's nasty smile was answer enough.

"Here's the thing," Lo said reasonably. "If I fail to return Kaethe's husband, she won't permit the dead to pass her gates. Which is a pretty serious problem for everyone."

Nona's eyes went flat. "A shame," she said. "But those troubles are not ours."

Jaskin swept into a low bow, wincing at the weight on his bad leg. "Most esteemed arbiters of fortune," he said in an oily tone, "perhaps we can come to an arrangement. These two—" he waved a hand at Lo and Morgen "—are of little consequence. Keep them as your servants, by all means. But I am far more valuable. Surely there is a higher rank befitting my skills and knowledge?"

The sisters burst into uproarious laughter. Jaskin straightened, scowling.

"You will have no higher rank in this house," Decima said.

Nona reached into her apron pocket and withdrew a spindle, still chuckling. She waved it through the air. Lo felt a tingling sensation, and then the weight of heavy, scratchy fabric against her skin. Looking around, she saw they were all clad in drab gray uniforms.

"You will fetch, clean, and hop when we say hare," Nona

declared. "Should you disobey or try to escape..." She looked meaningfully at the far end of the room.

Lo's gaze followed. Morta stood in the shadows, lank gray hair concealing her face. She raised a pair of gleaming shears and snipped them open and shut. *Whisk-whisk.*

The three prisoners recoiled.

"Now come along, little mice," Nona said, making a shooing motion. "There is work to be done!"

Twenty-Two

The sun touched the horizon, the sky dimming to the band of perpetual twilight between east and west, when the *Merry Maid* sailed into Yael. Cas stared across the choppy water, fixing his gaze on the squat warehouses along the harbor. It did his stomach little good.

The White Sea was notorious for its storms and swells. The first time he'd crossed it had been from Tjanjin to Aquitan, and he'd hated every moment aboard the flying ship. Now he'd gladly trade the pitching of the *Merry Maid* for the smooth motion of the *Wind Witch*.

Of course, that made him think of Lo. His heart clenched.

"We sail at the turn of the tide," the captain warned, striding past Cas's position at the stern rail. "Don't stay too long ashore."

"We won't," he promised.

As soon as the gangplank was lowered, the crew began hoisting casks over the side. The captain was offloading Galatian wine and buying grain to sell in Gilvra. Cas and Felippa disembarked and walked down the stone quay. Her boots were falling apart so badly that one sole flapped like a gossiping tongue.

"You need some decent shoes," Cas said, gulping a breath of salt air.

"Ah, but I can pick my big toenail without even taking them off," Felippa replied.

He managed a weak smile. "There's a cobbler on the high street."

"So you've been to Yael before?"

It was a port town at the tip of Clovis, the duchy where Cas had served as a Quietus.

"Orlaith sent me here many times," he said, "when they had trouble with the risen."

He glanced at the sky-blue cloak draped over his sister's shoulders. The hem, once dragging on the ground, now hung neatly at her ankles. She'd borrowed needle and thread from the bosun and stitched it up during their voyage from Prydwen.

"I meant to ask," he said. "That cloak. It belonged to someone who died, didn't it?"

Felippa nodded. "It must have. I found in a giant pile of clothes Magnus had stolen."

"We'll get you a new one, then."

Her fingers touched the crow embroidered on the right breast. "No, this suits me fine. It's warm and well-made. Best we save our silver for things we truly need."

Cas shrugged, though he'd expected her to jump at the chance to be rid of the grim reminder of her time as a captive of the mortifexes. But Lip had changed. Not much shook her anymore.

He focused instead on the simple pleasure of firm ground beneath his feet and a bit of exercise after a week shipbound. But as they climbed the hill leading to Yael's high street, he noticed the scars of recent violence. Blackened timbers and broken windows. Some buildings were girded with scaffolding, though there were no tradesmen rebuilding them.

"What in Bel's name happened here?" Felippa wondered as they skirted a pile of charred timbers.

"Let's hope it *wasn't* in Bel's name," Cas muttered, thinking of Brother Arnulf. Men like him had a way of coming back as sure as the unhallowed dead.

Luckily, the cobbler's shop was untouched. Its proprietor, a stout man with brown hair parted down the middle and a bright green coat, greeted them with a smile. "Welcome." His shrewd gaze landed on Felippa's shabby footwear. "Let me guess. Something for the young miss."

While the cobbler measured Felippa's feet, Cas nodded his chin toward the street. "You've seen trouble. Was there an attack?"

The man shook his head as he noted down the measurements. "No, this was our own folk turning on each other. Fear of the risen sparked a week of riots. Mobs tore through the town, hunting for any sign of necromancy." He sighed. "As if burning out their own neighbors would stop the dead from walking."

"That's stupid," Felippa said.

"Sense had nothing to do with it," the cobbler said wearily. "At least the watch finally put an end to it, though business has been terrible since." He forced a smile. "Come back in two days, and I'll have the shoes ready for you."

"Our ship leaves with the tide," Cas said. "We can't wait."

Felippa looked crestfallen. The cobbler thought for a moment. "I may have something that'll serve. More than a few orders were never collected." He disappeared into the rear of the shop.

Cas moved toward the front window. A patrol of the town

watch was headed up the high street. They ducked into each shop, emerging moments later to confer in low voices. After the riots, they were probably being careful, but...

A warning prickled the back of his neck. "Lip, I think it's time we—"

"These should do," the cobbler said, emerging with a pair of soft ankle-high boots. Felippa laced them on and took a few steps, then stamped her feet to settle the fit.

"Not too tight, I hope?" the cobbler asked. "They're a bit narrow for your measurements."

"They feel all right," she said. "My toes aren't squeezed, so I think they'll break in."

The cobbler smiled. "Off on a grand journey, are you?"

The patrol was one street away now. Cas quickly counted three silver ferries from his purse. "Aye, and we don't want to miss our boat." He dropped two extra copper pyres onto the counter. "For your trouble. Come on, sis."

Felippa threw a hurried thanks over her shoulder as Cas all but dragged her out the door. The town watch was nowhere in sight; they must be inside one of the other shops.

"We need to get back to the ship," he whispered.

"Why? What's wrong?"

"Just a hunch."

They were halfway down the hill when the patrol stepped out from the shadows of some scaffolding ahead. Both big men, a hand taller than Cas. Their surcoats bore the striped badger emblem of the local margrave. Thank Kaethe he didn't know them personally. They must be new.

Cas ducked his head. "Go," he hissed at Felippa. "Run!"

She hesitated only a moment before slipping into an adjacent lane. Cas squared his shoulders and kept walking, praying they'd let him pass. But the men crossed the street and blocked his path. One held up a hand, the other resting on the pommel of a short sword.

"Hold there!" he said sternly.

Cas stopped and forced a smile. "Bonny day, sirs."

"What's your name?"

"Herf Aubrey." He plucked out the first one that came to mind. Ironically enough, the old geezer he'd once shared a cell with in Swanton.

"Well, *Herf Aubrey*, you match the description of a man wanted for murder."

Cas frowned, even as his heart leapt into his throat. He should have stayed on the ship. If his stomach hadn't been so damned rough...

"Murder?" he repeated with a laugh. "You've got me confused with someone else. I just arrived an hour ago. Never even been to Yael before."

"Then you won't mind showing us your hand." The watchman's tone brooked no argument. "The man we want has the tattoo of a Quietus."

Cas readily held out both unmarked hands. He kept them palm-down to hide the welter of old scars, but everyone knew that Kaethe's mark was on the webbing between thumb and forefinger. "See? I told you."

The patrol exchanged a glance. For a moment, he thought they'd let him go. Then a stocky, white-haired man with the Redvayne phoenix on his scarlet cloak rounded the corner. Cas knew him well from previous visits to Yael. Gefreid Quincey, captain of the watch. His eyes widened with recognition. "It's Castelio zah Nerides! Arrest that man!"

The guards were reaching for him when an ominous creak froze them in place. The wooden scaffolding above their heads shuddered, then collapsed with a roar. Cas leapt clear as the watchmen went down in a cursing tangle.

A small figure barreled out of the alley. Felippa. She must have snuck inside and knocked out the supports. Cas caught up with her and they ran into the labyrinth of Yael's cobbled streets. Angry shouts echoed close behind.

The town was built on steep hills and Felippa soon started to flag. Cas pulled her into a narrow gap between two houses. They crouched behind a fluttering clothesline as the watch pounded past.

"We can't ... go back to the harbor," Cas whispered, trying to catch his breath. "That cobbler will tell them .... we came by ship. They'll have it ... watched."

"The warrant." She swallowed, lips dry. "It's really for murder?"

He nodded grimly. "Like I told you when I first came to Prydwen. Orlaith tried to poison me. She put nightshade in a bottle of wine." He glanced at the talisman around Felippa's neck. "That saved me, but my friend Esme drank it and died. Orlaith made it seem I'd killed her."

Felippa bit her lip. "What do we do?"

"Get out of town. Come on."

They crept from street to street, ducking out of sight whenever footsteps drew near. Pale spirits lurked in the deep shadows beneath eaves and north-facing walls, but didn't try to attack. Most of the living seemed to have abandoned Yael. Those who remained hurried along with shoulders hunched.

No one paid them much mind and soon they neared the outskirts. At the rocky headland above the bay known as the Great Salt Pond, they dropped to their bellies and crawled until they had a view of the town below. Cas swore. As he feared, a dozen gold cloaks of the watch were visible moving about the harbor.

"All our things are aboard the ship," Felippa said despondently.

"I know." He patted his pocket. "But I have the letters from Brennos. We can still deliver them."

She eyed him doubtfully. "It'll be a long way on foot."

"Aye, but we'll be safer if we travel the northward leg through the Boundary. I know every league of it." He squeezed her hand. "We can do this, Lip. We can make it to Mystral."

She squeezed back, and he felt a rush of gratitude that she'd insisted on accompanying him. "I believe you, Cas."

They slipped into the fringe of woods and hiked for hours, putting as much distance as possible between them and Yael before making a cold, miserable camp in a hollow. Felippa curled up in her cloak. She had that pinched look that reminded him of their years in Swanton. His own belly ached with hunger, but Cas ignored it, keeping watch while she fell into an exhausted slumber.

After a few hours, he woke her with a gentle shake and they set out again under leaden skies that threatened rain. Her steps were dragging by midday. Lip just didn't have his reserves.

"Listen," he said. "There's a village called Cerf not far ahead. We need provisions."

"You can't show your face, Cas," she said, alarmed. "What if they're looking there, too?"

"I won't," he said. "But maybe we can … I don't know, snatch a pie from a windowsill."

"I'd give my left tit for a bite of pie," Lip said wistfully. "But we must be careful."

The woods gave way to farmland. Then they passed a gated lichyard Cas recognized, the headstones furry with moss. "Cerf's just around the next bend," he said. "There's not much to the place, but I still have some coin. And they won't be looking for *you*."

"They might be," she replied shrewdly. "That captain got a look at me when we were running away."

They were debating whether to cut through the woods when the sounds of a commotion drifted down the road behind them. Felippa grabbed his hand and tugged him behind a tree. Within a minute, the source came into view.

A lone figure stumbled along the lane, vainly shielding itself with its arms. One of the risen — a man of middle years with the lean, weathered look of a farmer. The villagers were herding him with torches and sharpened sticks. A few threw stones, hurled curses.

"That's horrible," Lip said in a low voice.

Cas tensed. He thought of the weeping dead boy he'd met in the woods. He thought of Sarra's husband, trampled into the mud and buried under a bier of snow, only to rise and wander. A thousand others. Fathers and mothers, sons and daughters.

His hands balled into fists. Before he could think better of it, he was striding into the road. "Stop! Leave the man be!"

The villagers turned, startled at first. Then hostile expressions closed their faces.

"He ain't a man," one snarled. "Not no more."

Cas tried to assess the hostile crowd. Maybe he could intimidate them with something scarier. "Kaethe will judge you harshly for this," he said in a calmer tone. "Just move on, I'll deal with the risen."

A few seemed to weigh his words, but the leader scoffed. "Kaethe abandoned us, don't you know." He spat in the dirt. "That's for the Drowned Woman. She's either dead or a devil herself, and it don't matter which."

Shock rendered him speechless for a moment. Kaethe was

revered near the Boundary. Never had he heard someone speak of the goddess so — not openly at least.

Felippa appeared at his elbow, casting him an anxious look. "My brother used to be a Quietus," she said loudly. "Let him manage the dead man."

"Lip," he warned under his breath.

"They're about to string you up, lummox," she hissed back. "The warrant doesn't matter now."

There was a taut moment. Then the leader thrust his torch at the dead man, who was walking in circles. He gave an inarticulate cry and started shambling down the road again.

"You don't give orders here, stranger," he said. "These are our lands. Get out!"

Cas struggled to master his temper. "Look at him. He's not harming anyone. You've no cause to—

"No cause?" interrupted a stout flame-haired woman in mourning black. "Where were you when they rose up and took my Ayleth?"

A rumble of assent went through the crowd. "And my Jo!" someone shouted.

Cas pointed. "Was it that man who killed them?"

The woman glared. "Well, no... But they're all the same!"

"You're wrong. Most still have a piece of the person they used to be. I'm guessing this man was your neighbor?" He could tell from their faces that he was right. "He didn't choose this. Would any of you want to be treated this way? Where's your decency?"

For a fraught minute, no one spoke. Then the man with the torch took a step forward. He aimed to be menacing, but his eyes were as blank and shiny as the dead man's. Cas realized that for all his bluster, he was terrified. "Shut. Your. Mouth," he growled.

"Take 'em to Goram's barn!" someone shouted.

"Aye, the barn!"

The villagers formed a ring of torches and sharp sticks, forcing Cas and Felippa up the road. The dead man shuffled ahead, the three of them herded along like sheep. After a few minutes, they reached an old barn with a sagging roof. A new wooden bar sat in place across the door. Cas stared at the dark, filthy windows high above. Cold sweat broke across his brow.

"What's in there?" he demanded.

None of them would meet his eye.

"Please," he begged, "let my sister go. She's only thirteen."

The stout woman took Felippa by the arm, her fleshy face softening a fraction. "Come on, girl, you can come to my house—"

Lip yanked her arm free. "Feck off, I'm not leaving my brother!"

Her mouth firmed into a hard line. "Then in you go."

The bar was lifted. Men with torches stood to either side as Cas and Felippa were shoved through the door. The dead man came behind, sprawling on the dirt floor. An instant later, the bar thudded into place. Outside, with a feral rumble, the skies opened and rain began to drum against the roof.

Cas waited for his eyes to adjust to the dimness. Gray light filtered down through four windows, all too high to reach. Felippa pressed close, trembling. He glanced at the hayloft. It would do for now. "Up there. Go!"

She scurried up the ladder. Cas backed toward it, never taking his eyes from the dead. A flash of lightning illuminated more than a dozen figures standing motionless in the dark. Men, women, even a few children, their eyes reflecting the stormlight.

The villagers must have been herding them in here for weeks. Cas jumped as thunder boomed somewhere close by. It was just like that night when Ma came back, leaving muddy footprints on the boards...

He drew a steadying breath. No. He was no longer that boy. And he knew now that weapons — iron knives, Kaethe's Tears — they weren't what made a Quietus. Gui had said it for years, but Cas didn't really believe him.

Not until every tool of his trade had been stripped away, even his tattoo.

What made a true Quietus was something inside. Something you could never lose unless you chose to.

Compassion.

He paused with his hand on the ladder. Then he dropped it and began walking toward the dead gathered at the other end of the barn.

"Cas!" Felippa hissed from the loft. "Are you daft? Get up here!"

The risen's eyes tracked him, and he watched them back, ready to run for the ladder if he needed to.

Cas cleared his throat and spoke in Tongues. It felt rusty, as though his knowledge of it was fading, just like his tattoo. That worried him. But as he began to talk, the words came more fluently.

"I have traveled to the Cold Sea," he said. "It's a beautiful place, with dawn on one horizon and dusk on the other."

The risen made no move to attack, only watched. Did they understand?

"I have seen Dandariel, the Last Beacon," he continued, remembering the feeling of peace that had swept over him. "It's a lighthouse that guides souls on their final journey to the far shore. I swear I will do all I can to help you reach it."

"Cas! What are you saying?" Felippa called down, her face a pale moon in the darkness.

He felt sick and feverish like he had that night in another

barn ten years before. Caught in the grip of some power larger than himself. He looked up. "I understand what I have to do now, Lip. The living and the dead must unite—"

He trailed off as the gleam of torchlight lit the high windows. The townspeople had come back. Then Cas caught a whiff of kerosene and understood.

They weren't there to free anyone, but to burn the whole barn to the ground.

"Get back down here!" he called to Felippa. "Hurry!"

Her gaze sliced to the dead. She didn't move.

"It's all right, I promise. They won't ... hurt you." He coughed. Smoke was seeping in through the cracks around the doors. "Just do what I say!"

She looked terrified but climbed down the ladder. Cas cupped her thin face. "Listen to me. We are *not* going to die here. I have a ... plan." He coughed again, eyes stinging. "Stay low. The air will be clearer."

Felippa dropped to hands and knees and crawled as far as she could from the risen, then sat with her knees to her chest and the hem of her blue cloak across her face. Cas didn't waste time banging on the doors or begging for mercy. These people had let their own fear devour them. There would be no quarter.

Instead, he groped along the walls, probing for a weak spot. The glimpse he'd had of Goram's barn before they were shoved inside showed a decrepit structure, likely abandoned for some time.

Who knew? Maybe Goram was in there with him right now.

It was hard to see much in the thickening smoke, but his fingers finally brushed a plank that felt partly rotted through. He slammed his heel against it three times. The boards creaked in protest but held. He turned to the risen. "Come here, to me! Gather and push! All of you together!"

A corner of the barn was on fire now. Flames raced along the support beams and then leapt to the rafters and ceiling joints. The risen shied away, confused and frightened.

"Here!" Cas shouted in Tongues. "Come here and push!"

The raw desperation in his voice finally caught their attention. One by one, the dead drifted over to the rotten board. Cas backed out of the way, careful to avoid their touch. Two, then five, then a dozen pressed against the wall. It gave a groaning shudder and collapsed outward. Rain gusted into the barn.

When the dead stumbled out, the townspeople fled. Felippa took his hand and they ran into the field just as the roof collapsed in a shower of cinders.

"Are you okay?" Cas gulped down a lungful of clean air.

She nodded, blue eyes huge. "They saved us. The risen saved us."

Cas drew another shallow breath, throat still raw. Through blurred vision, he saw them starting to wander off in all directions.

"*Stop!*" Power resonated in his voice, and the risen halted in their tracks. "Come back!"

The dead turned around. In twos and threes, they shuffled toward him like a flock to their shepherd. Felippa gripped his arm. "What are you doing?"

"I'm not leaving them here to be tormented. They're coming with us."

She stared at him for a long moment. Then she touched his forehead. "You're burning up." Felippa spoke slowly, like she would to a very young child. "They're not stray cats, Cas. You can't make pets of them."

He grinned. "Can't I?"

"You're not thinking straight—"

"No, it's the opposite." He held up a palm to the risen. "That's far enough. Follow and you'll be under my protection."

He began to whistle a discordant tune in a minor key that had worked in the past to lure risen from the shadows. As one, their heads cocked. They waited for him to start walking, then trailed along in a ragged line up the muddy road.

"This is madness!" Felippa whispered. "You're like the Pied-fecking-Piper of dead people!"

He stopped whistling. "What if one of them was Ma? Or someone else you knew and loved? Would you want them wandering about, lost and alone, prey to whatever cruel shit happens along?"

She grudgingly shook her head.

"They saved us, Lip. Now we're returning the favor. The dead are respected in Mystral. They'll be safe there."

He resumed whistling and they walked without speaking for a few minutes. When they passed through the tiny village of Cerf, shutters slammed and doors banged as people hid from the macabre procession, but no one came out to confront them.

"Well, I don't suppose anyone will dare arrest you now," Felippa remarked.

He cocked a brow. "I'd like to see them try."

She gave a strangled laugh. Together, they led their strange company northeast, into the wild, misty passes of the Boundary.

Twenty-Three

Brother Arnulf rode into Pagelin, a backwater halfway between Cavet and Clovis, the low sun casting its rundown buildings in reddish light. Once it had been a thriving mill town, but then the river dried up and so did all the custom that came with the mill. Now it was a place of grinding poverty and boredom and general resentment, which was exactly the sort of hamlet that Arnulf found most fruitful.

His horse's hooves drummed on the dusty dirt road, empty at this hour. He longed to lift the goat-hair shirt away from his neck but resisted. The itching rash was penance for his failure.

He dismounted outside the sole inn, a building with moldy thatch and a sign proclaiming it the Ram's Head. Inside, Arnulf settled at a corner table, ignoring the hostile glances from the other patrons. An elderly barmaid set down a tankard of watered ale and a bowl of stew without a word.

As he ate, Arnulf's thoughts returned to Prydwen. Foul magic and death, all behind him now. It mattered not who had claimed victory in the end. Sir Richart Mortimer or the rebel scum — heretics all. When Bel returned, He would scourge the pretenders and unbelievers. Burn away the impurities of this world like base metal refined in a crucible.

Arnulf would be the god's instrument, His shining sword. And the false Strategos Brennos Fearghal... His jaw clenched around a bite of stew. The whore and his filthy demon would suffer a long, slow punishment.

But for now, his task was clear. Rebuild Bel's army and resume his important work.

He'd been forced to kill a wagon guard on the road. The man had gone into the woods to piss and Arnulf crept up behind, catching him with his breeches around his knees. A quick twist of the head and it was done. Now a blade rode at his hip, though not nearly so fine as the one Mortimer's gold had bought.

But soon, soon, the tide would turn again.

Arnulf closed his eyes, swept into visions of Bel's imminent return. Each night, the dream grew more vivid. The god's chariot racing across the heavens, His divine light bathing the land. Bel's presence seared his mind, holy commands thundering through his skull.

Kaethe and her coven of witches bore the blame for the rising dead, of this fact Arnulf harbored no doubts. He would not stop until he'd sent each and every nun to hell. Only then would Bel return in Glory.

Arnulf tossed a few coppers on the table and stood, his chair scraping loudly against the floorboards. The other patrons averted their eyes as he strode outside and made his way to the market square, dark eyes alight with purpose. The townsfolk parted before him, mothers pulling their children close.

He was vaguely aware that his kilt was stained with mud and blood, his hair unkempt from days of hard travel. No matter. They would heed Bel's call all the same.

He climbed atop an empty wagon, the wood creaking under his weight. "Good people of Pagelin!" Arnulf's voice rang out. "Hear the word of Bel, the one true god!"

Faces turned toward him, some curious, most wary. Arnulf met their gazes, unflinching. "The dead walk among us, an unholy plague unleashed by the bitches of Kaethe. Who among the righteous will stand against this tide of darkness?"

He stabbed a dirty finger toward the hills, where a convent crouched like a poisonous toad. "Cast down the handmaidens of evil! Burn their foul nests to ash, and Bel shall return to save us all! His light will scour the land clean!"

Mutterings rose from the crowd, a low angry buzz. Arnulf drank it in, stoking their budding rage. "Who among you has the courage to be Bel's champion? Who will take up the sword of faith and smite the wicked?"

A few pimply-faced young men elbowed each other, showing mild interest. Farmhands, smithy apprentices — good strong boys. Just like the army Mortimer had paid him to raise before Brennos deceived them and led his legion astray.

"Come forward!" Arnulf beckoned with a smile. "Brave lads, the bards will sing of you one day..."

He trailed off as the youths blanched, staring at something past Arnulf's shoulder. His new recruits melted back into the crowd. Townsfolk quietly scattered, hurrying down lanes and into houses. In moments, the square stood empty.

Arnulf whirled, hand dropping to his sword hilt. Two figures in white tabards approached, their movements too graceful, too sinuous to be human. Winged creatures crouched behind them. *Demons.*

"Begone, spawn of Kaethe!" Arnulf snarled. "Bel rebukes you! Bel casts you into the abyss!"

The demons regarded him with expressions of amusement.

Arnulf's heart thundered against his ribs. He prayed for Bel's fire to engulf them, to sear their tainted flesh from bone.

Nothing happened.

"Back to the pit that spawned you!" His sword slid free with a heroic rasp of steel. If Bel would not strike them down, His servant would do it. Arnulf brandished the blade. "Come closer! The Ninth Hell awaits!"

The demons halted a few paces away, near enough for Arnulf to feel the chill emanating from their flesh. To see the flames that danced at the center of their pupils. One sported a thick black beard braided into a fork. The other was yellow-haired with a single blazing eye.

"You think that's really a Son of Bel, Orm?" Forked Beard asked in dubious tone.

"Dunno, Skegg," One-Eye answered, squinting. "Looks more like a crazy beggar."

Arnulf drew himself up, ignoring the sweat trickling beneath his hair shirt. "I am Strategos of the Sons of Bel. Their commander!"

Forked Beard laughed. "Where are all your followers?"

Arnulf ground his molars. "Waiting nearby," he bit out. "Hundreds strong."

Both demons laughed then, long and hard. Arnulf sensed the cowardly villagers watching through parted curtains.

"What do you want of me?" he demanded, leveling his sword at Black Beard's barrel chest.

"We've been sent by the Empress Beatriu," the demon replied, "to root out every last priest of Bel from this land."

Arnulf blinked, struggling to comprehend through the fog of righteous rage. Empress?

One-Eye raised a meaty hand. Its fingers gently unfurled. "Since you love your god so much, allow me to return you to his keeping."

Fire erupted, everywhere, all at once. And that was the last of Brother Arnulf.

ABOUT THIRTY LEAGUES FROM PAGELIN, Lucius paused at the crest of a weed-choked road. Raising a hand, he signaled the long column to halt. Brennos and Gui reined up beside him as an eerie cry floated down, quickly answered by another.

Brennos tipped his head up, but there was little to see through the thick canopy. "I thought we lost them in the foothills."

"They're persistent," Gui muttered.

"It's time to stop anyhow," Brennos said. "We'll wait for them to pass."

Lucius had spotted the mortifex riders on the horizon days ago while the company rode through northern Galatia. It was sheer dumb luck that he'd seen them first and not the other way around. They'd managed to gallop to a deep fold in the rolling grasslands and hide there until the hunters had moved on.

It would have been suicide to continue across the open plain, so he'd guided them farther north into the wild Cabrian Mountains, using ancient byways that no longer appeared on any maps. They were forgotten by all except Lucius, whose memory extended back centuries. The terrain kept the riders from landing, but there were many of them and they flew high, covering vast swathes of territory.

"There's a spot not far ahead with a stream that will serve," Lucius said.

The Sons of Bel made camp in a sheltered dell. It was their fifth day without tents or fires and a dispirited atmosphere hung over the legion. Brennos moved among them, clasping shoulders, sharing a jest or encouraging word. The men seemed to take heart from his presence. When he finished his rounds, he sank down beside Lucius on a flat boulder.

"Do you think they know we're here?" he asked in a low voice.

Lucius shook his head. "We would already be ashes."

Brennos nodded, unwrapping his own cold rations. "Tell me about Pompeii," he said, biting into a withered apple.

Lucius eyed him in surprise. "No analysis of battle plans? More questions about the strengths and weaknesses of my kind?"

Bren gave a half smile. "You've told me enough. I'd rather speak of something else tonight. So tell me about the land of your birth."

Lucius thought for a minute. "I knew it before the Sundering. It was a different place afterward. People called it the Kiln. It was like the desert of Rhun, if you have ever been there. A parched, desolate wasteland."

"But that's not the land you grew up in," Bren prompted.

"No. The city I knew was lovely. It was a desert city, but we had many fountains and public parks. The date trees ... I remember those. And the ancient olive groves. My parents were makers of talismans, as most Vatras were."

"But you became a soldier."

Lucius sighed, though he found the old wounds were less painful now. "King Gaius was a charismatic man. I believed everything he said, at first. That we had been taken advantage of by the other clans, when in fact we were better than them. It shames me to admit it, but there was a part of me that enjoyed feeling superior. And a part that relished paying back the perceived slights."

"Yet you finally rebelled against him. Why?"

Lucius saw no judgment in Bren's face, only curiosity.

"Because the war... It only grew worse and worse. It was barely even a war. More like a slaughter. Yet still I did as I was ordered, growing more resentful and conflicted. There seemed no way out of the madness. Then one day I realized that it is not evil people who will be the ruin of the world. It is the good people who fail to stop them."

Brennos nodded approval. "And you won in the end."

Lucius gave a dry laugh. "Well, *I* lost. But the ones who came after me won. Gaius is dead now, his poisonous legacy of hate destroyed. I have been told all the clans are living in harmony again."

Brennos covered a yawn. He'd barely rested in days. "Get some sleep," Lucius said. "I will tell you more about my ill-spent youth tomorrow."

Brennos grinned and wrapped himself in his cloak. "Kiss me," he murmured sleepily.

Lucius glanced around. Other than the sentries, the men were all swathed in their own blankets. Half already knew their Strategos and First Flame were more than brothers-at-arms and didn't seem to care.

Lucius leaned forward and gave him a soft kiss. His lips tasted of apple. Brennos touched his cheek, made a grunt of contentment, and lay down on the cold ground. Lucius, who was not tired at all, watched the three moons rise, silvery light glimmering through the pine boughs.

Their time together was drawing short. He suspected Bren knew it, too.

After a few hours, they resumed marching. It wasn't long before a shallow gorge loomed ahead, with a river at the bottom. A limestone bridge arched above the churning water, pitted and worn by centuries of wind and rain. Lucius, who had forgotten about this particular feature of the route, eyed it with dread.

In his favor, it had started snowing. At least he didn't have to deal with direct sun *and* swift-running water at the same time.

"How old is that thing?" Gui asked, reining up next to Lucius and studying the bridge with a creased brow.

"Old," Lucius replied. "It was built by the first of the Do Santillan Ducs."

"Will it bear the weight of the horses?" Brennos wondered.

How tempting to suggest the long way around! But a detour would add days to their journey, and supplies were already low. A quick test with strands of earth power told Lucius the bridge was sound.

"It'll hold," he said tightly, missing his old dishonest self more than ever.

Brennos gave the order, Lucius relayed it, and the priests started forward, riding in twos and threes across the stone span, careful not to overload it. Lucius hung back until only the two of them remained on the near bank. He'd had Gui lead their horses across for fear he'd fall out of the saddle and straight into the water.

"Can you manage?" Brennos asked.

Lucius nodded firmly. "I'll be fine." If only the bridge were higher; but the river rushed just beneath it, so close that a layer of mist hung in the air. "Let's go."

They started across, side by side. Within seconds, a wave of nausea doubled him over. Lucius gripped the edge, fixing his gaze on the trees. Anything but the roaring monster beneath his feet.

"I'll carry you," Brennos said, his tone matter-of-fact. "Just say the word."

Humiliation burned at the thought. He was First Flame. He would not be hauled across like a sack of flour in front of his own men. "No," he ground out. "I can make it."

Lucius forced himself onward, one step at a time. Sheer stubbornness kept his back straight, his head high. They were halfway to the other side when a chilling cry split the air. His gaze snapped to the sky. An abbadax wheeled overhead, its dark wings outlined against the falling snow.

More shapes dropped out of the clouds, speeding closer by the second. At least two dozen riders, armed for battle.

Twenty-Four

Orlaith's needle stabbed through the tiny stocking, darning the hole in precise stitches. In the center of the canopied bed, Beatriu made a small hump under the brocaded coverlet. The child empress slept, her ringlets arrayed across a silk pillow.

Orlaith's gaze drifted to the window, where a damp breeze stirred the curtains. Once she'd found the view of her own vineyards soothing, but her mind wandered to the cellars below where her husband languished in chains. She knew she should visit Robert again, but the thought of descending those dark stairs filled her with dread.

What if she met the risen corpse of Lady Voisin, pointing a bloody, accusatory finger?

At least the noblewoman's body had not been discovered. Orlaith had made it seem that Lady Voisin had fled rather than bend the knee to her new sovereign, and Beatriu believed her. A warrant for the woman's arrest had been issued, which might have been funny under different circumstances.

Orlaith glanced at the slumbering eleven-year-old despot.

Beatriu's latest obsession was eradicating the Sons of Bel. Conquering the Moon Courts no longer held any interest. And whenever Orlaith tried to wrest back some modicum of control, she found herself thwarted by Beatriu's undead knights.

Her gaze flicked to Janus, standing sentinel by the door. His aquiline features betrayed not a flicker of emotion. Orlaith had grown so accustomed to the mortifex's constant presence that she often forgot he was there. Yet surely he must see the way Beatriu's grasp on sanity slipped a bit more each day. The way her left eye twitched, measuring the pendulum swings of her moods.

Did Janus realize his mistress's mind crumbled? And if so, did he even care?

Five days prior, Beatriu had decided that she could fly. When she declared her intention to soar like an eagle, Orlaith made no attempt to dissuade her. In fact, she suggested that Beatriu might have greater success if she started from a high point. With Janus absent — a rare occurrence — they climbed the stairs to the roof together.

Beatriu stepped to the edge, arms outstretched, face tilted heavenward. Her white gown fluttered around her tiny frame. "Behold!" she cried. "The mighty wings of Kaethe's regent unfurl!"

With that, the little empress pitched herself off the roof. Of course, she dropped like a stone ... only to be caught at the last moment by her knights below. As Orlaith ground her teeth, they lowered Bea gently to the courtyard, a rose petal upon the breeze.

Yet if they *hadn't* ... Orlaith felt sure that not even the Grand Menotte would have saved her.

She resolved to try other means. Brute force was out; after the flying incident, Beatriu was never alone. Orlaith considered the dwale berries secreted in her vanity drawer. It would be all too easy to sprinkle a lethal dose into the iced cakes Beatriu favored.

But even as the thought crossed her mind, memories of Enrigo arose. Tears stung Orlaith's eyes and she curled her hands into fists, fingernails cutting bloody crescents into her palms. No. She could not murder another child. *Not that way.*

In the end, Orlaith placed both their fates in the hands of Kaethe. When the summer rains arrived, ushering in fever season, she saw her chance. The pestilence ran unchecked through the city, feeding upon the unburied dead. It was a simple thing to dispatch Albion to procure the blanket of a fever victim.

That night, after Beatriu had gone to bed, Orlaith spread the contaminated cloth over her, tucking it close. Then she curled up at the girl's feet like a loyal hound.

There was a strange peace in surrender. The weeks of fear, the scheming, the grief and guilt — it all fell away, replaced by numb acceptance. She welcomed the release the plague would bring. At least it would end the long days of solitude and regret.

Orlaith's mother had taught her that a woman's highest calling was to please her husband and give him strong, healthy sons to carry on the family name. At this, she had failed by every measure.

Ghosts haunted the manor. Sometimes she heard Enrigo's shout of laughter echoing through the halls, the patter of small feet and Jak's sharp barks. She no longer dared walk in the vineyards for fear of glimpsing a flash of golden hair among the leaves.

A sense of being followed prickled her skin. Lucius, come to gloat over her misfortune? Or worse, the son whose death she...

A jab of pain pierced Orlaith's reverie. She glanced down to see crimson welling from her thumb. Clumsy. She must have pricked herself with the darning needle. Bringing the wound to her mouth, she sucked at the blood. A shadow fell across her sewing basket.

Beatriu loomed over her, storm-gray eyes stark against pasty skin. For a frozen moment, Orlaith thought her a wraith. Then the girl gave a rattling cough. "I thirst for spiced wine," she rasped.

"Of course, Your Majesty." Orlaith set aside her mending and hastened to fetch a silver chalice.

As Orlaith poured, Beatriu wandered the chamber, trailing listless fingers over the vanity. She touched the ivory combs, the pots of rouge and face powder, her gaze distant.

"Come, Your Majesty. Back to bed." Orlaith eased her down onto the silken pillows. She drew the covers up to Beatriu's chin and smoothed back the damp tendrils of hair. "Drink. It will soothe your throat."

Beatriu took a sip and sank back, cheeks flushing. As Orlaith took the chalice, her fingers brushed the Grand Menotte clasped around the child's thin wrist. The metal was so cold it burned. She marveled that Beatriu could stand its constant touch.

The girl's eyelids fluttered. Her breathing slowed, each exhale a faint wheeze. Studying that fragile form, Orlaith felt the dormant instinct of motherhood rekindle in her breast. How many times had she nursed Enrigo through childish colds and ailments?

"They hunger," Beatriu murmured. "So hungry, all the time. It never stops."

Orlaith's heart stuttered. "Hush now, Your Majesty," she soothed. "Let me read to you."

She selected a volume from the bedside table, a swashbuckling adventure full of romance and daring exploits. One of Enrigo's favorites. "Chapter Six," Orlaith began. "As the *Sea Serpent* sliced through the waves under the rising moons, Captain Leroux gathered his crew on the deck.

"Men," Orlaith read, deepening her voice, "tonight we make for the Nether Caves to claim the treasure of the dread pirate Yardley. But beware, for these tides be treacherous, and it's said a beast lurks at the entrance, guarding the hoard with jaws that can crush a galleon to splinters.

"The sailors muttered amongst themselves, making the sign of Bel. The captain stood tall and unafraid at the bow. 'All ye who be brave enough to face the perils, step forward and pledge your cutlass to the quest!'"

Beatriu's eyes had slipped closed again, her breathing even. Orlaith read a few minutes more, until she was certain the girl slept. Then exhaustion took her and she dozed off in the chair, the book splayed across her lap.

Sometime later, she woke to Beatriu thrashing and moaning, the covers twisted about her legs. The fever blazed. Orlaith tried to force more wine past her cracked lips but Beatriu knocked the chalice away. Red droplets spattered the white counterpane.

"Captain," Beatriu called weakly, struggling to sit up. "Attend me."

The mortifex glided to her bedside. Beatriu gazed up at him, her eyes glassy. "Go to the convent. Bring the nuns to pray over me."

Janus hesitated, gaze slicing to Orlaith. Leaving the empress alone with her clearly nettled him.

"You heard your mistress," Orlaith snapped. "Go!"

"Heed her," Beatriu whispered.

Janus inclined his head and strode from the chamber. Beatriu collapsed back onto the pillows, her slight frame wracked with coughs. "I would like to confess my sins to you ... should the sisters not come in time."

Oralith frowned. "Don't speak so, Your Majesty."

"I am dying." Beatriu fixed Orlaith with a cold stare, her old forcefulness returning. "I must unburden my soul. *You will listen.*"

Orlaith's protests died. She took Beatriu's hot little hand between her own. "Very well. But you must lie back and be at ease."

The child empress sank into the pillows. In a rasping whisper, she began. "My brother Tristan and I were close from the cradle." A wistful smile played about her cracked lips. "He called me Scarpetta. Little slipper. And I called him Lupo. Wolf, for his fierceness ... Always there to protect me from the others."

"The others. You mean your siblings?"

Beatriu nodded. Her fingers tightened on Orlaith's. "I loved him best of all. If only it were just the two of us ... But my sister Gentil ... she was jealous. And when Tristan rose to the throne, she had him murdered."

Orlaith made a noise of dismay.

"I know ... because I followed her to the orchard that day," Beatriu continued between wheezing breaths. "There was a long ... colonnade. I walked there often ... with Enrigo."

"Yes, I remember. What transpired?"

"I hid myself behind a pillar." Her words came faster now. "Gentil bribed his guards to drug and betray him. But she wanted Tristan to know who had ordered his death. So she stood over him and watched the life fade from his eyes."

"Merciful Kaethe," Orlaith murmured. The depravity of it chilled her to the marrow.

Beatriu's narrative was broken by a coughing fit. Orlaith

held a handkerchief to her lips until it stopped. The lace came away crimson.

"Your Majesty, you must rest now—"

"No! You will hear the rest ... A sip of wine first." Orlaith helped her drink. It seemed to give her strength, for Beatriu's voice firmed. "I bided my time. Waited a full year, pretending I didn't know. I combed Gentil's hair. Kissed her cheeks and called her dear sister."

"And then?" Orlaith breathed, on the edge of her seat.

A savage light kindled in the child's eyes. "Then I poured lamp oil over her bedclothes and burned her as she slept. I drugged her first, just as she'd done to Tristan."

"Oh my." Orlaith swallowed. "Well, she deserved it. You avenged him, Your Majesty."

"Did I?" Beatriu croaked.

"Masterfully. And what of your other sister, Ursola?" Orlaith asked, fascinated by the whole affair. "I heard a demon claimed her life." This much she had learned from Lucius.

"A demon of her own conjuring." Beatriu nodded, her brow damp with sweat. "She meant it for me, but her own sorcery ensnared her instead."

"How ghastly! You poor child."

The girl made no reply, sinking deeper into the pillows as if the speech had drained her. She was nearly as white as the bed linens. A mere wisp of a thing to bear the mantle of empress.

After a long moment, Beatriu stirred. "Read to me," she whispered.

Orlaith reached for the leather-bound book with hands that shook ever so slightly. As Captain Leroux's exploits unspooled once more, she marked the labored rasp of Beatriu's breathing, the restless twitch of her arms and legs beneath the covers.

The child's death-watch had begun, the shadow of the Veil gathering close.

Beatriu went still — so still that Orlaith thought she had slipped away. But no, a pulse still fluttered in the blue vein at her throat. Orlaith found herself reaching for the girl's hand, clasping it between her own as if she could anchor her to life through sheer force of will.

"Do not be afraid," she said. "Kaethe must love you very much to summon you home."

Tears welled hot and bitter, spilling down Orlaith's cheeks in scalding runnels.

Slowly, slowly, the faltering rise and fall of Beatriu's breast quieted.

Orlaith sat in numb silence. Her gaze strayed to the vanity, to the drawer where the dwale waited, a sweet promise of oblivion. She could join the poor child, couldn't she? Join all the other ghosts at Redvayne manor. What a great host they had become!

Footfalls sounded in the hall, shattering her reverie. The doorknob rattled, voices rising on the other side as the nuns found it locked. When had she turned the key? It must have been after Janus left.

But ... if she didn't act now, someone else would come along and take charge. That wouldn't do at all. Not after everything she had suffered.

The Grand Menotte slid easily over Beatriu's birdlike bones, eager to bind itself to a new mistress. As it slipped onto Orlaith's wrist, she gave a little cry. The icy cuff shrank tight, hinges fusing shut.

She gave a wordless howl as a hundred alien minds flooded her. Blood-thirst gnawed at her belly, clamoring to be sated. She teetered on a knife's edge, her own identity unraveling. The immensity of it drove Orlaith to her knees.

A flash of movement in the oval standing mirror snared her gaze. Wide, feral eyes stared back from a mourning hood, tendrils of golden hair framing a face that looked far older than its thirty-six years. The madness receded a step as memory stirred. Her name was Orlaith Redvayne. Wife of Robert, mother of Enrigo.

Her purpose crystallized: to avenge her family's ruin.

The pounding on the door intensified. Orlaith staggered upright, gripping her head. An animal sound tore from her throat.

"No, no, no, no, no." The words tumbled out, half moan, half prayer. "Go away. Go away!"

Orlaith clenched her fingers around the Grand Menotte until the cold of it bit deep. She used the pain to center herself, to leash the forces raging through her and bind them to her will. Reaching out with her mind, she sent a single shrieking command: *RETURN TO ME.*

Blessed silence fell, broken only by the frantic drumbeat of her pulse. In the eye of the storm, Orlaith found a semblance of calm. *If I controlled Lucius, I can control a hundred of his kind. I must!*

She strode to the door and unlocked it. Five nuns stood in the hall, bearing a shroud and the foul-smelling quicksilver concoction they used to wash the dead. One look at her face and they shrank back, fingers sketching Kaethe's nine-pointed star.

Janus loomed behind them, his chiseled features inscrutable. He dropped to one knee, dark head bowed. How many times had he ignored her presence completely?

Justinian. That is his true name.

How she knew this, Orlaith could not say, but it was right. She let him kneel and addressed the nuns, her voice amazingly steady. "Take Beatriu to the temple and prepare her for Kaethe."

"Yes, Lady Redvayne," the abbess stammered.

Orlaith brushed past them without bothering to correct the form of address. Titles meant nothing. True power was finally hers, and that is all that mattered.

She snapped her fingers at Justinian. He fell in behind her, a towering shadow at her heels as she swept through the secret door by the kitchens and plunged into the maze of underground passages.

The disused wine cellar waited at the end. Inside, a gaunt figure surged to his feet, chains rattling. Tears pricked Orlaith's eyes. "It's all right now, my love. Our time has finally come."

She turned to the mortifex captain. Surprise, tinged with revulsion, came through the menotte. Her temper flared. What right did he have to judge her? He was as dead as Robert! The only reason he looked like a man was because he drained the life from others.

I will be merciful for now. There's no time to waste punishing him.

Orlaith moved forward, selecting a smaller key from the ring. It had been so many years since it was used, she prayed it still worked. But with a rusty groan, the manacles fell away.

"Fetch my husband's horse," she ordered curtly. "We ride for Hellgate."

Twenty-Five

Cas knelt by the mossy rocks, scooping water into his mouth with cupped hands. Beside him, Felippa leaned down and stuck her face straight into the stream.

He glanced over. "You drink like a horse."

She gave a loud neigh, startling a crow from its branch above. "Aye, well, hiking for days on end makes a body thirsty."

Cas stood, knees cracking. It was the third day trekking north through the Boundary. A pair of stolen blankets from one of Yael's farms provided warmth at night, but the autumn chill seeped into his bones. At least Felippa had good sturdy shoes now.

As they walked on, Cas breathed in the familiar loamy scent of the forest. Shafts of misty light slanted between the pines. The Boundary had always been sparsely settled, but now it seemed empty of people entirely. The further they went, the more at ease he felt. It was the land of his birth, and part of it had never left him.

Leaves rustled behind. Cas whirled, hand going to the knife

at his belt. But it was only a silver fox watching them from the shadows, pointy ears pricked. He had seen plenty of animals on the journey. Deer and beaver, bear and lynx. Interestingly, none were afraid of their fellow travelers.

Gossamer shapes drifted between the trees; the risen from Yael, and others he'd met along the way. Their bodies had mercifully given out, leaving wisps of pure spirit.

Cas whistled a bittersweet tune as they crested a hill. He'd known exactly where they were, yet his chest still tightened at the sight of the old farmhouse nestled in the valley below, its stone walls crumbling, roof sagging under the weight of years.

Felippa squinted. "Too bad. I suppose whoever lived there is long gone."

Cas glanced at her, then back at the ruin. He cleared his throat. "It's our farm. You wouldn't remember. You were only four when we left."

Felippa blinked, staring intently at the homestead. "Did you bring us here on purpose?"

"Aye," he admitted. "When I passed through not too long ago, Ma's garden had some carrots and such left in it..." He trailed off. "What?"

She stopped walking, fixing him with her don't-feck-me-around look. "You came for carrots?"

Cas had to laugh. "Well, not only for that. I thought..." He shrugged. "We should pay our respects. Not just pass it by. We had a lot of good times here, you know." He studied her face. "I'm sorry, I've been an ass. Your worst memory is probably here. Mine, too. Let's go around—"

She drew a deep breath. "No, you're right. I want to see it."

They picked their way down the hill, weaving between ancient oaks and overgrown briars. Cas paused by a rusting wagon tilted on its side in the tall grass. "This was Teo's. He used to give you rides, remember?"

Felippa half shook her head. He couldn't tell if it was a yes or no.

"And this..." Cas bent and dug a scrap of faded gingham from the dirt. "You used to dress your little straw dolls in this. Ma would give you the leftovers from her good fabric."

A smile tugged at Felippa's lips, there and gone like a darting minnow. She ran through the grass and picked something up. "Look!" She held up a child's spinning top, its once bright red paint peeling.

"Da carved that for you and I painted it." Cas swallowed hard. "You carried it everywhere until you lost it one day. Gods, you screamed and fussed."

"I did not!"

His grin faltered as he regarded the house. The roof had collapsed in several places. Purple finches nested in the crumbling walls, their agitated alarm calls — "pik pik pik!" — piercing the quiet as Cas and Felippa entered what remained of the kitchen.

He rummaged around and found a cast-iron frying pan, still solid despite the rust blooming across its surface. A few chipped plates, a dented kettle — he set them out on the weathered plank table.

"You check the garden, I'll catch us some supper." Cas headed for the Forkings River, his boots leaving deep prints in the sandy bank. Lying on his belly, he trailed his fingers through the chill water, searching for telltale shadows.

A flicker of movement. Quick as a snake, Cas plunged his hand in and seized the trout, feeling the solid weight of it thrashing against his palm. Some skills never left you, no matter how many years passed. He returned to the ruin with his catch, gutting the fish with deft strokes of his knife.

Felippa emerged from the tangled garden, her arms full of wild bounty — pungent herbs, a few stubby parsnips, even a precious handful of late peas. She'd woven a wreath as she foraged, daisies and nodding periwinkle harebells.

"Lord of the Boundary," she declared, setting the circlet solemnly on Cas's head.

He grinned, striking a regal pose. "The wood nymphs will swoon at the sight of me."

They built a small fire beneath the lightning-scarred oak that had shaded countless family meals, its branches still sturdy despite the seams of char running through the trunk. The trout sizzled in the pan, the flaky white flesh flecked with herbs.

As they ate, Cas found himself thinking of roads not taken, the strange turns of fate that had shaped their lives. If Justinian had never come to the farm that night, if their ma still lived...

"Do you think I'd have made a good woodward, Lip? It's what Ma always wanted for me."

She tilted her head, considering. "There's no way to know, is there? You might have been terrible at it. The worst woodward in the history of green lore."

Cas flicked a pea at her, and she laughed. "I think we all turned out all right," she said. "Even Teo."

He was quiet for a minute. "Would you like to visit Ma's grave?"

Felippa hesitated, then nodded. They made their way down to the willow by the riverbank, its trailing fronds stirring in the breeze. She knelt near the pile of smooth river stones that served as a marker. "I wish I remembered her," she said.

Cas gently tugged her braid. "You look so much alike. She'd be proud. Always said you had a spark too bright to extinguish." He paused. "Not for lack of trying."

She elbowed him in the ribs, a fond jab, and they lapsed into companionable silence. Cas could feel Ma's presence in the wind bending the grass, the song of a lark.

At last, they returned to the farmstead, spreading their

blankets by the old oak where golden leaves drifted thick. The spirits clustered under the eaves of the trees, glowing faintly like marshfire.

"Cas?" Felippa said. "I just thought of something."

"Aye?" He rolled over to face her.

"Do you still have that letter? The one from Brennos?"

Cas frowned. "Aye."

"We should open it," she said, propping herself up on an elbow. "If something happens and you lose it, wouldn't it be better if we knew what it said? Then you can still deliver the message."

He hesitated, a strange reluctance tightening in his chest. This was the point where they needed to turn east and begin the long walk to Mystral. That was the plan.

"I suppose so," he said slowly, making no move to retrieve it.

Felippa held out a hand. "Give it here. I'll read it."

With a sigh, Cas dug the folded parchment from his coat and passed it to her. Felippa broke the wax seal and scanned the lines.

"Brennos pledges his aid to the Moon Courts," she read aloud. "He says he'll march for Hellgate." She looked up. "How far is Nyons?"

"More than a hundred leagues to the border, and farther still to Mystral," Cas admitted. He read the letter himself, then carefully refolded it.

"Then it might be too late by the time we get there," Lip fretted. "What do we do now?"

"Let's sleep on it. Morning will bring clarity."

Cas drew his blanket around his shoulders and stared up at the star-flecked sky. Hellgate would be much closer, sitting at the northern reach of the Boundary. One of the Greater Gates to Kaethe's Dominion. Of course, it would be closed like all the others.

But his gut told him that Beatriu might take her army there. It was the place where east and west had clashed once before...

A flash of pale wings caught his eye. Cas turned to see a spectral raven perched on a branch, its dark gaze fixed on him. A sign?

He drew a steadying breath. "Kaethe," he whispered, the first time he'd prayed since leaving Orlaith's service. "Show me how to carry out your will."

The raven quorked once, then launched itself into the sky. Cas tracked its flight until it vanished, then let the rush of the nearby river lull him into slumber.

He dreamed himself beneath the weeping willow, its branches trailing in the water. The grass over his mother's grave was dotted with white asters. Mist curled around the willow's roots, and from its shifting tendrils a figure emerged, pale and terrible.

"Castelio." The goddess's voice echoed as if from a great distance. "You've done well to show kindness to the lost souls who wander."

He knelt, gathering his words with care. "My Lady, they are suffering. Why do you punish them? Have we done something to anger you?"

Her face hardened. "The way will open when Delilah returns with my husband at her side."

Cas shook his head, pulse racing. "I don't understand. Where has she gone?"

"I still have faith in her," Kaethe said, though he sensed an uncertainty that chilled him. "But the paths are unraveling. All may yet be lost." Her eyes were two depthless pools. "Go with my blessing, Quietus."

“Go where?”

“Hellgate. You will know what to do.” Her form began to dissolve.

“Wait!” Cas charged forward, but his fingers passed through empty air. “What does Delilah have to do with any of this? Tell me!”

Silence. The goddess was gone, leaving curling mist in her wake and dread in the pit of his stomach.

He woke to a hand patting his cheek. Felippa leaned over him. “Cas? Wake up. I found breakfast.” She grinned and held up a withered tuber. “Carrots!”

He struggled upright and made to rub his gritty eyes — then froze. There, stark against the skin of his left hand, was the Lady’s nine-pointed star, his oath restored as sharp and blue as the day it was inked.

Twenty-Six

The storeroom of the Fates' apothecary shop was a symphony of smells that tickled the nose and stung the eyes. Lo knelt in her gray dress, scrubbing the flagstone floor. Shelves stretched from floor to ceiling, each laden with labeled flasks, jars, and tins. A pair of oil lamps lit the room, their flames dancing in the cool draft that seeped through the mullioned window.

Morgen stood at the central table, head bent over a mortar and pestle. The rhythmic grinding of dried herbs filled the air. Lo paused in her work, watching as Morgen's hands worked with practiced efficiency.

Lo knew little about herbs so she was treated like a scullery, sweeping floors, dusting shelves, and lugging heavy deliveries. Morgen's work was much lighter, but Lo didn't resent her for it. Her own lies had led them both into the trap.

Morgen had already died once since coming here. Five days before, a customer had come to the door and Morgen made a break for freedom. She didn't get more than four steps past the threshold before collapsing like a puppet with its strings cut.

Lo had been forced to drag her back inside and wait for her to revive. Then they all got a stern lecture from Decima about breaking the rules.

"Listen, I really am sorry," Lo said for the tenth time.

She didn't expect a response — the woman hadn't spoken to her in a week. Morgen didn't look up, but her hands faltered. The pestle mashed her fingers, and she cursed under her breath.

"Are you okay?" Lo asked.

Nothing.

Lo sat back on her haunches. "What you said to me before… You were right. I used you when it was convenient. If you'd known that Jaskin didn't have the Grand Menotte, I was afraid you'd leave me in that swamp." How she despised admitting the next part! But it was part of her new honesty regimen. "And I didn't want to be alone."

Morgen finally looked at her, a cold stare. "Is *that* the truth, or another lie?"

"The truth."

Morgen regarded her for a long moment. "You were right to be afraid. I *would* have left you." She took a salve from one of the shelves and rubbed it into her bruised fingers. "However," she added, her voice softening a fraction, "I can't blame you for all of it. Those women reeled us in like perch on a line. I suspect that no matter what choices we made, all roads would have led to this cursed house."

A squeaky shoe sounded from the hallway, the telltale sign of Nona's approach. Lo returned to her scrubbing as the plump, rosy-cheeked Fate entered the kitchen. "Sneaky Mouse," she said to Lo. "When you're done with the floors, you will dust the shelves." Nona turned to Morgen. "As for you, Grumpy Mouse, there's a customer at the door. I need a blend of catmint, comfrey, and hound's tongue."

Morgen nodded curtly and set about preparing the order. She located each herb, then mixed them in a bowl and poured the contents onto a small sheet of wax paper, which she folded into a square. Lo kept scrubbing, head down, as Nona watched. When the order was ready, the youngest Fate left, her squeaky shoe receding down the hallway.

Lo glanced up at Morgen. "There's more," she whispered. "Since I'm coming clean."

Morgen arched a brow.

"I wasn't really chasing Jaskin. I was chasing Bel."

"The sun god," Morgen said flatly.

"You know him as Nabu-bal-idinna."

Now Morgen laughed aloud. "Kaethe's consort? The gentle man who was always puttering about the kitchen, baking cardamom cakes? Who dandled me on his knee and sang silly songs?"

Lo regarded her grimly. "I know it sounds unlikely, but Kaethe has been holding Bel prisoner in her tower since the Sundering, and Jaskin Cazal ran off with him. Kaethe ordered me to bring him back. It's why she closed the gates to her realm."

Morgen returned to grinding herbs. "If you are going to lie again, at least come up with something plausible."

Lo threw her scrub brush down. "Think! Didn't you notice the scorched places we passed on the way to Loris? That was Bel's doing. He's starting to remember who he truly is. It's why I needed the god's bane. Not for Jaskin, for Bel!"

Morgen shook her head, her expression hardening. "This is ridiculous."

"Fine," Lo muttered. "Don't believe me. But I'm not scrubbing floors for eternity. There has to be a way out."

Before Morgen could respond, Decima strode into the room, her bony, austere face flushed with impatience. "I need a decoction of burdock and wormwood, Grumpy Mouse, three to one, mind you. Quick!"

Her ill-tempered gaze turned on Lo. "And you, Sneaky Mouse, go dust the spinning chamber."

"But Nona said to dust the shelves—"

"No backtalk! Or I'll send you to Morta."

Lo sighed and dragged her bucket to the spinning chamber, where they kept baskets of yarn. The afternoon dragged on, a monotonous routine of cleaning and hauling. Customers came and went, their needs attended to by Morgen and the two sisters. By the end, Lo's feet ached and her fingers looked like they belonged to a mummified corpse.

She found Morgen in the apothecary storeroom, replenishing jars and tins. Nona's humming drifted from the next room, where she sat filing receipts and logging sales.

Lo grabbed a pinch of salt from a nearby bowl and sprinkled it onto the table. She traced the word "sorry" in the white crystals. Morgen gave her a brusque nod. Lo erased it and wrote "allies?"

Morgen's gaze flicked to the doorway. She nodded firmly and brushed the salt into a cupped palm.

Lo felt a surge of relief. Together, they could escape, she felt sure. She gave Morgen a tight smile and mouthed, *Follow my lead*. Morgen nodded again and moved back to her worktable.

"Think you're so high and mighty, don't you?" Lo said loudly.

Nona's humming stopped.

"Me?" Morgen retorted with a crooked smile at odds with the acid in her voice. "You're the one who got us into this mess in the first place! Deceitful wretch."

"Oh, poor you! I'm doing all the hard work, while you're their little pet." Lo propped her hands on her hips. "Grumpy Mouse, make us a package of herbs. Grumpy Mouse, smile at the customer. Meanwhile, I'm down on my knees in the dirt. This is bullshit!"

They launched into a heated argument, voices rising until Nona hurried into the room, shoe squeaking. "Enough! The little mice will each do as she's told and not complain."

They donned resentful expressions and hung their heads. "Yes, mistress," they mumbled in unison.

"Sneaky Mouse, go prepare supper! Grumpy Mouse, finish with those jars."

Lo stomped off to the kitchen. She banged the pots and pans as she set about preparing a pot of rice. But as soon as it grew quiet, she kicked off her shoes and crept back down the narrow hallway. Up ahead, she could hear the soft murmur of Nona and Decima's voices. The door to the spinning room sat ajar. Lo edged closer, peering through the crack.

Her breath caught. It was transformed from the mundane chamber she had dusted earlier that day. Rosy light illuminated an elegant veranda with a white marble balustrade that belonged in a fairytale palace. Lavender mountains loomed in the distance, their peaks wreathed in mist.

Lo hesitated, then gathered her courage and slipped through the doorway. Her bare feet sank into thick, sun-warmed clover. A warm breeze caressed her skin, carrying the scent of honeysuckle and jasmine. The peaceful beauty of the place made her heart ache.

At the end of the veranda, Nona and Decima leaned across a long stone table, engrossed in their work. Nona's nimble fingers spun thread from mounds of a cloud-like substance, while Decima measured each strand with her distaff before winding it around a spindle.

Lo crawled closer, concealed behind a row of columns. Each thread must represent a life, for they glowed with a warm, pulsing light. The sisters worked with practiced efficiency, their movements precise and purposeful.

She could make out snippets of their conversation now. Decima was talking about the last customer of the day, a pretty woman with a dusky complexion and cheerful demeanor.

"Poor thing," Nona clucked, shaking her head as she examined a particular thread. "She has no idea that she will die tomorrow when she steps in front of a cart."

Decima glanced up from her measuring. "You have seen the larger weave, sister. If she does not trip and fall beneath the wheels, she will travel to Gaio and bring back a plague that kills dozens." She placed the measured thread into a basket. "It is for the greater good."

Lo had thought the Fates cold-hearted, but now she reconsidered. Perhaps they weren't evil, precisely. Just impartial. The complexity of their work, the way they perceived the ripples of each life within the larger ocean, was staggering. She was pondering this when her ears pricked up again.

"What should be done about this childish bickering between Grumpy Mouse and Sneaky Mouse?" Nona complained.

Decima pursed her lips. "Grumpy Mouse has proven herself the most useful of the three. Do we really need to keep the other two? Lazy Mouse" — that was their apt nickname for Jaskin — "is worthless. And Sneaky Mouse seems like trouble."

Oh, you're too right, bitches, Lo thought.

"Sneaky Mouse is also our sister's hunter," Nona snapped. "Let us not forget that."

Lo didn't know why they hated Kaethe so much, but the malice in her tone was unmistakable. Speaking of which...

Where was the scariest bitch of them all? Lo hadn't seen her since that first day. Her neck prickled and she glanced over her shoulder, half-expecting to find Morta behind her, shears glinting, but the veranda was empty.

Well, it was time to slip away before the others caught her.

Lo cast a final look at the purple mountains, the fields of wildflowers and sparkling lakes. Part of her longed to escape into this beautiful fantasy world, but she couldn't abandon those she loved. Besides which, Kaethe wouldn't open her gates until she had Bel back.

Fucking blackmail, but there you had it.

Lo crept back through the doorway. As she made her way to the kitchen, she passed Jaskin's cramped quarters, a converted broom closet housing a straw pallet. The door was half open and she couldn't resist pausing to spy.

Jaskin sat on his pallet, his trouser leg pulled up to reveal a neatly healed scar. He rubbed some salve into it, then sprang to his feet with apelike agility, not a hint of a limp in sight. Of course, the reason they called him Lazy Mouse was that he claimed his wound still pained him and he couldn't do any work. *Liar.*

Shaking her head in disgust, Lo continued to the kitchen. She warmed the rice and set out bowls and spoons. The Fates never ate; only the three little mice.

Not one to miss a meal, Jaskin was the first to arrive, followed by Morgen, her face set in its usual scowl. Jaskin limped to the table with an exaggerated grimace.

"How's your leg?" Lo asked.

He drew a deep breath through his nose. "I am loathe to voice endless grievances, but I fear the bad humors have returned," he moaned, easing himself into a chair.

"Aw, that's terrible." She slammed a bowl of rice down. "Let's have a look at it. I'm sure Morgen would be happy to whip up a poultice to ease your suffering."

He buried his face in the supper, shoulders hunched. "No,

no, that won't be necessary. It would be unseemly for a young lady to gaze upon my bare calf."

Lo made a noise of sympathy. "But you're clearly in so much pain. Surely your modesty would allow an expert opinion."

Jaskin shoveled the rice into his mouth as if it was his last meal on this earth. "You are very kind, but I already have a salve. Rest is all that's needed. Demoiselles!" He sketched a bow and hobbled from the kitchen, his limp even more pronounced than when he'd entered.

Lo held a finger to her lips when Morgen rolled her eyes. They finished their meal in silence, the only sound the scrape of wooden spoons against bowls.

"I cooked, so you can do the dishes, Fancy Mouse!" Lo announced as she stood.

Morgen's eyes flashed. "You call that cooking? The lowest convict in Blackwater Jail ate better than this."

"Then you can make your own supper tomorrow," Lo retorted, spinning on her heel and stalking out of the kitchen. She strode down the narrow hallway and pushed into the cramped room she shared with Morgen.

The space was scarcely bigger than Jaskin's closet, with two narrow pallets. Lo sank onto her bed, the straw crackling beneath her weight, and stared at the rough-hewn ceiling beams. Her mind raced, tumbling over the implications of what she'd overheard.

At last, the door opened and Morgen slipped inside, her face unreadable in the dim light of the single candle. Only when they were both tucked under their itchy blankets, the candle extinguished, did Lo share her most important discovery of the day.

"I overheard the Fates talking," she whispered. "They

didn't know we faked that argument. They think we really hate each other."

There was a pause as this sank in. "So they can't see everything," Morgen whispered back. "But ... how can that be? They've manipulated us from the moment this journey began. Or even farther back, most likely."

Lo bit her lip. She'd already considered this. "I think it's because we're inside their house. It's the one place they're blind. Just the way you cannot see the ground under your own feet."

"Or," Morgen said dryly, "they are playing with us like cats. It amuses them to watch us scurry about."

"You could be right," Lo admitted. "There's no way of knowing unless we try." She hesitated. "I have an idea, but it requires two people. I understand if you don't want to take the risk."

"No," Morgen whispered immediately. "I will join you. Being their slave is worse than my last death."

The two women reached across the gap between pallets, their hands finding each other in the dark and squeezing tight. A pact sealed.

"Even if we manage to escape, how do we stop Morta from taking our final lives once we're gone?" Morgen wondered.

"She must be behind that locked door. I've heard the sisters call it the cleaving chamber." Lo allowed herself a brief shudder. *The cleaving chamber.* Where souls were parted from their life threads.

Morgen's breath hitched in the darkness. She'd already lost her eighth life to Morta's shears.

"I was scrubbing down the hall when I saw Nona put the key into a little clay pot shaped like a pig," Lo whispered. "If you keep her and Decima occupied, I can sneak inside."

"And then what?"

"I'll steal the spindles holding our lives. If Morta doesn't have our threads, she cannot cut them."

Morgen's eyes gleamed in the dark. "You would creep up on Morta?" she asked dubiously.

Lo gave a grin of bravado, though her stomach roiled at the prospect. "I'm Sneaky Mouse, remember?"

THE NEXT DAY dawned gray and damp, the air thick with impending rain. Lo and Morgen rose and went about their usual routine, careful not to draw undue attention from the sisters.

As Lo swept the front of the shop, she heard Morgen's voice drifting from the apothecary storeroom. "I must admit," she said in her usual cool tone, "I am impressed by the depth of your knowledge."

Nona murmured something inaudible. The Decima spoke. "You have a solid grasp of the basics, but if you pay attention, there is much you can learn." Morgen started peppering them with questions about arcane herbs and their precise combinations. The ploy worked; soon, the three of them retired into the drying room in the rear of the shop, their voices fading.

Nerves tingling, Lo abandoned her broom and tip-toed down the hall. There, on a shelf, sat the clay pig with the key to the cleaving chamber door. Lo paused to listen. Morgen was still yammering away. Just as she reached out a hand, the faint tinkle of a bell sounded.

A customer. Well, shit. The timing was very inconvenient! She silently willed the unwelcome visitor to leave, but the bell chimed again, more insistently.

Biting her lip in frustration, Lo set the pig back on the shelf and went to the door. She opened it, a polite greeting on her tongue, but the words died as she took in the man on the threshold.

He was tall and bearded, with a wild mane of dark hair and eyes that seemed to pierce right through her. Pride radiated from the tilt of his chin and the set of his broad shoulders. He wore only a thin white tunic that left his muscular arms bare. Despite the snow coating the steps, he wore no shoes, either.

Something about him set her nerves on edge. She fought the urge to slam the door in his face. "Welcome to Tinctures, Tonics & Yarn," she said. "How may we assist you today, good sir?"

The man's gaze flicked past her shoulder, scanning the shop's interior. "I seek a rare herb," he said, his voice deep and confident. "I was told you might carry it."

Lo swallowed. "Come in, then. I'll fetch the owners."

She stepped aside and he crossed the threshold, bringing with him the scent of ripe strawberries. It was a pleasant smell, but there was something at the edges of it, a burnt, smoky note, that made her heart thump even faster.

"What herb are you looking for?" she asked with a manic smile.

"I will tell your mistresses," he replied, his own face darkening. "Fetch them at once."

There was no need. At that moment, Nona and Decima appeared, Morgen trailing behind. The sisters looked about to faint. Nona's plump hand flew to her mouth. Decima's jaw merely sagged open, making her gaunt face look even longer.

The man gave a cruel laugh, savoring their reaction. "You did not see me coming because I have no thread for you to spin, Moirai."

Decima recovered first. "What do you want?" she demanded, crossing her bony arms.

He smiled, though there was no humor in it. "I have a

message for my wife." The last word dripped with fury and Lo realized that it was fucking *Bel* standing there. Her own jaw flapped in the breeze for a moment before she shut it with a snap.

"Then tell her yourself," Nona retorted. Her composure was returning, and she lifted her chin defiantly.

Bel's eyes flashed. "I would love nothing better, but Kaethe is hiding from me. She's your sister," he growled. "I'm sure you can find a way." He stepped closer. "Tell her that I will make her pay for what she did to me. In the meantime, my children will wreak havoc!"

Lo's breath caught. So Kaethe was right. Bel *was* an asshole. She glanced at Morgen, who had drifted to Lo's side, and saw the same fear and awe reflected in her eyes.

"Loris will burn to ash," the sun god snarled. "You will not be able to cut threads fast enough to keep up, crones!" He gave another taunting laugh. "I am immortal, beyond your reach. There is nothing you can do to stop me."

Nona's lips twisted. "You were a terrible match for Kaethe. We tried to warn her, but she wouldn't listen."

"She loved me at first," he snapped. "She would have done anything for me."

"Including banishing her own sisters when you demanded it," Decima said bitterly. "We told her you would be her downfall, but she was blind."

Lo watched the exchange with bated breath. If she looked hard, she could make out Nabu-bal-idinna lurking behind Bel's handsome, arrogant face. They *were* the same man, but their personalities were so different it caused a profound physical change. Then she noticed Nona edging closer.

"Get the gods bane," she hissed. "Quickly!"

Morgen gave an obedient nod, eyes wide. She and Lo slipped away, leaving Bel trading barbs with his sisters-in-law.

"So they really have god's bane?" Lo asked in disbelief. Why this was the most important question to pop into her head she couldn't say, but it was irksome.

Morgen pulled down a dented tin from a high shelf. "That waif at the market wasn't lying. They have every known herb here, and more I've never even heard of."

Lo set a kettle to boil, her mind racing two steps ahead. "We can still salvage the plan," she whispered. "Once he's drugged, we drag him back to Kaethe."

Morgen crumbled the leaves into a teapot with trembling fingers. It was the first time Lo had seen her icy composure falter. "Portals don't work. We've both tried."

Lo poured the god's bane tea into a cup. The amber liquid glowed faintly, promising oblivion. "Yes, but we didn't have Bel before. If Kaethe is watching, she'll open all her gates to get him back. Now grab a funnel!"

Understanding dawned in Morgen's eyes. She ransacked a drawer as Lo juggled the hot cup. They hurried back to the front of the shop, Lo hiding the knockout tea behind her back. Bel was still ranting about his revenge, and all the horrible things he had planned for everyone.

"Let the dead walk," he cried. "Let them dance a jig through Kaethe's temples. I don't care. They will burn along with the living. My fire children will see to that. Even now, they march for the darklands!"

Lo crept up behind him, the tea steaming in the cup. She caught Nona's eye and the woman gave a slight nod.

Lo and Morgen pounced.

Bel roared as they wrestled him to the ground. Light burst from his eyes and mouth, casting the room in blinding radiance. It dimmed slightly as Morgen jammed the funnel between his lips. Lo upended the cup, pouring the tea down his throat.

Bel thrashed and gurgled. Slowly, his struggles weakened. The fire dimmed in his eyes, leaving them glassy and vacant. His face rippled weirdly, its imperious lines fading, until he resembled the gentle, scholarly Nabu-bal-idinna once more.

They stepped back, breathing hard. Nona glared at Nabu's still form, then bellowed, "Lazy Mouse!"

A long minute passed before Jaskin came limping out, his expression aggrieved. Then he spotted Nabu and drew up short. "How ... how did he find me?" Jaskin spluttered.

Lo closed her eyes and prayed to Kaethe. *I have Bel! Let us through!* She tried to form a portal to the Lady's tower. Nothing happened. When she looked up, Decima's cold gaze bored into her.

"Sneaky Mouse is up to something," she hissed. "I knew we should never have trusted her."

In a flash, the sisters were upon her. One on each side, with grips like iron manacles, they dragged Lo down the hall toward the forbidden room. The cleaving chamber. The door swung wide at their approach, though no hand touched it. Morgen shouted something, but the blood buzzing in Lo's ears drowned it out.

Then the two Fates were shoving her through the dark doorway. She landed hard and threw out a pleading arm as the door slammed shut with the finality of a sealed tomb.

TWENTY-SEVEN

Nathan Ouvrard gazed at the parchment rolled up on the table as he might a poisonous asp. They'd all read it more than once. It was the reason he was here at the Boundary garrison, along with Chaos and Caul Courtenay, and Duc Caino Scalici of Alessia.

A summons for the regents of the Moon Courts to attend the Empress Beatriu at Hellgate.

"Regents," Caul spat for the fifth time. "As if she's already folded us into her so-called empire. The nerve of the girl!"

Chaos laid a calming hand on her sister's arm. "At least she did not threaten us this time. It has more the tone of an invitation."

"That's cause for optimism, I should think," Scalici put in, running a thumb along his ruddy nose. "By Kaethe, it's cold in here," he muttered. "Can you stir up the fire a bit?"

Nathan caught his mortifex Vigo's eye and gave a slight nod. Flames roared up from the dying embers in the hearth. Scalici moved closer, palms extended to the warmth. A stout, grandfatherly man, he wore a yellow doublet embroidered with a rosette and lion beneath a heavy cloak.

Nathan shared his aversion to the cold. This unseasonable winter was most unpleasant, and his own coat — black, naturally, and bearing the argent Hand Sinister of his house — while fashionable, did little to ward off the chill. Across from him, the Courtenays wore thick layered skirts and dark shawls that made a stark contrast to their masses of curling white hair.

At the tower door, Vigo and the Courtenays' mortifex Mace kept vigil, eyes glowing faintly.

"An invitation?" Caul, the taller and more impetuous of the twins, made a rude noise. "If so, it is one we dare not ignore. It is a command, make no mistake."

Nathan cleared his throat. The same argument had gone round and round for days.

"Setting aside the girl's arrogant tone," he said, "I hold out hope of reaching an accommodation. Beatriu has the Grand Menotte, but we are not completely without leverage."

They would need to tread carefully, but there had to be a path through this mess that avoided another disastrous war. He refused to believe otherwise. Caul looked unconvinced, but she held her tongue. Chaos nodded, shrewd and thoughtful as always.

"It will depend on what Beatriu hopes to gain," Chaos said. "And what she might be willing to concede. But I agree, we must at least try for a treaty, unpalatable as it may be."

Scalici sank his bulk into a chair with a grunt. "I brought my most seasoned troops. We are ready for anything. But let us see what comes of this council first."

Caul snorted. "Beatriu doesn't need to make open threats. We all know what she's capable of." Her bone bracelets clattered as she gestured sharply. "She could unleash her army upon us with a word."

Chaos leaned on her left cane, idly tapping the right. "I wonder ... Could the power of so many mortifexes be capable of disturbing the Sundering itself?"

A heavy silence descended. They had all glimpsed it — the sun breaching the horizon over the Nightwood. For a few terrible moments, golden light had spilled across a land that knew only darkness. Then, mercifully, it sank again.

Yet even that brief flash had wreaked havoc on the fragile ecology. Leaves curled and withered. Bats fell from the sky, blinded. Nathan had found Chaos clutching one to her breast, trying to bring the poor creature back to its senses.

"If Beatriu can make the sun move in the sky," Nathan said, "we have no choice but to cede to her demands, whatever they may be." A muscle in his jaw ticked. "Otherwise, our home will be destroyed."

Caul growled, a sound of pure frustration. Nathan understood. Every fiber of her being balked at the thought of kneeling to a child.

The tower door opened and one of Scalici's border captains entered, snowflakes swirling around his cloak. At his side stood the green-haired centaur Astris, her equine body filling the doorway.

"My lords, my ladies," the captain said with a bow. "The child queen and her retinue have arrived at the Clovis garrison."

Nathan squared his shoulders. "Then let us go and greet her."

They descended the winding tower steps and emerged into the twilight of the Boundary. Hellgate sat before them, a narrow mountain pass with steep cliffs rising on either side. At its center, a lake of black ice marked the border between Alessia and Clovis.

Their own camp spread out along the shore, an orderly

collection of tents and cookfires. Centaurs, humans, and loup garou moved among the banners of the Moon Courts — the stooping Nightjar of Nyons, the Hand Sinister of Vendagni, the Rosette and Lion passant of Duc Scalici's own armies.

Across the ice, torches flared to life outside the cliffside garrison of Clovis, where Kaethe's nine-pointed star fluttered from the central tower. Riders were alighting in the snow, Beatriu's so-called Knights of the Vanguard. A column of soldiers in mail wound down through the pass. That must be her regular army. Nathan didn't care about them. It was the mortifexes he worried most about.

"Do you see her?" Chaos whispered in his ear.

Nathan scanned the knights. They were gathering around a figure in a red cloak. "There."

An honor guard was moving across the ice now, approaching the center of the frozen lake. The four nobles of the Moon Courts shared a look, then strode forth to meet it. As they drew closer, a new banner unfurled from the Clovis garrison tower. The phoenix of House Redvayne.

Nathan's steps slowed. Something was amiss. But turning back now would be certain to cause offense. Six mortifexes glided across the ice, pale cloaks rippling in unison. They surrounded a pair of riders with hoods raised.

Mace and Vigo flanked Nathan, ready to unleash hell at his command. Scalici was sweating and Caul muttered an oath. Only Chaos remained unruffled, her silver canes tapping lightly against the ice as she walked.

They met the opposing party at the middle of the frozen lake. Mist curled off the ice, mingling with the swirling snowflakes. As they'd all agreed, Chaos stepped forward and inclined her head. "We welcome you to the Moon Courts," she said with formal politeness, "and hope that we can sit down as cousins and not enemies—"

The lead rider threw back her hood in a cascade of golden hair. The wind seized it, whipping bright strands against her scarlet cloak. Orlaith Redvayne, cold and imperious. The heavy iron cuff of the Grand Menotte gleamed darkly around her forearm, drawing the frail light into itself.

Nathan hadn't spared Orlaith a thought these last weeks. Yet here she was, wearing the most powerful relic in the darklands.

He was so surprised that it took him a moment to register the trembling horse beside her, and its grisly rider. When Castelio claimed that Duc Robert Redvayne was reanimated all those years ago, and that his wife kept him chained up in his own wine cellar, Nathan had laughed.

It wasn't so funny now. Wisps of white hair clung to Robert's leathery skull, his eyes small shriveled things nesting in sunken sockets.

"Esteemed lords and ladies of the Moon Courts," Orlaith said mockingly. "For twelve long years I have awaited this moment. Now Bel has returned to us, and His light shines upon my purpose."

Her gaze swept them, blue eyes glittering. "You thought us defeated when last we met here. But the phoenix of House Redvayne rises from the ashes, stronger than before. Soon our standard will fly above your shattered keeps."

Orlaith raised her fist, the Grand Menotte dark against her pale skin. "You will kneel and beg forgiveness, or be swept away. The choice is yours, necromancers."

Nathan could only stare, his mind reeling. Around him, the others stood equally stunned.

Then Caul spoke up, scorn in her voice. "You speak of necromancy. What of your husband? He is a ghoul!"

Robert snarled, baring yellowed teeth. Orlaith's answering smile was razor-thin. "That is different from your foul magic," she retorted. "It was done by necessity." Her gaze fixed on the Courtenays' mortifex Mace, burning with hatred. "You killed my husband! And for that, I will see you suffer eternal torment."

"Killed your husband?" Caul erupted. "Robert murdered our parents under a flag of truce! Enticed them to parley and then drew steel." Her fists clenched. "The man had no honor. He was a lying snake who deserved a far worse death than the one Mace gave him!"

Orlaith stared at Caul with loathing, then turned to Duc Scalici. "You see how she speaks of our dear Robert?" she exclaimed. "Come, old friend. You were always loyal to House Redvayne. I forgive your error in judgment, allying with our foes. Join me now and all will be as it was."

The old duc shook his head gravely. "That device on your wrist, it is evil. You know in your heart that I am right, Orlaith. You must rid yourself of it." He reached out a pleading hand. "I know you took Robert's death hard, but there is enough blame to go around. The Courtenays are not their parents. There's still a chance to set aside old grudges. Surely we can find a way to destroy the menotte together."

Orlaith's rigid expression seemed to soften as Scalici spoke. Nathan held his breath. Perhaps reason would prevail after all. But then Scalici glanced around, brow furrowing. "Where is Enrigo? Is he not with you?"

In an instant, Orlaith's face turned to stone, all traces of warmth vanishing. "My son is dead," she said flatly.

Scalici reeled back. "Dead? How? When did this happen?"

Orlaith's angry gaze found Nathan. "You betrayed my trust. Forced me to seek allies in Galatia. I went to Vellio to betroth my son to Beatriu, and he..." She swallowed jerkily. "He died there. This is your fault!"

Nathan stared back, incredulous. "And what of Beatriu?

Where is she?" A suspicion began to form. "Did you murder her, too?"

Orlaith went white to the lips, incandescent with sudden fury. She spun to the dark-haired mortifex at her side. "Will you let him speak to me so, Justinian? Kill him!"

With a thrill of deep-seated horror, Nathan realized it was the mortifex who had come to Castle Cazal all those years ago. The same pitiless eyes that had looked down on him as his parents lay slaughtered in the next room.

So fixated was he that he scarcely noticed when Caul seized his arm and wrenched him aside. A heartbeat later, a gout of flame roared through the space where he'd been standing, close enough to singe his hair.

Vigo and Mace stepped forward in unison, hands outstretched. Twin walls of fire raced toward Orlaith like the jaws of a demon from the ninth plane. Nathan glimpsed the horses rearing up, hooves flailing.

"Run!" Caul shouted. "Make for the garrison!"

"Forgive me, my lady," Nathan murmured, sweeping Chaos into his arms.

She gazed up at him with dark eyes. "You are forgiven. Now go!"

With Scalici to his left and Caul to his right, Nathan ran as fast as his long legs would carry him. The inferno roared higher as Vigo and Mace took the rear, covering their flight with gouts of flame.

"So much for reaching an accommodation," Scalici panted, half sliding on the ice.

Nathan didn't waste breath on a reply. He stopped just long enough to set Chaos on her feet and draw a knife from his belt. The blade was chill against his arm as he carved a shallow gash and pressed it to his own lips, tasting the hot salt of blood.

"Urthrok!" he cried, the syllables wavering in the air like a heat mirage. "I summon thee!"

A desperate gambit, but he was nothing if not desperate. The pressure in his ears shifted as if he'd plunged into deep water. The draugr was an invisible presence, ancient and avaricious. Inhuman laughter rasped against his mind like scales over stone. Yet it had aided him before...

Then the clouds boiled down from the twilit sky, and all restraint vanished. Soldiers in crimson surcoats poured forth, the Redvayne phoenix emblazoned on their chests. They crashed against the shields and spears of Scalici's army like a bloody tide.

Arrows hissed down in dark swarms as the centaur archers took up positions on the flanks. Then the loup garou appeared, prowling from the shadows. They wore the faces of beautiful women until they dropped to all fours and became white teeth and blurring speed, tearing into men with savage glee.

Nathan, Scalici, and the Courtenays regrouped at the top of the garrison tower, where they could observe the battlefield and work their spells to greater effect. Lady Chaos murmured an incantation, and a seething mass of bone-spiders skittered forth, mandibles clacking. Lady Caul conjured a vortex of hot ash that coalesced into human shapes who waded into the fray. Nathan focused his will on the draugr, which stalked unseen through the fighting, pausing here and there to bite off a head or rake its six-inch claws through heavy plate armor.

The mortifexes retaliated with elemental fury. Whirlwinds of flame and lances of jagged ice slashed through the snowy air. Creatures screamed as they died by the dozens.

Yet Nathan knew it could have been worse.

It *should* have been worse.

"She's holding back," Chaos observed, voicing his

thoughts. "Orlaith could end this now if she chose to. Burn us all to ash."

"Yet she hesitates," Caul said slowly. "Why?"

Nathan studied the chaos below, searching for Orlaith's telltale golden hair. "She's waiting for something," he murmured. "There's no other explanation."

"Reinforcements?" Caul shook her head. "She hardly needs them. A weapon? Again, she already possesses the greatest weapon ever devised."

Scalici frowned. "Then what could it be?"

No one spoke for a long moment. Chaos looked thoughtful, tapping her cane against the toe of her boot. "Not what, I think," she said at last. "But *who*?"

Twenty-Eight

Lucius's horse clipped a hoof on a loose stone as he wound his way through the high mountain pass, and he palmed its flank, murmuring soft words. Gray peaks stabbed the sky on either side, funneling the legion through the narrow defile.

He had expected an attack on the bridge, but the mortifex riders had pulled out of their dive at the last moment, circled around, and flown away eastward. He was grateful, but he didn't know why, and that troubled him. Had their mistress changed her mind about destroying the Sons of Bel?

"I got to know Beatriu during the brief time she held my bond," Lucius said. "There's a chance she'll listen to me."

Brennos glanced over. "You think she can be reasoned with?"

"She's not all bad. I believe she has her own sense of justice, twisted though it may be."

Brennos arched a dark brow.

"She allowed Morgen to kill Vaszoly Marcel," Lucius reminded him. "I feared she would order me to intervene, but she didn't. She said, and I quote: 'While revenge is an act of mortal passion, vengeance is an act of immortal justice. Like the Lady's due, it may be long or short in coming. But when a person has been grievously abused, come it will.'"

Brennos ran a hand over his four-day beard, considering. "I almost like her," he said dryly. "But she is a devotee of Kaethe. And thanks to Arnulf, in her eyes we are all the enemy."

"I can vouch for your character. Explain to her that you *stopped* the attack on the convent."

"And if she doesn't believe you?"

"I can be very convincing," Lucius said firmly.

Brennos nodded, though it was obvious he harbored doubts. He was right to. Most likely, Beatriu was no longer the girl Lucius had known in Vellio.

The narrow mountain pass twisted through snowy crags and knife-blade ridges. Lucius scanned the skies. Dark specks wheeled high above — riders on their winged abbadax. They'd followed for days but made no move to swoop down and attack.

Then one of the forward scouts returned in a lather. "The fighting's already begun, Strategos," he reported.

Lucius and Brennos exchanged a look. "So soon," Brennos muttered. "Who is winning?"

"It is hard to say," the scout replied. He looked shaken. "There is dark magic at work."

Brennos dismissed him, fingertips lightly tracing his scars as he considered this news.

"Let me go alone," Lucius proposed. "I'll try to reach Beatriu. I still believe she might listen to me."

Brennos frowned. "We have not come so far to turn back now. Nor to abandon the allies *you* urged me to support." He lowered his voice. "And I will not send you into battle alone. You are my First Flame. You will remain by my side."

Lucius pressed a fist to his chest. Bren gave him a slight smile, then turned his horse and rode onward, as Lucius relayed the order to resume the march. At last, the track spilled out of the final pass, revealing Hellgate's icy lake below. On the near side, the three Moon Court banners flew over a large encampment of tents, half of them in flames.

It came as no surprise. Lucius had smelled blood and smoke for the last hour.

Across the border, a second garrison raised the crimson phoenix of the Redvaynes. And between the two, armies clashed, the sounds of ringing steel and screams borne away by the wind.

Twelve years ago, Lucius had stood on this same ground overlooking a different battle — but one hardly less brutal. Again, it was east against west. Lucius, still in thrall to the Redvaynes, had been forced to fight for a man he despised. Now, for the first time in ten centuries, he could choose his own path.

Scanning the chaos, he sought a glimpse of Beatriu's slight form. Instead, his gaze snagged on a fair-haired woman standing on the roof of the garrison tower, surrounded by a heavy guard. *It couldn't be. Could it?*

Then Orlaith's head turned and unerringly found him like a hound scenting a plump rabbit. He felt the cold weight of her regard across the distance that separated them.

Lucius realized he'd led them into a trap. He had convinced Brennos that they might negotiate with Beatriu, reason with her, but Orlaith? The widow whose husband he'd failed to protect at this very pass? Not to mention her son. Lucius had told the boy every rotten thing his mother had done. She probably blamed him for that death, too, even though it was her own hand who poisoned the wine.

Lucius's grip tightened on the reins as a wave of self-loathing washed over him. After all his long servitude, his first act of freedom had been to lead good men to their deaths. *Yet again.*

Brennos stood with his back to Lucius, dark hair lifting in the wind as he conferred with his Second Flames. He turned at the sound of Lucius's approach, the scars on his face livid in the fading light.

"Strategos," Lucius said, his voice low and urgent as he dismounted. "A word."

Brennos held up a hand to his captains, and they retreated a few paces, leaving the two men in a small bubble of privacy. Brennos's eyes were dark and steady, and for an instant, Lucius was transported back to their first meeting — the fierce young priest, masked as the Red Rogue, defying Duc Marcel with nothing but conviction and courage.

"What is it?" Brennos asked.

"Orlaith Redvayne wears the Grand Menotte, not Beatriu." Lucius fought to keep his voice level. "My eyesight is keen. I saw her atop the garrison, surrounded by her mortifex slaves."

Brennos frowned. "I take it this is worse."

"Much worse. She is mad with grief and hate. She blames the Moon Courts for her family's fall from grace. There will be no parley, no mercy — only slaughter."

"And what would you have me do?" Brennos asked, his voice mild.

"Retreat. Pull your men back into the pass. We can bide our time until—"

"Until what? Our allies are wiped out entirely?" He shook his head. "No. This is the place. This is the hour."

"The legion will die," Lucius said, hating the truth of it. "All of them."

"Perhaps." Brennos looked past Lucius to the lake. "But

there are greater forces in this world than a single talisman. If Bel wills it, we will live this day."

Never had Lucius hated the man's blind faith so much. "Listen to me," he snarled, seizing Brennos's arm. "In my long life, I've watched a hundred religions rise and fall. The words of their prophets are twisted to fit whatever comes to pass. None are worth dying for."

Brennos didn't pull away. Instead, he placed his hand over Lucius's, warm flesh against cold. "You're wrong. Truth, loyalty, honor. Those are all worth dying for. You died for them, did you not, Legatus Claudius Quintus?"

His old name struck Lucius like a blow. Memories crashed through his mind — his own legion, their faith when he ordered them to protect a Danai village from his king's bloodthirsty madness.

"That was a different time," Lucius argued, the words ringing hollow. "A different man."

"Was it? I don't think so." Brennos laid a palm on his chest, above his heart. "I think he's still here."

Before Lucius could respond, a horn sounded from Orlaith's camp. Brennos turned to his captains. "Form the lines," he ordered, and they hurried to obey. Then he climbed onto a rocky outcrop where all in the legion could see him.

Lucius watched the Sons of Bel assemble. Half were barely more than boys. Down on the frozen lake, the forces of the Moon Courts were regrouping — humans who had learned to live alongside the night creatures, fighting for their shared lands. Among them, the tall forms of centaurs pawed at the ground, and the loup garou paced back and forth, ready to bound into the fray again.

"Brothers!" Brennos's voice rang out. All faces turned to him, standing against the smoke-darkened sky. "Today we face an enemy who is stronger. Who outnumbers us. Who wields fire."

A murmur ran through the ranks, but Brennos raised his hand and it stilled.

"I see fear in your eyes. Good. I am afraid, too. Only fools feel no fear before battle." He moved slowly along the outcrop, his gaze sweeping over the men. "They expect us to break. To run away. But they do not know us." He paused, his voice rising. "We are the torch against the dark. The lantern in the long night. We are the Sons of Bel!"

A ragged cheer went up.

"Look to your brothers beside you. Look to our allies before you. We stand not just for ourselves, but for all who would live free in these lands." Brennos unsheathed his sword, the blade glimmering in the twilight.

"They believe we are outmatched. That Hellgate will be our grave." His voice dropped, and the men leaned forward to catch his words. "But I say this. If today is the day we die, let us die so gloriously that songs will be sung of us for a thousand years. Let us die with such courage that our enemies will count themselves honored to have slain us. Let us die knowing that we were blessed to fight this day!"

He raised his sword, gazing heavenward. "And maybe we will not die, brothers. For Bel's eye is on each and every one of us now. His fire burns in our veins. Let His will be done!"

A roar went up from the priests. They beat their spears against bucklers, a thunderous affirmation that echoed off the steep walls of the pass.

Something stirred in Lucius — something he had not felt in centuries. Hope, perhaps. Or the simple joy of standing for what was right, no matter the cost. The feeling he'd known as Claudius Quintus, general of the Tenth Legion, before death and centuries of bondage had ground it out of him.

Brennos leapt down from the outcrop, his captains gathering around him as he gave his final orders. Then he turned to Lucius. "Will you ride out with me, First Flame?"

For some reason, Lucius thought of Justinian at that moment. His own trusted captain, who had stood with him to the end. Who had died minutes after Lucius did.

"I will ride with you." Lucius mounted and drew his own blade. "To whatever may come."

Brennos's smile was like the sun breaking through clouds. He leapt into the saddle and turned to his legion once more. "For Bel!" he shouted and charged down the slope toward the frozen lake.

The legion surged forward, a wave of crested helmets and streaming cloaks. The defenders gave their own battle cry, centaurs galloping to the flanks, loup garou leaping ahead in the vanguard. Across the ice, Orlaith's army moved to meet them, red and gold banners snapping in the wind. Behind them strode the dead daēvas bound to her will.

I will not call them mortifexes any longer, Lucius resolved. *They are my kin, and they have no more choice about whom they fight for than I did twelve years ago.*

Lucius spurred his horse after Brennos. He would stay close, protect him for as long as possible. It would not be enough, but he would try.

The armies crashed together on the ice with a sound like thunder. Steel met steel, flesh met flesh. Men screamed and fell. The air filled with the scent of blood and the acrid tang of sulfur as daēvas unleashed their elemental powers.

Lucius fought his way through the press, keeping Brennos in sight. The priest fought like a wolverine, fast and vicious. For a self-taught swordsman, he had natural talent. But talent alone would not save him from the fire-wielding Vatras. Lucius fended several off, repelling their attacks with infernos of his own.

Then he caught sight of a familiar figure cutting a swathe through the Redvayne troops — Mace, the Courtenays' servant. He was brown-skinned like his mistresses, tall and wearing only a sleeveless leather jerkin. Tattoos of sea serpents wound around his heavily muscled arms; before he died, Mace had been one of the seafaring Marakai clan.

Twelve years ago, Lucius had killed Chaos and Caul's older brothers at the Battle of Hellgate. He still remembered the look on Mace's face when he'd come upon the bodies, the hatred in his eyes. It had not dimmed with time.

As if sensing Lucius' gaze, Mace's head snapped around. Their eyes locked. Mace's hands came up, wreathed in fire, and Lucius knew he was about to be incinerated.

He dug his knees in, making the horse dance to the side just as a fireball hurtled past. His mount screamed and reared up on its hind legs, nearly throwing him from the saddle. Gripping the reins with one hand, he used the other to slam a wall of air into Mace, driving him back three steps. "I'm not your enemy!" Lucius shouted. "I'm here to aid Nyons!"

Mace only snarled wordlessly. He thrust his arms forward and twin lances of white flame shot toward Lucius, who countered the attack with another blast of frigid air. Fire and ice collided in a hissing maelstrom. Through the roiling steam, Lucius glimpsed Mace gathering himself for another assault.

Lucius urged his reluctant horse forward, bending low over its neck. Hooves skidded on ice as he bore down like a charging lance. At the last instant, Lucius launched himself from the saddle and dragged Mace down. They hit the ice, grappling and kicking. Mace's hands found Lucius's throat and clamped down with crushing force.

"You fucking bastard," he ground out.

Lucius slammed his forehead upward and was rewarded with a grunt of pain. With a quick hook of his legs, he flipped their positions and yanked the dagger from his belt. Lucius pressed the edge to Mace's throat. "Move and I'll saw your head off," he warned.

Mace glared up at him. Blood bubbled from his nose.

"Just *listen* for a minute," Lucius said tightly. "My bond is broken. I no longer serve the Redvaynes."

Mace went still beneath him. "You lie. Our bonds don't just break."

"Mine did. I'll prove it to you, if you promise to behave."

Lucius eased the dagger from Mace's neck and staggered to his feet, bracing himself to fend off another attack. But Mace just sat and spat blood on the ice. "Show me," he rasped. Lucius pushed his shirtsleeves up. Mace's eyes widened a fraction as he took in the naked white skin.

"I want nothing more than to see Orlaith dead," Lucius said. "Painfully if possible, but quick works as long as she's gone for good. It's the only way we can win this fight."

Mace searched his face for any sign of duplicity. Then he gave a slow nod. "A truce," he said, "until that bitch is dead."

They waded back into the fray together, eventually joining Nathan Ouvrard's white-haired Valkirin daēva Vigo to rain fire and destruction down upon their foes. Hours bled together as the battle raged on. Time and again, Lucius tried to penetrate the ranks and reach Orlaith, but there was no getting through her daēva guards, who ringed her five deep.

In fact, that was the only reason the battle wasn't already over. She was holding them in reserve to protect herself.

Finally, Lucius's horse balked. It simply stood there, trembling all over. He didn't blame it; part of him felt the same. With a silent command, he took pity and sent the beast galloping south toward Mystral.

It hardly mattered anyway. The Alessian lines wavered on the verge of collapse. Lucius swayed on his feet as he hurled another fireball, which was answered by the daēvas bound to Orlaith. He was so tired, he barely noticed the sky lightening to a pale grey. It was only when the sun crested the granite peaks that he understood what was happening.

Bel's fearsome eye has opened...

Lucius sank to his knees in the churned-up slush and flung out an arm to shield himself. He could feel blisters rising on the exposed flesh. Crawling to a patch of shade seemed like an excellent idea, except that his limbs refused to cooperate.

Then hoofbeats rang against the ice. He squinted painfully as a handsome face swam into view above him. "Up with you!" Brennos shouted.

Lucius reached out a hand, face averted. Brennos gripped his wrist and hauled him across the saddle. Through stinging eyes, Lucius glimpsed the rosette and lion passant of Duc Scalici still flying from the garrison tower. Then they were through the thick archway, Brennos half-dragging him down from the horse. He slung Lucius's arm over his shoulders, bearing him up when his knees buckled.

"I came as fast as I could. Does it hurt?" Brennos asked. His face was streaked with mud and gore, his dark hair plastered to his brow.

"You see?" Lucius croaked. "This is why I prefer Kaethe."

Brennos stared at him for a moment before breaking into laughter. Lucius braced a hand on the wall, forcing his knees to hold. "Go, I can make it from here." Brennos searched his eyes, then nodded and strode off, already barking fresh orders.

Lucius climbed the spiral steps to the round chamber at the top. He slumped down against the wall below the narrow window embrasure, but not before he saw Orlaith's captive daēvas falling back to the Redvayne garrison. The sun burned them, too.

What a terrible device Jaskin Cazal had made. Not simply in the power it granted, but the suffering it inflicted on those enslaved to it. How long would the cycle go on? There had to be a way of destroying the Grand Menotte. He just couldn't see how.

Then he heard Brennos's voice coming up the tower stairs. Nathan Ouvrard and the Courtenays entered the chamber with him, their faces drawn and haggard. Scalici leaned on Lady Caul, blood seeping through his brigandine. When she saw Lucius, she scowled deeply. Chaos ignored him.

"My thanks," Nathan was saying to Brennos, "for coming to our aid. It was unexpected, to say the least."

"So you never received the letters I sent?" Brennos replied. "They were with Castelio. He was traveling by ship to Mystral."

"Then we would have missed each other," Nathan said. "We left Mystral a week ago at Beatriu's summons." His face darkened. "Though she is not the one who met us. How Orlaith came by the cuff, I have no idea."

Lady Chaos spoke up. "We are not accustomed to the light of the sun—"

"Nor do we wish to be," her sister cut in tartly, then fell silent when Chaos shot her a look.

"But we are grateful for the reprieve," she finished. "At least it drove our enemies back."

"You have Bel to thank for that," Brennos replied. "But I do not know how long it will last. We cannot hold them if it grows dark again."

Nathan shook his head. "We cannot hold them any longer, period. Our casualties are too great. We must pull back. Retreat and live to fight another day."

"Retreat?" Lady Caul looked like she'd just bitten into a wormy green apple.

"If you do not, the Moon Courts will be left with no rulers at all," Brennos said grimly, and for once Lucius agreed with him. "Gather your people and make for the Nightwood. We will hold them off long enough for you to escape."

Mace and Vigo exchanged a glance. "Permission to remain behind, Your Graces," Mace said. "We can do more good here than in the Nightwood."

The Courtenays nodded, as did Nathan.

"Are you certain about this?" Duc Scalici asked. His skin had a gray cast, but he stood on his own now, one hand braced against the table. "I dislike abandoning an ally to Orlaith's jackals." He didn't say it aloud, but his expression made it clear he believed Brennos's offer to be suicide.

"If the pass is left open, you won't make it far," Brennos replied.

"But won't they simply fly over it?" Scalici pointed out.

Lucius pushed off the wall. "No," he said. "Orlaith wants to capture me first. She hates all of you, but I suspect she hates me even more. As long as I remain here, so will she." He glanced out the window. The sun was already descending. "If you mean to pull back, do it now," he warned, "before dark falls."

"I still despise him," Lady Caul muttered, casting a baleful eye on Lucius, "but he talks sense. And the fallen will rise again soon. There is no time to debate."

The lords and ladies of the Moon Courts departed to gather what remained of their people. Brennos joined Lucius, staring out at the red-churned snow and black ice littered with bodies. "Bel is with us," he said. "Why else would the sun rise now, if not as a sign?"

Lucius sighed, scrubbing a hand over his face. "I hope

you're right. But we are still sorely outnumbered. How many men do you have left?"

"Twenty-seven."

"Kaethe's frosty tits," Lucius muttered. It was worse than he thought.

Brennos turned from the window, self-controlled as ever. "The pass can be held by a handful of men if they are brave and true."

"That is what the bards say about heroes," Lucius grumbled. "Except that they're usually dead ones."

Brennos stepped closer, reaching up to trace his sharp cheekbone. "We are bound together," he said softly, "in this life and the next."

Lucius took his shoulders and leaned in so their foreheads touched. "Forget the next. I want you to live," he whispered. "To grow old and fat."

Brennos laughed. "Perhaps I shall. But I seem to recall you saying a daēva life span is akin to an oak tree, while we poor mortals are mayflies." His eyes were gentle. "Time is nothing to one such as you. I only ask that you wait for me once you have gone on to the Fields of Asphodel."

"I swear it." The words caught in Lucius's throat. "And if you get there first, you will wait for me."

"I swear it," Brennos agreed.

Their lips met in a long, lingering kiss. Then the two men stepped apart. Together they descended the tower steps for the last time, striding out to where a fresh pair of horses waited. There was no other path but forward into the dying light.

Twenty-Nine

The clay mug steamed in Morgen's hands, yet still they felt cold. Since Lo had been dragged off to the cleaving room, the other two Fates never let Morgen out of their sight. Nona, in particular, watched her like a cat fixated upon a mouse hole when she prepared the god's bane tea each day.

Now Nona paused outside the kitchen, tilting her head. "Make sure it is extra strong. We must keep him docile."

Morgen nodded curtly and stepped through the door. Bel was their cook now, which the Fates seemed to find amusing. He believed himself to be an alchemist named Nabu-bal-idinna, though Morgen could no longer think of him as anything but the sun god.

In the kitchen, Bel stood motionless at the cutting board, knife dangling from limp fingers. Silent tears tracked his cheeks. A half-chopped carrot lay abandoned, bright orange against the scarred wood.

"My children," he muttered. "They make war upon each other."

"Your children?" Nona repeated sharply.

His voice was the barest whisper, but Morgen caught the words. "The Avas Vatras."

Few knew that name on this side of the White Sea, but Morgen's mother had an expansive collection of books that included volumes of ancient history, and she had read them all. He was referring to the fire daēvas. The mortifexes.

Morgen spoke before Nona could stop her. "They are fighting one another?"

Bel's face was desolate. "No, they kill those who keep the faith."

"Keep the faith… The priests, you mean?"

"Enough," Nona snapped, shooting Morgen a quelling look. "I think you had a bad dream," she said to Bel in honeyed tones. "But your tea will make it all better."

He stared through her, lost in whatever vision tormented him.

"Must there be so much suffering?" Morgen asked her captor quietly. "Can't you do something?"

Nona's plump face was impassive. "The threads have been spun and measured, the tapestry woven. It cannot be altered."

Morgen lowered her gaze, feigning meekness, but she was done sitting here while the world bled — and Bel was her only chance to escape. For the last two days, she had weakened his dose of god's bane. It only made him melancholy. She needed the arrogant, lightning-hurling god who had arrived four days ago.

It was time for stronger measures.

With a sharp jerk, she pretended he had jostled her elbow. The tea splashed across the flagstones. "Clumsy fool," Morgen snapped.

"I… I'm sorry," Bel muttered, brushing clumsily at her skirts.

She pushed his hand away. "Never mind. I will make more."

Nona's mouth pinched in irritation. "Quickly, Grumpy Mouse." She whirled away, apron swishing.

In the apothecary storeroom, Jaskin sprawled in a chair snoring, a broom resting between his knobby knees. Morgen kicked the chair's leg as she passed. It toppled with a satisfying crash. Jaskin jerked awake, limbs flailing. His glare held murder. "You did that on purpose, you black-haired harpy!"

Morgen matched his glower. "Too right I did! You're meant to be sweeping the floor, you shiftless lout."

Jaskin swung toward Nona, beseeching. "Mistress, I protest! Such abuse is uncalled for. Why, 'tis hardly a fortnight past that I suffered a mortal wound—"

Morgen tuned out his bleating. Nona stood with arms crossed, shoulders shaking with mirth. Neither noticed as Morgen's fingers deftly swapped the tags dangling from two identical tins. To the nose, catmint and god's bane were one and the same.

Her palms sweated as she brewed the tea, the ritual now rote. Steam curled from the pot, bringing the sharp scent of mint. She tried not to let tension show in the set of her shoulders as she carried the mug back to the kitchen, Nona squeaking along behind her.

Bel slumped at the roughhewn table, bearded chin propped on one hand. His bloodshot eyes stared at nothing.

"Your special tonic is here!" Nona sang.

He looked up and summoned a tremulous smile. "Ah, thank you."

Morgen set the mug before him and watched Bel raise it to his cracked lips and gulp it down. Of course, the fact that it was scalding hot didn't bother him. And if it tasted any different than usual, he made no comment. The knot in her chest eased a fraction.

Nona studied him, apparently satisfied. How long before the last dose of god's bane wore off? Morgen worried at her lip. Catmint would soothe his nerves for a time, at least.

"Supper will be ready soon," Bel declared, resuming his chopping as if nothing had happened. "A hearty pottage with plenty of thyme. I hope you have an appetite!"

She forced a smile and turned to Nona. "By your leave, mistress, I'll return to my duties in the storeroom. And make sure that shirker Lazy Mouse pulls his weight for a change."

The Fate flicked a hand in dismissal, already drifting toward the door. Morgen glanced once at Bel, then followed on leaden feet. Wake up, she silently urged. And do it soon!

THE CLEAVING ROOM was the largest chamber Lo had ever seen. The ceiling was so high above her head as to be an indistinct blur, and its walls vanished into gloom in all directions. Perhaps, she thought darkly, it had no walls at all.

Here, at the heart of the Fates' domain, Morta perched upon her stool like a cunning old spider, snipping threads of life with shears that glimmered in the faint light. Each time she did so, the thread's spindle disappeared, marking the end of someone's life. Lo had counted them at first, until the weight of those numbers crushed her spirit and she stopped. Now she simply dragged basket after basket of spindles to Morta's feet, her body growing weaker with each passing hour.

Or day. Or week. Time had lost all meaning in this place.

When Nona and Decima first locked her inside the cleaving chamber, Lo had dashed past the hunched figure with the shears, determined to find a way out. But no matter which direction she fled, she'd found herself back where she began.

She finally gave up and approached her lank-haired adversary. "What do you want?" she had asked. "If you meant to kill me, you would have done it already."

Morta had simply pointed to a basket, her ancient face unreadable. So Lo had brought it over. Then another. Then another.

The work was mindless, but Lo's thoughts remained sharp. This was apparently her punishment for being a Shadow Soul, a creature with nine lives divided between the worlds of the living and the dead. Though she still did not understand why that made the Fates so angry.

"Just tell me one thing," she pleaded, as she hauled another basket to Morta's feet. "Why do you hate us? What have we ever done to you?"

If she hadn't been half-mad with hunger and thirst, she wouldn't have found the courage to voice the question. Morta was the scariest being Lo had ever encountered, and that was saying something. The silence stretched so long, she doubted the Fate would answer. Lo was turning away when she spoke. Her voice was old and powerful, but it was not unpleasant.

"I hold no hatred for any living thing." The shears paused, half-open. "But my sisters are different. Shadow Souls are an affront to them."

Lo sank down beside the basket, waiting.

Morta's milky eyes fixed on Lo. "The threads of a Shadow Soul are not spun and measured by Nona and Decima. They are unraveled from the substance of the Veil itself. You are the only creatures in this world outside their influence. My sisters take this personally. I do not."

She resumed her snipping while Lo pondered this bit of information.

Her soul was *woven from the Veil*. Well, it made a strange sort of sense — her cursed luck, the way death seemed to follow her like a loyal hound.

"But we're not outside *your* influence," Lo said. "You cut one of Morgen's threads when she tried to escape. You could end me right now if you chose."

"This is true." Morta tilted her head. "But I find it more interesting to let chance take its course. You are a puzzle, a mystery, and there are very few of those to a being such as I."

"Wait. So you don't know what my last death will be?" Lo asked, a small spark of hope kindling in her chest.

Morta snipped more threads, the spindles fading away to nothing like smoke dispersing in a breeze. "I cannot see the manner of it," she admitted. "But your final thread grows very short. It is barely there at all."

This came as no surprise; she could feel Death's chill shadow at her shoulder. The weight of failure dragged her down. Was all this meant to be? Did she have no control over her own destiny?

Then Morta's voluminous skirts shifted, and Lo saw a basket half-hidden between her feet. Unlike the others, this one contained only three spindles. Lo's breath hitched in her throat.

You know your own soul when you see it; the recognition was immediate and visceral. Lo could pick out her spindle from a thousand others. Nine threads braided together, eight dark and lifeless, only one still glowing with a faint, pulsing light. And that light was dimming.

At Morta's imperious gesture, Lo forced herself to her feet and fetched another basket of spindles. Each step was a battle against her own frail body, but she refused to crawl. She would not give the woman that satisfaction.

I will not die here, she vowed, *not by your hand*.

"If your sisters didn't weave our threads," Lo asked as she set the basket down, "how did you get our spindles?"

Morta took the basket and selected a thread, positioning her shears. "Shadow Souls are strange creations," she mused. "The spindles only appeared after you came here."

"Huh. So whose idea were the night-ghasts? Decima, I bet. It's the kind of thing she'd come up with."

"If you did not die in their cookpot," Morta replied, "then you were not meant to. But it wasn't Decima who willed it."

Lo shook her head. "I don't believe you."

"Your belief or disbelief changes nothing," Morta said with maddening calm.

Lo looked past her shoulder. "Well, here she comes, let's just ask her."

As Morta's head began to turn, Lo made her move. She lunged forward with a desperate burst of speed, fingers outstretched. But Morta was faster — impossibly fast for one so ancient — seizing the spindle with reflexes like lightning.

"Are you so eager to die for the last time?" Morta growled, her mask of civility slipping to reveal something cold and terrible beneath. "Then so be it!"

The ancient shears snicked open, blades glinting. Lo's breath caught in her throat as Morta positioned them around her final, fragile thread.

A furtive step sounded. Morta squinted into the gloom.

"Who is it?" she called, voice sharp. Silence stretched. Then Morta let out a grunt of recognition. "I know you are there, Morgen of Juniper Isle."

Morgen stepped forward into the dim light, the whites of her eyes large against her brown skin. She clutched a key — the one from the ceramic pig, presumably. "Put your shears down," she said.

Morta gave a dry laugh. "I don't answer to you, little

mouse. I answer to no one. I lived before the dawn of the first day, and I will outlive the twilight of the world. I am above the gods."

"Are you?" Morgen replied. "Then tell that to him."

As if on cue, a second figure shuffled forward, his movements slow and uncertain. Lo's heart leaped as she recognized Bel, a faint golden aura emanating from his form. In its light, she could see the confusion etched upon his face, the sweat beading his brow.

"What is happening?" he asked, his voice wavering between the mild tones of Nabu and the deep, commanding timbre of the sun god. "Where is this place?"

"You are in the house of your enemies," Morgen snapped. "They are keeping you as a pet!"

Before Bel could respond, running footsteps — one squeaking — came from the darkness. Nona and Decima rushed up, Jaskin close on their heels. A triumphant grin split his sharp features.

"I told you they were up to something!" he crowed, pointing a finger at Morgen. "I saw her steal the key!"

"Stupid, stupid girl!" Nona hissed. "You will spend the next ten years in the root cellar for this!"

Decima's glare took in all three Shadow Souls. "Let them all rot in darkness until they learn their place. Defiance will not be tolerated!"

Jaskin's eyes bulged. "What? But I have not defied you. I am *loyal*," he spluttered. "I deserve a reward, not punishment! I've been naught but faithful, and yet—"

As he continued his bleating tirade, Morgen strode up to Bel. "Wake up!" she growled, slapping him hard across the face. Once, twice, the force of the blows rocking him back on his heels. "Wake up! You are the Prince of Dawn. Keeper of the Celestial Fire. Kaethe's sisters have tricked you!"

At last, Bel's eyes cleared, the fog of the god's bane lifting. His gaze fixed upon Nona and Decima. Slowly, his expression hardened, a glint of molten gold sparking in his eyes.

"Now you listen—" Nona began sternly.

Brilliant light flooded the chamber. The Fates threw their arms up, howling in rage. Lo took advantage of the distraction to wrest both the scissors and her own spindle from Morta's grasp. Her eyes darted to the basket at the ancient Fate's feet, and she snatched up Morgen's spindle, too, tossing it to her friend.

"Run!" she cried as Morgen snatched it from the air.

Bel wavered between his two identities — Nabu's pathetic confusion and the sun god's awakening fury warring within him. His aura pulsed light and dark, as Lo and Morgen each seized one of his arms, dragging him toward where the door should have been. But the twisted space of the Fates' realm betrayed them, and they found themselves once more facing the enraged sisters.

"Kaethe!" Lo called desperately. "Let us pass into your realm!"

Nothing happened. She concentrated, trying to form a portal as she had done before, but something blocked her power. Beside her, Morgen attempted the same, with identical results.

Nona and Decima advanced, their faces promising retribution. Behind them, Jaskin watched with gleeful malice. Lo looked down at her spindle and the single glowing thread that kept her tethered to life.

She knew what she had to do. Had known, perhaps, all along. There was only one sure way to get Kaethe's attention.

As the pulsing light of Bel's aura washed over her, Lo raised Morta's shears. Her final thread, the ninth and last, seemed to tremble beneath the blades. She hesitated for the space of a heartbeat, then whisked them shut.

In the instant before her soul slipped its mortal coil, she saw Morta's knowing, enigmatic smile. The scissors slipped from her hand. Her final thread shriveled. The spindle vanished like mist in sunlight.

Peace washed over her as the two halves of her soul, so long divided between the world of the living and the dead, finally knit together. The hunger, the thirst, the pain—all faded. Morgen's hoarse cry reached her as if from a great distance. *"What have you done?"*

Then Jaskin stepped forward, desperate eagerness on his face. A vortex of light and shadow was forming at her feet. The necromancer broke into a run, bony legs pumping.

"Wait for me!" he cried.

The cleaving room grew dim. Her last sight was of Morgen's lips forming words she could no longer hear, and the golden light of Bel's true form blazing in the darkness like a newborn sun.

Thirty

The rocky pine forest at the northern end of the Boundary was usually full of birds. Inquisitive gray jays, territorial shrikes, and chattering merlins. If you were lucky, you might see a barred owl peering down, grave and scholarly, from an overhanging limb.

But today it was eerily quiet as Cas hiked through the snow, Felippa at his side wrapped tight in her blue cloak, cheeks pink from the cold. Behind them, hundreds of spirits followed, pale shapes that wavered among the trees like candles burning low.

"Look." Felippa pointed.

Through a gap ahead, an orange glow painted the clouds. It had to be Hellgate. The faint tumult was audible now: a hum of steel on steel, screams and shouted commands. Beneath it all was another sound Cas recognized — the hiss and crackle of flames.

He stopped walking and turned to his sister. "This is as far as you go."

Felippa's elfin face hardened. The silver talisman winked at her throat as she crossed her arms. "You can't tell me what to do."

"Feck's sake, we're too close already," Cas said, glancing over her shoulder. "The battle's right there. I can't be worrying about you when—"

"When what? You go down there? I didn't come all this way to get left behind!"

"You're no soldier, Felippa," he said with exasperation.

"Nor are you," she parried with a sniff.

Cas raked a hand through his hair, fingers catching in the tangled waves that fell to his collar. "Well, you're right about that," he admitted. "This is madness. I should never have brought us here." He glanced at the spirits. "Nor them."

"Didn't Kaethe tell you to?" she reminded him.

"Aye," he grumbled.

"And she said you're her servant again, right?"

"Well, she didn't say so outright, but...." He held up his left hand, where the blue ink of the Lady's nine-pointed star stood fresh and sharp. "This is all I've got!"

Felippa studied him, her gaze steady. "It'll be enough."

"Now you sound like Gui," he said, a half-smile touching his lips despite himself.

"Of course I do. Because Gui is always right."

Cas was opening his mouth to reply when a young man appeared at a stumbling run through the trees. He wore the uniform of the Sons of Bel: a dark pleated skirt and tunic, both badly singed. He'd lost his helmet, revealing sweat-matted blond hair. A deep cut on his forehead bled freely, and the skin of his hands was blistered red.

When he spotted them, he froze, his gaze slicing to the spirits beneath the trees. Terror flashed across his face.

"Don't be afraid." Cas raised his palms. "They won't harm you."

The young man's chest heaved with panicked breaths.

"What's happening down there?" Cas jerked his chin toward the mountain pass ahead.

The question seemed to bring the soldier back to himself. He swallowed, his gaze darting between Cas and the spirits. "Monsters," he whispered. "Flying monsters with fire in their eyes. They encircled us."

Cas's heart sank. "How many are still alive?"

"I don't know. Not many." The boy wiped blood from his eye with a trembling hand. "It makes no difference now." His gaze hardened and he gestured at the forest. "Run, if you've got any wits!"

With that, he limped away, disappearing into the gathering dark before Cas could ask more.

"We must help them," Felippa said, her voice anguished. "Gui's down there."

Cas gave a hard nod and approached the spirits. They drifted closer, forming a loose circle around him, as if they'd expected this moment. He spoke in Tongues, the harsh, guttural syllables coming fluently.

"I thank you for coming with me," he said, glancing at Felippa. "With *us*. I don't have any right to ask more of you, but I will say this. You might be trapped on the wrong side of the Veil, but you still have free will. The ones down there are slaves to an evil talisman."

The gathering watched in silence. As always, he couldn't be sure how much they really understood. *Keep it simple.*

"I'm going to fight," he said. "To aid the living. I hope you will join me."

He couldn't blame them if they didn't.

Cas was turning away when a mountain lynx prowled forward, its spectral eyes gleaming. Behind it came two centaurs, bows clutched in their ghostly hands. They were followed by men and women, farmers by their clothes, with a pack of loyal dogs, tails wagging. A spirit-hawk circling above gave a piercing cry.

The rest of the dead came. More people from all walks of life. Animals both meek and fierce. Rabbits and stoats, brown bears and shaggy gray Boundary wolves — or maybe the last were loups garou. A magnificent stag with a rack of antlers wider than his spread arms. They gathered around, not with the restless hunger of the dead he'd banished in his days as Orlaith's Quietus but with purpose.

He looked to Felippa, whose face shone with wonder in the growing dark. "Stay close to me," he told her. She gave a tight nod.

They all went together toward the orange glow, emerging where a steep hillside careened down to the lake. From this vantage point, Cas could see the full scope of the battle — or what remained of it.

Fires smoldered in the narrow pass beyond the Alessian garrison. Bodies lay in mounds across the frozen ground but most thickly at the entrance to the pass, where a small knot of defenders still held out.

Mortifexes, both on foot and riding the "monsters" the soldier had described, hurled fireballs. Their barrage met with an invisible shield. When a volley of flames came back, Cas realized that at least one mortifex must be fighting with the Sons of Bel. Lucius, no doubt.

He drew a taut breath and gripped Felippa's hand, letting the dead flow around them. The mountain lynx bounded forward, followed by the centaurs and the hawk, which soared ahead. Within seconds, a soundless avalanche of spirits was descending on the valley below.

The first of the mortifexes noticed the ghostly army when it was halfway down. Her warning cry carried over the sounds of battle. One by one, the others turned, their attack faltering. Cas could see the defenders in the pass now — a dozen men, bloodied and exhausted, standing in a tight circle with their backs to each other. He spotted Vigo and Mace towering over the human survivors, though he didn't see Lucius.

The spirits reached the bottom of the embankment and swept across the ice, surrounding the living in a protective circle of white light. The mortifexes milled in confusion, then pulled back. They seemed reluctant to engage the spirits, though how long that would last, Cas had no idea.

He quickly scanned the defenders again, searching for Gui. At last, he spotted one of the fallen, a tall, broad man, his skin dark against the snow. The heart-shaped bald spot was visible even from a distance.

No, no, no.

Cas half slid down the slope, scraping his palms raw on loose pebbles. He ignored the riders circling overhead; if they wanted to kill him, there wasn't much he could do about it. Once he hit the ice, he broke into a sprint. Somehow Felippa kept pace, her face white and pinched.

Cas reached Gui and dropped to his knees, panic clawing at his throat. Gui lay curled on one side, blood staining his tunic. His chest rose and fell with shallow breaths, and Cas whispered a silent prayer. He leaned down, touching his shoulder. "Gui, it's me."

Gui's eyes fluttered open, their blue-gray depths clouded with pain. Recognition dawned slowly. "Cas," he murmured. "You came."

"How bad are you hurt?"

Gui winced and shook his head. "Can't tell. A rider... claws..."

"That's better than getting poked by a sword," Felippa said

briskly, lifting up his tunic to look. "Why, it's just a scratch. I bet you've had worse shaving."

Gui's laugh turned into a wince.

"Take this." She hung her talisman around his neck. "It's not supposed to work without a daēva, but sometimes it does anyway."

The hairs on Cas's nape lifted. He turned and saw a white-cloaked figure watching them from twenty paces away. Justinian's dark hair was wild, his eyes flickering red. No nine-pointed star contained his old enemy now. For a long moment, they just stared at each other.

Three seconds. That's how long it'll take him to close the distance and kill us all.

But to Cas's great surprise, Justinian broke away, his cloak swirling as he strode in the opposite direction, toward the Redvayne garrison. Within moments, he vanished into the smoke.

"Hold on, Gui," Felippa ordered, her small hands working to staunch the blood flowing from the slashes along his ribs. "We're taking you someplace safe."

Cas looked around at the besieged pass, at the flames leaping from the arrow slits of the Alessian garrison and the riders wheeling in the soot-stained skies. "Where the feck is safe?" he wondered.

Gui's hand found his wrist, gripping with surprising strength. "You brought safety with you," he whispered, nodding toward the spirits. "It's what I tried to pound into your thick skull all these years."

"What's that?" Cas slid an arm beneath Gui's shoulders and helped him sit.

Gui's lips formed a pained smile. "The Quietus isn't in the staff or the symbols," he said. "It's in you."

Thirty-One

Lucius knelt at the edge of the ice, watching the spirits flow into the valley like a river of light. It all seemed a dream, yet he could feel the slush seeping through his clothes, the hot sting of his burns. The stillness of his heart, a heavy stone in his chest.

He brushed a stray lock of hair from Bren's forehead. He looked peaceful, as if he'd only closed his eyes to rest. The bonewood blade had pierced him through the heart, a merciful death. Lucius had seen it happen, had tried to reach him, but the crush of combat had kept him away until it was too late.

Brennos hadn't yet risen, but he would. Lucius refused to leave his side until it happened. He would take care of him. Not let him wander lost, like the others.

Around them, the fighting ebbed. Where had the dead come from? They'd appeared as the battle reached its darkest moment, delaying the inevitable, but he could see his enslaved kin regrouping. No doubt their mistress was ordering them to end it.

Lucius felt a curious sense of juxtaposition as if he existed in two places at once. Another field, another desperate stand against a superior force. Then, as now, he had known it was hopeless, yet he'd chosen to fight. His men had followed him without question, just as the Sons of Bel had followed Brennos.

He had died in a place much like this one, except that it was covered in ash instead of snow. In the end, every battlefield looked the same.

For a moment, he couldn't tell if the pair of approaching riders was real or a figment of memory. The first horse carried a woman in black, strands of golden hair bright under a lace mantilla. On the second horse slumped a pathetic figure, his skin gray, his face a rigid mask.

Real, Lucius decided. She has come to gloat.

Orlaith reined in her mount a few paces away. Her blue eyes were glassy. "So," she said, leaning forward in the saddle. "Now you know how it feels to lose everything you care about, Lucius."

He could see from the emptiness in her face that the victory was hollow. Robert moaned, his head trembling like an old man with palsy.

"Lucius is not my name. My name is Claudius Quintus. And I pity you."

Orlaith jerked as if he'd slapped her. Then she gave a brittle laugh. "*You?* Pity *me*?"

"Yes. Shall I tell you why?"

Her mouth worked but no words came out.

"Your husband and son are still dead," he said. "You've won nothing but a worthless piece of ground, since the Courtenays escaped your clutches. They will regroup in the Nightwood, while you slowly lose whatever remains of your sanity."

Livid spots of color bloomed on her white cheeks.

"And one day, on another field of battle, they will kill you," he continued relentlessly. "That future would not be possible if the man I love didn't give his life to buy them time to flee. So I am at ease. We did what we set out to do." He eyed her with contempt. "While you will be forever remembered as the monster who brought ruin to Aveline."

Orlaith's scream of rage echoed off the sheer rock walls. "You dare? You dare speak to me thus? You … you pale shadow of a man. You are *nothing*!" She turned to the daēva who had just stepped to her side. "Strike him down," Orlaith snarled. "Cut off his head. Cut him to pieces!"

Justinian looked unhappy, but he unsheathed his blade. "Forgive me, legatus," he said, using the old title. "I must obey."

Claudius Quintus got to his feet. His wounds ached, and his elemental fire had dimmed to embers.

"I understand you better than you think," he told Justinian wearily. "To be trapped in this half-life is surely hell, and worse to be bound to a madwoman." He drew his own blade, the weight of it heavy in his hand. "But I am not an untried boy like your other victims. We will see who emerges with his head intact—"

His words faded as a crack split the air.

Orlaith walked her horse back, eyes bulging, as the black ice began to splinter, hairline fractures spreading outward. A wind rose, even colder than the bone-deep chill of the pass, and with it came a collective sigh from the spirits. The daēvas who were poised to slaughter the last Sons of Bel lowered their blades.

"What is happening?" Orlaith shrieked, looking around wildly. "Heed my command! You belong to *me*!"

But whatever authority she wielded was gone with the melting ice. A whirlpool formed at the center of the lake, a vortex of light and shadow. Claudius recognized it immediately. Hellgate was opening.

Robert Redvayne flailed and toppled from his horse, which promptly raced away, mane streaming. The dead Duc writhed for a moment like a turtle on its back, then rolled over and began to drag himself to the lake.

"No!" Orlaith dismounted in a flurry of black skirts and ran to him. "Don't leave me!" she screamed, hysterical. "Stay with me, Robert!"

But the pull was too strong. The current took him, and Orlaith, who clung stubbornly to his arm, was dragged along into the black water. Her shrieks cut off when it filled her mouth, and both Redvaynes sank into the Gate.

Claudius watched as the spirits entered of their own volition, prowling or walking or flying, and then the daēvas who had been enslaved for so long, and the mortal dead from the battle on both sides. Whatever was happening, it broke all allegiances. Vigo went, and so did Mace. Only the handful of living were spared the inexorable pull of the Greater Gate.

Justinian stood waist-deep in it, his dark hair whipped by the wind. Their eyes met, and a thousand years fell away. They had been brothers once, comrades in life and death. Justinian nodded, a simple acknowledgment. Claudius returned the gesture. His former captain gave a faint smile, looking like the man he'd once known. Then he turned and waded deeper, and deeper, until he was lost to view.

Lucius was the last. He stood there for a minute, resisting, and then he carefully and deliberately laid his sword down and lifted Brennos into his arms. The water rose around them; it was not cold at all. Just before it closed over his head, Lucius glimpsed someone on the far shore of the lake. A woman with snakelike black hair and large black eyes. She raised a pale hand in what might have been greeting ... or farewell.

Then the Gate closed, and Hellgate was silent once more.

Thirty-Two

The stone corridor stretched to an infinite point, doors marching into the distance. Kaethe's house was just as Lo remembered. It was *she* who had changed.

Her other deaths were half measures, temporary jaunts behind the Veil. This time, she was here fully, severed from the world of the living forever.

"Your hair," Morgen said. "It's..." She drew a sharp breath and shook her head.

Lo touched the braid that hung over one shoulder, long enough to brush her waist. "Oh, that's weird," she whispered. "What else do you see?

"You're pale, but you always were. How ... how does it feel?"

"Lighter," Lo said after a minute. "Weirdly okay."

"That's good." Morgen swallowed hard. "I feel different, too." She flexed her fingers as if testing whether they still belonged to her. The other hand gripped her spindle, with its single glowing thread. "As if ... I've been living with only half my senses, and suddenly they've all come alive at once."

"Because you are whole now. I can sense it. The halves of your soul are joined again." She threw her arms around Morgen and hugged her tight. "Thank you for not leaving me."

Her Shadow Sister stiffened, a startled gasp escaping her lips. Slowly, hesitantly, her arms came up to return the gesture of affection.

Lo pulled back to search Morgen's dark eyes. "Keep your spindle with you always. Guard it carefully. Your fate is your own to decide now."

Morgen twisted it in her hands. "But what about you?"

Lo was about to reply when a crash came from nearby, followed by raised voices. The argument was coming from the kitchen.

"You pompous ass!" Kaethe's voice spilled through the door. "After everything I've done for you—"

"Everything you've done?" Bel's resonant baritone shot back. "Such as making me forget my own identity? Keeping me prisoner in your tower? Treating me as your servant?"

Something else shattered — a plate, perhaps, or a cup.

"You were happy!" Kaethe screamed. "And Nabu made a far better husband than you ever were. In bed, too!"

"Don't you dare—"

"I only did what I had to! You were out of control—"

Bel gave a sinister laugh. "I'll show you out of control, you devious, snake-haired fishwife!"

"Fishwife?" Kaethe shrieked. There was the distinct crack of a hand slapping flesh, and a muffled curse. Another crash came, the loudest yet, as though the large oak table where Nabu used to chop vegetables had been upended.

Lo winced, but then it grew ominously quiet.

"Do you think they killed each other?" she whispered.

Morgen raised an eyebrow. "They're immortal."

"Fair point. But..." Lo cocked her head, listening intently. "It doesn't sound good. We'd better go see."

Together, they crept to the door. Lo eased it open just wide enough to peer inside.

Amid the wreckage of the kitchen, Bel had Kaethe pressed against the cold stove, her pale hands tangled in his hair. His robe was half-undone, revealing a bronzed shoulder. Their lips were locked like randy teenagers.

Lo shuddered. *I'll never unsee that.*

She cleared her throat. The pair broke apart and turned to glare. "Did you need something?" the goddess of death demanded.

Lo tried to ignore the way Bel's hand rested possessively on Kaethe's breast. "I just... We just..." She tried again. "Did you destroy the Grand Menotte?"

Before Kaethe could answer, Bel pulled her close again, his lips brushing her neck. "Get back here, my watery wench," he growled. Kaethe giggled and turned to kiss him again.

"Perhaps we should—" Morgen began, but Lo cleared her throat a second time, louder.

"What is it now?" Kaethe broke away from Bel with obvious reluctance. Her hair writhed vigorously.

"The Grand Menotte?" Lo reminded her. "Your promise to destroy it? The reason I am now dead and stuck in your tower for eternity?"

"Oh, that," Kaethe replied lazily. Her attention was still half on Bel, who trailed kisses down her pasty neck. "Yes, it's done."

Before Lo could ask for proof, Kaethe flicked a finger. The kitchen dissolved and she found herself in a vast circular chamber. Morgen made a retching sound and steadied herself on Lo's shoulder. Being tossed about used to make Lo dizzy too, but she felt fine. One of the perks of being dead — no more nausea.

They were in the Chamber of Souls, a replica of the Dominion in miniature, complete with tiny forests, mountains, and rivers. At the center of the model stood Kaethe's tower, a slender spire, and around it lay the Greater Gates that connected her realm to the world of the living.

As they watched, the dark gates began to flicker with pale green fire. From each came a trickle of glowing sparks — trapped souls, freed at last. The trickle turned to streams, and the streams to rivers as thousands upon thousands flowed through the gates, crossing Kaethe's domain before disappearing beyond her borders. The dark shoreline, Lo knew, marked the Cold Sea, where the spirits would undertake their final passage.

A phantom ache bloomed in her chest as she watched them moving onward. She would never follow their path. As a Shadow Soul, she was bound to Kaethe's realm forever.

"I wonder where they end up," she said softly.

"No one knows," Morgen replied. "But I believe it is a good place."

They stood in silence for a while, watching the spectral procession. Eventually, Lo turned away, and Morgen followed her out of the chamber and into the corridor.

"Do you remember coming here when we were children?" Lo asked as they walked.

Morgen's brow furrowed. "I do. But I've spent so many years with my memories divided between Morgen and Mara that having them all mixed together is very strange."

"You were scared of everything," Lo said with a rueful smile. "The first time I saw you, you were hiding behind a bookcase in the library, terrified that Kaethe's hounds would find you."

"And you decided that the best way to help was to tell me that the hounds could smell fear," Morgen recalled, shaking her head. "You said they'd eat me if I wasn't brave."

Lo winced. "I was a little shit, wasn't I?"

"You were," Morgen laughed. "You used to hide behind curtains and jump out at me. Once you convinced me that the water from Kaethe's mouth was magic and that if she kissed me goodnight, I'd drown from the inside."

Lo laughed, then quickly sobered. "I'm sorry for all that. Truly."

"You are forgiven." Morgen was quiet for a moment. "When I was Mara, I hated how weak and fearful I was. When I was Morgen, I disdained emotion altogether and tried to feel nothing at all."

"Now you have one life to simply be yourself, the woman you were always meant to be," Lo said. "I'm so glad for you."

They turned a corner and paused at a balcony overlooking the misty gardens. "Strange how the tower looks solid from the outside," Lo said, "yet once you're inside it, there are windows and terraces. It's hard to tell what is real here and what is illusion."

"A pretty cage," Morgen agreed, "but a cage nonetheless. It will be hard for me to enjoy my new freedom knowing you are stuck here."

Lo leaned over the railing. A koi pond lay below, surrounded by lush green lawns. "That's the bargain. Nine lives… but nothing after except for *this*."

"A bargain we never agreed to," Morgen said with one of her old scowls.

"True. But it still binds us. And I am content that the Grand Menotte has finally been destroyed. It was worth dying for that."

Morgen laid a hand over Lo's. "Still too high a price.

Kaethe should not have demanded it of you. She could have broken the talisman anytime she wished!"

Lo snorted. "I find it futile to argue with gods. And don't forget, one day, you will join me here. We can keep each other company. In the meantime, you must go find Dravka and take her home to Juniper Isle."

Morgen's fingers tightened. "I hate to leave you here alone," she muttered.

"I'm not alone." She wove their fingers together and pressed the fist to her chest. "You are in my heart. Now go, sister, before Kaethe sets you some impossible task."

A reluctant smile tugged at Morgen's lips. "I never thought I'd see her playing the lovesick maiden."

"All the more reason to leave while she's distracted." Lo released her hand. "Besides, I need you to carry a message for me."

Morgen nodded. "Of course. What is it?"

Lo leaned close and whispered in her ear. When she was done, Morgen nodded. With a twist of her fingers, she conjured a shimmering portal. They embraced once more, and then she was gone, the doorway winking out of existence in her wake. Lo stood for a minute in the sudden quiet, watching the spot where her friend had been.

Just for the hells of it, she tried to make her own portal. Of course nothing happened.

A word popped into her head. *Unbearable.*

She let it fade back into the murk. No use thinking like that now.

The gardens. A walk would do her good.

She wandered down meandering pathways, climbing roses and clematis perfuming the air. Topiary hedges towered on either side, sculpted into fantastic beasts — chimeras, manticores, griffins. After a while, it began to rain. Somewhere in the trees, a nightingale sang its little heart out.

When the rain grew heavier, her steps led her back to the kitchen. Lo entered warily, but inside she found order restored. The oak table was righted and dusted with flour. Nabu-balidinna puttered about humming to himself. Cardamom filled the air, warm and comforting.

She knew it was him at once, even before he spoke.

"Ah, Delilah!" His face creased into a pleased smile. "Just in time! I'm baking a cake, your favorite. It will be ready soon."

Lo settled onto a stool, breathing in the fragrant steam. "It smells wonderful," she said. And it did. But though her nose twitched appreciatively, she found she had no desire to taste it.

At least that urge to scheme, to manipulate, to twist the truth to suit her purposes — it was gone. Completely gone, like a broken fever.

Nabu perched on the stool beside her, brushing cardamom from his purple star-spangled robes. They chatted about small, inconsequential things — the rain, the cake, how lovely the roses were this time of year.

Kaethe had won in the end, as she always did.

The days flowed by like the Dominion's swift rivers, and Lo continued to explore the gardens within Kaethe's vast house. Some were formal affairs with straight, wide paths and geometric beds. Others had wild meadows of columbine and hyssop, snakeroot and anemone.

Her favorite place was a shaded bank beneath a willow where silver fish darted in a deep pool. She would sit for hours trailing her fingers in the water and letting her mind drift.

She wondered if her mother and father were grieving, or if

they didn't know and were searching for her, the way she had searched for them. How she missed dear Thistle! And all the daēvas she had known back in Nocturne.

But it was Cas she thought of most often, with his cockeyed grin and easy laughter. He'd understood her in a way no one else did. The poor man was probably heartbroken. But there was no use dwelling on that now. She'd made her choice, and it was the right one. Morta had said her last thread was growing short anyway. At least she had ended it on her own terms and made it count for something.

One day, Kaethe summoned her to the Chamber of Souls. When the goddess wasn't canoodling in some shadowy corner with Nabu, she spent most of her time there, prowling her miniature realm, keeping a close eye on its goings-on.

"I have news from the living world," Kaethe announced. "The centuries-long blight of the risen is finally over."

"Really? That's wonderful," Lo said. "But how?" Her gaze narrowed. "Were you behind that, too?"

Kaethe shot her an offended look. "The Grand Menotte was the root cause, a perversion of the natural order. Now that its power is broken, the Veil has mended itself."

Lo chewed a ragged nail. "What about your sisters?"

"We made peace. I should never have let Bel talk me into banishing them to Loris. I told them they could come back if they wished, but they claim to like living there." Kaethe stopped to peer down at one of the glowing gates. "Remind me, what is the name of their shop?"

"Tinctures, Tonics & Yarn." Lo would never forget it. "What about me? Are they holding a grudge?"

"Nona and Decima demanded that I turn you over."

"But you talked them out of it." *Please oh fucking please.*

"Not I." Kaethe smiled. "Morta. She convinced the others

that it is enough to keep Jaskin Cazal as their servant until the end of days. A fitting punishment, I think."

"He must be pissed." Lo tried to feel sorry for him but couldn't quite manage it.

"I am merely relieved it is they who must listen to his mewling," Kaethe replied, "and not us."

In the days that followed, Lo tried to distract herself. She read poetry and histories in the Lady's gargantuan library. She tried her hand at the instruments in the music room and played chess and backgammon with Nabu. But inside, an emptiness took root.

"You could petition the Lady to release you, as she did your mother," Nabu suggested one day, sensing her malaise.

Lo shook her head. "Kaethe said resurrecting my mother was her greatest mistake. She'll never grant such a boon again."

Still, the loneliness gnawed at her. Finally, she contrived to escape the tower, just for a little while. She found Nabu hunched over a tome in the library's fourth gallery, his purple robe stained with what appeared to be tomato jam.

"Good afternoon," she said sweetly, as if time had any meaning in Kaethe's house.

He startled, dropping his book. "Oh! Delilah. I didn't hear you come in."

"I've always been light on my feet." She retrieved it and sat beside him, peering at the mystical symbols. "What are you reading?"

"A treatise on the movements of celestial bodies and their influence on the tides between realms." His smile was full of boyish enthusiasm. "It's fascinating, actually."

"I'm sure it is." Lo smiled back, eyes wide and innocent. "I was wondering ... since we're good friends, might I trouble you for a favor?"

He flushed with pleasure. "Of course, if it is within my power to grant."

She'd grown fond of Nabu-bal-idinna, but the man was still comically gullible.

"A small favor only," she assured him. "I've been cooped up in this tower for so long. I was hoping I might take a little stroll through the woods. The real woods, not the garden. Just to stretch my legs."

A hand caught his dark beard, tugging at it. "Oh, I don't think Kaethe would approve."

"Please?" Lo pressed. "I won't go far."

Nabu hesitated. He kept glancing down at his book, clearly eager to return to its arcane formulae. "I suppose a short walk couldn't hurt. But you must stay within sight of the tower."

"I promise," Lo said, concealing her triumph. "I wouldn't *dream* of wandering far." She gave an ostentatious shudder. "I don't want to meet any dead people. They give me the creeps."

Nabu led her to the tower's single entrance and exit, a massive black door of some unknown material that resembled volcanic glass. He retrieved a large ring of keys from inside his robe. Lo couldn't believe Kaethe still trusted him with it.

"Remember," he said, aiming for a stern tone, "come back soon or I shall have to send the hounds after you."

Lo nodded eagerly. The instant the door swung open, she squeezed past Nabu and gave a little hop of glee.

Freedom!

Perhaps she could find the shore of the Cold Sea. She might not be able to cross it, but at least she could look—

"Oh dear," Nabu muttered. "Oh dear, oh dear. Kaethe won't like this."

Lo squinted. There, sprawled across the hillside below the

tower, was a camp — tents and small fires with figures moving about. As she watched, the figures stilled, one by one, until all eyes turned toward her. A hubbub of voices erupted.

"Mouseling!" The world tilted beneath Lo's feet as her mother raced up the hill with her father close behind.

"You foolish, brave, impossible girl," Nazafareen cried, pulling her into an embrace. "What have you done?"

Before Lo could reply, more friends appeared. Tijah, her hair in tight braids and a scimitar poking over one shoulder. Achaemenes, grinning broadly.

"Took you long enough," Tijah said, her tone gruff but her eyes moist. "You think we don't have better things to do than sit around in Kaethe's backyard?"

Lo laughed through the tightness in her throat. "Sorry. The goddess can be heavy-handed."

"You don't have to tell that to the person she tossed through a portal," Tijah said with a sniff.

Lo was wearing a white dress with blue flowers embroidered at the neckline that she'd found in the wardrobe of her bedchamber. Now something soft brushed against her bare leg. She looked down to see her beloved Thistle, fat as ever, his gray tail curling around her knee. She scooped him up, burying her face in his fur. "I missed you, you terrible thing," she whispered.

"And I you," Thistle hissed, his voice the rattle of dead leaves in a lonely lichyard. "Though your absence did give me time for a pleasant visit with Mother."

More people surrounded her, all the friends and family she'd never had a chance to say goodbye to. Her grandfather Victor, black-haired and fierce. Culach, the strapping Valkirin whose camp she and Cas had stumbled upon in the Vale of Harran. Nicodemus with his flame-red hair and sea-blue eyes, who had crafted the silver talisman she'd given to Felippa. Meb, the tattooed queen of the Marakai daēvas. Javid and Katsu, who had raised her after her parents disappeared.

There was much embracing and happy tears. Only one person hung back, standing at the edge of the gathering with his hands shoved into his pockets. His hair had grown shaggier, falling into his heavy-lidded brown eyes. He watched her carefully, his expression unreadable.

Lo gently disentangled herself from the crowd, batting away their questions, and made her way to Cas. She felt suddenly awkward. "I wasn't sure if you got my message," she said, making a weird face that felt like a cross between a smile and a grimace.

His gaze was stormy. "Morgen sought me out," he said. "She told me what happened. I came through a gate the instant I heard. Thistle gathered the rest of them." He scowled at the tower. "We've been pounding on that door for weeks."

"Weeks?" Lo echoed. "You've been here all this time?"

He nodded. "Kaethe answered the door herself. She refused to let us in and slammed it in our faces. After that, she just ignored us."

That lowdown, double-dealing fishwife. "Of course, she never mentioned it." Lo hugged her arms across her chest. "I'm not sure how much Morgen told you, but ... well, I'm ... not who I was."

He stepped closer, his voice low and fierce. "I don't care if you've used up your last life, I love you and I'm not leaving."

Her throat tightened. She still felt sensations in her body if the emotion was strong. "I don't know what I am, exactly. I mean, I'm definitely not alive in the normal sense. But I don't speak Tongues." She touched her braid. "My hair grew back, even longer than before. No idea why. Will it keep growing now, or stay this way forever? There's so many things ... I have no idea ..." She realized she was babbling and shut her mouth.

Cas reached for her hand. She tried to pull back, but he was too damned quick.

"Do I feel cold?" she asked anxiously. "Be honest."

Cas brushed a thumb across her knuckles, eliciting a delicious shiver. Well, *that* still worked. "No," he said, a hint of surprise in his voice. "If anything, you feel feverishly warm."

"Whew," Lo said, relieved. "I wouldn't like to be cold *and* dead. But let's not talk about my problems. How's your family?"

Cas squeezed her hand. "All fine. They've gone back to Prydwen, for good. The west is still unstable, but it's better than it was, and there haven't been any reports of the dead rising. Not a single one." He searched her face. "You did that, didn't you?"

"Kaethe did it, but only after I met her terms. Which I couldn't have managed without Morgen. I suppose she didn't mention that?"

"She told me very little other than that you were ... in the house of the Lady of Shadows," he finished diplomatically.

Lo grinned, relaxing a bit. Gods, it was good to see him. "Well, the Fates had other plans for us, but—"

She frowned as the tower door crashed open. Kaethe stood in the doorway, her hair wiggling like a swarm of eels. "Begone, trespassers!" she commanded with an imperious sweep of her arm. "All of you. Go home!" Her glare settled on Lo. "Back in the Tower with you this instant."

Nazafareen stepped forward, her expression mutinous. "She's coming with us."

"Pshaw. Under the covenant of the chthonic deities," Kaethe declared, "a Shadow Soul cannot pass onward, nor can she return to the land of the living. Delilah must remain here." She cast Lo a reproachful look. "I have treated her like my own daughter. Now the rest of you, shoo!"

A tempest erupted. Victor delivered a series of dire ultimatums. Tijah unleashed a torrent of salty curses. Culach offered several wry objections, and Queen Meb made an eloquent plea. Her mother, of course, shouted loudest of them all.

Only Cas stayed silent, watching with an amused curve to his lips.

The cacophony grew until Thistle let out a demonic howl that silenced them all. "I carry a message," he announced, "for the Lady of Shadows from her illustrious cousin Khaf-hor, Lord of the Thalassic Deep, Prince of the Abyssal Trench, Imperial Immortal of the Five Gods of the Cold Sea."

Lo glanced at Cas, whose smirk had widened. He caught her eye and winked.

Kaethe's face tightened in displeasure. She lifted her chin. "Well, what is it?"

Thirty-Three

The Laughing Gull buzzed with a congenial crowd, a far cry from the empty tavern Cas had visited before. Baba-hor's rusalki crew sat in the corner, weaving lotus crowns and flipping clam shells into a mug. All the curtained booths were occupied, and more patrons crowded the tables. A pair of boo-hags sipped lavender dream vials, water babies wailed by the flowerpots, and a trio of trolls rolled bones in the corner. In short, business was booming.

"You should've seen Kaethe's face," Cas said to Baba-hor, "when she heard your father was collecting on Lo's debt."

"Gnashed her teeth!" squawked Bilmek.

"Tore her hair!" Golguth shrieked.

"She was livid," Lo agreed with a grin. "But she couldn't do a damned thing about it. The bargain with Khaf-hor preceded my last death and has to be fulfilled before she can claim me."

Bergmann wiped a dream vial with a cloth. "Bargain?"

Lo leaned an elbow on the scarred bar. "I gave up my..." She tilted her head, lips silently counting. "Seventh life to reach the bottom of Khaf-hor's Trench and beg his aid. He told me where to find Magnus the Merciless. In exchange, I vowed to return the favor when called upon."

"So what's the favor?" Bergmann asked.

Cas drained the dregs of his ale, grimacing at the fishy aftertaste. "Hunt down the fugitive humbug Talon. Arrest him and bring him before the Five. He's accused of using Magnus and his mortifexes to steal dreams from his rivals."

Bergmann gave an approving nod. "It's past time that scheming fraud was brought to justice. It's his own fault that he lost his license. Selling nightmares and phantasms..." He paused to scratch his chin. "Of course, Talon's a four-toed humbug. They can look like anyone."

Bergmann was a shapeshifter, too, though Cas saw his true form now. A rather average-looking man with jug ears, a mop of greenish hair, and eyes that stuck out like a goldfish.

"Yep," Lo said happily. "So it'll probably take a long time to find him."

Baba-hor chuckled, flashing his pearly baby-shark teeth. "My father hinted there may be additional jobs after that as well. It's unlikely you'll be back at Kaethe's tower anytime soon." He lowered his voice to a conspiratorial whisper. "Between us, the Five were also furious about Kaethe locking her gates. Unless she wanted to risk all-out war..."

"She had to back down." Lo raised her mug. "To blackmail!"

"Extortion and racketeering!" shrieked Bilmek, bobbing his black head.

Golgoth let out a raunchy guffaw. "Skullduggery most foul!"

Cas and Lo clinked mugs. She barely touched the ale to her lips before setting it down on the scarred bar.

"Well, we'd best be about it." Lo stood, her stool scraping through the sand on the tavern's warped floorboards.

"Rumor has it that Talon is hiding in the Nether Caves north of Sat-bu's Maelstrom." She dropped a bulging purse on the bar. "I don't suppose there's a seaworthy vessel for sale?"

Bergmann eyed the purse with a frown. "Coin's no good in Dreamhaven, Delilah. You know that."

She pushed it toward him. "Oh, it's not coin. It's seeds. Chestnut, birch, apple. Cherry, pine, maple, oak. Cas gathered them for you. A gift."

Wonder dawned on Bergmann's face as he loosened the drawstring. Cas smiled, recalling their earlier conversation. "You said Dreamhaven had lost its forests for firewood. These are all special varieties that thrive in the half-light of the Boundary. They should fare well here."

Bergmann lifted his gaze, eyes glistening. "I ... I don't know what to say. Thank you, truly. This means more than you can imagine."

Baba-hor had been watching the exchange, his seaweed cloak gently undulating in some unseen current. He cleared his throat. "The Dream Collectors' Collective gave Bergmann and me the *Reverie*, the brigantine that Magnus once used to terrorize these waters. We've gone into business together." His black eyes glittered. "So I'd be willing to return your *Wind-Witch*, for the right price."

Cas groaned openly. "Let me guess..."

"A riddle." Baba-hor flourished his cloak. "Answer it true and the ship is yours."

"And when we lose?" Cas asked dryly. "Will you take the clothes from our backs? Because that's about all we own."

Baba-hor stroked his long, mottled gray chin. "If you lose, you may keep the seeds."

"What?" Bergmann clutched the pouch to his chest. "You can't bet my seeds!"

Lo made a quelling gesture, her eyes never leaving Baba-hor. "I won't lose," she said softly. "Let's have it."

Bergmann made a noise of dismay as Baba-hor leaned forward. "I am everywhere but cannot be seen. Can be captured, cannot be held. No throat but have a voice. What am I?"

Lo's forehead puckered for an agonizing minute. At last, she turned to the open window, lined with bright flowerpots. A breeze stirred her raven hair. She laughed with delight. "The wind."

Baba-hor swept a graceful bow. "The *Wind-Witch* is yours."

Bergmann heaved an audible sigh of relief. Lo shot Cas a smug look, as if to say, "Was there ever any doubt?" He just shook his head, a reluctant grin tugging at his mouth.

They bid goodbye to Bergmann and Baba-hor, who wished them luck on their quest, and ambled down the hill toward the harbor. "Baba-hor gave me an easy one," Lo remarked.

"Aye," Cas agreed, his gaze catching on the creaking sign that read *Talon's Roost*. Their quarry's old tavern. "So let's enjoy it. I suspect it'll be the last test we pass so easily."

"It's funny," she said. "Bergmann didn't look like Javid this time."

"Same here. I saw Gui when we first met him, but now I'm pretty sure I saw his true form."

"Green hair?"

"That's it."

"Why don't we see the illusion anymore?" Lo wondered. "Bergmann doesn't do it on purpose. Our own minds conjure up the person we trust most in the world."

Cas ran a hand lightly down her back. She turned and leaned in, rubbing her check against his beard stubble. "Maybe," he said, "it's because we're already with each other."

Lo smiled. "Now that makes perfect sense."

They rounded a bend and the harbor spread out before them, bustling with ships of every description. Sloops and schooners, brigantines and barques, bobbing up and down on the aquamarine water of the Cold Sea.

And there, tied up at the end of the stone quay, was the *Wind-Witch*.

Cas's heart lifted at the jaunty lines of her hull, the way she strained against her moorings as if eager to be off. Thistle crouched on the foredeck, licking his claws with studied indifference. His ears cocked as they approached, though in the manner of cats, he didn't deign to look up.

"Baba-hor took his tooth back," Thistle remarked, "but he replaced it with a proper mast."

Cas eyed the new spar. Seasoned oak, by the look of it, straight and true.

"He treated the ship well," the cat added grudgingly. "Though you'll need to sweep up the rusalkis' soggy flower petals. They're *everywhere*."

Lo leaped from the pier, landing lightly on the deck. Cas thought back to the last time they'd arrived at Dreamhaven, when she'd tripped and almost pitched headlong into the water. But the Quickening's influence was gone now. She moved like a stalking panther. It reminded him.... Well, it reminded him of Lucius.

Cas crossed the gangplank with rather less grace and helped her raise the sails. The breeze freshened, snapping the canvas taut. He glanced at Lo. The wind teased strands of hair across her face. She looked wild and utterly beautiful. Unable to help himself, Cas caught her chin and kissed her, long and deep. Lo made a small noise in her throat and kissed him back, her body pressing against his in all the right places.

Then she pulled away with a wicked grin. "To our latest misadventure," she declared, guiding the ship toward the harbor mouth.

"To trouble and mayhem!" Cas agreed as the *Wind-Witch* sliced through the waves.

"Hijinks and escapades," Thistle growled from his customary spot at the bow.

As they glided past the other ships, lightning flickered along the horizon. It mirrored the flames that danced at the center of Lo's blue eyes.

THE TANG of ink and fresh parchment filled Felippa's nose as she bent over the angled writing desk, quill scratching busily. Sunlight poured through the shop's large windows, setting dust motes aglow and warming the honey-colored floorboards.

She finished the last flourish on the deed of property and handed it to the waiting customer with a smile. "There you are, Master Teague. That should be everything in order."

The portly merchant counted out one silver ferry and two copper pyres. "My thanks, Mistress Nerides. It's a rare treat to find a scribe with such a fine hand."

Felippa inclined her head at the compliment, already reaching for a fresh sheet of parchment as he departed and the next client stepped up. Her hand ached from the hours of writing, but it was a good ache. An earned ache.

The line of customers stretched out the door of Bel's Quill and halfway down Guppy Lane. Felippa had been up since dawn, but she didn't mind. This was her dream made real — her very own scriptoria, a place where anyone, rich or poor, could come to have their letters and documents scribed. She had plans to expand, to take on apprentices, but that was for later. Now there were bills to be paid.

Felippa was so focused on the task at hand, she didn't notice the shadow that fell across her desk until a gentle voice said, "I've brought you dinner."

She glanced up to find Sarra standing there, a pail in hand and a kind smile on her face. Felippa's stomach rumbled as the scent of fresh bread and stew reached her nose.

"You're a lifesaver," she said, stretching her cramped fingers. "I didn't realize how famished I was."

"You work too hard," Sarra tutted, but her eyes twinkled with pride.

Felippa took the pail gratefully and followed her outside. Da and Gui were ensconced in their usual spot beneath the awning, a plank balanced between two barrels to serve as a makeshift bench. Teo sprawled beside them; he always stopped by for a quick meal when he could.

Gui looked up, his seamed face splitting into a grin. He set aside his pipe and stood to buss Sarra on the cheek. They made a funny pair, grizzled Gui with his bad leg and round, rosy-cheeked Sarra who barely reached his shoulder. But there was an easiness between them, a tenderness in the way his hand lingered at the small of her back. Felippa was glad of it. They both deserved some happiness after all they'd been through.

Da puffed on his pipe, blue smoke curling about his head. "How fares the shop?" he asked as she plopped down beside him.

"Busy as a brothel on payday," Teo answered for her, popping the lid off the pail. "Can't you see the line out here?"

He swiped a chunk of Felippa's bread, popping it into his mouth with a wink.

"Hey now, get your own!" she swatted at his hand.

Teo rolled his eyes. "What, and deprive my dear sister of the chance to show her generosity?"

Gui chuckled around his own pipe stem. "Bel's Quill… I do believe there *is* a brothel of the same name near Amon's Wharf."

"That's because it's the sort of lewd pun Cavettis can't resist," Da muttered.

Felippa pretended ignorance, though her lips twitched. "I surely have no idea of what you speak, father."

Gui cleared his throat. "Well, I knew you'd do well for yourself, lass. You've got your mother's quick mind and your father's willingness to work like a three-legged mule."

Teo burst out laughing. Da frowned. "Is that a compliment? I can't always tell with you, Harcourt."

A sudden lump formed in Felippa's throat. She busied herself eating stew to hide the shine in her eyes. It still didn't seem real that the shop was hers. Gui had bought it for her, sinking the coin he'd saved over a lifetime of service into this ramshackle building on a shabby street.

When she'd protested that she could never repay him, Gui had just waved a hand. "I've no family nor heirs. Who else would I leave it to but you, Lippa? You've earned it, and more besides."

She'd flung her arms around his neck and peppered his white beard with kisses, heedless of his grumbles about getting too old and fat for such nonsense. In truth, she didn't know what she would have done without Gui. He'd been a steadfast presence through all the dark days of Prydwen's growing pains.

Felippa leaned her shoulder companionably against Teo's. Together they watched the passersby, hawkers and housewives, merchants and mendicants. Prydwen's lifeblood flowing past, vibrant and irrepressible.

Teo stretched out his long legs. "I hear you're teaching the little ones their letters down at Mother Morrigal's. Saint Lippa, patron of lost causes."

"It's hardly saintly," Felippa demurred. "Besides, you're one to talk. Da says you've been helping rebuild, and joined the civil guard to boot. Turning respectable in your dotage, brother mine?"

Teo clutched his chest in mock affront. "Slander! My reputation will never recover."

Da chuckled, exhaling a stream of pipe smoke. "Leave off teasing your sister. I'm proud of you both."

Teo ducked his head at the rare praise, intent on his lunch. Felippa's own smile faded as she reached up to touch the silver pendant at her throat. Her good luck charm. She hoped Cas was well, wherever he was now. More than anything, she wished him happiness.

But her new shop, the children at Mother Morrigal's, this sun-drenched city rising from the ashes ... it was home now. And despite everything, there was still hope to be found.

Nathan wove through the crowd of revelers, the wild flutes of the centaurs thrumming in his ears. The cavernous dining hall of Castle Cazal had been transformed, its long trestle table shoved against the wall, blue witchfire leaping in the hearth. Creatures and mortals alike spun to the frenetic music, a victory celebration of darkness over light.

Chaos sat in a chair at the edge of the dance floor, tapping the beat with one of her canes. She wore a dress of midnight velvet, and a tiny elf owl roosted in her upswept white hair.

"My lady," Nathan murmured, sketching a bow. "You look radiant tonight."

Chaos lifted her chin. "Idle flattery does not suit you, Nathan."

"There is nothing idle about it." He offered his arm. "Would you care to take the night air? I confess, I find parties to be highly overrated."

She hesitated, then gave a cautious nod. "I would like that."

Chaos accepted his arm and levered herself up, leaning on him slightly as they made their way out of the hall. Outside, the triple moons hung low in the sky, waxing gibbous.

"Do you miss Mace?" Nathan asked.

"Very much," she admitted. The elf owl gave a soft hoot of agreement.

"Vigo was like a father to me," Nathan said. "The keep is lonely without him." He gazed up at the stars. "Yet I am glad they both moved on. It was time. A thousand years of service is long enough."

The Duc of Vendagni and the Ducissa of Nyons strolled along the ramparts under the silvery light, until the music faded behind them and there was only the wind howling across the misty chasm.

"Would you dance with me now?" Nathan asked, his pulse leaping.

For the first time that night, Chaos smiled.

Morgen turned the brittle, yellowing page of the grimoire *Arbatel de Magia Veterum*. The magic of the ancients. She was curled up in her favorite reading nook at Juniper cottage, Jaelle beside her. "I don't understand," the girl said, wrinkling her nose. "Why would anyone want to summon a *lemon*?"

Morgen laughed aloud, squinting at the tiny letters. "It's a misprint. What do you think they really meant?"

Jaelle chewed her lip. "Demon?"

"I imagine so," Morgen said wryly. "Somewhere along the line, a half-blind scribe got it wrong." She smoothed the girl's pale hair. "Though I suppose a lemon could be useful if you were making a particularly tart potion."

Jaelle giggled, and Morgen felt a rush of warmth. It was good to hear the child laugh. She'd been so solemn when she first arrived, weighed down by the trauma of her past. But slowly, day by day, she was starting to heal. They all were.

The ring of steel against steel drew Morgen's gaze to the octagonal window looking down on the beach below. Dravka was sparring with Luzia da Matos, known as the Red Jackal, a Galatian swordmaster Morgen had hired to instruct her. The little terrier watched them, his stub of a tail wagging energetically. The pup barked with excitement every time they crossed blades, but he was smart enough to keep back.

Dravka lunged. Luzia parried, then riposted with lightning speed. Dravka barely got her sword up in time to block, staggering back a step. Blood trickled down one cheek. Another dueling scar to add to her collection. The Galatians called them *beijos de aço*. Kisses of steel.

Jaelle grabbed Morgen's arm. They watched through the window with bated breath. *Don't trip...*

With a roar, Dravka found her feet and attacked, teeth bared in a fierce grin.

Claudius Quintus stood on a shore of black sand at the farthest border of the Lady's realm.

His journey through the gate was already half-forgotten. All he knew was the deep pull that drew him onward.

And that somehow, somewhere, he had lost Brennos.

Six of Kaethe's hounds watched him from the water's edge. They no longer seemed interested in tearing him to pieces. He wasn't the unnatural creature who had trespassed through their mistress's lands with… who was it? He struggled. Found the name at last. Castelio.

But the thought faded quickly, just as his physical body grew thin and frayed like a garment worn too long.

There was a boat. He waded out to it.

A wind filled the sails, carrying him away from shore. He sailed on and on, passing the sweeping beacon of Dandariel and the still waters of the Thalassic Deep. At last he spied a fair green shore. Golden light suffused the air. It grew brighter, and then brighter still.

There was no pain in this light. Only warmth, like an embrace after a long absence. Claudius let it claim him until there was room for nothing else. His last thought was that it felt like grace.

Epilogue

Sixteen years later

The boy loved to run.

He ran everywhere, bare feet slapping against the sand, the dust-laden desert wind rushing through his hair.

The Vatra capital was the most beautiful city in the world, he felt certain. What place could compare to its lofty glass buildings, their panes of emerald, topaz, and ruby catching the light and reflecting it back in bright shards.

Now he skidded to a halt in front of his family's compound, catching his breath. Nicodemus said he'd been found on the doorstep when he was an infant, tucked inside a cradle of willow reeds. An orphan and a mystery.

When the boy turned ten, he started to have vivid dreams. Sometimes he was a soldier, and sometimes he was a slave. When he told Nicodemus about these dreams, his adopted father would ruffle his hair and say only, "The old blood runs strong in you."

A caravan of gaudily painted Yezudi wagons emerged from the heat haze like a mirage made real. The boy dashed inside the workshop, kicking up puffs of ruddy dirt. "The traders are here!"

Nicodemus looked up from the talisman he was shaping with air and fire, his hands stilling. "Aelia, my love," he called. "Our friends have arrived."

The boy bounced on his toes as Nicodemus and Aelia took their places on woven rugs under the shade of a pavilion. The Yezudi approached, their layered robes billowing in the arid breeze. Greetings and blessings were exchanged, along with a ritual pressing together of palms. His uncle Atticus brought out a tray of protective talismans. Then the bargaining began in earnest.

As the boy served cups of steaming mint tea, he felt the prickle of eyes. He glanced over and met the frank gaze of a Yezudi boy about his age. This insolent newcomer had a proud aquiline nose and dark curls, damp with sweat. Faint pits, the mark of a childhood fever perhaps, stippled his cheeks. They only enhanced his striking good looks.

The boy looked away and focused on pouring the aromatic tea without spilling a drop, though he remained intensely aware of the other's regard. Where had his self-assurance gone? He felt wrong-footed, like he'd stepped on a dozing sand snake.

After the last round of tea was served, he retreated to a shady corner and pretended to examine the leaves of one of Aelia's potted lemon trees. From the corner of his eye, he saw the Yezudi boy watching. An instant later, he unfolded his lean brown limbs and strolled across the sun-drenched tiles. "What's your name?" he asked.

"Liber."

"It means 'free', yes?" The Yezudi intonation made the words into a song.

Liber blinked in surprise. "You speak our tongue."

"Some. My mother taught me."

Liber scuffed the sand with his toe. For the first time in his sixteen years, he noticed how dirty his feet were — and actually cared. When he looked up, the boy was studying him with a creased brow. He had the unsettling feeling of being weighed and measured to the ounce.

"What's *your* name?" he asked in a rush.

The Yezudi smiled, a dazzling flash of white teeth. "I am David," he said. "It means beloved."

Afterword

First of all, thank for you reading to the end of this epic adventure! If you haven't read The Fourth Element trilogy yet, it kicks off the whole twelve-book daēva cycle and tells the story of Lo's parents Darius and Nazafareen, as well as Tijah and Achaemenes, and the sometimes wicked, always cheeky necromancer Balthazar (who appears later in my Gaslamp Gothic mystery series). *The Midnight Sea*, book #1 of the Fourth Element, is free to download everywhere.

My next project is Lord of Everfell, the prequel series to my Nightmarked books (which seem to be a fan favorite). The first book, *Dark Bringer*, comes out in August 2025.

Anyway, thank you again for reading my stories and supporting me as an author, it means the world to me! If you want to keep up with new releases and ramblings about my writing process, you can find me on Substack at https://katross24.substack.com/.

Warmest, Kat

Acknowledgments

Thanks as always to Carol Edholm for her eagle proofreading eye! I'm still not sure how I muddled through without you, Carol.

To Laura Pilli for her hilarious emojis, and the fabulous team at Acorn.

To Mom (also an amazing proofreader) and Nick, my darlings.

To Moose, Bean, Spike and Big Man, the house would be far too quiet without you.

About the Author

Kat Ross worked as a journalist at the United Nations for ten years before happily falling back into what she likes best: making stuff up. She loves myths, monsters, magic, and doomsday scenarios.

Join Kat's list, *The Sorcerous Pen*, and never miss a new release!

Her ravens will also deliver a free ebook, along with early access to sales, giveaways, diabolical potions, and arcane lore.

If you haven't read the Fourth Element trilogy, which tells the story of Lo's parents, Darius and Nazafareen, Book #1, *The Midnight Sea*, is free to download on all retailers.

www.katrossbooks.com
kat@katrossbooks.com

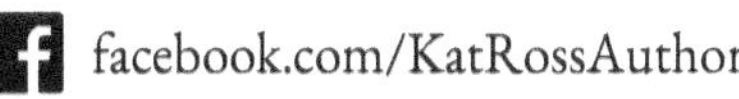

facebook.com/KatRossAuthor
instagram.com/katross2014

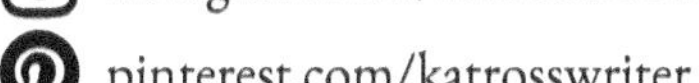

pinterest.com/katrosswriter

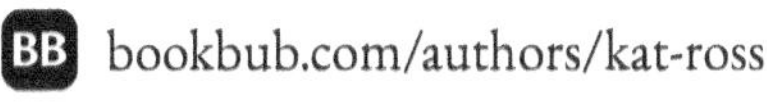

bookbub.com/authors/kat-ross

Also by Kat Ross

The Fourth Empire Series

Savage Skies

Rogue & Revenant

A Wicked Wind

Shadow Soul

The Fourth Element Trilogy

The Midnight Sea

Blood of the Prophet

Queen of Chaos

The Fourth Talisman Series

Nocturne

Solis

Monstrum

Nemesis

Inferno

The Nightmarked Series

City of Storms

City of Wolves

City of Keys

City of Dawn

The Lingua Magika Trilogy

A Feast of Phantoms

All Down But Nine

Devil of the North

Gaslamp Gothic Collection

The Daemoniac

The Thirteenth Gate

A Bad Breed

The Necromancer's Bride

Dead Ringer

Balthazar's Bane

The Scarlet Thread

The Beast of Loch Ness

Standalone Dystopian Sci-fi Novel

Some Fine Day

www.ingramcontent.com/pod-product-compliance
Lightning Source LLC
Chambersburg PA
CBHW031306280626
47169CB00017B/354
* 9 7 8 1 9 5 7 3 5 8 1 9 2 *